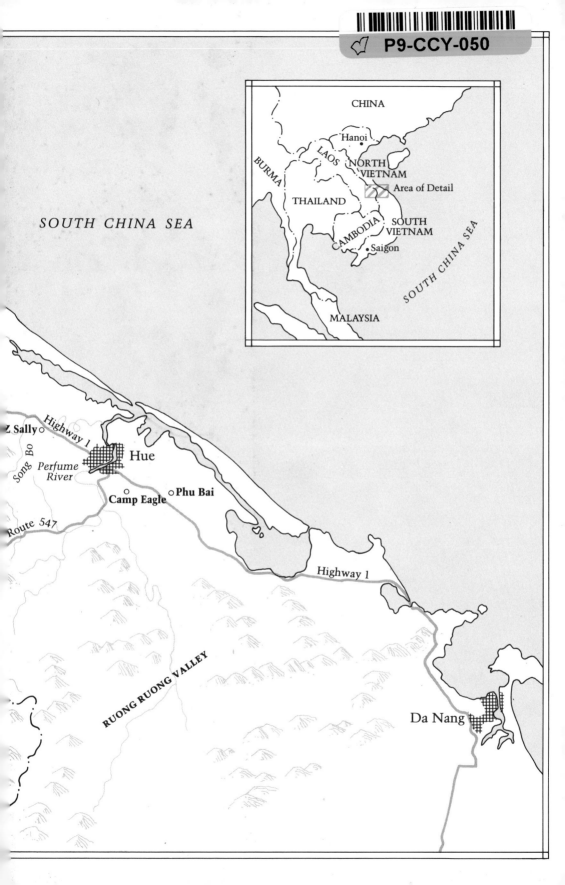

P9-CCY-050

CHINA

Hanoi

LAOS

NORTH
VIETNAM

BURMA

Area of Detail

THAILAND

CAMBODIA

SOUTH
VIETNAM

Saigon

SOUTH CHINA SEA

MALAYSIA

SOUTH CHINA SEA

Highway 1

Z Sally

Song Bo

Hue

Perfume
River

Phu Bai

Camp Eagle

Route 547

Highway 1

RUONG RUONG VALLEY

Da Nang

CW2

CW2

LAYNE HEATH

WILLIAM MORROW AND COMPANY, INC.
New York

Recognizing the importance of preserving what has been written, it is the policy
of William Morrow and Company, Inc., and its imprints and affiliates to have the
books it publishes printed on acid-free paper, and we exert our best efforts to
that end.

Library of Congress Cataloging-in-Publication Data

Heath, Layne
    CW2 / Layne Heath.
    p.   cm.
    ISBN 0-688-05265-7
    1. Vietnamese Conflict, 1961-1975—Fiction.   I. Title.
PS3558.E263C9   1990
813'.54—dc20   89-13773
                                                                        CIP

Printed in the United States of America

        3   4   5   6   7   8   9   10

BOOK DESIGN BY PAUL CHEVANNES

For those who left something there.

And for Laurice.

BOOK I

CHAPTER ONE

"**W**ELCOME TO Charlie Company," said a voice beyond the screen. Billy Roark gave a final glance across the camp—clusters of sandbagged hooches, sheet-metal roofs, rusty barbed wire—then turned and stepped inside. A large man with a dark mustache sat slumped in a chair, legs outstretched and propped, dressed in an olive drab T-shirt, faded fatigues rolled to his knees, and tire-soled sandals. Across his belly was a harried paperback. "God, I'm glad to see you, whoever you are," he said, and stood and held out a beefy hand. "My name's Jeb Brady."

"Billy Roark," he replied. "You must be going home."

"You got that right," said Brady, falling into his chair with a dreamy smile. "One and a wake-up." He was silent a moment, then asked, "You processed?"

"Captain Crable took me around."

Brady snorted. "What did you think of him?"

"Seems a bit stiff."

"He's a turd. You want a beer? You look like you've been in the sun."

Brady was wearing nothing to indicate rank, but Roark was certain he was a warrant officer. "I'd kill for one," he said.

"When you've been here awhile you'll lower your price. Sit down, take a load off. You'll be flying your butt soon enough." He went behind a short bar.

"I guess I'm not used to the heat," Roark said. His face and arms glowed red. Muddy rings circled his neck.

"It'll take about a month. Better here than down south."

Roark sat in the breeze of an oscillating fan and gazed around the hooch—a simple shed of bare plywood, screened above four feet, weather drops propped open on a circling sandbag wall. Along a hallway were doorless cubicles partitioned to eye level, open rafters and sheet metal overhead. In the gangroom were four turquoise café chairs, a plywood bar, a refrigerator, and Brady's rocker—a dominant piece fashioned of sandbag cloth and two-by-fours. Ammunition crates formed low tables while all around lay a sprinkling of sand and flattened cigarette butts. A shaft of sunlight burned through a thumb hole in the roof. When Brady delivered the beer, Roark pulled deeply, gasped in reaction, then held the cold can against a cheek. "So where do we fly?"

"The A Shau," Brady said flatly.

"So how's it been going?" he lied. All he had heard since he hit country was about the 101st Airborne and the A Shau Valley. The cadre in Long Binh had smiled when they announced the ones going to I Corps. *Northern* Eye Corps, they said. Then they laughed.

"We're getting our butts kicked," said Brady. "The gooks are dug in and they're not running. We're on general support now, but we were on direct for the Third until Airborne."

"Airborne?"

"A firebase on the edge of the A Shau. Got overrun in broad daylight. We went in with ammo and tried to carry out the wounded. Lost three ships and eight men, and half the grunts. That was about two weeks ago, which is why you're here." Brady pushed his face into a strange smile. "Anybody come with you?"

"No, just me. I'd begun to think the war was over—I've been sitting down at Group for four days."

"That's about right," Brady said. "And Crable tried to make me fly today. I told him to get corned, I'm going home. If they're going to kill me now, they're going to have to come in here to do it." A loaded M-16 hung from a sling on the back of his chair.

"So what do we do on general support?"

"Everything. We fill in with whichever company is on direct, helping them shuffle troops around the jungle, and we fly logistics for grunts in the field, hauling food and ammo—sort of like airborne trucks. We also support the ARVNs in Quang Tri and the MACV advisers in Hue. All that and CCN."

"What's CCN?"

"You'll find out soon enough."

Roark turned the can up and finished in two long drafts. "I've got a lot to learn," he said. "Where can I put my gear?"

"Take your pick," Brady replied, gesturing toward the hall. Roark walked the length of the passage, sticking his head into each cube. Four of the eight were empty, but at the doors of two, printed in black marker on gray tape, were the names Moore and Dansworth. He selected one without a name, leaned the M-16 inside, then went out to fetch his gear.

The cubicle, six feet by eight, contained a spring-wire cot with a shriveled mattress enclosed in a mosquito net tent. At the foot of the bunk stood a narrow plywood closet—a rusty pipe rod and a few rusty hangers. On the opposite wall were shelves above a low cabinet, and a writing shelf served by a folding metal chair. Roark slapped at the netting, then dragged the mattress free and kicked it loose of its dusty load. He found a hobo's broom at the end of the hall and set about making a home. He was absorbed in thinking about the A Shau Valley, wondering what had happened to Moore and Dansworth, when he heard Brady behind him. "You got Cathron's room," he said.

"There was no name."

"CCN," Brady said, "is Command and Control North. It's flying recon teams into Laos, then going in to get them out when they're discovered."

"Where are Moore and Dansworth? And Cathron?"

"They're gone."

They went to the gangroom then, not talking so much, but more at ease with each other. It seemed strange to Roark that his war was about to begin while across from him sat a man whose war was almost over. But this isn't exactly World War II, he thought.

Someone approached beyond the screen, wearing chest armor, carrying a flight helmet. He stomped dust from his boots and opened the door. "You must be Billy Roark," he said, extending a hand. "I'm Gil McCawley. Captain Hood told me we had a new guy." McCawley was almost twenty-five—four years older than most warrants—and looked and sounded like a country boy. He was two inches shy of six feet, bowlegged, and walked on the edges of his feet as if he were wearing cowboy boots. His cap was pushed back on sandy waves, and his narrow face was open and tan. Pale green eyes were almost blue, friendly creases all around. He freed the broad Velcro band at the waist, then slipped the sweat-soaked armor over his head and leaned it against the wall. "You eaten yet?" he asked.

"No."

"Well, I don't recommend it on a regular basis, but I feel like a challenge. Let's go to the mess hall, then I'll show you around." He turned to Brady. "You eating lurps?"

"That's right," Brady said. "Chili with beans. Give you something to remember me by."

Walking beside the weathered McCawley, Billy Roark felt conspicuous. With his shabby flight suit, salt-rimmed cap, faded patches, and sand-scrubbed boots, McCawley looked like a moving part of the environment. Roark, sunburned and wearing fatigues still stiff with newness, boots still smooth and black, might as well have been suited out in civvies. McCawley named a few of the features they passed and explained the layout of the camp. Roark already knew some of it from the time he had spent with Crable, but didn't mind getting it again.

Camp Evans was the northernmost Army helicopter base in Vietnam. It sat at the western edge of Highway 1, halfway between Hue and Quang Tri. East and north of the camp were flatlands— partly barren sand and tidal traps, the rest paddies and hamlets. Ten miles away was the South China Sea where the coastline slanted across the map northwest to southeast. In the opposite direction low brushy terrain rolled four miles to a great escarpment, beyond which were endless mountains. About a mile in diameter, Evans was divided by a hard-surfaced airstrip. It housed the rear elements of three infantry battalions, six company-size aviation units, portions of two artillery battalions, a company of engineers, a surgical hospital, a detachment of Seabees, plus various support units—all randomly arranged. While the officers' hooches of Charlie Company were on high ground adjacent to the 18th Surgical Hospital, the administrative segment and the quarters of the enlisted men lay east beyond another unit's flight line. North across a road, between the Seabees and Headquarters Company, were the hangar and parking area of the Hueys of Company C, call sign Phoenix.

Supper was round steak, sliced into shapeless chunks and fried to plywood, hardtack biscuits, watery gravy with no cracklings or pepper, and runny potatoes from dehydrated base. A square of melting green gelatin was the finishing touch. There were half-pint cartons of a warm liquid advertised as reconstituted milk and a murky vat of water tinctured Kool-aid red. A few flight crews were coming in, as well as men from aircraft maintenance and the motor pool. At the CO's table the commanding officer, Major George Andrews, sat opposite his executive officer, Captain Phillip Crable. After speaking, the two pilots sat at the most distant officers' table.

Roark had met the CO when he arrived, receiving the standard briefing. Andrews was a compact man who wasted few words. He had short black hair that lay tight against his scalp and dark eyes that were sharply intelligent. He appeared to be a man not to be crossed, but one who could be depended on never to make an unplanned move.

Crable was a different story, one that Roark had not yet defined. After almost two hours together Roark knew only that they did not particularly like each other. The captain seemed impressed with his position, very aware that he outranked every man in the outfit but one. His every word, every glance, carried a raw, challenging edge as if he had not quite accepted his own authority and assumed that neither had anyone else. The man looked physically out of place. His thinness lacked the muscle to be lean, and his pasty skin denied the tropical environment. His face was sharply narrow, with the gristle of his arched nose showing whitely through. Pouting lips of an odd purplish color had difficulty covering teeth bunched in front. But the eyes were the strangest part, pale gray—near white—with an uncertain cast of green. Roark had decided that something about the man did not quite fit. Crable wore his hair clipped hard against the skull, his fatigues were clean and crisp, and the double-leather toes of his paratrooper boots were spit-shined to perfection. All like a professional soldier, but with something critical left out. The captain was unconvincing in his role. That's it, Roark thought, glancing across the room. He looks like a grown, weird kid playing Army, an actor playing a part, and all this is nothing but a gigantic game of pretend.

Phillip Crable chewed the beef with begrudging precision, feeling elastic strands accumulating between his teeth like rubber bands. Across the table Major Andrews, whose teeth were disgustingly short and straight, gnawed at the coriaceous fare as if he expected nothing else. Phillip could hardly wait to get back to his hooch to floss. The way the Army ate was a disgrace; since coming to Vietnam he had eaten both at Navy and Air Force facilities, and any comparison with the mess before him was ludicrous. The Navy in particular ate better in Vietnam than the Army ever had back home. But it was not as if he hadn't had a choice; in fact, it was that very Spartan aspect of Army life that had caused him to decide upon it. Sometimes that was difficult to remember.

Major Andrews almost never uttered a word during meals, so Phillip occupied himself with studying the new warrant officer, watching him through stolen glances. He was not sure what it was, but something about Billy Roark raised his hackles, made him feel the cold metal fillings in his teeth. The kid was so clearly excited about arriving at his marvelous war, so brightly confident, arrogant with youth. Peachy and lean, he was outrageously average. Because he was a W-1—because of changes that had happened within that rank—the kid-pilot unwittingly represented everything that was happening to the Army. The decision to make this a helicopter war had been the beginning of it. Requiring men with the intelligence to operate complicated aircraft and the ability to handle responsibility and pressure, while at the same time restricting their actual authority, made the rank of warrant officer the obvious choice. The machinery was put in motion to produce them by the thousands. The lure of wings without a degree was the incentive, while the pressure of the draft guaranteed that quotas would be filled. But the combination of youth, intelligence, and sudden advancement—worsened by the certain cockiness of rapid proficiency in a live-or-die environment—produced a Frankensteinian monster of considerable proportions. Suddenly the Army was filled with strutting young roosters who saluted with their hands flat against their faces and an unmistakable fuck-you-very-much-sir look in their eyes. And the situation was growing quickly worse. Crable felt that the commissioned officers, men like himself, were losing control of the entire Army because of an unwillingness to knuckle down on green and confident kids like Billy Roark, a situation which, he decided, could only be overcome a single man at a time.

When he finished his meal, Crable dabbed at his lips with a paper napkin, then walked over to Roark and leaned across the table, completely ignoring McCawley. "Drop by to see me tomorrow morning," he said, then flashed his cadaverous teeth.

The sun had fallen beyond deep green peaks; flat beams of apricot dissolved across the sky. Camp Evans was alive with helicopters, circling beyond the perimeter, landing here and there, hovering along the oiled ravines. The earth beneath Roark's feet pulsed with little pats of sound. On the red cross outside the hospital a Medevac bird discharged a load of stretchered men, then rose and plunged southward, nose low and pulling hard. Immediately overhead, Loaches and Cobras of the 2d of the 17th Cav passed low on final. Roark looked up at the men looking down and resisted a childish urge to wave.

Charlie Company's flight line lay along a ravine north of the main road through camp. The far end abutted the perimeter facing the village of Phong Dien, while on the high ground near the road stood the maintenance hangar and Phoenix Operations. Recently built by the Seabees, the shining sheet-metal building had five bays for maintenance, plus a sixth enclosed for parts and arms and ready rooms below, Operations overhead.

When they crossed the upper edge of the flight line, Billy Roark could feel his excitement grow. He was in the midst of it now, and everything within his vision was thrilling. There were several Hueys already in the revetments, some with blades tied down, others still running or coasting to a stop. A ship was on short final, and another hovered slowly up the hill toward the hangar, sending out a faint halo of dust. The shrill sigh of turbines shutting down pierced the throbbing Huey sound that filled the air. Along the length of the ravine, pilots and crews were moving around their ships; gunners walked with machine guns on their shoulders. Roark watched it all and believed he was somewhere near the peak. Whatever it meant to be part of all this, whatever it meant to fly these marvelous machines, could not possibly fail to be worth the price.

A pilot with his back to the door was leaning across the counter in Operations. Beyond, against a bank of radios before two corner windows was a very tall black kid who flashed a wide and oily smile when he spotted Billy Roark. "Well, I'll be. Lookie here," he said, "a fucking new guy. An FNG. All right!" He held his arms above his head and wiggled his narrow hips in a dance of celebration. "You're dead meat," he said, "but you're live meat now, and that's what counts." He danced again and said, "Welcome to 'Nam, sucker."

Roark could feel himself blush. The pilot at the counter had turned around and was checking him quietly. "That's Motormouth," McCawley said. "He runs the company. And this is Steve Sharp. Steve, Billy Roark."

Sharp was a year older than Roark, but the difference in their ages seemed greater. He had black hair and light blue, distant eyes. His skin looked older, and there were acne scars on his cheeks. His inspection of Roark complete, he turned to McCawley. "Am I flying tomorrow?" he said, looking like he wanted a day off.

"How are your hours?"

"Just passed one-twenty. One good day would peg me out."

McCawley shook his head. "The Old Man says we're going to one-forty."

The hope drained from Sharp's face. "Okay," he said, "try to make it light. My butt's in the dirt." He lifted his helmet and M-16 and walked slowly out of the room.

McCawley watched the empty doorway. "I'm the unit instructor pilot," he said, "but I'm filling in as scheduling officer for first platoon. The guy that had it got killed, along with our platoon leader."

"Moore and Dansworth?"

"Yeah. You're going to get some sort of extra duty besides flying. That's probably what Crable wants to see you about—to stick you on a shit detail. You might want to think about scheduling."

"What's involved?"

McCawley led him behind the counter to the aircraft status board. On the left was a column of numbers, some of which had been scratched out. "We're supposed to have twenty ships," he said. "Ten to a platoon. Right now we're four short, and there's always one or two in maintenance. That's okay because until we get more pilots we won't be able to man more ships."

"So where are the pilots?" Roark asked. "They're cranking out four hundred a month, and that's just warrants."

"Some are rotating," McCawley said. "We're also running about forty percent casualties, half dead, inside a year. Some of the new ones have probably been going to Tay Ninh—there's been a bunch lost around Parrot's Beak with the Big Red One. And the 1st Cav, wherever they are, are sure to be leaving their usual trail of junk. The 101st Battalion at Eagle is in about the same shape we are. Their three lift companies lost at least nine birds in the past month."

Two more pilots had climbed the stairs and were standing at the counter, turning in their flight time and SOIs, the radio code booklets. A rotating beacon from a hovering Huey swept a red swath across the ceiling, and the entire building buzzed with sound. McCawley explained the scheduling system, and it seemed simple enough, the only drawback being the requirement to be at Operations between 2300 hours and midnight when maintenance released the list of flyable ships. Roark agreed to take the job as soon as McCawley had him trained. "We'll come back down later and go over it," McCawley said. "You'll be flying with me tomorrow."

Roark was surprised. "Don't I need a checkride?"

"Like I said, I'm the IP. We'll combine it with the mission."

The stars were brightening as they left the hangar, the glowing trace of the Milky Way beginning to show. Though there was a comfort in having the seasoned pilot at his side, Billy Roark felt very much alone. Tomorrow he would be a helicopter pilot in Vietnam, flying a combat mission in the fabled northern I Corps, doing what he had trained and waited and wanted to do every moment for a solid year. Powdered earth splashed beneath his feet with little plops, swirled around his boots and the bloused bottoms of his pants, lacing them with dust, making them seem not quite so new.

I remember the day I heard Gary Pederson had been killed. That's not when it began, but that was the day I began to give up pretending. That was the day my mind began making the changes it needed to make to get me ready. When I look back, when I let it all slide past in reverse, I bump to a stop on that day like sliding down a rope with a knot.

It was the summer after my junior year. Jay Brewer and I were hanging out at the Mixer, leaning against the windshield and watching the Saturday night cruisers. The juices were flowing pretty well by then, and we both were about to die. Patti brought us cheeseburgers, onion rings, and tall cups of ice. She was divorced with two kids, but still had a good butt on her, and we watched her walk away, groaning a little so she could hear.

We had a fifth of Bacardi and a six-pack of Wink in the cab of the truck, and we mixed drinks and got back on the hood. Jay had been with some guys who had made a liquor run to Dallas, and they'd stashed the rum and two bottles of Swiss Colony in a brush pile near the lake. Jay told me about it, and we went out and stole the stash, then drove to the sandbar to swim in the sunset and start getting drunk. We waded out deep—me to my shoulders and Jay to his chin—and watched the changing patterns of red and gold and blue, a jigsaw puzzle with pieces that moved. We talked about fishing and girls and a canoe trip we were going to make down the Brazos and never did. Finally, we talked about Vietnam and the draft, and all that. It was getting hard to see, and we dried ourselves on our dirty clothes, put on fresh Levi's and T-shirts, and headed for the Mixer.

It seemed like half the town was on Main Street that night. We howled at the girls and shot fingers at our friends. Charlie Coogan came creeping along in his squatting '60 'Vette with its half-flat racing slicks and purple metal-flake paint. It was a piece of junk, but it was fast junk, and he took it to the Valley on weekends. Charlie was a year out of school, and had lied his way into a 4F classification, then had to brag about it constantly because it made him look like a coward. He finally began picking fights with almost everyone he met.

Melvin McDaniel and his younger brother Mike skidded up in the rusty clunker they called their GTO—about a '54 Pontiac. They had cut the top off with a blowtorch, and there were old sofa cushions covering the springs where the seats had rotted out. The shocks were blown, and it sounded like a tractor, but the car had good tires.

Melvin was drunker than Cooter Brown, which was how he seemed to stay since school got out. He was wanting us to go to the circle for some beer. We'd have gone if he hadn't been so wasted, just to have something to do. There was always the chance we'd be attacked by a carload of girls who had eaten Spanish fly. Or maybe we'd be murdered; you never knew about Dallas. Anyway, we didn't go.

I could tell he was leading up to something, and finally Melvin said, "Hey, d'you hear about Gary Pederson"—one of those questions where you know what's coming next as soon as it's asked. "No," we said, "we didn't." "Little fucker got blown to pieces," he said. He went on, talking like it was some kind of joke, but I wasn't listening. I sat there feeling the rum move through me, feeling heavy. A breeze blew the trash from the cheeseburgers off the hood and into the street, and I just let it go.

Gary wasn't someone I knew well, but he was someone I knew. He was a face and a voice and a personality. That was the moment when Vietnam stopped being some faraway place where strangers died. From then on, it was a place where people I knew got killed. It was a place I knew I'd be going.

CHAPTER TWO

"**R**OARK."

"Yeah."

"Oh-four-hundred." Everything was laid out to find by feel—pants and shirt on nails, boots and socks beneath the bunk, helmet and armor beside the door. The M-16 stood next to his head where he slept; the .38 was beneath his pillow. Other names were called, with answering grunts, then the weaving flashlight moved down the hall and out the door. Slow groans, bare feet on the wooden floor, scratching fire to cigarettes. Someone pulled a beaded chain; light shot through the rafters.

He laced his boots and smelled the smoke and recalled the woodcutting mornings. Sometimes in winter they rose early like this and loaded the tools and chain saw, then hitched the red trailer to the old blue truck, packed a sackful of egg-and-cheese sandwiches and a steel thermos of coffee, and set off for the far side of the lake. His father smoked, and the truck was filled with a rich and manly aroma.

"You ready?" Gil McCawley stood in the door, a cigarette dangling, smoke wreathing past his eyes.

"Yeah." He lowered the armor over his head, secured it at the

20

waist, then grabbed his cap and rifle, his helmet and ammunition. "Okay if I take this?" he asked, lifting a camera. The first thing a new pilot did in Vietnam was buy a Seiko watch and a 35mm camera.

"Sure. Most of the guys carry them."

They walked to the mess hall for biscuits and coffee. The entire camp was awake, preparing for the day. Roark watched in serious silence, filled with a sense of importance—today he was going to war. Then he was struck by the melodrama and felt foolish. Everyone seemed bored or exhausted, moving like zombies with shared purpose. No jutting jaws and clenched white teeth and noble looks of glory; just a lot of tired young men doing a job where people got killed.

Phoenix Operations was full of pilots getting mission assignments and contact frequencies. McCawley signed for his SOI code booklet, dropped the attached security cord around his neck, then slipped the pamphlet into the pouch on his chest protector. Motormouth was on the radio, and he turned and waved for them to wait. "That was Lumberjack," he said. "One of their units just got hit north of Blaze. They need ammo."

"Is it hot?"

"Didn't sound like it."

Gil McCawley looked at his new pilot. He had assigned his ship to a log run for the 3d of the 187th to give Roark some orientation time before plunging into something more serious. The battalion had been pulled out of the valley for a breather, and companies Alpha and Charlie were on three-day standdown, a period to recuperate. Bravo and Delta were at Firebase Rakkasan and had elements scouting the mountains between Firebase Blaze and Camp Evans. Any mission could turn hot, but routine logistics was the best way to start a new pilot, at least until he had shown how he would react under fire. Even so, some who seemed cool as ice would fly apart when their own guns went off, and others that looked mousy would maintain control while their windshield was shot out. The first few days with a new guy could be worse than flying alone. "Think you can handle a hot LZ?" he asked.

Roark had anticipated the question, but he reacted without thinking. "If I didn't think I could handle it, I wouldn't be here," he said, too firmly and too loud, too much like a hero. Everyone heard him. Eyebrows shot up and impressive faces were made. He's *bad*, someone said. Roark was at once terribly embarrassed, astounded, and a little angry. He had spent a year training for this moment with newspapers and televisions and flight instructors telling him daily that he was likely to get his brains blown out, and he hadn't come this far to have someone blandly inquire if he thought he could handle it.

"Relax," McCawley said. "It's just that some guys don't do so well their first time out." Roark wanted out of the room, but he leaned against the wall and held steady eyes on the heckler. "Tell Lumberjack we'll be there ASAP," McCawley said, then left with his peter pilot trailing close behind.

They crossed the flight line in silence. Figures moved past in the darkness—gunners and crew chiefs struggling with cans of ammunition, pilots doing preflight inspections or trying to locate their ships. Roark had cooled enough now to begin to worry; McCawley had asked a legitimate question. He thought he could handle a hot LZ—he certainly hoped he could—but it was not the sort of thing determined by discussion. He almost hoped they would get shot up today just so the matter could be settled.

Specialist 4 Piermont was working busily on his Huey when the pilots walked into the glow of the dome light. The cargo doors were back and pinned, and the cockpit doors stood wide, the left-side armor turned out. The aircraft log, the 2408, lay open in the cargo bay. Working by flashlight, the crew chief stood on the flat toe of the left skid, reaching into the chin bubble on his belly, chasing sand through the drain port with a whisk broom. "Morning," McCawley said.

There was a grunt of escape, and Piermont backed out of the hole. "Morning, sir," he said, then he saw Billy Roark and smiled. "We got the new guy," he said, nodding approval. "That's good—we can train him right before the screwups get hold of him. Morning, sir," he said to Roark.

"Good morning," Roark responded. Piermont had a build similar to McCawley's, but without the parenthetic legs. His movements were quick and efficient, the cockiness in his voice friendly. He carried a dark towel in a hip pocket, and when McCawley had put his armor into the seat and hung his helmet on the hook above, he moved back into the chin bubble and cleaned it carefully.

Roark hung his helmet and stood his armor on the right, then followed McCawley to the log book to check the aircraft time and the dash-thirteen, the write-up page where discrepancies regarding the ship were recorded. "Have you seen Dusty?" McCawley yelled to Piermont. "We've got an ammo run."

Piermont was standing inside the left pilot's doorway, leaning over the front of the ship, gently wiping the windshield. "He's in the arms room spit-shining his babies," he said. He jumped down and jogged away toward the hangar.

McCawley watched him go, then turned to Roark with a smile.

"He comes across a bit smartass," he said, "but most good gunners do. The thinkers and kissers kind can't stay with it."

There was no time for the finely detailed preflight he had planned for Roark, and he began moving over the ship quickly with a flashlight, speaking rapidly of stress, tolerances, vibrations, and lubricants. Roark observed that the engine deck was spotless, and that the dark skin of the ship gleamed a reflection of the distant hangar lights. They worked down the left side, around the tail and forward. Things were moving very fast for Roark. He followed Mc-Cawley around, listening to the information, trying to stay close so he could see what was being checked and still be out of the way of the next move. He was awash in sights and sounds. Other parts of his brain were fixed on Hueys that were cranking and the movements of men who hurried to prepare their ships. The odor of burned JP-4 filled his lungs and soon flowed in his blood.

When they climbed up to do the topside inspection, the filter screens covering the engine air intake had already been removed, together with the upper half of the particle separator; the parts were lined up neatly on the far side of the deck beyond the cowling. McCawley pulled the inner screens and foam filters, then checked the lower assembly for the usual load of pebbles and twigs, but Piermont had done it all. He reassembled the parts, and when they had inspected the main rotor, mast, flight controls, and hydraulic servos, they moved back to ground level.

They were completing the exterior check when Piermont and Dusty came down from the hangar on their second trip with a 1500-round can of ammunition between them. They walked hurriedly, shuffling with effort, their loaded arms pulled straight and long, their free ones jerking for balance. When they heaved the rectangular can to the cargo deck, both were panting and dripping with sweat. Dusty gave Roark a blank look and turned and hurried away to get the guns. Piermont pulled the can into place against the mounting post, secured it with a bungee cord, then removed red, green, yellow, purple, and white smoke grenades that were stacked on top and hung them by their spoons around the lip of the can. He pulled a ten-foot section of belted bullets free, checked for kinks, restacked it so it would feed without snagging, then moved to the other side and repeated the procedure.

Several other ships, assigned to missions in the A Shau, were hovering down the flight line for takeoff when Roark and Mc-Cawley strapped themselves into their seats. Piermont stood at the front of the ship and held the tip of the main rotor until the birds were past. McCawley moved faster now, passing his hands over the radio console and across the overhead panel of switches, working by memory more quickly than Roark could follow. "Beep it down and set the throttle," he said. Roark held the RPM switch back for about ten seconds, rolled the throttle to full open, then back against the flight idle stop. He pressed the indent button, retarded the throttle just past the stop, and said, "Throttle set."

"Clear and untied?" McCawley yelled.

"Clear," yelled Piermont. "Clear," came another voice. Dusty had installed both guns and was standing on the right side of the ship with a fire extinguisher in his hands.

With the stick fully down and a firm grip on the throttle, Roark pulled the trigger beneath the collective control head. "Coming hot," he said. McCawley punched the clock twice to start the sweep second hand and flicked his eyes across the gauges. There was a low moan and a rapid click of igniters, then a thin climbing whine above a growing growl. The main rotor blades began sweeping past the windshield, right to left, and the needles of the gauges lurched to life.

"Forty percent," McCawley said, and Roark released the starter. He waited for the exhaust gas temperature to stabilize, then slowly rolled the throttle to flight idle. The aircraft commander began going through the systems checks, working from memory, calling it out to Roark as he went. Normally one pilot read from a checklist while the other performed the required task and announced, "Check." Roark sat holding the list, watching McCawley work through it as if he were reading. McCawley smiled at him. "You'll be able to do this in a few months," he said, "but we still use the checklist. Later, you'll be so tired your eyeballs will be hanging out, and it's easy to miss something that'll kill you."

He called their departure to Phoenix Ops on the FM, or Fox-Mike, the low-frequency radio used primarily for ground-to-ground and air-to-ground communications, asking Ops to relay to Lumberjack that they would be on their pad in two minutes. Rakkasan rear was less than a mile away, but the FM was a line-of-sight transmitter, and a hill and two metal hangars were in the way. He flipped his selector to UHF. The more powerful radio, used for most air-to-air calls, sent signals bouncing off the ionosphere, broadening its range. "Coming up," he said on the intercom.

"Clear up left."

"Clear up right." Roark turned in his seat as much as the belt and harness would allow. He could see the crew chief in the left well, helmet on and harness secured to the bulkhead, leaning forward and looking back toward the tail boom. Dusty, in the right well behind Roark, was beyond his vision. McCawley checked the instruments, then eased the collective upward, holding the grip of the cyclic gently between his fingers, feeling for balance as the ship lightened on the skids. The nose of the H-model began to rise, and the throb of the rotor blades deepened, sending pebbles and sand scurrying out of the revetment. The heel of the right skid left the ground, then the heel of the left. "Coming back," he said.

"Clear back left."

"Clear back right." The gunners' helmets were connected to control panels in the ceiling by long cords with hand buttons. The Huey backed slowly, gracefully, out of the revetment to the center of the narrow flight line, then turned ninety degrees right. The eastern sky had begun to green above the hooches of the Seabees. "You do the takeoff," McCawley said. "I'll call clearance."

"I've got it," Roark said, and thought, Oh, shit.

"You've got it."

He gripped the controls as if he had never had them in his hands. The Huey jerked firmly and rose two feet while he screamed silently at himself to be calm. Then the control came, and the helicopter settled obediently against the cushion of air at a three-foot hover. Roark could feel sweat streaming down his sides.

"Evans Tower, Phoenix Two-four."

"Phoenix Two-four, Evans."

"Roger, Evans, Phoenix Two-four in the nest for departure, right break, Rakkasan rear."

"Phoenix Two-four, current altimeter three-zero-zero-two, winds zero-niner-zero at zero-five. Negative outbound arty. Cleared for takeoff, right break. Call short, Rakkasan pad."

"Phoenix Two-four, wilco." McCawley waved two fingers. Roark checked the instruments and eased the cyclic forward, pulling in a touch of power in spite of himself as the aircraft dipped going into translational lift. His spirit soared as the craft climbed away, and he felt his blood moving through his veins. The Huey was strong and lunged eagerly into the sky. Any doubts Roark had about what he was doing vanished forever in that instant.

"Clear right," Dusty said. Roark began the turn, and soon they were approaching five hundred feet. He lowered the nose, reduced power, and managed to peg the altimeter, intensely aware that this was part of his checkride. McCawley had that nonchalant look, gazing out the window or dragging lidded eyes across the instruments on his way to looking somewhere else, that instructors display to encourage their students to relax. Roark was certain the aircraft commander was quietly coiled and ready, completely aware of his aircraft and the untested pilot on the controls.

The Huey was special, as anyone who flew them knew. There was a surging strength, a vibrancy in it approaching that of a living creature which made it impossible to regard it as merely a machine. It breathed, it pulsed, it lived. A pilot tasted its breath in his own, felt its heartbeat through his flesh, knew the scream of life surrounding him. And when he had flown them long enough he began to think of himself, if not as a helicopter, then at least as a helicopter's mind.

Somewhere the sun moved, caught the floating particles in the limits of the sky, beginning the refractive trickery of dawn. A thin strand drew the level of the sea below distant polka dots of purple. The red-lighted instruments were suddenly dimmer, and the ground was visible below.

When they landed near the southern perimeter two young men who looked like beach bums began loading ammunition. They wore fatigue pants and jungle boots, no shirts and no hats, and had skin the color of old copper. Roark watched as Piermont and Dusty stacked the cargo against the firewall to keep the center of gravity aft. One of the loaders gave the frequency, call sign, and coordinates to McCawley who recorded the information in grease pencil on his plastic-covered map. He marked the position, studied the surrounding terrain, and fixed a picture of the place in his mind. He would be able now to find it from memory. "I'll take it," he said. "You're going to want to do a lot of looking." He handed the map to Roark. "Try to keep track of where we are."

When they crossed the perimeter, headed south, Roark looked back at the new pine crates, wondering if a round through the floor would blow them to bits. He smiled. Piermont and Dusty raised their machine guns from the nose-down position, cocked and loaded them, and began looking for targets.

The eastern horizon was red, the polka dots now edged in pink. Shafts of blue and purple and thin vermilion reached across the sky. The tangle of growth that covered the foothills was gloomy and flat, deceivingly without depth. Ahead, the 2,000-foot face of the mountains showed darkly green with just a blush of dawn color. McCawley radioed for artillery clearance south from Evans to the Song Bo and along the river to Firebase Blaze, then switched the Fox-Mike radio to the ground frequency. They were climbing steeply, and by the time they cut the corner and picked up the blue line, there were fifteen hundred feet between them and the jagged terrain. As he would do throughout the day when not making calls, McCawley talked tirelessly to Roark, beginning the transfer of the encyclopedic mass of information a pilot had to know to survive in Vietnam.

"Juniper Kilo, Phoenix Two-four."

The canyon of the Song Bo was steep-sided, but not vertical. The lower slopes were lush elephant grass, palms, bamboo, and choking blankets of vines. The larger trees became increasingly dominant higher up until they finally meshed into a solid canopy. The river, so green and clear with sparkling rapids in full sunlight, was a thin, fairly straight strip of gray cutting through the forest, reflecting the brightening sky.

"Juniper Kilo, Phoenix Two-four."

"Hello, Phoenix," came the response.

"Morning, Kilo. We're inbound your location with some dang-dang, 'bout zero-five out. What's your sit-rep, over?"

"Got a negative sit-rep, Phoenix. Charlie left over an hour ago. Been quiet ever since."

"Roger, Kilo. I'll call a minute out."

"Kilo, roger." Roark was having no trouble keeping track of their progress; he was accustomed to maps, and following the river made it a cinch. Every turn, every tributary, was there on paper exactly as on the ground. The X McCawley had drawn lay in a small saddle on a jutting finger halfway between the ridge and the river, and already Roark thought he could see it through the haze. The sky, the river, and the air in the canyon were slowly becoming blue. The Huey began to descend.

"Juniper Kilo, Phoenix Two-four. Pop smoke."

"Roger, Phoenix. Smoke popped."

While they flew toward the LZ, waiting for the smoke to rise and spread, McCawley explained the procedure. "After you call for smoke," he said, "wait, identify, then tell them what color you see. They'll confirm it. Sometimes a screwball will tell you what color he's going to pop. If that happens, don't land. Make them do it right, and with a different color. The gooks have radios and smoke grenades, and what they'll do is pop the same color somewhere nearby and blow you away when you land to it." A growing purple cone lay almost horizontal in the push of air moving down the canyon wall. "Juniper Kilo, got your goofy grape."

"Affirmative, Phoenix. Come on in."

McCawley kept the ship over the center of the canyon until the landing zone was out his door, then began a descending S that kept them far from the ground until they were almost upon the saddle. The landing zone did not look good, but it was the only spot in the area where a ship could get in at a low hover. The jungled wall of the canyon loomed above the saddle, most of it from an angle that the doorgun could not reach. Once they landed, the Huey would be practically defenseless while every gook on the mountain could throw down whatever they had. "Make it fast," McCawley said on mid-final, but the gunners could read an LZ. Sensing McCawley's nervousness, Roark held his hands close to the controls, tensed his body, and waited for the war to begin. Ahead, the jungle became suddenly real, a garden gone mad, an uptilted ocean of stormy green with no apparent bottom. The figures of the men on the ridge were as insignificant as insects in a field of weeds.

The deep grass in the saddle lay down when the Huey came to a hover, rippling silver and green and running away like water. The gunners seized the cases and quickly threw them out; in less than ten seconds the ship was empty. "Just a minute, sir," Dusty said. A man who had been crouching to the right with a rucksack, a steel pot, and an M-16 hurried forward, handed the items up, then moved away. "We're up," said Dusty.

"Up left." McCawley was ready. The take-off path was clear ahead, but he turned the ship quickly at a high hover and left the way he had come, dropping into the canyon with a quartering tail wind to get away from the ominous wall, then turning and climbing to altitude above the River Bo.

"Somebody DEROSed this morning," Dusty said. Roark looked back at the rucksack sagging across the rifle. It was dark green nylon, swollen and lumpy on a paint-chipped metal frame. Across the top was a burgundy-black stain. Wind moved over the pack, shaking it, making the flaps and tiedowns flutter. On the elastic camo band around the helmet was a message in black ink printed in a youthful hand: *Goldwater Was Right.*

CHAPTER THREE

T HE SKY looked like November on the Great Plains when early winter winds shove sheets of ice ahead at altitude, making the sunsets spectacular. The sun hung red and clear above the mountains of the Chaine Annamitique as the pilots approached the hooch, sloshing through dust that followed in pink phantoms. Billy Roark was satisfied; his war had finally begun, not with the blast of violence he had expected, but quietly, unobtrusively, invisibly. They had logged more than seven hours flying from Evans to Firebase Rakkasan and units in the field with mail, ammunition, food, and replacements. Between graduation, leave, in-country orientation training, processing and sitting at Group, it had been eight weeks since he had flown. All his early landings were something less than standard, but Gil McCawley had the infinite patience that good IPs must have and a talent for explaining with exactly the right words. Roark's head felt like pulp until the burst of exhilaration at the end of the flight.

They had taken four hits. When the big blades coasted to a stop, Roark stared up at two jagged rips, one near the tip of each blade, exposing streaks of foil honeycomb, not looking anything like bullet holes. He called to McCawley, still strapped in his seat with the log book in his lap, and they began going over the ship. Piermont found the holes in the tail rotor, a novelty since the high-speed blades were regarded as waiting for the slightest excuse to fly apart. The rotating blades had dispersed the weight of impact; no one had any idea when they had taken the fire.

The hooch was empty except for the sound of a working broom. Dust boiled into the sunlight. Roark stepped forward and met a familiar face. "Hey, Baker, where'd you come from?"

"Hello, Roark. Good to see you. I just got here a little while ago from Eagle."

"But I was there—uh—yesterday morning. Where were you?" Yesterday already seemed a long time ago.

"I just got there yesterday," Baker said. "They processed me this morning and put me on a bird this afternoon." He rested bony hands atop the dilapidated broom. His light brown hair was bleached almost blond on top, and blue eyes shone in a face that was Arizona tan. He studied Roark in his flight suit and chest armor, still clutching his helmet, sunburned and sweaty and looking very comfortable in his gear. "You've only been here one day?" he asked.

"One long day," Roark said, smiling. Gil McCawley stuck his head into the cube, and Roark introduced them.

"Let's go get a beer," McCawley said with his usual friendly grin. Everybody agreed it was a great idea.

The sun was down but the evening light seemed especially clear, even through the dusty haze that always hung around a helicopter camp. The mountains that stood higher and higher away toward Laos were as still and impassive as a photograph.

"Hark, an Aardvark!" McCawley said, entering ahead of Roark and Baker. A muscular, handsome pilot named Jim Tyler looked up glumly from his table, but his face quickly formed a smile. His teeth were even and white, and his eyes were large and brown with lashes too long for a man.

Gil McCawley was a rarity among the more experienced aircraft commanders, shunning a tendency among older hands to congregate like herd bulls, excluding the new guys. His teaching extended beyond his position as instructor, and he made a point of associating with new pilots. He waved to some men across the room, then he and the new guys pulled out chairs at Tyler's table. There were introductions all around.

The Phoenix Club was built by the officers of Charlie Company, but Jim Tyler and a few others from Alpha Company, as well as most of the pilots of Delta, enjoyed it as their own. The club was L-shaped with a bar along the side of the L and tables in the base. The windowless building was eternally under construction. The floor and walls were bare plywood, as was the finished portion of the ceiling. Near the rear lay a stack of materials traded away from the Seabees in exchange for rides to Da Nang. Blocks of foam rocket dunnage were being used as insulation, and each time a few more pieces became available another sheet of plywood was nailed to the rafters. There were plans to install carpet, upholstered furniture, and an icemaker—all of which the Seabees had promised to help procure. Speakers hung from the wall, and a reel-to-reel played music behind the bar where a buck sergeant named Keeper served drinks.

"So what's happening in the Big Valley?" McCawley asked. A number of Phoenix aircraft had been used that day for a big assault in the A Shau, and most of the crews were not yet back. Two gunnies sat at a table against the far wall, and around another were three pilots from second platoon. A thin haze of cigarette smoke was beginning to spread.

"You guys weren't there?" said Tyler.

"No. Will be tomorrow. We worked close in for the Rakkasans today. Baker just got here. You?"

"Most of the day," Tyler said. "We came back early because of a chip detector light. They're putting a firebase on the valley floor."

"The *floor?*"

"That's right. Calling it Currahee. We inserted troops this morning, then Chinooks brought steel posts and concertina wire and about a thousand bales of sandbags. When we left, those guys were digging like crazy."

"Can't say I blame them," said McCawley. "That's going to be mortar city. I wonder why they put it on the floor?"

"Beats me," said Tyler. "Maybe there's a reason—they probably want it for artillery coverage—but it almost looks like they're doing it just to show the NVA we can."

"Shades of Khe Sanh?"

Roark and Baker listened carefully. Neither knew enough to contribute more than dumb questions, so they kept quiet. One of the gun pilots was making diving motions with a hand, his face brightly animated. McCawley yelled at him. "Okay, kamikaze, come tell us your lies." The gun pilot stopped in middive, then the two grabbed their beers and walked over. McCawley stood between them with his arms on their shoulders to make the introductions. "These are front-seat Foreskins," he announced.

"Redskins," they both corrected.

"I'll compromise," McCawley said with a grin. "Red Foreskins."
Lieutenant David Luskey and Warrant Officer John Deiterman
laughed and pulled chairs near the table. "Now what's all this
about?" McCawley asked, making airplanes of his hands and in-
scribing a series of overlapping loops and dives that resembled a
dogfight. Deiterman laughed, and Luskey, who was fair, blushed
vividly.

"We knocked out a fifty-one today," Luskey said, regaining his
composure with the gravity of the statement. "The one that shot
up Two-one." He was in his early twenties. Thin lines bracketing
his mouth deepened when he smiled.

"Two-one?"

"You didn't hear? You got a bird shot up today."

"Steve Sharp?"

"I think so. Dark hair, eyes like a husky? They got shot to shit
near Hamburger. Took some rounds through the console and fuel
cell, but made it back to that new firebase, just barely. Nobody
hurt."

"Ops didn't say anything about it."

"It happened late—they might not have heard yet. Me and Duffy
just got back a little while ago."

"What happened?" McCawley asked. Roark and Baker leaned
forward with their arms on the edge of the table.

Luskey was not unaware that he had an audience of new guys.
"Near noon," he said, "a company of grunts was inserted on a ridge
off Hamburger. They kept receiving fire from up on the hill, but
could never pinpoint the source. It looked like a setup, so when
they said they wanted extra ammo for the night, Sharp called us.
Sure enough, right after he landed the fifty-one opened up. He took
off and cut away hard south. That's when he took the rounds in
the belly. John was front seat with Parsons, near the bottom of
their pass, with us coming around on top. It was right in front of
us. Duffy just rolled out early, dumped the nose, and started sending them home." Luskey's eyes were vivid with the sight of the
twin trails of smoke tightening down to the target. He had sprayed
the minigun into the roiling dust as they came out of the dive, but
it was only a token punctuation.

McCawley looked thoughtful. "They should be bringing in
Steve's bird pretty soon," he said to Roark and Baker. "You guys
might want to go take a look."

"I don't think so," Deiterman said. "The last I heard, they
couldn't get a Hook. Said they were just going to leave it there and
bring it back tomorrow." He had olive skin and a dark, perfect
mustache.

McCawley shook his head. "Those boys at Currahee are going to be pissed at us," he said.

"Why's that?" Roark asked.

"They're going to get mortared tonight. They probably would have gotten it anyway, just being where they are, but a Huey gives the gooks twice the reason, and it makes it look like it's our fault." He turned to Luskey. "Is the ship inside the perimeter?"

"Perimeter? They don't have a perimeter," Luskey said. "Those suffering bastards are sitting out there in foxholes with no bunkers, no perimeter, no nothing. Just a Huey for registration."

There was a moment of silence at the table, then McCawley began to laugh, softly at first, then harder as it took hold. The others, except Roark and Baker, caught the image and joined him. Soon they were wiping tears from their eyes. The new guys laughed with them, but not nearly so hard since they didn't really understand what was so funny.

He awoke on the floor, the scream and explosion shuddering through his body. It had been very close. Meaty thumps resounded throughout the hooch; an exhausted voice said in irritation, "Son of a *bitch*." The camp siren began its orphan's wail, rising and falling as it turned round its base. Roark listened, then jumped quickly for his pants, flopped to the floor, and arched his back to pull them on. His bare feet were stuffed into boots and his flak vest was across his shoulders when he heard the second round, far off on a suicide dive, screaming louder and louder. He groped for his mattress, but there was no time, and he scurried into the dust and cobwebs beneath his bunk. The rocket was a vomiting roar that filled his head, seemed to pass through it. *KA-BAAAAAM!* The trailing sound was metallic.

He jumped to his feet and roughly tied the loose strings, grabbed his steel pot and rifle and bandolier, chambered a round, and moved quickly down the hall and out the back. In the deep shadow beneath the eave he crouched against the sandbags, rubbed the selector with his thumb, and scanned the darkness. The weapon was cool and reassuring in his hands. Across the drive at the front of the hooch a number of men were hurrying into a huge sunken shelter that had a steel and sandbag roof. Roark watched and shook his head. A man in that hole was a blind man who had turned his life over to luck. He would take his chances in the open where he could see.

Another scream came, ripping the sky, and he fell against the bags and pressed himself into the earth like putty. When he was twelve, he and a friend had been playing beneath a trestle, sitting on the concrete ledge between the steel beams that held the track, when a freight train came. The train passed over them three feet away, and though they drew their bodies into tight fetal positions and clamped their palms against their heads, every living part of them understood that death was taking place. It was a sound that could have been heard without ears, different from a rocket, but with the same explicit message. It came to Roark that this rocket was his; it would land between his shoulders, and in the morning they would find his meat-filled boots, a few tattered rags clinging to the clotheslines, mongrels worrying with the scraps. Then the rocket was suddenly past, and he turned and followed the sound. There was a white-orange flash among the hooches of Headquarters Company, and the rattle and puff of concussion.

Camp Evans resembled an anthill someone had kicked, warriors lashing futilely at an unseen enemy. Illumination flares drifted across the camp on white parachutes. The 155mm howitzers were firing toward the mountains, groping blindly for the launching site. Two Cobras climbed away to the north.

Forty-five seconds later the next round came on the same path, but crashed into bare earth behind the Phoenix hangar, lacing the steel wall with shrapnel and producing a sound like a booted drum. When several minutes passed and nothing happened, those in the bunker began coming out. Some stood on the roof. The big siren stopped, then another began, smaller and moving toward headquarters. Roark became aware he was soaked in sweat; sand covered his arms and stomach and face. His muscles were pumped, and he blinked to moisten his eyes. He sat a long time in the shadows, then stood and moved back to the door. "Hello, hooch," he said loudly, and stepped inside.

He stripped and toweled away the sweat and sand, then lay nude and gritty on the quilted poncho liner, staring into the darkness, waiting to come down. When he finally closed his eyes and slept, his ears remained awake, keeping watch, listening to every sound. The pebbled perspiration on his body caught the moon glow and the fuzzy shadowed hatching of the screen.

CHAPTER FOUR

FLYING A helicopter involves continuous coordinated movements of both hands and feet. It is balancing and juggling combined. The collective stick, rising obliquely on the left, determines the pitch in the main rotor blades, thus the speed of flight, or power. The cyclic stick, which stands between the pilot's legs, controls the tilt, or path, of the main rotor plane. The pedals adjust the pitch of the tail rotor blades which counteract the torque produced by power delivered to the main rotor; the pedals are also used to cause the aircraft to pivot at a hover. The controls are integral through flight; a change in one ultimately requires corresponding adjustments of all.

A helicopter demands more of a pilot than fixed-wing aircraft. The traditional airplane essentially flies itself once put in a condition to do so; adjustments must be made periodically for flight to continue, but the operation of the simpler craft compares to that of an automobile with a third dimension applied. No such comparison can be made with the helicopter. Though it may appear graceful, it flies strictly by brute force. The pilot is always aware he is performing a feat of magic. He must be forever alert, totally sensitive to the creature he only partially controls. He feels the ship's condition through his hands, his feet, and the cheeks of his butt. He listens to the different threads of sound—the hungry suction of air at the intake, the muffled blast of flame inside, the jet exhaust, the rumble of gears turning round, the heavy blades beating overhead, and the soprano song of the tail rotor. All these things he hears and feels and watches.

Next come the usual flight duties of navigation, checking instruments and keeping gauges within proper parameters, operating three or four radios, watching for other aircraft, contemplating emergencies, and negotiating all types of weather, day or night. In combat there are also enemy fire, artillery, formation flight, low-level obstacles, stump-studded landing zones, fatigue, and emotional trauma. When all combinations of these elements have been weighed and provided for, the pilot so inclined may then enjoy the unique occasion of flight.

There are four stages in the development of a helicopter pilot. The beginning is pure chaos bordered by absolute panic. This is the time the young aspirant suddenly becomes aware he is in the depths of a nightmare, and that *no one* could possibly make an eggbeater hover. Many students drop out in the first week of training. There then follows a period of basic learning, with marked progress in all areas. This stage peaks out at about one hundred hours in the air when the pilot begins to believe he can do anything. Now he is truly dangerous.

The third stage requires an environment like the military. It begins when the pilot is made painfully aware how stupid, ignorant, and incompetent he is. The people who bring this about are the older brothers with hundreds, sometimes thousands of hours at the controls, and experience in almost every conceivable situation. Now the true learning begins.

After somewhere around a thousand hours another change takes place. The pilot never knows when exactly, but one day he looks back and realizes the difference. From then on, when he wants the aircraft to do something, it simply happens. There is no conscious link between the pilot and his helicopter, and it leaves the impression that if a surgeon were instructed to separate the two, he could not be certain exactly where to begin his cut.

They were approaching Three Forks where the branches of the Song Bo came together. Out Roark's window was the scenic canyon of the Rao Trang, a continuous sequence of deep clear pools with bouldered bottoms, short rapids and low falls, gray and green with jungle dawn. The forest tumbled down the mountains, fan-

ning in protective fingers above the rocky boundaries of the
stream. The lush and gloomy canyon with its self-made mist and
water rushing nowhere seemed a world apart, a place that knew
nothing of armies or war.

"Our area of operation, or AO," McCawley was saying, "is essentially the northern fifty miles of South Vietnam. It'll change
some when the monsoons come, but for now ninety percent of our
flying is done inside a triangle formed by Quang Tri, the A Shau,
and Camp Eagle." As he spoke, McCawley's eyes were constantly
in motion, flicking across the instrument panel, scanning the sky
ahead and to either side, then back to the vital gauges. "The country here will fool you—everything is out of whack from the way it
seems it should be. The A Shau is almost due south of Evans, and
if you fly straight north you end up in the ocean."

"What about RPGs?" Roark blurted, feeling suddenly stupid.
"We heard about them constantly in flight school. I mean, I know
it's a rocket-propelled grenade . . ."

"That's really a misnomer," McCawley said. "It's actually an
antitank weapon that penetrates a foot of armor steel. The gooks
use them on us at close range from the edge of a landing zone."

"We get hit with one of those babies," Piermont said, "and you
can spread your legs, bend over, and kiss your ass good-bye. It'll be
all over but the crying."

"Phoenix Two-four, Bulldog Three."

"Three, Two-four."

"Two-four, got a unit in contact on Hill Nine-nine-six. Divert to
the upper pad at Blaze for resupply. Call en route."

"Two-four, roger." The dove-gray sky toward Laos was cast with
violet. With new tail rotor blades installed and patches of hundred-
knot tape concealing the silvery slashes in the mains, they were en
route to the A Shau. The mission was direct support for the Third
Brigade, headquartered at the mountaintop Firebase Berchtesgaden—
nicknamed BG—which stood on the brink of the valley. Their initial instructions had been to report to the battalion commander at
Currahee, but Bulldog Three, deep in a bunker at BG, had overall
control. McCawley turned to Roark with a wry smile. "We're
going to get you that hot LZ yet," he said.

"Looks like it," Roark replied impassively. He was already excited, simply being in the air, having his hands on the controls.
Merely flying the Huey was a thrill, but today he was bound at last
for the infamous A Shau Valley. He had an imagined instant with
lead zinging past, little splats through the windshield. He braced
his left leg against the collective, then checked his belt and harness

by feel. McCawley noticed, but looked out the window toward the dark textured mountains.

Firebase Blaze sat in a crook of the main tributary of the Song Bo, ten kilometers south of Three Forks, thirty klicks from Evans. It was connected to division headquarters at Camp Eagle by a dirt road, Route 547, and later to the A Shau Valley until the monsoons washed the road off the canyon wall. Emplaced around the forward supply point were a battery of 155mm guns, a long-barreled 175 that could shoot twenty miles, and an eight-inch cannon which lobbed two hundred pounds half that far. The 175 fired into Laos, sending hundred-foot smoke rings curling far into the sky. Blaze was a red-orange gash in what had been a beautiful jungle valley. Before the firebase was established, a recon team found a road beneath the canopy, a branch of the Ho Chi Minh Trail. So the Ranch Hand crews were called to spray defoliant, and the slopes were bombed until the earth lay cratered and bare. When it rained, the narrow valley slithered away to silt the rapids of the Song Bo.

A shirtless loader popped a smoke grenade so the pilot could know the wind, then stood at the upwind edge of the pad, his arms held in a T. On either side were stacks of wooden crates, and next to them were three loaders. Roark had visions of impaling the man on the pitot tube projecting from the nose of the ship, but managed to stop in time. Yellow smoke rushed away in a tight stream, spread, and climbed in hairy wisps outside the rotor, then dived down through the blades. The scent of sulfur filled the cockpit. The men leaped to work, and in a few seconds the Huey was loaded with a thousand pounds of grenades and bullets and claymores and one small bundle of black plastic. One of the loaders yelled something to the crew chief, then gave the thumbs-up and moved aside. "We're up, sir," said Piermont. "This guy says we've got two more trips."

"Must be expecting a war," McCawley said, "or they're in one." He took the controls and departed in a climbing hairpin, then followed the twisting canyon west and south. The jungle covering the mountains was various green, billowed like the surface of a thundercloud. "Bulldog Three, Phoenix Two-four."

"Two-four, Three."

"Roger, Three, we're zero-two off Blaze en route. Do you need us to evac any wounded?"

"Negative, Two-four. A Dustoff just came out, and one's touching down. Contact Lima Chuck X-ray up this push."

"Three, is there gun support on station?"

"Negative. They're en route to Eagle to rearm. ARA will be out here shortly for a combat assault if we need them. The landing zone is cold, but you might be taking mortars."

As soon as McCawley rogered, Piermont said on the intercom, "Might, my ass."

"You're about to see some mortars," McCawley said. "Unless the grunts are getting murdered, they usually make light of what's happening. Don't want to discourage anybody."

Nine-nine-six was a sister hill in the same mass as the more famous Nine-three-seven—Dong Ap Bia, better known as Hamburger Hill. Named for its elevation in meters, it was one of those many knobs where a lot of men died a few at a time for a long time, and so never earned a reputation with the press. It overlooked the canyon produced by the Rao Lao, the narrow stream that drained the A Shau westward into Laos. It was spitting distance from the Laotian border where thousands of NVA troops were embedded in the steep slopes. The terrain surrounding Nine-nine-six was aggressively held by the enemy, permanently occupied. The NVA, cocky and sure of themselves, could dart across the border with their bellies full of hot chow, launch an attack, and make it back to the underground complex within a few hours. That is why battalions of NVA appeared and disappeared so quickly, and antiaircraft positions sprang up along the A Shau like mushrooms.

McCawley was silent as they climbed above the rising canyon. Far below, a thin clear stream tumbled between gray boulders. The massive mountains that held BG and Eagle's Nest loomed to their right. Slowly a blank space developed beyond the ridge ahead, and the A Shau Valley lay spread before them.

The A Shau ran northwest to southeast, roughly parallel with the border for thirty miles. Perceived as crucial by both sides, the valley provided passage through some of the most rugged mountains in the border region. Through its eastern passes a network of wide trails yielded downhill access to both Hue and Da Nang. The farming hamlets once occupying the valley were now abandoned, and the flat floor was pale green with deep elephant grass and encroaching brush. A few trees grew tall and lank with limbless gray trunks as if survivors of an older forest. The eastern side of the valley was banked by steep mountains with low passes near the middle and at the southern end; on the west a progression of foothills grew quickly into a great ridge of peaks along the border; and to the north the valley was open-ended, passing the buttressed limestone walls of Tiger Mountain and merging end to end with the southern reaches of the twisting Da Krong Valley.

They passed what would become Firebase Currahee, still little more than trenches and sandbags, and a Huey that looked out of place. The Medevac bird screamed past, its apparent speed doubled, en route to the 22d Surgical Hospital at Phu Bai. McCawley radioed Lima Chuck X-ray for a situation report and was told that the LZ was still cold. "Make a hover kickout on the southern side," the tired voice said. "We got mortared with both the Dust-offs." McCawley rogered and began a steep descent. He dropped to treetop level and increased airspeed. Piermont and Dusty checked their guns and ammo belts and leaned tautly over their weapons.

Nine-nine-six had been blasted bald, so landing there in a rush was simple. McCawley skimmed the treetops, weaving a crooked course past Hamburger's scowling face. Suddenly he turned up-slope and began a measured flare. Almost at once they were in the LZ. "Get on the controls with me," he said. The gunners jumped forward and began the kickout while the wind-whipped grunts knelt in their holes. Roark sat tensed and ready, staring at a dead gook just behind his feet. The man was wearing black pajama pants, rolled above the knees, and nothing else. The body was folded, limp as a dishrag. Around the LZ were several others, and sprawled among them were dead GIs. Roark looked out his side window and into an empty face that could have been dead but wasn't.

Ka-WHUMP! The round landed to their right, and every man on the hill jerked as if connected to one nerve. After a short delay the barrage began, one round per second, moving across the LZ. Roark heard the measured beat, saw the red-orange flashes marching toward him, the gray puffs they left behind.

"We're up!" Piermont yelled. McCawley spun the ship around to the right and plunged southward, pulling the collective high beneath his arm. A moment later Dusty opened up with his sixty, the barrel aimed straight down, then Piermont began to fire. McCawley zigzagged and dropped back toward the jungle. "I saw three gooks," Dusty said after a sustained burst. "About two hundred meters off the LZ."

"We took some hits," McCawley said. "You got it," he said to Roark. "Put it on the deck, but watch for trees." Roark took the controls and let the Huey slide earthward, flying the way he had seen McCawley do, trying to avoid good fields of fire, continually changing course. His breath was deep and steady, his eyes quick and alert, and he felt as if he could live forever. His butt muscles ached.

"Bulldog Three, Phoenix Two-four."

"Three, go ahead."

"Roger, Three, we've got three gooks in the open just south of Nine-nine-six." He read the coordinates from the map.

"Okay, Two-four, we'll put some arty in there. Remain low level."

McCawley acknowledged. When they landed at Blaze, while Dusty helped the loaders, Piermont jumped out and checked his ship. He plugged his cord in and said, "We've got three holes through the tail boom, but it looks okay." The tail rotor drive line lay along the top of the boom beneath a cover. It was tough, but could be knocked out with small arms. The thin cables controlling the tail rotor pitch ran inside the boom and would be severed by a direct hit. If either occurred in forward flight, the minimum result would be a running landing at Evans; from a hover in a rough LZ, even an expert pilot was likely to crash.

The second run to the hilltop was much like the first. Mc-Cawley dropped to low level as soon as they entered the valley, then slipped beneath the gun-target line and approached the hill from the northeast. The area south of the LZ was thick with reddish dust and pale gray smoke from impacting artillery. When they came to a hover, McCawley said, "You've got it," to an astonished Billy Roark. The mortars came again as before, but quickly bracketed the aircraft, peppering it with shrapnel, making two white chips high on the windshield. He held his hands steady on the controls, held himself in check, not blinking. Then they were out again and racing away. The adrenaline rush was on him, and he pushed hard on both pedals to hide the trembling in his legs. He began to laugh before they reached Currahee, and McCawley laughed with him.

"Phoenix, Chuck X-ray."

"Go ahead, X-ray."

"Don't come back, Phoenix," he said, out of breath. "We can't stand any more of this. Please don't come back."

Bulldog Three was monitoring the transmission, and he released them to Currahee. "I've got a couple more runs for you," he said, "but they can wait."

A small U.S. flag hung limply on a stalk of antenna pipe outside the pit that was quickly becoming the command bunker. Shirtless men were digging trenches, filling sandbags, their pants soaked through. Steel stakes had been driven into the soil where the perimeter wire would be. "Don't shut down," McCawley said, then grabbed his map and baseball cap, and started toward the flag. Roark rolled the throttle to flight idle and gazed at Steve Sharp's Huey. The mortars had come in the night. None had struck directly, but the windshield was splintered, and the rotor blade angling above was speckled silver. The tail boom looked like it had been shotgunned. Both gunners got out to have a look.

Eight Hueys crossed the pass in formation, then turned southward, slowly separating, preparing for a one-ship LZ. Nearby and higher were two Cobras looking like evil fish.

Suddenly the mortars began to fall. Roark rolled the throttle and yelled unnecessarily at the crew. Piermont slapped at McCawley's open door and leaped aboard with Dusty. They looked for McCawley, didn't see him, and pulled pitch. The door flapped loosely in the wind.

Alone at the controls above the valley floor, Billy Roark was beginning to believe that this might all be real. His war had begun, and it was exciting and strangely wonderful. When McCawley radioed that he was ready, they landed quickly. When he was aboard, Piermont rushed forward to close his door since he couldn't do it himself because of the armor. Roark took off while McCawley secured his belts. When he was strapped in, his helmet on, the aircraft commander lit a smoke. "You passed your checkride," he said, grinning. Roark returned the smile, but said nothing, not sure he was supposed to be enjoying this.

They made a series of sorties carrying mail and rations between Blaze and units in the field, most at the bottom of deep hover holes in the gloomy jungle. Later, when they were departing a broad meadow on the northern valley floor below Airborne, McCawley reduced RPM to simulate a heavy load, then showed Roark a complex technique for squeezing the last bit of energy from an overloaded Huey. "Just for an emergency," he said. Near noon Bulldog Three sent them back to Nine-nine-six.

There were eight bulging bags in a pile. The grunts tried swinging one up with a man at either end, but it struck the side of the ship and fell. After that, three men worked with each, shoving them roughly aboard, banging hard against the floor. The last was heavy in both ends, empty in the middle, and when they threw it aboard it twisted and rolled forward against the console at Roark's elbow. They were halfway to the morgue, Graves Registration, before he realized they had not been mortared. He could smell the blood and bowels, and a terrible feeling moved through him. Remembering the dead gooks, he wished bitterly that there had been a hundred. But that number seemed small compared to the load that pressed against his seat.

"Here comes the prick," said Motormouth.

"Hush," Captain Hood hissed. But the spec 4 was right; the wall

supporting the stairs carried the sound of footsteps clearly, herald-
ing all but the stealthiest climber. Phillip Crable had a signature
like no other, calculated and emphatic, wanting to be known.
Hood turned back to the wall and resumed the simple but satisfying task of sticking red and yellow pins into a map of northern I
Corps, adding to the bright clusters already rimming the A Shau.
Each pin was a confirmed enemy antiaircraft position—yellow for
12.7mm—.51-inch—weapons, called fifty-ones by the pilots, and
red for 37mm guns or quad-fifties. Withdrawn only when a position was destroyed, the pins depicted the situation as worse than it
actually was, but correctly displayed concentrations of force. The
tightest group, thirty-four, completely covered the hill at the valley's southern tip where the NVA route called the Yellow Brick
Road cut through a protrusion of Laos on its inexorable course. But
today the new pins decorated Hamburger Hill and the ravines and
ridges that tapered toward the border. Hood stepped back to examine his work and study the squiggly lines; he had never seen any of
the terrain in real life.

Crable marched through the door, shoulders squared, chest in-
flated, accentuating poor features that would have gone unnoticed.
His eyes were milky and opaque like a snake too early out of hibernation. Before he could say anything, Motormouth jumped up and
announced, "Time for me to go take a shit," and walked immediately out of the room. Crable ignored him. "Good afternoon," he
said to Hood. He spray-starched and ironed his fatigues himself,
and they were almost as neat as when he had put them on that
morning. The seat of his pants hung empty.

"Hello," Hood replied. He was a thin man with glossy black hair
and a tanless face who flew only minimum hours. His war was
largely an illusion represented by squawking voices of the radio,
painted pins in a map, perforated Hueys the Chinooks brought
back, and faces that arrived and disappeared. "What can I do for
you?" he asked. Crable rarely entered Operations except to brief
the nighttime duty officer, or for his own monthly four-hour flight.

"Have you seen that new warrant officer, Billy Roark?"

"Briefly," Hood said. "He's been flying with McCawley and
training at night to schedule first platoon."

Crable frowned. "Do you know when they'll be in?"

"They just called from POL, topping off with fuel. Should be no
more than a few minutes."

"I need to speak to him," Crable said. "Mind if I wait?" The
question was absurd. Hood waved a hand. Ordinarily working as
much as possible on his feet, he now sat with his back to the room,
taking calls from returning aircraft. Crable sat on a bench and

crossed his legs in the squirmy manner of women and old men. Several minutes passed, and though it was the busy time of the evening, Motormouth did not return.

The stairs began to rumble, and a flow of pilots moved through the room. Crable kept his eyes averted, listening carefully to the incoming calls as each pilot reported flight termination and their bird's expected status for the following day. When he heard Mc-Cawley's voice he went behind the counter to the corner windows where he stood thumbing through a sheaf of intelligence reports, watching for Billy Roark. Captain Hood divided himself between radio calls and taking SOIs and URC-10 emergency radios from pilots at the counter. At last Crable spotted Roark walking with McCawley up the rise, and he quickly hung the clipboard on its nail and left the room. When he reached the landing he realized the timing was wrong, and he feigned interest in something in the shop below before moving slowly down the stairs. His feet were at head level when the pilots rounded the corner, and he stopped and gazed down with all the force he could find.

"Mr. Roark," the captain said.

The pilots were looking at Steve Sharp's Huey, now parked in front of the hangar, pointing at different holes and laughing. They turned abruptly at Crable's voice. "Yes, sir," Roark answered, and he smiled up at the captain. He climbed three steps before he realized the XO wanted him to stop. McCawley moved past Crable to the top of the stairs, then turned on the landing to watch.

Crable assumed his most withering look. "Mr. Roark," he said, "I believe I asked two days ago that you come see me."

It had completely slipped Roark's mind. The two twenty-hour days had left it far behind. "Sorry, sir," he said. "I've been flying."

"I can see that," Crable said testily. "The point is, Mr. Roark, you have made no effort to contact me. In case you are unaware, a request by a superior officer is *not* a request. It is an implied order, and you are expected to make an effort."

Roark made his face a blank and said more calmly than he felt, "Sir, I had no idea it was an order. I am a pilot, and I have been doing my job." The sarcasm was intentional.

"You will recall, Mr. Roark, that you were made an officer *before* you received your wings," Crable said. "That was to remind you that you are an officer first, and a pilot second. Flying is secondary to the performance of your military duties." This was an old line the warrant officers never bought. They had joined the Army to fly—were recruited as prospective pilots—at a time when none of them knew or cared what a warrant officer was. The day prior to graduation from flight school and the awarding of the wings they were given warrants because that was the lowest rank a pilot could have. But it was the wings that mattered, not the bars.

McCawley intervened. "Captain, I've been with him almost all the past forty-eight hours, and there hasn't been much time to track you down." Crable turned and found himself at eye level with McCawley's boots. "We've been up here until midnight both nights." McCawley's words were forceful, but his face was wrinkled in a good-old-boy smile.

"I am aware of that," Crable said, "but I have an extra-duty assignment for him." His voice was more civil now.

"He's taking over scheduling for the first platoon," McCawley said flatly. Roark was forgotten.

"Who gave him that position?"

"No one. He took it like I did when Mike got killed."

"Well, that's most admirable, but since Captain Dansworth is no longer with us, I am in charge of the platoon."

"This is the first I've heard of it."

"What?"

"This is the first time anyone has said anything about you running our platoon. Danny's been dead three weeks, and the platoon has been running itself. I took over scheduling—nobody gave me the job. Now I'm passing it on to Roark."

Crable knew he had lost. He could bull his way through, ordering Roark to another position, but that would leave a flank exposed. Since the two had taken the initiative, they would have a solid case if they went to the CO—unlikely since warrants took pride in butting heads with superiors, but still a possibility. "Very well," he replied abruptly. "Roark will do scheduling." He spun about and descended the stairs without even a glance at Roark.

Once they were inside the door of Operations, Roark turned to McCawley and thanked him. "That's part of WOMPA," McCawley replied. "Warrant Officers Mutual Protection Association." Roark smiled, but only briefly. He could not escape a feeling that he was on a collision course with the posturing captain, something there would be no way to avoid.

When Crable walked out of the hangar he passed directly in front of Steve Sharp's Huey. In his haste to track down the errant Roark he had failed to notice it before, but now he slowed, turned, and finally stared in astonishment at the damage, unaware that part had been caused by mortars. The windshield and tail boom were obvious, but what got his attention most was inside between the pilots' seats. The radio console was destroyed, and the over-head panel and both greenhouses were shattered. In the floor behind the console were three monstrous metallic eruptions, huge exits above. Crable's eyes grew wide, and he felt as if he were in a tunnel. He could not look at the fist-sized holes without seeing the chunks of hot lead rising from the jungle in slow motion, blasting in stop-action sequence through the floor, the metal curling back like opening blooms, the gush of dust and exploding fragments erupting in a soundless vacuum. The projectiles tumbled, blasting oblong holes through the roof, destroying the hydraulics above and biting off chunks of blade, still carrying enough power to sever a leg or head from a body on their unstoppable course through the sky.

Afraid he was being watched, and that his fear might be known, Crable walked forcefully toward the mess hall. But he could not shake the slow-motion sequence. It was what he saw on the screen of his mind when he closed his eyes that night; what later awoke him, terrified and gasping, completely drenched with sweat.

One of our drills in Basic was with pugil sticks—*five-foot poles with hard padded ends*—which we used to beat each other to a pulp. The stated purpose of the drill was to teach the use of the bayonet and rifle butt in a hand-to-hand situation. Mainly it taught gut-ripping aggression, and how it feels to be beaten sense-less, knowing it was the same as dying.

After weeks practicing basic maneuvers in a field, we went to the sand pits where each platoon circled round while two men squared off for battle. We wore helmets which made it appear our heads were protected, but provided only an additional surface to be crushed against our skulls. One of the drill sergeants had dis-liked me from the beginning, and when it became my turn he put me in the ring with the biggest man in the platoon. I didn't last long, and when I was down on my knees with the sand weaving before me and the black edges of unconsciousness moving in, the big bear Luke Johnson was there, apologizing for hitting me so hard. When he helped me up, the drill sergeant, Garcia, was standing with a smirk on his face, and it was only then that I understood.

Everybody went through twice, and when it was my turn again

the rules changed. Garcia put two men against me. Fear and anger were the only hope I had.

The man behind moved first. I heard the crunch in the sand and whirled with a butt stroke and caught him beneath the jaw. I saw him start to flip, then I spun and ducked a wild swing from the man in front, made a quick full circle, and brought my stick down like an ax on the back of his neck. He went to his belly and stayed there. Then the first one tried to get up, and I took him out hard on the ear while he was still off balance.

I whipped around toward Sergeant Garcia and stood in the ready position, hoping the slimy fuck would put on the gear. He didn't, but he left me alone after that. He knew I'd made the turn.

CHAPTER FIVE

T HE HOOCH smelled of buttered popcorn, cigarettes, and cold beer. Allen Baker and Steve Sharp, wearing sweat-stained olive T-shirts and holding cold cans, slouched comfortably in the gang-room. Behind the bar Andy Ross rattled a skillet on a hotplate, its rimmed lid rising slowly with white explosions. A blue fan turned its head dumbly back and forth, following the conversation. Roark had not yet encountered Andy Ross, and he sized him up quickly: a tall, lean kid with a flat chest, slumped shoulders, platinum hair, and light brown, evasive eyes. A round St. Christopher hung on a chain with his dogtags. Roark nodded, but Ross looked away as if he had missed the greeting. "Hail!" McCawley said.

"Hell, yes," Sharp replied, saluting with the beer, clearly not his first.

"What d'you do today? Hood said you pissed-off a colonel."

"I carried a turd in my whirlybird," said Sharp, silly with new-found wit. "Fucker wouldn't roll his sleeves down."

"Anybody we know?" McCawley and Roark lowered their helmets and armor and removed their shirts. Ross poured hot popcorn into an earless C-ration case, then reached into the fridge and set two beers on the bar.

49

"Naw," Sharp said, "just some asshole from Saigon. Made us sit forty minutes in Hue with the blades turning just so he wouldn't have to wait for us to crank. So I decided to fuck with his mind, find out how good a grip the old fossil had on what's left of his life. I told him to put his sleeves down. He said no, he'd leave them the way they were, thank you, and told me to take him up to Nancy. I said I was sorry, I had orders not to carry anyone with their sleeves up unless it was a combat assault. He said he'd been riding around all morning with his sleeves up, and I said it had slipped my attention. Then he pointed at the little smashed birdie and said, 'I'm a colonel, goddamn it, and I'm ordering you to take me to LZ Nancy!' I said, 'Yes, sir, I'm going to do that, sir, but my orders are from a two-star general, sir, and he says you have to have your sleeves down to ride in one of his helicopters.' He about had an aneurysm on that one. 'I want your name, soldier!' So I gave him one of my cards." He handed a business card each to Roark and Baker. In the center was a red-and-blue phoenix with outstretched wings. Stacked in one corner were his name, rank, call sign, and unit designation. Around the others were COMBAT ASSAULTS, LAOTIAN EXCURSIONS, and A SHAU SERVICE. Below the phoenix was HOT EXTRACTIONS OUR SPECIALTY.

"Did he put them down?"

"He definitely did." Steve's eyes were moist and a little wild. "I said, 'Yes, sir, *sir*, just following orders, *sir*, trying to do my job, *sir*, up your ass, *sir*.'" The others laughed, more at the change in personality than his words.

"Think he's going to do anything?"

"He's already done it," Sharp said more slowly. "He called Group, Battalion, *and* the CO. Andrews jumped my ass about it, and I acted dumb. The sombitches can't touch me. I'm doing my job, following their chickenshit rules. God, I love this war!"

It was plain there was more working on Steve Sharp than just a jerk colonel; going down in the A Shau was finally hitting home. "You're off tomorrow," McCawley said.

"Hell, I don't want a day off. I'm having fun."

"We're down to thirteen birds," McCawley said. "I red-Xed mine for air holes, and Esch's is in for periodic."

"I'm sure glad they put us on general support so we could recover," Sharp said snidely.

"You're off, too, Roark," McCawley said. "You're duty officer tomorrow night. Baker, you're flying with me."

"Great." Allen Baker was plainly anxious to get back in the air. "Say, I went to the PX today," he said. "I was thinking it'd be nice if we had some music and a TV. We can get a reel-to-reel with speakers, plus a tube, for about thirty-five bucks a person. What do you guys think?"

"I'm in," Roark said.

McCawley considered it. "Well, Steve and I are going to DEROS when September gets here, but I'm for it. Steve?"

"Yeah, I'll go."

"Wait a minute." It was the first time Ross had spoken. "Not everybody here has the same time left," he said. "We ought to pay according to how long we've got left."

"Okay," said Sharp. "So tell us, how long do we all have left?" Ross silently looked at the popcorn.

"Are we agreed?" McCawley asked.

After the others answered, Ross mumbled, "Yeah," then retreated to the rear of the hooch, leaving a baffled silence; he had only been in-country two months.

The sun was down, light fading, darkness moving in. The young men sipped their beer. Steve Sharp dozed in his rocker, and soon the talking ceased. Several silent minutes passed, no one wanting to break the spell, an evening pond without a ripple. "Anybody going to the mess hall?" McCawley said.

"I'll go," said Baker.

"No," Roark said. "I'm going to go find Tyler." Captain Hood had announced that Alpha Company had lost another bird in the A Shau. The three went outside, closing the door quietly, leaving Steve Sharp asleep in his chair. The last of the creamy sky glowed up from beyond the mountains, and the camp was painted in shades of brown and black and gray. Far off to the west the red flash of a rotating beacon marked the progress of a ship coming home.

Jim Tyler was at a corner table, his back to the door, with Deiterman and Luskey. The gun pilots nodded at Roark, but Tyler kept his eyes on his drink. Luskey announced he was going to the hooch. Deiterman said he would join him. "See you guys," said Tyler.

"Yeah," they answered, and walked away. There was an empty moment, then Roark asked, "Were they friends of yours?"

Tyler nodded. "Yes," he said. "Terry Smith and I went through flight school together, and Harwell bunked next to me."

Roark looked around the club. "You off tomorrow?"

"Yes," Tyler said.

"I'm going to Eagle Beach. You want to go?"

"Never heard of it."

"They mentioned it at Group. Thought I'd check it out."

"How are you getting there?"

"Catch a bird, the only way you can."

"I don't think so," said Tyler. "I need to write some letters."

"I'll be at Battalion at oh-nine-hundred if you change your mind. See you later. Sorry about your friends." He left Tyler facing the corner, turning his drink in a glassy puddle.

Billy Roark looked down from a Huey en route to Eagle Beach. The polished sky in the paddies was freckled with fresh green sprigs; pillowed clouds were trapped behind a traveling web of dikes. Peasants worked the fields—old men with bamboo whips rode the glistening mud on wooden harrows drawn by gray buffalo; women in slick black silk, bony rears in the air, stabbed sets into the dun-colored soup. In the corners of the miniature fields tiny plats of seedlings grew like green hair.

At the opposite end of the seat Jim Tyler sat with his cap in his hands, looking ahead toward the sea. His eyes were narrowed against the wind, the stretch of his face resembling a smile. Between the two pilots sat a pair of silent soldiers straight out of the field.

Roark was pleased that Tyler had come. He found him waiting at Battalion, standing in front of the hooch smashed in the rocket attack. It was the first round, rather than the third, that had done the damage. A captain from Headquarters Company, still in his bunk, was the worst of four wounded. A chunk of iron entered above the collarbone and plowed through most of his body. His heart was still pumping when the ambulance came.

They found a clerk at Battalion who had heard of the beach, but had never been there. No one seemed to know exactly where it was. Finally they caught a courier to Camp Eagle, which dropped them at Group where they discovered that the beach run was a regularly scheduled mission.

When they boarded the Huey, the grunts moved to the center, away from the doors. Roark smiled at the man on his side, but drew no response. When they were high above the colorful paddies he tried again. "Where you guys been?" he yelled. The man looked at him. For an instant it seemed he would respond, then his eyes dulled and wandered away. There was no rudeness, and the man was not stoned; he had simply gotten lost in search of an answer. Roark turned away, but unobtrusively studied the soldier at his side. He may have been nineteen. His fatigues were faded and tattered, and the patch on his shoulder was torn partway off. His boots were raw leather and bleached nylon, ripped and slashed and fuzzed, stained red with clay and deeply bent. The exposed skin was tanned, and he had a fresh haircut that looked unnatural. He smelled, and there were sores on his face and the backs of his hands.

The slender white boundary was quickly in sight. Between the beach and paddies, centuries of onshore wind had heaped the sand into a huge running hill, and in its lee beyond the moat produced by the mashing weight of sand, tiny hamlets had taken shelter. "What's that?" he yelled across to Tyler, pointing along the beach.

"A refugee camp." The compound was large and rectangular, set back from the beach on sterile sand, a tight repetition of tiny steel rooftops shining like silver-blue scales. There were no boats, no garden plots, no fields to work; no trees for shade, no palms or bamboo; only orderly, metallic desolation. Roark wondered if the people could find their homes if set free, and he wondered if they called themselves refugees.

Eagle Beach was a hundred meters of azure sky, ivory sand, and limpid water surrounded by loops of concertina wire. Guards with machine guns kept watch in towers. The bathhouse was divided, one section marked, hopefully, WOMEN. When they had changed, Roark and Tyler carried their bags through dimpled sand where cigarette butts stood like stumps of a clear-cut forest. About thirty GIs were scattered along the beach. Some sat in pairs with cigarettes, talking in low voices, not looking at each other; others lay alone and belly down; a few were in the water. Nearby, Roark spotted the two grunts who had shared their flight. They were sitting identically, facing the water, their legs drawn toward their chests and wrapped with their arms, smoking. Their bodies were sickly white where their fatigues had been, and dark-tanned Vs stabbed at their chests. Both wore cutoff fatigues. The one who had sat next to Roark had damp sores on his legs, and where others had been were purple scars like stains from grape juice. Beyond them, a GI's effort at horseplay drew a snarl. The sun baked the sand and the soldiers, a cool breeze came in off the sea, and the gentle sound of surf filled the silence.

Jim Tyler had an honest face that could hide very little. He had been quiet most of the morning, occasionally trying to be friendly, then lapsing again into periods of silence. Once he was on the beach he seemed to brighten. The sun bent the lines of his face and tipped the brown hair with gold. When they sat in the warm sand, Roark noticed he put a wedding band in his bag. "How long you been married?" he asked.

"Four years," Tyler replied. "Are you married?"

"Heck no," Roark said, "I'm still a baby, just twenty."

"You really are," Tyler said, "but I was married at your age. Got a girl?"

"No." Roark looked down the beach through the loose coils of razor wire. Offshore lay a band of thunderclouds low to the water. He did not smoke, but he wished he had a cigarette. It had been his choice, not having a girl back home; he had wanted to come clean and unencumbered. "Got any kids?" he asked.

"Two." Tyler's eyes warmed. He reached into his bag and produced a photograph. It showed the four of them, dressed as if going to church, with Tyler holding a little girl on each arm. They were twins and had their mother's honey-gold hair, pulled back and tied with red ribbons. Twisting tendrils had escaped and framed their little faces. Their eyes were large and brown like Tyler's. "They're just over two," he said. "My wife's name is Susan, and the girls are Michelle and Sheri."

"You know, I never really thought about being a daddy," Roark said. "I can't even imagine it, but I guess a pair like that could change your mind. How'd you end up here with kids?"

"I keep wondering that myself," Tyler said. "No, really, I was in ROTC when I got married."

"Doesn't it bother you—?"

"Having kids? Yeah, it bothers me," Tyler said. "I can't say I regret it—I wouldn't take anything for the girls—but I'd be lying if I said I didn't think about it. Sometimes I wish we'd waited. It was sort of an affirmation of faith."

"Why'd you join Rotcy?"

"Money. My father was killed in a wreck when I was small, and there wasn't much when I was a kid. It looked like a good choice. I worked summers and some on weekends, and what I got from ROTC was enough to make it through school. Trouble was, when I got out I owed it all to Uncle Sam."

"Didn't you know you'd be coming here?"

"Not at first. It was '63, and we didn't have very many people here then. I figured on going to Germany or Japan. That had all changed by the time I graduated, but I was locked in. So when I went active, I applied for flight school, and here I am. It's like I've been coming here for years, and it just took this long to happen."

The clouds were closer now, their reflection making a dark smudge on the water. "Let's get wet," Roark said. The water was cold and perfectly clear. Even chest deep he could make a shadow and see the bottom. Rolling explosions of sand boiled away from his feet no matter how carefully he moved.

"What about you?" Tyler asked. "How'd you get here?"

"I wanted to fly," Roark said. "School wasn't working out, and I wanted to get on with my life."

"Got any brothers or sisters?"

"A brother, five years older. My folks sent him to UCLA, then he dropped out in his final semester. He was in San Francisco about two years ago—the last anybody heard. Probably hiding from the draft."

"Everybody's making decisions."

Roark nodded and leaned against the waves with Eagle Beach before him—the flat white ashtray, silhouetted wire, silent guards, empty faces. No sound of gunfire, no stench of flesh or powder, no blood. Just a glimpse of war at the edge of an ocean. "Let's get the hell out of here," he said.

A gust of wind dulled the water as they padded through the sand. The kid with the sores was lying faceup, mouth open, lids partway closed, staring at the sky.

CHAPTER SIX

I MUST be overdressed for the occasion, he thought, hefting his gear. He was rigged in his flak vest and steel pot with a bandolier of ammo across one shoulder, an M-16 in his hands, and a revolver on his hip. He hesitated at the door, realizing that anyone he encountered outside would be dressed simply in fatigues or a flight suit and wearing a baseball cap, making him look even more ridiculous than he felt. Only a few hours ago he had been on the beach in a swimsuit. Suddenly he turned and sent the vest and pot crashing into his room, pulled his cap down tight, and stepped outside with just the weapons.

Captain Crable had not arrived at Operations to brief him, so Roark sat on the bench, thinking about his job. Between 1800 and 0600 each night, the company duty officer was the CO's representative, a role that seemed a lot of responsibility to a new guy. "You the CDO?" Motormouth asked, leaning across. "Come on over and I'll get you started. Maybe we can finish before the shithead shows up." Captain Hood snapped his head around; Motormouth held out a hand. "Sir, you know yourself this outfit's full of shitheads. I could be talking about 'most anybody."

"They're going to hang you one of these days, Butler," Hood said. "You're going to hang yourself."

"That's all right, sir. I got a long neck." That was true enough; Motormouth looked like black rubber, heated and stretched, every part long and thin. He began going over procedure with Roark, the use of the landline and radios and the keeping of the duty log. "I'll be here in case you've got questions," he said.

"You?"

"Why, sure. I'm the nighttime RTO, the commander-in-chief of Charlie in the midnight hours."

"I thought you worked days."

"No, I hang out here days. I work nights." There was the rumble of a truck downstairs. "That's probably Wiley," he said. "He's sergeant of the guard tonight. You might want to go down and meet him. He's a good head. He can tell you what you need to know about the perimeter." Captain Hood was on the phone trying to locate Crable.

Sergeant First Class Harlan Wiley was standing at the tailgate of a three-quarter-ton truck, one hand on his hip, the other waving loosely through the air. "Come on, boys," he said in a deep, patient tone as if talking to cattle. "We're running behind." His legs were spread for balance; his drooping belly looked low on air. The guards were loading guns and ammo cans into the truck. "That's good," Wiley said. "You four wait here with the rest of this gear." He locked the arms room while six guards climbed into the rear of the truck. He seemed too busy to be bothered, so Roark let him drive away, then followed on foot toward the perimeter. The four remaining guards slumped against the steel hangar wall, smoking and talking quietly, spitting on the black oiled dirt.

A Huey was crossing the wire on final and another rounding the perimeter from POL, so Roark veered left along the high ground near Battalion. He could see the entire flight line, a concave portion of the perimeter, and, in the distance, a few of the houses of Phong Dien peeking through the bamboo not far from the bunkered walls of an ARVN fort. A narrow strip of abandoned paddies edged the perimeter, and beyond lay rough, brushy ground marked occasionally with Vietnamese graves. The oval concrete walls of the graves resembled goldfish ponds, open at one end—excellent fighting positions for the enemy. That thought made him stop and look around. There were eighteen open revetments—low walls of dirt-filled steel plate—which afforded only minimal protection. A shallow ditch began near the hangar and coursed the length of the ravine and another edged the road, but nowhere was there a bunker or a prepared position. Just bare oiled earth. He frowned and continued toward the wire.

Sergeant Wiley had manned the first three bunkers, and when he saw Roark he turned the truck and pulled up beside him. "Evening," he said, glancing up and down in open assessment. "Are you the CDO tonight?" he asked, but his tone seemed to say, Are you the best they could do?

"That's right," Roark said bluntly, returning the look. Wiley had dark hair, close-cropped and gray at the sides, black across the brows. His face was gray and pink, and one cheek stretched around a wad of tobacco. He had a wide mouth, and there were brown stains on his lips.

"Get in," he said, making it sound like an order. Roark looked toward the perimeter. He would have preferred to go on alone, but he got in the truck. Wiley drove in silence, leaning to spit out the window, bouncing comfortably behind the wheel. Roark lacked the weight to compress the cushion, and as the truck jolted along he felt daylight spring beneath him. Wiley steered loosely, letting the wheel whip through his hands while the tires found a path.

Roark watched him slide out at the hangar, heard him ordering the men to do what they were already doing. Good head or not, he was not sure he liked this old fart.

When the men were posted and Wiley was returning the truck to the motor pool, Roark walked the perimeter. Charlie was responsible for a five-bunker sector. He checked each position, meeting the men and familiarizing himself with the layout while it was still light. The bunkers were ominous, clumsy structures with sandbags layering the steel-plate roofs and deflecting slopes all around. Sturdy as they were, they seemed marginal with openings too large, roofs that could not withstand a direct hit, and doorways behind the guards that could neither be closed nor defended. Inside, the machine gun rested on a sandbagged ledge, and behind it the guard sat on a thick plank. Before him lay an array of detonators attached to a tangle of wires that led through the slot and underground to claymore mines and drums of Phougas. On the plank sat a hand-cranked phone, called a landline, on which hourly reports were made. Against the rear wall was a gritty cot. Roark checked the weapons, ammunition, and flares, feeling awkward. Most of the guards knew a lot more about what they were doing than he. Each time he looked out the slot he was struck by how near the rough ground seemed.

He returned to the hangar with a growing sense of unease and was about to climb the stairs when he remembered his flak vest and steel pot. They no longer seemed so ridiculous. He turned toward the hooch to retrieve them, unaware that Captain Crable was at the window above his head.

"Where have you been?" Crable shouted when he returned. For a moment Roark was struck dumb, standing in the doorway with his gear. Three pilots were at the counter, and they glanced at Crable, then Roark. Motormouth mumbled something about his bowels.

"I've been doing my job," Roark said, deleting the "sir."

Crable seemed ready to burst. His eyes enlarged and his nostrils flared. A blue vein pulsed at his temple. Then all at once the rage drained from his face, and he said in a natural tone, "I need to give you your briefing."

Roark was stunned by the transformation. "Motormouth has already shown me everything up here," he said. The words came reluctantly. "I checked out the perimeter. I've pretty well got it down." He still could not bring himself to mouth the "sir" he didn't feel.

"Nonetheless, I need to brief you since this is your first time," Crable said pleasantly. Roark listened while the XO went through the routine by rote; he did not interrupt with questions. Motormouth had covered it all, except the last. "The most important thing of which you must be aware are the rules of engagement," Crable said. "Situated as we are with Phong Dien so close, we must be especially prudent in the use of firearms. The perimeter was purposely placed along the low-lying areas to provide a shield of terrain between us and the village. However, we must still exercise extreme caution. The sergeant of the guard has been instructed to tell his men to aim low, *if they fire at all*. Other portions of the perimeter enjoy the freedom to occasionally recon by fire—what they call a mad minute—but our particular sector is prevented by circumstance from doing that. The *only* time we may use our weapons is when we are actually under attack. Is that clear?"

"What if someone sees a gook?"

"The guards have been instructed to call in and report. You, or the sergeant of the guard, will then go to that bunker, make a confirmation, then call Battalion. The BDO will contact the colonel for permission to engage the enemy."

"You mean the guards have to have permission from the colonel to shoot a gook?"

"If we are not under attack."

"Is this for real?"

"I assure you, Mr. Roark, this is very real."

After midnight, when Gil McCawley and a warrant officer from second platoon named Simpson had finished scheduling, Roark went downstairs to look for Harlan Wiley and to get some coffee. The maintenance crew kept a pot going in the corner beside the ready room, and Wiley was there, leaning on one arm against the wall, holding a cup on the slope of his belly. "You got a minute?" Roark asked.

"Got all night," Wiley said. With him was a red-haired, similarly shaped staff sergeant named Donner who ran the night crew. The maintenance man tossed a paper cup toward a yellow drum and went to check two men riveting patches beneath a tail boom. Wiley refilled his cup and poured one for Roark. "So what's up?" he asked.

"Nothing really," Roark said. "I'm just trying to figure out what's going on." Wiley sipped his coffee and waited. "Did Captain Crable give you a briefing this evening?"

"No, but he has."

"Did he mention the rules of engagement?"

"He mentioned them," Wiley said, staring blankly out the hangar doors.

Roark had hoped that Wiley would volunteer something, but his reticence was understandable. There were officers, there were enlisted men, and then there were warrant officers, men who seemed to fit neither category. Enlisted men with bars, or officers with stripes—until you knew the man it was hard to know which you were talking to. "Okay, Sergeant Wiley," he said, "I'll stick my neck out first. I think Captain Crable is an asshole. If he's a friend of yours, I'll go back upstairs. If not, I'd like to talk about what's going on around here."

Wiley looked at him without expression. "What do you want to talk about?" he asked.

"The rules of engagement."

The sergeant drew a flattened package from a hip pocket, dipped a hooked finger into the fragrant tobacco, and stuffed a wad far back in his cheek. He rolled his tongue around until everything was in place. A brown bit of leaf clung to the corner of his mouth. The rivet work was loud between the metal walls, so he stepped inside the ready room and sat on a cot. Roark sat opposite, sipping his coffee and waiting.

"I'm not what you'd call a combat soldier," Wiley said. "I'm a supply man. But what I'm *not* is an idiot. Nobody is going to put me on a bunker where people are trying to kill me, and then tell me I can't shoot the bastards without permission. Being there with a gun in my hands is all the permission I need, and no colonel lying in bed is going to decide whether I live or die. I tell the boys what I'm supposed to, and then I tell them to use their heads and don't let some idiot rules get them killed. The number-one rule is stay alive. One of the big problems here is that some of the commanders have seen very little real combat. You take our battalion CO. I don't know his personal history—this is just an example— but when he goes back to the States his record is going to show that he's got another year in a combat zone, just like mine is. But neither of us is in combat. The difference is, if we both come back here, I'll be issuing canteens and he'll be telling kids how to fight the war. Out at Berchtesgaden there's a colonel, the commander of the Third Brigade. He lives there, and when they get mortared he gets dirt in his face. When the gooks come through the wire it's *him* they're coming after. When they got hit a while back, the first sergeant killed a sapper *inside* the command bunker. So that man is having to live by the rules he makes, and you can bet your balls he tells those guards to shoot any goddamn thing that moves.

"I don't want to kill any civilians. I also don't want my boys to die. So you've got to use your head. What it comes down to is each man has to decide how the war is going to be fought. He's just got to be sure his ass is covered because when things turn to shit they're going to be looking for somebody to blame. And that's all I've got to say about that." Wiley had become angered by his own speech. The gray was gone, and his eyes and face were red. He stood with effort and left the room. Roark sat thinking a long time before going out into the hangar. Harlan Wiley was nowhere in sight.

By 0130 he was beginning to feel leaden. When he and Jim Tyler returned from the beach, he had borrowed McCawley's fan to try to get some sleep. But it was no use; the sheet-metal roof turned the hooch into an oven. The poncho liner and every part touching it were soon soaked. Now, with gravity pulling at his face, he was certain he could sleep in the morning, fan or no fan. "How did you get stuck with this job?" he asked. Motormouth was writing in a spiral notebook.

"I volunteered," Motormouth said. "Before me, they used to rotate it like CDO. But I like it. Nobody fucks with me. It's quieter at night, I don't work too hard, I'm awake when we get hit, and I don't have to pull guard. 'Sides that, folks don't know it, but everything that happens in this outfit—everything that matters—sooner or later goes right through this room. I got the radios, I got the switchboard, I hear things. I know more about what's going on than anybody, including the CO, which is why he calls me when he wants to find out the facts. It's air-conditioned, and I run things. I plan to extend."

Roark was too tired to argue any of the points. He yawned and said, "I'm going to check the bunkers. I need to do something to wake up." He put on his flak vest and steel pot, then lifted the rifle and bandolier.

"You look like GI Joe," Motormouth said. "Go get 'em, Killer." Roark flipped him a finger on the way out the door.

The camp was quiet, just the throaty sound of generators singing to one another across the hills like lonely frogs. Though a bright moon silvered the sky, the inside of the first bunker was blackly invisible. Roark could see only an outline of the guard against the moonlight. Through the slot the various shades of black were threatening. "See you later," he whispered.

The sand along the bunker line was white, hauled in from the beach to fill bags, the remainder spread by boots and weather, making it easier to see. Roark walked without a sound, looking past the wire toward the dangerous black brush, almost directly at the first explosion when it came. With no awareness of getting there, he was on his belly in the sand, then was up and running toward the second bunker, shouting that he was coming in. Mortar rounds began a steady beat, progressing obliquely across the perimeter. Just as he plunged into the bunker there was an explosion in the wire ahead, sending metal hornets whizzing past. Both guards were on the floor. "Shoot!" Roark yelled. "Get up and shoot!" He stuck his rifle through the slot, thumbed the selector, and emptied a clip toward the brush. Then the guards were on the sixty, blasting through the wire, sweeping the barrel around. The other bunkers opened up and laced the night with tracers. Red ricochets wobbled over Phong Dien.

The mortars walked into the flight line, then back through the wire and forward once more. Roark was loading his third clip when he realized they had stopped. "Hold your fire," he said, but the gunner could not hear. Then he yelled and grabbed his arm, and the gun stopped firing. He ran outside with a white hand flare and fired it high. It made a falling starburst, revealing nothing but empty wire. Slowly, one bunker at a time, the firing stopped. Two Cobras climbed away from the runway with a flareship close behind. "Battalion's on the line," said a guard.

He took the handset, breathing hard. "Yeah."

"Is this the Brown Sector CDO?"

"That's right."

"Are you in contact?"

"Negative. We took about thirty mortar rounds. I haven't had time to check for casualties. Tell the gunships the mortar tube is either in or on the edge of Phong Dien."

"I'll relay the info," the voice said, then, "Wait one." There was a pause of several seconds, then another voice came on the line, deeper and older, with authority. "Phoenix, I understand you are not in contact. Did you receive ground fire?"

"We took a bunch of mortars on our position."

"I know that, I can hear! Did you receive ground fire?"

"Not to my knowledge."

"Then what are you shooting at?"

He realized by then that he was talking to Colonel Walters, but no identification had been offered. "We were shooting to break up a ground attack," he said.

"What ground attack?"

He paused. "The one we didn't have," he replied flatly. There was silence in the handset. He gave it to the guard and went outside. Two parachute flares were drifting slowly across Phong Dien, casting a weird amber light, making the shadows shift and move. The Cobras were circling the village. High above, another flare flashed and began to burn. "Ho Chi Minh's a motherfucker!" somebody shouted toward the wire. Roark checked each of the bunkers and spoke to the men. Everybody was all right. He walked slowly, feeling numb and tired, but wide awake. His ears were ringing. A fire truck crossed the flight line with its siren wailing, moving toward the scattered pieces of a Huey. The first flare sputtered and died, its wasted parachute fluttering to earth unseen.

When things had completely settled down, it was time to wake the oh-three-thirty crews for the A Shau. He went up the hill, dazed and tired, still shaken by the attack. It had been totally unlike watching mortars from a helicopter where, even when they were hitting all around, there was a definite sense of unreality. But in the bunker it had been real; the ground shook and he could hear the whirring pieces. Then the battalion commander called to chew his butt in his pajamas.

The moon was low. A third of the sky and all the mountains shone in a blue-white haze. He stepped up to the flat shelter roof to look. Along the foot of the escarpment for several miles lay a luminous mound of fog, and the blue hills were edged in silver. All at once it came together—the machinery and mortars and corpses, the colonel and Crable and jungle fog. That was the instant when

Billy Roark understood that it takes more than traveling to reach a place; he knew then that he had finally arrived in Vietnam.

It was exactly 0700 when he came to attention, saluted, and said, "Reporting as ordered, sir."

"Good morning, Mr. Roark," Major Andrews said, returning the salute. "Please stand at ease." Though the major was small, he projected considerable force. He had olive skin, black eyes, and only a trace of gray in his sideburns. His fatigues were not starched.

Roark spread his feet and crossed his hands at the small of his back. He liked Major Andrews. "Good morning, sir," he said, then quickly glanced around the room. The major's desk stood directly before the door. There was an unmarked map of Vietnam tacked on the wall, a couple of padlocked cabinets, some military books on shelves, and a box fan in the window. On a gray chair nearby, Captain Crable sat with his arms and legs crossed, his lips pursed, his eyes poisonous. Roark understood that the captain was the reason he had been called before the commanding officer, but knew nothing more than that. Following the attack, Crable had climbed the stairs to Operations, sputtered a command, and stalked out of the room. Roark assumed the CO wanted a report, but there seemed to be more. He remembered the colonel's words, sharp and disdainful, but was beginning to think that was just the way colonels were.

"Mr. Roark, you're here because of last night's incident," the major said. "I realize you have not yet slept, but there is some urgency involved—I have a meeting at oh-eight-hundred with Lieutenant Colonel Walters regarding the matter. I will be brief as possible. First, tell me exactly what happened." Roark told his story, beginning with the initial impacting round and concluding with the call from Battalion, omitting the details of the dialogue. "Why did you order the guns to fire?" Andrews asked.

"Sir, when I hit the bunker, both guards were on the floor. A round had just landed real close, so they had a right, but if gooks had been in the wire they wouldn't have known it. It seemed like a good tactic. The flashes had us blinded; there could have been gooks right in front of us, and we wouldn't have been able to see them. So I ordered the guards to shoot. I shot, too."

"And you received no returning fire?"

"No, sir."

"How long did you shoot?"

"As long as the mortars were falling. Maybe forty-five seconds.

It seemed longer." He was gaining confidence. The major projected the somber sensibility of a judge.

Andrews pushed away from his desk and studied him. At last he said, "Mr. Roark, what I need most to know is whether you disobeyed orders intentionally or simply lost control."

"Huh?" Roark frowned and leaned forward. His mouth was open, his eyes went dumb. He wondered if he had fallen asleep and missed something. The major repeated the question. "Neither one, sir," he said.

"How's that?"

"Neither one. I don't know what you mean. I was in control, and I didn't disobey any orders, sir."

"Yes, you *did*!" Crable shouted.

Roark had until then completely ignored Crable, but now he turned and gazed steadily at him before addressing the major. "I don't know what you are talking about, sir," he said. His voice was deep and flat, his face completely blank.

"You were briefed last night by Captain Crable?"

"Yes, sir, I was."

"And what did he tell you regarding the rules of engagement?"

"That we were not to fire without permission from Battalion unless we were under attack."

"Unless you were receiving *fire*!" Crable shouted.

So there it is, he thought. "Sir, the words the captain used were *'under attack.'* I don't know if he was listening, but Motormou— Spec 4 Butler was there, sir."

Major Andrews looked hard at Billy Roark, then gazed at Phillip Crable. The captain was shaking his head, but avoiding his eyes. "That will be all, Mr. Roark," the CO said. "This afternoon when you have gotten some rest, I'd like you to write a brief report on last night's action."

When he left the office Roark started automatically across the ravine toward the hooch. He was exhausted. His eyes felt sandpapered and seemed locked open. Then he remembered breakfast, and he turned and walked stiffly up the slope toward the mess hall. The sun was brilliant above the hooches, and when a shadow interfered he stopped and looked. A tall column of black smoke rose through the still morning air, boiling thickly across the sun. Shitcan, he thought. The odor filled his head and reminded him of the pisstubes, and then he could smell them as well. He was on the steps of the mess hall before he could smell the food, and by then his appetite was nearly gone. He made a plate of hard biscuits and bacon spotted white with grease, skipped the putrid powdered eggs, and poured a cup of drain-oil coffee. When he was seated at a table he stared at the plate, the thrill completely gone. He munched a biscuit and drank some coffee, and thought of the lines: *I'm an airborne trooper, I eat with a poopie-scooper. Life out here ain't super-duper, But I'm tough.* He looked up then and saw Harlan Wiley seated at the NCO table, eyeing him like a frog. The sergeant belched, licked his teeth, and walked over. He rested both burly hands on the table.

"You got any more questions?" he asked.

"Not a one," Roark said.

The sergeant grinned an ugly grin, then began a slow laugh. His breath was foul. He walked away with his feet splayed, his weight far back on his heels. He was still laughing when he reached the door.

CHAPTER SEVEN

"I HEAR Crable stepped on his dick," Baker said. He and Mc-Cawley had been released early from a mission, but Gil was still flying, giving a pilot a checkride.

"That's right," Roark said, thinking just how close the captain had come to stepping on his as well. He was feeling anything but triumphant. Baker sat in the sand and began to remove his boots.

Roark had slept until noon when the heat of the popping roof finally overwhelmed the fan. He spent the afternoon doing laundry in a bucket and writing letters, then caught a ride to the Post Exchange to buy sodas and beer and Mateuse rose, and two cartons of cigarettes for trading. Then he changed into shorts and carried Brady's abandoned paperback, *King Rat*, out back where the shadows had begun to grow. Soon there was a sound inside, and Allen Baker came out carrying two beers.

"So what d'you do on leave?" Roark asked.

"We split it between Texas and Tucson," Baker replied. He had met and quickly married a girl from Denton—a college student—while stationed at Fort Wolters, then took her along to Fort Rucker while he finished training. "How about you?"

"Nothing special," Roark said. "Stopped by Vicksburg on the way home. Walked around that hill with all the graves."

"What for?"

"I don't know. Seventeen thousand guys just like us, I guess. I spent ten days in New Mexico, backpacking and fly fishing. Then I just wandered around that dead-end town, trying to find some girl who wasn't married or pregnant or had the clap."

"Do any good?"

"Yes, once I realized I'd set my standards too high."

Their attention was suddenly captured by a nurse leaving the hospital emergency hut. The covered walkway between the inflatable Quonset-type units was almost directly behind the hooch. They saw very little of the woman, just the briefest glimpse of a face as she emerged, then chocolate hair and baggy fatigues with that important difference in the rear. "She looks like Paula," Baker said.

"I've got a feeling that pretty soon they're all going to look like Paula."

"I didn't know there were any women here."

"Just a handful of nurses."

"A handful is better than none at all."

"Not if it's not my hand."

"I guess you're right," Baker said, laughing. He watched the sidewalk where the nurse disappeared.

There were more sounds inside, and Steve Sharp walked out. He plopped down in the sand with a beer, leaned against the bags, and said, "Ninety-four and a wake-up." When he had taken a long drink he stared straight across at the next hooch and said, "You did exactly right last night. You just learned one of the big secrets— we're fighting more here than gooks."

Roark appreciated the support, but was not reassured. He kept thinking about what might happen if there was another attack the next time he was on duty. He was not sure he could sit without ordering the guns to fire.

"Maybe some good came from last night," Baker said. "Hood says Group agreed to turn loose some birds and pilots. We're supposed to get three brand-new H-models this week."

Sharp snorted. "They're not doing us any favors. We're just being set up to go back on direct for the Third. Bravo's getting their butts wiped. You new guys are gonna be learning fast." No one said anything while he drank his beer. "And speaking of learning," he said, turning to Roark, "schedule us together tomorrow for that CCN. May as well get on with your education." Roark looked at him. "There's a big one going out. Eight birds instead of the usual two or three. Should be lots of fun."

Baker walked over and pissed on the back of the dental clinic. Sharp tossed his can between the sandbag wall and hooch. "Let me tell you something about Crable," he said. "Being a captain is important to him. He needs that rank, so he's gonna use it. But you've got to remember there's always a way of balancing things. Someday it'll come. Don't hunt for it, don't pledge revenge—revenge is for children. It's a lot more satisfying to fuck with his mind. Just keep your eyes open and wait for the chance. Then take it for everything it's worth." He slumped against the bags and closed his eyes.

Roark emptied his can. Suddenly a torrent of scenes of the past few days came rushing forth. It seemed a really weird war. But tomorrow he would be flying CCN, going deep into Laos where there were lots of enemy troops, maybe not so many rules, and no Phillip Crables at all.

There was a sense of genuine danger north of the Ba Long—the river the maps called Thach Han—the awareness of a powerful enemy nearby. Though a division of Marines and a brigade of mechanized infantry gave the appearance of American dominance, everyone realized the North Vietnamese were capable of annihilating all opposing forces within twenty miles of the demilitarized zone. Several divisions of NVA troops were massed along the 17th parallel and in the mountains north and west of the Rockpile, and if they decided one drizzly night to walk down and massacre all of Quang Tri Province, there was little that could stop them.

Steve Sharp had said nothing since departing Evans, but now he began to point out important landmarks, mentioning that from farther north a red flag could be seen in North Vietnam. Roark looked, but saw only haze. The flight separated into groups of two and made preparations to land.

The CCN compound stood away by itself, a small cluster of hooches with none of the signs and ornamentation of less serious outfits. The Hueys landed in a grassy field within the enclosure and shut down to await briefing. Two Cobras of aerial rocket artillery, ARA, call sign Griffins, were already there, and soon a pair of Marine E-model Huey gunships made their usual spectacular arrival, a style the Army pilots referred to as controlled crashes. They dusted everyone thoroughly before setting down. The Paragons were outfitted similarly to the Army C-model Hueys which the Cobras were replacing, and they bristled with armament. When the pilots climbed out of their ships, Roark's mouth fell open. "*Silk scarves?*" he said.

"It's a glorious war," Sharp replied. "They're good guns. They seem to think they should be issued wheelbarrows to carry their balls around, but you can't beat them for cover. Ignorant bastards will go up against anything."

The crews gathered in a standby hooch to sip sodas and coffee. There was joking and friendly chatter, though many were strangers. Soon a captain in camouflaged fatigues and a black beret appeared. "Briefing, gentlemen," he announced.

When they were seated in a blue windowless hooch, the door closed and a guard posted outside, Captain Davis stepped to an easel supporting a draped map. He was blond with a good tan—a regular recruiting poster, square features and blue eyes. "I see new faces," he said briskly. "Who has never flown Command and Control North?" Roark and Baker raised their hands. "Please come up, gentlemen. There is a form for you to sign."

When they returned to their seats, Steve Sharp leaned forward and whispered, "Wouldn't want you boys embarrassing the president."

"Today, gentlemen, we are going here," the captain said, raising the cloth cover and using a short pointer to indicate a spot almost halfway across Laos. "The red zigzag line is our approximate route of travel. It will keep us clear of known antiaircraft positions, but radar-guided thirty-seven mike-mikes and quad-fifties may be encountered anywhere. We will be flying at six thousand feet indicated, but at that altitude you stand little chance against those weapons. Should you encounter airbursts, do not attempt to climb above them. You can't. I suggest the flight break up and get to the deck as quickly as possible, but that decision will be up to your flight lead. In that event, the mission will be aborted and we'll regroup here if no one is hit. The hatched areas you see are booby-trapped with bombs a thousand pounds or larger, rigged with magnetic detonators sensitive to low-flying aircraft. Air America has reported Russian helicopter gunships in the area, but we have not encountered them on any missions. We don't know their intentions, so keep your eyes open.

"You will be carrying a twenty-eight-man team aboard six ships, the seventh and eighth serving as chase birds to pick up anyone who goes down. If you must make an emergency landing across the border, pull the radios and guns. We have fastmovers on standby in Da Nang, and they will destroy the ship in place. If anyone goes down, and we're unable to get you out, I suggest you E and E west rather than trying to make it back here. The terrain is easier, and there will be fewer enemy the farther you go. Try for Udorn in Thailand. An alternative is Ubon, about a hundred miles southwest. We have Air Force facilities at both locations.

"I need the aircraft commander from each ship to come up following the briefing to sign for a blood chit." He held up a green sealed plastic envelope. "This contains an American flag and a statement in several area languages offering a reward to anyone who assists you to safety. However, you should attempt to avoid contact as long as possible; the enemy gives rewards, too. There is also some foreign currency in case you have to buy food or catch a cab." The remark drew a few stiff, obligatory chuckles. "Gossamer has seen the landing zone, and will be directing you into it. It is a one-ship LZ. Once he gives you a mark you will drop to treetop level, circle this low mountain on the southern side, and approach from the west. The first ship will be talked in with bearings and distance. When you depart, make a sharp left, circle the mountain again, low level, well to the right of the approach path. Do *not* return to altitude until you are south of the mountain. Chase birds, maintain a high orbit to the east. Griffins, establish a covering orbit slightly farther than normal west of the LZ, but do not escort the ships. Paragons will provide low-level cover, remaining to the right of the approach path. There will be no prep, and no shooting unless we stumble onto the enemy, and then only on a return-fire basis. We do not want the exact location of the team known, and the terrain will hide a lot of what we are doing."

Davis then announced the operational frequencies, departure time, and the expected winds en route. He noted the call sign of each ship and their respective positions in the flight, asked for questions, and closed the briefing. There was little talk among the pilots. Allen Baker, next to Roark, said in a low voice, "Serious shit."

The LRRP team—half American, half Cambodian mercenaries—gathered in ugly groups near the aircraft. They wore soft boonie hats, camouflaged fatigues, and their faces and arms were painted in dark jungle colors. Most carried crisscrossed loops of belted ammunition. There were eight machine guns, a half-dozen grenade launchers, and several light antitank weapons. The men with rifles wore several bandoliers of clips, and those with launchers had lumpy bags of high explosive and buckshot rounds. Hand grenades hung everywhere.

The blades were untied and turned; the pilots strapped themselves in and waited. Hands found little things to do while the minutes crept past. At last came the click of igniters, a minute early. Others joined, and soon all the blades were turning, flashing in the sunlight, fanning the clearing with a confused breeze. The special grunts helped each other from the ground and moved toward the ships in heavy, slow-motion steps. Each backed up to the edge of the bay, lifted his legs and swung around, then scooted across on his butt, pushing with a free hand and the heels of his boots. They sat against the firewall, or back-to-back, their weapons angling upward or out the side.

Steve Sharp and Billy Roark were the second bird, chalk two, so there were five men aboard their ship. An LRRP with a grenade launcher sat with his back against the console, and while Sharp did the run-up and tuned the radios, Roark removed his helmet and spoke to the man. "What did he say?" Sharp asked when he again had fastened his chin strap.

"They're taking out an enemy village," Roark replied.

Sharp gave a strange look and almost smiled. "Everybody dies," he said.

The Paragons led the departure, followed by the Hueys in pairs, then the faster Cobras. The flight formed a staggered formation with the Marines ahead and to one side, the Cobras holding far back where they could watch for enemy fire with room to roll in on target. They flew westward, climbing steadily, and crossed the mountains between the gap of the Ba Long River and the massive Marine fire support base Vandegrift. They passed above the canyon and blasted skeleton of Route 9, the black rock falls at the edge of the plateau, the grim and wasted bunkers of Khe Sanh. The Air Force forward air controller, or FAC, call sign Gossamer, overtook the flight just before they reached the Xe Pon River at the border of Laos.

They crossed between Co Roc with its tilted strata and the flat-topped Arrowhead, both broad mountains acknowledged as important North Vietnamese headquarters. Neither mountain showed signs of bombing, but stood unscathed in shades of virgin green. Large mountain ranges lay to the north and south, but beneath the flight the ground formed long running hills, giant waves in an ocean of elephant grass. Dark clumps of trees lined the low areas and dotted the hillsides. Puffy white clouds made round shadows. Nothing had been defoliated, and only a rare crater marred the beautiful countryside.

Soon they passed open signs of the enemy. Broad gravel highways, graded and maintained, followed the flow of the land. Tank trails led through the grass to trampled bivouac sites, then southward back to the road. Thatched hooches peered from the edge of woods, and funnels of blue-white smoke rose from small fields.

There were cultivated crops, wooden foot bridges, and woven bamboo fish traps waiting in the streams, but no people could be seen.

Roark watched the ground, wondering what it would be like down there afoot, living off the land for however many months it took to reach safety. His father's long sermons about survival were making more sense than ever before.

The formation loosened to two hundred meters. Soon the rolling ground gave way to ancient mountains eroded down to broad low hills caped with jungle. Gossamer moved ahead to locate the landing zone and quickly radioed that it was in sight. The Hueys began to descend and to take up a thirty-second separation.

The LZ was an old cornfield, now being reclaimed by the jungle. Gossamer dropped to a discreet thousand feet, called "Mark, mark," as he crossed, then held his course so the spot would not be obvious. He made a few decoying turns, then returned to altitude.

Unlike McCawley, Steve Sharp said very little that was unnecessary during a flight. Roark had lots of questions, but kept silent. He studied the new terrain, checked the instruments, and listened carefully to the radio calls. "Gil says you like low level," Sharp said. "Here, take it on down."

Roark was astounded. "I've got it," he said. Soon they were a few feet from the trees, the sensation of speed exhilarating. But this time it was more difficult, watching the treetops, keeping the lead bird in sight, maintaining proper airspeed. He felt the perspiration begin to flow. The radio calls came quickly—Gossamer, flight lead, the guns, Gossamer, flight lead, Gossamer. He was tense with concentration.

"Lead's in." The ship had disappeared into the jungle. The separation seemed too close, but Sharp said nothing. Then the flashing disk of a main rotor was rising out of the trees ahead. "Lead's out."

"Chalk Two, short," Sharp said on the UHF, using his foot switch. The LZ was on them in a rush. The first men in had moved to each side to form a perimeter, and were almost invisible in the foliage. Roark brought the Huey to a five-foot hover, and the ship wobbled as the men jumped out. "Chalk Two's out."

"Three's short." In less than three minutes the insertion was complete, the men had vanished into the forest, and the invading flight was en route back to Vietnam.

It was almost 0100. Wake-up would be at 0330 for the A Shau. The 155mm howitzers were firing, and the sound he had learned to sleep through now was chiseled on the night. Each round made a lingering mental image like a leftover imprint of light. He lifted the netting, pulled on shorts, and fumbled through his duffel bag. He found matches in the C-ration box and two cans of beer in the refrigerator, and with them and a new package of cigarettes he went out front and sat on the bunker roof.

He smoked and drank and tried to make his mind go blank, but the man with the grenades kept coming back, the one he had talked to as they readied for the trip to Laos. He raised the beer and quickly emptied it, belched, and opened the second. He pulled hard on the cigarette, his first since the experimental days of junior high. The spark put a red-amber glow between him and the night, and the smoke was raw and painful in his lungs. Then came an image from the hills of Laos, of blood and bowels and roast-sized chunks of meat, of heads lying loose like melons gone bad, open mouths and waxy eyes, busy insects. Other images rushed forth; the hollow muteness of Khe Sanh's bunkers; the unblemished green of the mountains of Laos a few kilometers away; the zigzagging, secret flight, avoiding enemy locations on a mission to locate the enemy.

The big guns stopped firing when the second beer was almost gone. The alcohol was in his veins, and he could feel himself coming down. He thought about the day, the days before, the year of days ahead. The images spun, his mind went blank. He lit another cigarette.

III

Preflight Training was duckwalking across a field with Tac officers bending over us, screaming we would never make it past the month we had to spend with them. They were partly correct; two men quit then and there, a few feet from the chartered bus that brought us. They were taken with tears on their cheeks to a holding company to await the lonely trip back to Fort Polk and AIT. In disbelief, I watched them go. If I had to duckwalk to fly a helicopter, I would duckwalk, naked through grass burrs, if need be. I grabbed my ankles and cried, "Quack, quack, quack," feeling like a fool, but one with conviction.

A tall CW2, who I later learned had a broken back and a nylon leg below one knee, limped along on a cane beside me part of the way. He might have been twenty-two. His approach was different—he whispered. I had to stop quacking to hear him. He said that a .51 could go completely through a helicopter in any direction, and he explained how it would be when a round went up my ass and out the top of my head. "You think I'm kidding," he said. He told me that half the birds shot down exploded or burned upon impact, and when that happened my skin would crisp and melt, and no girl would ever see my face without curling her pretty lips *in revulsion. "If you've got any brains at all, if you ever want to have a wife and kids, if you want to live much longer than a year, you'll quit."*

"Quack, quack, quack, quack . . ." I waddled away.

A few days later the Tac officer, Mr. Mullins, was taking advantage of an early afternoon dismissal from classes by calling a few of us into his office for individual closed-door sessions. The guy who bunked next to me was married, and he came out crying, saying he didn't think he could take it much longer. Then my name was called. Fuck it, I thought, nobody's going to make me cry.

The office was the size of a walk-in closet. Mullins sat behind a tiny desk, and in a corner I couldn't see until I was already in the room stood another CW2. Like Mullins, he had a Purple Heart and silver wings pinned to his TWs. Unlike him, he didn't have any hair or eyebrows or ears. His nose and lips were almost gone, and covering his face was a layer of webbed tissue like pulled cheese. When I realized that the man was alive, and that we were staring at each other, I saw that one of his eyes was glass, though I couldn't tell which.

"Sir, Candidate Roark reporting, sir." Mullins waited for me to make a mistake, then finally returned my salute. I snapped my hand to my side, feeling the seams in my fatigues beneath the edges of my fingernails. He let me cook another minute before he spoke. I could feel the burned man's eye.

"I just wanted to see if you had thought any more about what we discussed the day you arrived, Candidate." He spoke real slow and gravely, nothing like the first day.

"Sir, Candidate Roark, I don't know what you mean, sir."

"We were talking about you dropping out of the program."

"Sir, Candidate Roark, I believe I'll stay, sir."

"You're a fool, Candidate."

"Sir, Candidate Roark, you stayed, sir."

I didn't realize the implication until it was too late. He sat there with his broken back and plastic leg and studied my stupid face for a long time. "You're going to die in Vietnam," he said. "Or maybe you'll just be paralyzed. Do you want to spend the rest of your life in a wheelchair with somebody wiping your ass?"

"Sir, Candidate Roark, no, sir."

"Then you're going to drop?"

"Sir, Candidate Roark, no, sir."

When Mullins spoke, his voice had changed. "The day's going to come when you'll remember standing here," he said, "and you'll be wishing to God that you'd quit."

"Sir, Candidate Roark, I'm here to stay, sir." It was the kind of bravado bullshit you'd expect a young stud to say, standing before life with my chest puffed out, yelling Bring it on, you son of a bitch, I can handle anything you've got. The two maimed men had scratched a line in the dirt, but there was never any choice of which way to go. In my bursting virility I would have died in my tracks rather than quit, but I left the room without looking again at the terrible man in the corner.

CHAPTER EIGHT

B Y THE last week of August, after seven weeks in direct support of the Third Brigade, Charlie Company of the 158th Assault Helicopter Battalion was a shambles. The official line for the period was that I Corps was pacified, and the media happily echoed this news back home. But no one mentioned it to the combatants on either side. While only two Phoenix birds were actually shot down during those weeks, almost every remaining aircraft in the company took hits from enemy fire. Hot LZs were a daily occurrence. While it did appear there were fewer large concentrations of enemy, it seemed more a matter of dispersal than withdrawal; the NVA and Viet Cong were everywhere, and they enjoyed shooting at helicopters.

The men of Charlie Company had good rapport with the infantrymen of Third Brigade. They felt a closeness and responsibility that stemmed from the grunts' dependency on the helicopters, from carrying them into combat each day and sometimes fighting to get them out. Nonetheless, no one was sorry when the period of support was completed, just as no one in Alpha was thrilled to be assuming the job. The switch to general support did not mean that Company C was out of the A Shau, but it did mean a reduction in the number of mornings when everything flyable flapped off in the same direction

78

before dawn. Only when large assaults were staged would the Phoenix birds be in the valley as a unit; the majority of the time they would be scattered from Da Nang to the DMZ, from eastern Laos to the South China Sea, performing every sort of mission that bored and wasted minds could contrive.

General support was anticipated by the crews as a chance for recovery. During the weeks in the A Shau, the men averaged less than five hours' sleep each night, and when there were probes on the perimeter, or when rockets or mortars fell from the sky, that was cut in half. Whenever a mission had a ten-minute wait with the engine running, it was common to see men slumped in their seats as if shot, strands of saliva hanging from their lips. Everyone learned the soldiers' secret of how to fall asleep in thirty seconds while someone kept watch. On general support, wake-up would normally not be until 0430, and the crews were looking forward to the extra hour of sleep.

Billy Roark had learned a lot. All his embarrassing newness was gone, and he felt very much at home in Charlie Company. His uniforms were beginning to fade—the green Nomex flight suits taking on a sickly mustard tone, and the fatigues becoming softer and paler each week. He had even grown a mustache. He knew the language and the routine, the missions and the call signs, and had a working knowledge of the area of operation. He loved the flying, and despite the bad days he would have turned down a chance to go home if it had been offered. The missions were rarely what could be called fun, but they were exciting beyond all things.

Greg Dooley thought he was alone. He sat in the big rocker with headphones clamped over his ears, eyes closed, electric sounds moving through his head. "Oh, wow," he said softly. "Oh, *wow*." He slapped a quick bongo beat on his thighs and began a whispering rendition of "Black Magic Woman," Roark and Baker stood in the doorway watching the spectacle, then Baker reached across and gave the volume dial a twist. Dooley screamed and jerked the headphones away, but when he saw the two he dropped to his knees. "My most humble apologies, Bwanas," he said. "I didn't know it was the great ACs, the defenders of freedom who rain piss and sometimes entire helicopters upon the heads of the heathen. But wait! Have I erred? Didst thou not become aircraft commanders this very day?"

Roark and Baker exchanged looks and went directly to the refrigerator. Greg Dooley, who had only been in the outfit two weeks, was shot down on his third day. The aircraft commander, a warrant named Luper with less than a month to go, made a forced landing to a sloped clearing, but the ship rolled and the doorgunner, Stoddard, was trapped. When the spilled fuel ignited, the others watched and listened while the man died.

Dooley was leanly muscular, very narrow in the hips, and had shoulders that seemed too wide for his chest. Unruly brown hair stabbed at green and adolescent eyes. "Well? Are you ACs?"

"We'd have had to crash on the checkride to keep from it," Baker said. Four pilots, including Sharp and McCawley, would DEROS within two weeks. Baker popped two beers and offered one to Dooley, who declined.

"I've got battalion duty tonight. Besides, I'm underage."

"Who isn't?" Roark went to his cube and soon came out wearing cutoffs and carrying his fan which he plugged in and turned directly on his face. Baker stripped to his flight pants, then bloused them above his knees. He added his fan to the effort, and the room began to cool. They propped both doors while Dooley watched.

"I guess when I grow up to be an AC I'll know how to keep cool," he said. Then something seemed to hit him, and his smile went abruptly away. He hung the headphones and switched on the speakers. Santana filled the hooch.

Becoming an aircraft commander was a formalization of what had already occurred. At about two hundred twenty hours the title of first pilot was bestowed, and the pilot then became commander of a ship with a copilot in his charge. He remained in the familiar right-seat position until the three-hundred-hour level when he was given a checkride in the left seat and officially pronounced an aircraft commander. Though that was the day of recognition, the truly important and scary time was the first day as first pilot. Near midnight one evening the platoon leader would walk in and say something like, "We're short of people for that big assault tomorrow. You're flying first pilot." Suddenly, a kid of twenty was in charge of a quarter-million-dollar warship and several men's lives, and unless he was an idiot he spent the few hours until wake-up thinking of all the things that could go wrong.

Charlie was on a one-day standdown, a day to patch up and clean up in preparation for general support. Early that morning Roark and Baker had flown their Hueys down to the Song Bo where they landed in the shallows and gave old-fashioned scrubbings to their beloved machines. It was one of the last few days of bare feet and sunshine.

Baker inherited his ship from a pilot bound for home. Well worn and proven, strong as a new one, the bird was comfortably into middle age. The Plexiglas windshield was pitted and scarred, with stress cracks at the corners. A clear patch covered a hole in the chin, and above was a metal one on the nose. The cockpit doors were chipped and boot-marked, and bare metal showed on the gray painted floors. The exterior had achieved a patina of age, exhaust smoke, and layers of Johnson's wax so that the original flat olive drab had deepened to a bullfrog color. Along the left side behind the crew chief's position was a diagonal row of three off-colored patches.

Billy Roark's Huey was brand-new. When Fred Luper lost his, he grounded himself. When the next new Huey arrived, it went to Roark, along with Luper's crew chief, Steve Kitchen.

As he carefully bathed his charge, Roark was as euphoric as a kid with a Corvette. The Huey looked as undeveloped as a tadpole, but the devotion to function and utility had its own beauty. The grace of the machine in response to his learning hands held him captive the way some women hold some men. When they returned to the nest, he helped Kitch paste-wax the skin, then buff it down with towels. They dusted and polished and cleaned, forgetting that the first LZ, the hurricane of dirt and twigs and trash, the muddy or bleeding men, would obliterate their work. When they were done, Roark doubled-up with Baker, whose ship needed more. They masked and painted the nose flat black, and the entire floor flat gray, then the skids glossy black with clean white toes, and put the same white on the stinger. They polished the windows, scrubbed the soundproofing, cleaned the decks with solvent, and wiped away every trace of oil.

Gil McCawley used the standdown to catch up on a perpetual backlog of checkrides, and to train the replacement instructor. He saved until last the two rides with his hoochmates, then spent extra time, turning each loose reluctantly since he would not be around to watch over them.

Baker had been right about the music. From the moment he connected the tape player, the hooch was transformed. Suddenly a chicken shed where dust seemed to propagate, where inch-long splinters lay in ambush for bare and shuffling feet, where the heat at midday could drive men outside like suffering snakes, was transformed to reasonable temporary bachelor quarters. Even Andy Ross agreed the money was well spent.

"Where's the rest of the guys?" Dooley asked.

"McCawley's on his way up," Baker said, "and Ross is still on the flight line. I think Turner just landed, and I haven't seen Sharp all day."

"He's in the club getting drunk."

"Roark!" Lieutenant Turner Wilson stood in the doorway ahead of McCawley, his cheeks flushed, golden hair showing beneath his cap. "I owe you one," he said. Wilson, the platoon leader, had arrived three weeks behind Roark and Baker. As the newest first pilot, he had drawn one of only two half-day missions assigned to the unit, a series of runs that MACV swore were essential to the continuation of the war.

"Why, Turner," Roark said, smiling, "MACV is one of my favorite missions. What'd they do to you?" Baker and McCawley also wore knowing smiles. MACV *was* good to work for, but they seemed to know little more about helicopters than that they could fly.

"I still don't believe it," Wilson said. "We picked up this gook and a spec five in Hue, then went up the street to a compound surrounded by barbed wire. They wanted us to hover beside an eight-foot pole so the gook could change a light bulb. So I've got the right skid beside the pole, and the ground is maybe five feet away. The gook is having problems trying to figure out how to hold on to the ship with one hand and still have two to change the bulb. Then it hits me what we're doing. So Fritz asks the interpreter, and sure enough we're hovering in a fucking minefield!"

"That's MACV," said McCawley. "Wait 'til you meet that new colonel up at Dong Ha."

A jeep pulled up to the hooch, sending dust boiling into the room. An orderly appeared with a bundle of mail. "Dooley," he called.

"Here!" It was Dooley's first mail. He glanced at the envelope, then stuffed it into a pocket. There was a copy of Stars and Stripes for the hooch, a care package for Allen Baker, and mail for Roark and Andy Ross. Roark took his letter to his cube and put Ross's on the bar, then sat with the others watching Baker. Allen carefully cut the tape with a small knife, moving slowly, making it last. Inside was a layer of newspaper, and beneath that a new issue of Playboy. There were shouts all around as he parted the pages to the centerfold. "Tomorrow you can look," he said. "Today it's mine." He kissed a glossy breast, then slipped the magazine beneath the box. Next was a Jackie De Shannon tape, and beneath that a tin of melted fudge, a softened stick of Cracker Barrel sharp, a small bottle of Amaretto di Saronno, and four boxes of Parodi cigars. "Groady Parodis," Baker growled with a grin. In one corner were several letters, and the scent of perfume quickly reached everyone. He went to the refrigerator where he deposited the fudge and cheese. "The candy's for everybody," he said, "and the rest is for me." He took his package to his cube, then returned with the tape.

"Hey, did you guys hear about the Redskins?" Wilson asked, his eyes suddenly bright. "They caught thirty-two gooks in the open up by Oceanview at first light, out in bare sand with no place to go. They were walking one behind another, and they just flopped down on their bellies. Luskey and Morton took 'em out on a single pass with the minigun. *Boy*, I'd like to have seen that!"

"No shit," Roark and Baker both said, smiling. The summer in the A Shau had enhanced everyone's vision and it had certainly defined their perspective. Baker flipped the switch, and De Shannon took over, singing "Put a Little Love in Your Heart." A trace of perfume still lingered.

"I'd like to put a little love . . ." Dooley said.

"Hush!" Baker turned the volume as high as the speakers could stand. The hooch trembled. Roark was the first to surrender, and he went to his cube and returned with his flight helmet and the vial containing his earplugs. He moistened the soft stoppers with saliva, then pulled his helmet over his head. Wilson and Dooley quickly did likewise, and Dooley lowered his dark visor. Baker got his helmet, but McCawley just squeezed his head between his palms.

Roark saw Captain Crable before he reached the door, and turned to pretend to not see him. Crable stood with an awful expression, a hand against his right ear. He seemed to be saying something, screaming something, but no one could hear him. Turner Wilson had his back to him, Dooley was clapping his hands and weaving around with the jack cord up his nose, and Baker was just staring blankly, mouthing, "I can't hear you, I can't hear you." Finally, Crable reached over and stopped the music. "I couldn't hear you, sir," Baker said.

Crable gave him a nasty look. "Mr. Roark," he said. Roark removed his helmet, then the earplugs. "I need you to schedule us to fly together tomorrow." The hell I will, thought Roark. "Mr. Roark? Did you hear me?"

"Yes, sir."

"I just need a few hours, so it doesn't have to be anything too long." He turned then and left the hooch.

"Captain Wonder flies again," McCawley said, relieved that someone else was getting the burden of nursing Crable through his single monthly flight. It seemed ironic that with Crable's dislike for warrant officers, it was always a warrant he chose to go with. McCawley began to chuckle, and the others made teasing remarks. Roark smiled, but there was no humor in his eyes. He was determined to find a way to get out of flying with the company XO.

When the speculation about Roark's dilemma subsided, Baker switched the tape player on at a normal level. He sat with the issue of *Stars and Stripes* and began reading about the war. The playful mood was gone; no one was wearing his helmet. Andy Ross walked through the door with long, easy strides. "Evening," he mumbled, then stopped to get a soda and to pick up his letter before retreating to his room.

"Personable fucker," Dooley muttered, and no one had anything to add to that assessment. Ross had never become part of the hooch. He spent his spare time in his cube writing long letters or reading, plainly preferring his privacy to the noisy gangroom. After five months in the outfit, there was still no one who knew him well.

The sturdy form of Jim Tyler appeared in the door. When Roark moved toward the fridge, Tyler waved him off and said, "I'll pass. I've got to get back." The lines of his face were solemn. He sat absently on a folding chair that Wilson brought from his room. "We lost two birds today," he said.

"Anybody hurt?" McCawley leaned forward.

"Yeah, we lost two men and some grunts. A new pilot named Quigley—I don't think you knew him—and the doorgunner, Pepper Beasley. Two grunts were wasted, and three more messed up pretty badly."

"What happened?" Wilson asked.

"Took an RPG near Airborne." Tyler knitted his fingers and frowned. "Beasley was blown to rags down to his waist, and Quigley got a hunk of shrapnel through the back of his helmet. The other ship was in a different LZ—Nelson was flying—and they just stuck the tail rotor into a stump and flipped over. Everybody got out okay." He turned to Roark. "Anyway, it'll come down from Battalion, but I just stopped by to tell you we're going to need a bird to help out tomorrow."

"Was that Bob Quigley?" Dooley asked.

"I think so. He'd only been with us a couple of weeks. Did you know him?"

"We roomed together at Wolters."

Tyler stood suddenly, cleared his throat, and said, "Well, I've got to go. Catch you guys later."

No one spoke for several minutes. The tape ran out, the machine turned itself off. "I didn't even know he was up here," Dooley said. His eyes were full of tears as he stood and walked toward his room. Everybody else lit cigarettes.

Baker turned to the two full pages of the obituary and began going through the hundreds. Soon he folded the pages and held them in front of Roark, his thumb marking a spot. "Remember Guthrie?" Roark read, then walked outside and lit another cigarette. McCawley came out and said he was going to rescue Steve Sharp, then patted Roark lightly on the shoulder and moved off toward the club.

When he went back inside, the gangroom was empty. Wilson

and Baker were both in their cubes, and the light that rose through the rafters made the rest of the hooch seem dark. He went to his room, read the letter from an aunt, then unlocked the cabinet and took out a diary. He made a few notes, then flipped to the front. At the bottom of a column that already held eight names he added, "WO Daniel Guthrie." He heard a sound, and when he looked up, saw the past issue of *Playboy* hanging from a hand at the top of the wall between his cube and Baker's. He sat looking idly at the girls, not interested. He flipped through the pages, reading the cartoons, and stopped at a small one by Gahan Wilson. With his pocketknife he cut out the cartoon, then taped it in the front of the diary across from the list. He sat and studied it, and read the names again. The bizarre cartoon with its sad humor seemed a fitting memorial to his friends, their foolishness and his, and to the insanity that claimed them all. It was a simple scene of devastation, of green and vaporous fog, of a soldier alone on a battlefield. His uniform was shredded, his hands still clutched his weapons, one arm was wrapped in gauze; his teeth were bitten off, his eyes were bulging and empty, and he stood in stupefaction, surrounded by conquered domain. Beneath his boots was the caption, *"I think I won!"*

It was almost midnight before Roark resigned himself to flying with Crable. He sat at the desk with his face in his hands and stared at the blank assignment sheet. "You do a good job, and you'll get to fly with the shithead next month, too," Motormouth quipped. Roark placed the maintenance report beside the list of pilots and running totals of flight time, and began. He worked quickly, matching ACs with their ships, juggling missions from previous days, dropping names on the duty roster, and assigning longer missions to pilots with low time. The high-time AC and pilot were given the day off, and the task was complete. "What'd you decide?" Motormouth asked.

"First ARVNs."

"That should do. Nothing too complicated, and a little pad time. From what I hear, you're gonna be doing all the flying." For someone who never flew, Motormouth had an unusual comprehension of what went on in the air.

Roark had wanted to go to the A Shau with Alpha, but there was Crable to consider. With ten months in-country, the XO had logged less than a hundred hours since flight school, and he had never been to the valley. Though the 1st ARVN mission would involve some work along the DMZ, a large portion of the day would be spent over terrain less demanding than the A Shau. He had assigned the Alpha mission to Andy Ross.

He walked up the hill toward the hooch, feeling the pull of fatigue. The morning and another mission were only a few hours away. He thought about Crable—what a pain in the butt he was, and how he played at being a soldier. That reminded him of Steve Sharp, and what he had said about balancing things out. Suddenly he stopped in his tracks, thought a moment, then hurried back toward Operations.

He met Spec 5 Steve Kitchen coming down the stairs. Kitch was nineteen, solidly built, and had brown hair that he combed straight back from a high forehead. His face was darkly stubbled with a long day's growth, and he looked worried and angry. "Glad I caught you, sir," he said. "We may have a problem tomorrow."

"Why's that?"

"The new gunner—the one that transferred in from the Rakkasans? Sergeant Caldwell assigned him to us to see what I think, and what I think is he's going to be trouble. He's got an attitude like you wouldn't believe."

"This is the guy who extended to get out of the field?"

"Yeah, and as far as I'm concerned he can go back. He was supposed to be helping us on the ship today, but he just laid around the hooch. The only thing he's done since he got here is try to impress everybody with what a badass he is, like he's the only one who's ever been to war."

"I heard he was on the initial assault of Hamburger."

Kitchen looked embarrassed. "Yes, sir, he was. I'm not trying to put him down—I'm sure he's seen some shit—but it's not like he's got a monopoly. Besides that, he *asked* to come to Charlie Company—something about us saving his butt one time. All I know is if he wants to be a doorgunner, he's got two days to get it together."

"I heard he was the only man in his squad who survived."

Kitchen looked away. "Okay," he said quietly. "Okay."

"We'll see about it in the morning, Kitch," Roark said, starting up the stairs. "Maybe it'll work out." Then he stopped. "Oh, yeah—we're going to have Crable, too."

Kitchen clamped his eyes. "Where are we going?"

"The A Shau."

CHAPTER NINE

B Y 0430 the arms room was loud with preparation. Belted bullets rattled across steel edges; smoke grenades fell in place with thin metallic twangs; oiled bolts were drawn and dropped and cycled like machinery; heavy cans of ammunition scraped the concrete floor; men grunted, belched, and broke wind as they strained beneath their loads.

"Hey, Cassini, let me help you with that."

"The name is Ca-*chee*-nee, dumbfuck, and I don't need any help!" The sounds stopped; Steve Kitchen stepped back. Rico Caccini was slightly shorter, but carried about the same weight as Kitch. He was thicker in the thighs, and his biceps filled his sleeves. If they fought, Steve Kitchen would have to strike first and hard. Caccini stooped, lifted the ammo can, and carried it in slow, choppy movements outside to the mule, a display of strength that impressed no one. When he returned for the second can there was sweat on his forehead, and when he came back for the guns it was streaming down his face.

"There's something you don't seem to realize," Kitchen said. "You're temporary. You've got two days with me, and then you're either a doorgunner or you're out."

"Fuck you," Caccini snarled. "I extended six months to be a doorgunner. Guaranteed."

"Wrong. You extended to get out of the field, and you're out. We didn't guarantee you anything."

"I'll get Caldwell to put me on another ship."

"Wrong again. And when you get bumped to maintenance or motor pool, there ain't *no* coming back."

"That's right," said a blond kid named Potter, oiling a sixty on the cleaning table. "If Kitch says you're out, you're out. Period." He made a clownish smile and went back to work.

Fuck it, Caccini thought. I'm out of the bush, and that's what counts. I'm alive, and that's what counts. I'm alive.

Rico Caccini was alive, and after nine months with Alpha, 3d of the 187th, he was the only member of his original ten-man squad who was. Two were gone before Hamburger, then five more were killed in the ten-day battle. Everybody DEROSed in a bag. He was flat on his belly at Eagle Beach when Hamburger Hill and what it meant finally hit him. What made it come was seeing the hill—blasted, vacant, and worthless—moving away from the Huey again and again. The decision to pull out when the hill was finally taken was fine with him—nobody wanted to stay—but it made it appallingly clear that nothing at all had been won.

From then on, Caccini was a survivor. He began to count the days to DEROS. Then Roundman went up in a geyser of mud right in front of him on point, and just he and Boomer were left. The day Boomer fell to a sniper that nobody saw, he knew what he had to do. He told no one, but two weeks later when they came in from the field he went to the CO and signed the papers, gambling two hundred seventy days as a doorgunner against ninety as a grunt. He had no choice at all, but that did not make the decision any easier.

Phillip Crable had always hated flying. In fact, it was with considerable reluctance that he had finally committed himself to flight school. He hated flying, but this morning he hated it more than ever. He felt the giddy, falling sensation, the helplessness that surged in his throat just short of hysteria. When they crossed into the A Shau north of Rendezvous, he was completely alone, forgetting the fourteen birds ahead and even Billy Roark an arm's length away. He stared through the chin bubble and fought an impulse to pull his feet into the seat as the ground plunged to the valley floor. They were descending toward that floor, and he watched for the glowing red rounds he was certain would come. The palms of his gray leather gloves were soaked.

The A Shau was a late summer playground, a trampled arena. Toward the moonscape of Hamburger Hill, Hill 996, and the slopes between, the bare blasted dirt and splintered stumps evoked images of other wars. They landed first at LZ Foxy, an airstrip on the northern floor, where fifteen birds from the Kingsmen of Camp Eagle sat with engines at idle. Huddled beside the caliche surface were Pathfinders in black caps directing traffic with portable radios. Six heavy Cobras parked at an angle toward the center of the strip, touching down on the toes of their skids, then rocking back and spreading the struts. Above the pass against a dawning sky came two more Cobras, and behind them a twin-rotored Chinook with a sling load of blivets for refueling. The commotion and confusion, the tangle of voices on the radios, and the ship again being in contact with the earth were all reassuring to Phillip Crable.

There were two moves to be made. Two companies of infantry in separate pickup zones were to be carried across the valley and inserted along ridges west of Hamburger Hill. Next would be an extraction of two ARVN companies from the Ruong Ruong Valley south of Eagle, and the insertion of those troops into the low hills at the southern tip of the A Shau. The operations were separate, but even combined they would not have been a large move by valley standards.

When the first mission began, the two flights departed in different directions with timed separation. High above and to the north, the guns at Berchtesgaden belched smoke as the bombardment of the LZs commenced. Phillip tightened his belt and tried to prepare himself. He had developed a theory that men who were subjected to constant danger secreted a mysterious chemical to help them cope, a dulling, stupefying agent that picked up where ignorance left off. He realized that he lacked that chemical, that his careful life prevented its development. He was simply too aware of what was happening; that was how he explained his fear.

Today was not supposed to be happening. He had always managed to avoid combat assaults, fulfilling his monthly minimums on administrative runs to Da Nang or VIP trips between the lowland bases. But now, inexplicably, Crable found himself in the heart of the A Shau on what could easily develop into a living version of his worst nightmare. The wind in the cockpit was not enough to dry the moisture from his bleached face.

There was a brief glimpse of the sun before they dropped deep into a gloomy hole on the eastern rim, hovering straight down into the bowels of the jungle. Phillip looked down at men of incomprehensible courage and stupidity staring blankly up at the ship that could crash and kill them all. The PZ, blasted out by wrapping trees with bangalore explosives, was rough and filled with shattered stumps. The Huey had to be boarded at a hover; the ship wobbled like a gyroscope as the five men struggled aboard with rucksacks. Then the vulnerable craft moved up and away from those who were left, straight up through the deep shaft where great boughs reached for the rotors. It was then that Crable understood how completely his life was in Billy Roark's hands.

Chalk Two drew fire off the first landing zone, a saddle west of the hill, and when he called to the rest of the flight, the rapping sound of his sixties piped the war deep into Phillip's head. The gunners dropped smoke grenades to mark the targets, and the Cobras rolled in with rockets and miniguns. The radios screeched with overlapping calls—*Taking fire; Gooks in the treeline; Red smoke's out; Chalk Three break left; Three-six going hot; Three's out; Four's short; Three's taking fire from the left; Flight remain low level; How many sorties left in the PZ?* To those who flew them daily it was an average combat assault. To Phillip Crable it was a day of pure terror.

The ARVN lift was more difficult and confusing. The ARVN colonel was not quite ready, and he put the mission on hold with five loads of troops already airborne. Then the first two sorties were inserted in the wrong LZ, and it was difficult to convince the Vietnamese to get back onto the ships. In the midst of the mission an artillery barrage began five hundred meters from one LZ with the shells raining down through the flight. It was finally discovered that another ARVN unit was staging a simultaneous assault with their own CH-34 Kingbee helicopters, and the unannounced artillery was coming from an ARVN firebase. Five-year-olds playing football.

At the completion of the lifts they were assigned to Bulldog Three at Berchtesgaden to perform routine logistics. By midafternoon, with fatigue dulling his consciousness, Crable began to acknowledge that he might survive the A Shau. It did not, however, occur to him that he had touched upon one of the ingredients of the mysterious chemical of courage.

By the time they landed at Firebase Berchtesgaden, Rico Caccini felt better about his decision. It was not the extra time in 'Nam that haunted him; it was everything he had left behind. It was waking each morning covered with a layer of old sweat and scum and grit as thick as a poncho, his lips swollen from mosquito bites, and black ants down his back; it was sleeping four hours that ended like a collision, and spending the rest of the night waiting to murder someone in an ambush or taking turns at watch or listening to shells overhead and wondering if one was going to fall short; it was getting hit, with the whole world an explosion, and being in the middle of it, and later when he was sitting in a hole full of empty shells and empty clips and half his grenades gone, wondering what he had done during those few seconds or minutes, and what had happened; it was zipping part of yesterday into every bag with some dead somebody; it was waiting for a chopper to come and take the useless thing away; it was humping a ruck through the netherworld green, and waiting each second for the earth to explode; it was slimy red clay and wait-a-minute vines and almost never seeing the shreds of blue up high; it was being dead without the relief.

But that was only half of it. The other was being gone, and the image of climbing out of a foxhole and just walking away from the others, leaving them and the ghosts of his friends to make out as well as they could on their own; it was no longer knowing how much being alive was worth, but moving blindly along, hoping a day would come when he would know what he was doing, what he had done and why.

Putting the grunts on the hill had helped, though he had not thought it would. The men were from the 506th, and though he knew no one there, he sat stiffly over his weapon as if he did not have time to notice them. Then, when they were on short final and they could see a Cobra in a dive, firing rockets into the next ridge, the grunt beside him slapped his leg. The soldier was preparing to jump and sat with his butt on the edge of the floor and his feet on the skid. Suddenly he hit Caccini and made a grimace that looked like a mad smile, getting ready for the hill. Rico smiled back and popped him on top of his steel pot. He felt his arms and legs prickle. "Go get 'em," he said, then they both returned their attention to the landing. When they were out and darting low level down the slope to the northwest, then around to the right between Hamburger and Tiger Mountain, Rico leaned over his gun and stared at the jungle as if he could see, blinking hard to clear his eyes. Now, sitting in a Huey at the top of a mountain with a cool breeze on his face, Caccini felt better. He looked out over the valley where he knew there were men in the jungle, but the leaves and trees that covered the hills were so far away they melted together like paint. The war was a little removed, transformed to a swirling breeze that sometimes sucked people away, nothing like where he had been. If he were killed now, it could not be helped. He had spent his time in the bush, had done what he had to do. Rico Caccini was alive.

*　　*　　*

Throughout the day the Phoenix ship was a supply line to troops around the A Shau. From the mess tent at Firebase Blaze they delivered murmite canisters of hot chow to BG, Currahee, Airborne, and Rendezvous. They carried mail, ammunition, flares, C-rations, bales of sandbags, and steel posts; two light colonels, a sergeant with a toothache, one dead teenager, and two sling loads of drinking water in black rubber bladders; one folding chair, a brand-new second lieutenant to replace one murdered by his own men, and a bound and blindfolded gook who trembled facedown on the floor with the tip of a rifle in his ear. They landed on windswept peaks, flew down and back into holes in the jungle where giant trees were overhead, hovered on bomb-blasted ridges in clouds of blinding dust, and squashed a path with rotorwash for a platoon that was lost in a forest of elephant grass. Routine logistics, the A Shau Valley, 1969.

Following a late lunch in the mess tent at Blaze, the summer afternoon became a desert of boredom and drowsiness. They shut down at Currahee for almost an hour, again at BG waiting for a colonel, and once more at Camp Eagle while the same man enjoyed coffee with cronies. While the gunners slept, Roark paced around the ship to keep himself awake. Later, between the abandoned firebases of Birmingham and Bastogne, his head rolled forward, and he awoke in wide-eyed terror, not knowing how long he had been asleep at the controls. Crable was gazing out the window, and never knew. Roark tuned the ADF radio to AFVN, turned the volume loud, and lit a cigarette. By late afternoon the rush to get everything done that had been put off began, and the day ran long. More than once Bulldog Three promised just one more sortie, then had to renege as another call came in. When the sun went down, Phoenix Two-five was the only ship left in the A Shau Valley, and Bulldog Three was still promising just one more sortie to go.

The succession of mountains between Berchtesgaden and Camp Evans were shaded folds in a black blanket when the Phoenix bird was released. The crew was quiet as each man began the mental slide toward the bunk or chair waiting back at the hooch. There would be a stop at POL to top off with fuel, but the long day was nearly done.

"Phoenix Two-five, Phoenix Two-five, Bulldog Three."

The voice was anxious. Roark resisted an impulse to turn the radio off and pretend he had not heard. "Two-five, go."

"Two-five, our unit on Hamburger is in heavy contact. Can you take some ammo in?"

"Affirmative," he said, beginning the turn.

"They'll be ready on the upper pad at Blaze. Contact Tango Two Zulu on the hill, up this push." When Roark acknowledged, there was a pause, then Three came back. "Thanks a lot, buddy."

They were less than a mile from BG, and when the ship was turned so the valley was again before them, no one said a word. The top of Hamburger was a bird's nest of red and green tracers, the enemy green far outnumbering the red. Roark turned again and nosed the ship over, then called Motormouth. He explained the situation and had him scramble a pair of Snakes. "Be careful out there," the RTO said.

Two stacks of crates were waiting at Blaze, and when the Huey landed between them six men lunged into action. Kitch and Caccini had to move quickly to keep from being crushed. They were loaded in seconds.

Daylight was gone. A slice of moon made a feeble light through cracks in a mackerel sky as they climbed above the black canyon. The instrument panel glowed crimson, and there was time to listen to the steady slap of blades. The gunners checked their weapons, ammunition, and harnesses, then sat back to wait. Roark checked the radios and instruments, tested his shoulder-harness lock, and pushed the tip of his revolver down tight beneath his butt so that the widest part of the weapon was across his genitals. Crable squirmed in his seat. When they could see across the rim and into the valley, he cleared his throat. "We can't fly into that," he said. The top of the hill was still a bright tangle. Red-orange bursts flashed and disappeared. When Roark did not respond, Crable said more firmly, "I mean it. We're not flying into that."

"We are if it doesn't stop before we get there."

"Now see here, Mr. Roark, I'm the ranking officer on this ship, and I'm saying we are *not* flying into that firefight!"

Roark waited to be sure before he spoke. "Sir, I'm in command of this aircraft," he said. "Those men need ammo; this ship is landing on that hill. I can let you out at BG."

"Don't be absurd," Crable snapped. He clamped his lips tightly around his teeth, drew his long neck down into his body, and sat helpless and silent.

"Phoenix Two-five, Redskin Three-six."

Roark switched his selector to UHF. "Hello, Three-six," he said, smiling because it was Luskey.

"Two-five, we're just coming up on BG. Say your poz."

"Two klicks north of Charlie Bravo heading two-seven-zero."

"Roger, Two-five, have you in sight. I take it that mess up ahead is where you're going?"

"Affirmative, Three-six. I'm dousing my nav lights now, and I'll cut the beacon on final. We're going in blacked out."

"Three-six, roger. I can't say I blame you, but if you go down we won't know where you are."

Suddenly the firefight stopped. A few red streams of tracers squirted out from the hill, splattering around like droplets, then there was nothing. The NVA had seen the approaching beacons and now were either withdrawing or waiting for the explosive target to land. Roark pondered what he should do. If the enemy were gone, he could use the landing lights, and it would be as easy as landing at Blaze or the nest. But if they were still there, waiting in ambush, then the lights would be the worst possible thing. Besides providing beams to guide the enemy guns, the entire top of the hill would be illuminated, the GIs placed in silhouette, their night vision destroyed. But a blackout landing could mean flying into one of the many tall stalks of shattered trees that stood around the hill; it could mean misjudging the approach and crashing on top of the men. A flareship was the best solution, but the one scheduled to spend the night at Currahee had not yet shown, and there was no time to wait.

"Tango Two Zulu, Phoenix Two-five."

"Two-five, Zulu."

"Roger, Zulu, we're two minutes out. You need to evac?"

"Negative at this time, Phoenix. I think we're all okay. We're almost out of ammo, though."

It did not seem possible no one was wounded. "Roger, Zulu. We're coming in blacked out. I need you to mark your position with strobes." Soon two white pinpoint flashes were pulsing in the darkness. The gunships established a pattern, and the Huey lined up on approach. "You guys are going to have to help me a lot on this," Roark said to his crew. "I can't see much from up here." The cockpit lights were dimmed, but the shining plastic windshield caught every image and threw it back toward the pilots. The gunners, with no lights in their faces and nothing between them and the ground, could see the outline of the hill and the different textures below.

When the throbbing strobes began to move toward them at what seemed a normal rate, Roark began the approach, relying on the instruments and the relative position of the strobes. He looked out the side window and could see the shape of a ridge, but could only guess at the distance. "Turn off the beacon," he said. Crable fumbled, but found the switch.

"You're coming in too fast," Kitchen said. "Angle looks good. Slow down. We're clear of the trees. Pull up. Pull up! *PULL UP!!!*" Roark jerked the collective hard, pushed the cyclic forward slightly to bring the tail up, and in the next flash of light the ground was suddenly beneath them. A man was crouched in a hole in front of the ship with his face in the dirt and both hands covering the back of his neck. A storm of sand blew across him.

Roark could hardly breathe. His heart was racing as he tried to hold the ship steady in the weird, jerking changes from brilliant light to absolute darkness. They had come within feet, perhaps inches, of crashing, and thinking about that made him forget the NVA. When they were again flying across the valley, he restored himself with deep, even breaths and thought about the next landing. The gooks were probably gone, but maybe not. The landing lights still seemed too great a risk. He called Two Zulu and had him place the strobes three feet apart to give a known distance for judging closure, then explained to the crew that the next time they would use the navigation lights, but still land in darkness. Phillip Crable sat silent, as he had done since they entered the valley.

The rotor blades had not yet stopped when Crable stalked out of the revetment. He still had not broken his silence. Roark watched him walk away, feeling a mixture of contempt and unease. Major Andrews was due to rotate in less than a week, and since nothing had been announced to the contrary, it was possible Crable would succeed him for the two remaining months of his tour. Crable had been wrong to challenge his command of the ship, and Roark knew no other way he could have handled it without giving up control, but if the captain became the CO he was likely to find some way of getting even.

It was past 2200 hours. Roark took a long time with the log book, stopping several times, envisioning the hill and the crash they almost had—the stumps, the fireball, the bodies. They had been awfully lucky. He forced himself to concentrate on the log book. A puff of air through the cockpit carried the scent of urine. Kitchen got the tie-down and port covers from the aft compartment, then secured the blade and checked the ship over with a flashlight. He was about to close Crable's door when he stopped and said, "I'm not believing this."

"What's the matter?" Roark asked. Caccini was pulling a can away from its post, and the dragging sound stopped.

"Look."

Roark leaned across the console. Beneath the right seat and trailing into the chin bubble was a drying puddle flecked with sand. Caccini came up, and everyone stared in embarrassed silence. "A guy I knew shit his pants," Caccini said, "but he got killed right after that." Roark suddenly felt sorry for Crable, and ashamed, like someone who has played a trick on a child. "I'm going after a mule," Caccini said. "I'll bring back some water." He disappeared past the tail boom, the crunch of his boots loud in the darkness. The sound stopped and his voice said, "I'm gonna need some help with the ammo cans, Kitch. I 'bout ripped my guts out this morning."

CHAPTER TEN

S TEVE SHARP lay sprawled unconscious on the flat bunker roof, one knee drawn and pointed toward the sky, an empty hand reaching for an empty bottle. "Where is everybody?" Roark asked when he entered the hooch. Gil McCawley sat motionless in the rocker, ash curving from his cigarette.

"Down at the club doing a wake," he said.

Roark sat down and pinched a cigarette from his shirt. Motor-mouth had been waiting in Operations and had almost gleefully delivered the news—Andy Ross was shot down on the 1st ARVN mission, caught between a pair of .51s up at Cam Lo, dived straight into the ground. Ross was killed, and Gary June and Spinach Wise-man, plus six ARVNs. The doorgunner, Keisler, was okay. Motor-mouth went on, rattling out details while Roark stood picturing the faces of the men. He saw them alive, then going down, then smashing into the ground. Then they were dead, and the faces in his mind were those of dead men.

The ash fell from McCawley's cigarette. Roark thought he heard it hit the floor. "They were flying my mission," he said. McCawley met his eyes, then looked away. "I had 1st ARVNs last night, then I went back and changed it so I could put Crable in the A Shau.

97

Then I damn near killed us, and Ross and June and Wiseman are dead."

McCawley dropped his cigarette and lit another. "So?"

"So? So they're dead, and I'm alive."

"What do you suppose it all means?"

"Come on, for Christ's sake! You know what I'm saying."

"Sure. You want to be dead? You're wearing a pistol."

"You're a lot of help."

"What do you want me to do, feel sorry for you? You want me to console you for not getting killed today? It wasn't your turn, that's all. And when it is, it's not likely anyone else is going to be saying it should have been them."

"But it *wouldn't* have been me," Roark said. "We'd have been earlier or later or higher or lower or something."

"Uh-huh. And maybe there would have been ten bodies out there instead of nine, and maybe Ross would have crashed on Hamburger and killed a dozen more."

"How'd you know about that?"

"I was in Ops," McCawley said. "How'd it go?"

"I almost flew into the ground."

"Look. What time did you get up this morning?"

"You know. Oh-three-thirty."

"What d'you log?"

"Twelve hours."

McCawley looked at his watch. "It's almost twenty-three-hundred now, and you got what?—three hours' sleep last night?"

" 'Bout that."

McCawley made a shrugging gesture with his hands. "When the Army figures out that helicopters aren't tanks, then the numbers will change. Until then, we're going to be crashing some birds. It's nothing but a complete miracle when a pilot gets a thousand hours here without screwing up."

Roark slumped in his seat. His eyeballs hurt far back in his head, and he kept forgetting to blink. He went to the refrigerator. "Motormouth said we're supposed to get a typhoon tomorrow. Canceled all the missions." The fragrance of beer filled the room as he returned to his chair.

"That's what they say."

"What day are you leaving?"

"Monday."

"Wolters, wasn't it?"

"Yeah. Me and Steve both."

"Well, I wish you were staying. It's nice having somebody around who knows what's going on."

McCawley shook his head. "I'm tired," he said. "Real tired. I need to go home while there's still some of me left. Get reacquainted with my wife. And there's Steve. Just look at the poor bastard. I don't know if he's an alcoholic, or if he just prefers being drunk. I'm glad he's going to be where I can keep an eye on him."

"Weren't you classmates?"

"We signed up together. But he wasn't this way. Nobody knows that. They just look out there and see him unconscious, completely missing the fact that they're looking at the entire situation on two legs."

"You want some help with him?"

"Yes, let's bring him in."

The two went out to fetch their friend. They carried him upright with his feet dragging like a dead man. He had pissed on himself, and he moaned when they put him on his bunk.

Billy Roark awoke in a dream, flying the ARVN lift again with Crable, reliving a forgotten moment. The ARVN artillery had just been discovered, and the flight was forced to low level, scurrying back to the PZ beneath the invisible arc of the shells. Crossing a canopied ridge, he glanced out his window and down and glimpsed a tiny hole in the jungle. Below was hard-packed earth. It was instantly gone, but he was sure he had seen a bamboo structure. He reported the sighting to the air mission commander, who was unconcerned. Of course he had seen something, the man said; the area was crawling with gooks. But in the dream, it all happened more slowly, and there was time to see. The earth between the trees was red-orange and struck with sunlight, and he noted the way the bamboo was lashed together.

Someone was hammering. He raised the netting, peeled away the poncho liner, then sat before the fan. He could see Allen Baker standing at the bar. "Coffee," he gasped. He pulled on fatigues and asked through a yawn, "What's all the noise?"

"Getting ready for the blow." Baker handed him a cup. He was smoking a Parodi, stinking up the hooch.

"They're serious?"

"Supposed to catch it this evening."

Turner Wilson walked briskly into the hooch. "Baker, Roark, what are you doing?"

"Preparing for the typhoon," Baker said, puffing his shriveled cigar.

"I need you guys to go down and start on the birds. Take Dooley with you. Gil's already there," he said. "Roark, when the work's done, I need you to inventory Ross's gear. Stack the issue stuff on his bunk and pack the rest in his duffel bag. Here's his keys." He tossed a ring, then marched off toward Crable's hooch, jotting notes on a clipboard. Roark glanced at the keys, then put them on the bar.

Dooley was working energetically with a hand saw outside, cutting a plywood panel for the screened upper half of the door. Roark and Baker sat with their coffee, commenting on the fine job he was doing. When the panel was nailed in place, Dooley propped the door, then dropped the tools on an ammo box. "My daddy's a carpenter," he said. "A real butthole, but a good carpenter. But my mama's nice." He smiled like a child.

They found McCawley at the hangar talking to Sergeant Donner. Repairs were halted, and maintenance personnel were moving parts and tools to the CONEXes and ready room. With the east side completely open, the hangar was sure to be filled with rain, if not blown completely away. Donner gave the pilots several coils of manila rope and rolls of hundred-knot tape.

Kitch and Caccini were at the revetment, driving steel stakes, securing the skids with cables. They tied the main rotor fore and aft with rope and lashed the tail rotor firmly to the vertical fin. They taped ponchos across the delicate windshield, taped the intake and exhaust covers, the sleeve on the pitot tube, the bleed air vents, and the edges of the pilots' windows. Then, for good measure, they ran a rope around the tail boom forward of the forty-two-degree gear box and secured it to each side of the revetment. When they were done, they doubled up on other birds, then stood around talking and fiddling with the ropes. No one seemed comfortable with leaving the ships.

Steve Sharp was slumped in the rocker with a stunned expression, holding a cup, barefoot and wearing nothing but the pants he had slept in. His chest was flat and pale with a small patch of black hair. "Need some help with that coffee?" McCawley asked.

Sharp shook his head slowly. "No," he said, and moved the cup carefully toward his mouth.

"Do you know how much you drank last night?"

"Enough, apparently."

McCawley paused. "You're killing yourself, fella."

"It's nice to have that option."

Baker emerged from his cube and sniffed the air. "Why don't you get out of those filthy pants and go take a shower?" he said, reaching for a soda.

"Why don't you bite my rumpled ass?" Sharp snapped. Baker glanced at McCawley, shook his head, and went out front. Soon everyone but Sharp joined him. Dooley came carrying the hammer and a limp paper sack that had nails poking through, and began working his way around the hooch. He lowered each panel over the screens to check the fit, then made latches to hold them tight before propping them open again. Roark climbed up on the roof, and Baker and McCawley doubled up to toss sandbags to weight the sheet metal against the wind. They scratched a shallow ditch across the rear of the hooch, filled the water jug and canteens, checked the candles, matches, and flashlights, and called it done. Then they went outside with beers. A veil of vapor hazed the sky like a cataract.

Soon they saw Crable and Wilson approaching. The XO had enlisted the lieutenant early that morning to help with the details of supervision by carrying his clipboard. Crable's pace slowed and his demeanor softened when he saw the pilots. "Is that all you men have to do?" he asked congenially.

"It's all we've got planned," McCawley said, then made a rubbery grin to suggest a joke. Wilson ducked into the hooch.

"Well, I think we're finally all done," Crable said pleasantly. "Mr. Roark, if you can spare a moment, I have a small matter I'd like to discuss."

"Sure," Roark said, and he hopped down from the sandbags. He could see that Crable was making an effort, and he still felt badly about last night. He let the captain lead him to the far side of the flat-topped bunker. They sat down to talk with their backs to the others.

Phillip Crable was so thrilled to get back from Hamburger Hill alive that it was the following morning before the career possibilities of the adventure occurred to him. It was all there when he opened his eyes. A good night's sleep and an active imagination had changed his perspective considerably. The A Shau Valley was not that big a deal, really, now that he was out of it. But just think how it would look on paper! He knew the hyperbole by heart: *nighttime emergency ammunition resupply . . . a desperate infantry unit completely surrounded and cut off by a numerically superior enemy force . . . a withering hail of mortars, rockets, machine gun and automatic weapons fire . . . complete disregard for his own safety in the face of overwhelming odds . . . above and beyond the call . . .*

Definitely. Beyond the call of common sense, sanity, and anything remotely approaching reason. He had decided that Billy Roark was an utter maniac; he was completely convinced that the peach-fuzz kid would have flown his Huey straight into that fire-fight if it had not ended. Unbelievable, but exactly the sort of thing to be expected whenever kids were fighting a war. Roark had ob-viously seen too many movies.

The set-to over command of the ship would have to be ignored for now; perhaps it could even be forgotten. Phillip had no delu-sions about personal heroics, but now that it was done, he decided, it may as well be put to good use. He removed a tablet from a cabinet and smiled as he began to write. Billy Roark was definitely a hero; he could hardly wait to tell him.

The roof of the shelter was only two feet above the surrounding ground and made an ideal place to sit as well as to sunbathe or stare at the stars. Roark sat first, and Phillip plopped down beside him. "Say, I didn't want to mention this in front of the other guys," Crable said, "but did you hear about last night?"

Roark stiffened. Crable was very close, his voice hushed, his at-titude intimate. "I guess not," he said.

"Well, they're saying at Battalion that those men last night are writing us up." He leaned toward Roark, made a fist, and tapped him with exaggerated gentleness on the shoulder. "You're a hero," he said.

Roark glanced over his shoulder. The gang was draped across the sandbags, solemn as a congregation of crows. When he turned back, he moved a few inches away from the captain. "What for?" he asked.

"For what we did. They're putting us in for decorations."

"We didn't do anything except nearly kill them."

"Sure we did! Those men were surrounded, and we went into a hot LZ with ammo. That's sure something!"

"It wasn't hot."

"Yes it was! I saw the tracers!"

"Bullshit."

Crable smiled. "You'll never get anywhere with that attitude," he said. "Look here, you're young, intelligent, and obviously coura-geous. The Army likes to reward men like you. You could get a Silver Star, and you'd almost certainly get a DFC. And you've still got more than eight months to go. When somebody gets decorated early, they attract attention. People will be watching, and the next thing you know you'll get another medal. Like Audie Murphy. Later, if you decide you want to stay in the Army, with the right decorations you could get a direct commission to captain. Think about *that*."

"Okay, if they want to write us up, it's fine with me." Roark started to stand, but Crable grabbed his arm.

"Wait, I'm not finished," he said. "The way these things work is by coordination. There are hundreds of write-ups sent to Division each month, and most of them are trashed. It's only the big ones that count—the ones that are written from several angles, and with lots of people testifying. I know how the system works, and I know how to write. I can talk to the people who were out there last night, coordinate this thing, insure that it's done properly, and we would be almost guaranteed decorations. All we've got to do is add our write-ups to this thing, and we've got it."

"Our write-ups?"

"Sure. You say something wonderful about me, and I say something wonderful about you. We put those statements together with the ones from the field, and that's it."

"You mean write ourselves up?"

"Well, I guess it does sound that way, but it's really just supporting everything else."

"No way, Captain."

"Don't say that yet." Crable waved a hand and smiled. "Think about it a couple of days. A Distinguished Flying Cross! At least a Bronze Star for valor!"

"I don't need to think about it," Roark said. "I'm not writing you up, and I'm sure as hell not writing myself up. That's all there is to it."

Crable was momentarily choked with anger. "You won't get too far in this Army thinking like that," he said.

"Damn." Roark snapped his fingers. "And I was hoping to make colonel."

IV

There was a tremendous sense of life excitement when we moved up the hill after Preflight. I remember those months as quiet amber mornings, clear blue days with cool and gentle breezes, and restless nights that stood between me and tomorrow. I have never been so happy as during those days of preparation.

The only cloud over Phase I was a man named Corbin. During that part of the war, rated warrants were required to serve two year-long tours of combat. They were shipped out straight from flight school following leave. The ones who returned and could still fly were often assigned to one of the flight schools where they were expected to pass along a portion of what they had learned. A year later they were again ordered to Vietnam.

CW4 Corbin was a helicopter pilot long before Vietnam. He flew 23s in Korea and did two tours in 'Nam as a scout in 13s, and that was in the days before doorgunners. The other Tac officers said he had logged over five thousand hours in sling-wing time, which placed him among a very select group of pilots. No one ever said so, but it was our impression he no longer flew.

Corbin was the head Tac officer for our flight. Our building was a white two-story rectangle with a wide foyer at the center. Corbin's office was there, and he lurked like a spider waiting for a WOC to wander past so he could lunge out and destroy him. We learned to use the end doors and to walk quickly with our eyes straight ahead as we passed the foyer.

Corbin was the most serious threat we faced in Phase I. We expected the normal attrition of flight school; every week someone washed out. Academics, physical coordination, the inability to divide attention, too many speeding tickets, getting thrown into jail, ulcers, second thoughts on the future, and simple fear of flying were part of the anticipated process of elimination. We were like a school of fish, and when someone was swallowed up, they were immediately forgotten. We looked ahead and swam harder.

Corbin was the predator in the pool. The other Tac officers wanted to weed out the weak and warn the rest of what was ahead. But Corbin wanted to weed out everyone. He was a dark man with dark skin and dark eyes, a tormented man with few illusions. He lived on post in a BOQ and drank straight whiskey to dull the things that were happening in his head.

He rarely spoke to us as a group, but when he did, the subject of self-control invariably came up. The most visible sign of self-control in a soldier, he said, is the control of what comes out of his mouth. Profanity is the oral expression of the environment of war, and it is very easy to allow it to take over and to command you. But it limits you, it describes you, it reveals you as something profane, something out of control. If you cannot learn to control your mouth, then you shall never be able to control anything about yourself. Some of you who survive Vietnam will be out of control when you return. If there is to be any hope for you at all, he said, you have got to begin now by controlling what you can.

One night just before lights out, 2200 hours, he came into the barracks drunk, carrying the dregs of a bottle. Almost everyone in the building was in their underwear about to go to bed. Our quarters were clustered together on the opposite side of the post from the married duty personnel, so there were never any women around. Our rooms had large windows which were not draped, and it was impossible to climb into an upper bunk without being visible outside. There was no rule against sleeping in the raw, but no one did, and a soldier in his underwear is not such a shocking sight on a military installation.

We heard Corbin coming down the hall. My roommate was in his bunk; I flipped the light and crawled between the sheets. Across the hall a tall kid named Jasper was getting things laid out for the morning when Corbin stormed into his room in a foaming rage. He braced the candidate to the wall, shoved his contorted face forward, and began to scream, saying the warrant officer candidate was a pervert, parading around half-naked with lurid intentions, obviously a queer who should be kicked out of the program. He said every degrading thing he could think of, then repeated it all. Our ambition made us hobbled sheep, but it would have been hard to find a witness if Jasper had decided to break the tether. But he already knew about self-control. Finally Corbin staggered down the hall, promising before he left that Jasper would be shipped out the first thing in the morning.

He stopped when he reached the foyer and finished his bottle. From there the entire flight could hear him, and everyone was listening. He launched a short tirade on his favorite subject. "You goddamned sniveling little cocksuckers got to learn to control yourfuckingselves!" he roared. Then he threw the empty bottle down the hallway. The shattered glass slid along the polished concrete floor like shards of ice.

When he was gone, it was lights out. We put on our boots, then got brooms and mops and cleaned the hallway by flashlight. I don't recall discussing it, but I think each of us decided to keep quiet unless Corbin went for Jasper, which he never did. It seems now that we must have understood something even then: CW4 Corbin, whatever he might be, was one of us.

I have often thought about Corbin, but this is the first time I have been able to see him so clearly. I remember him from the perspective of a clean and eager kid, but I am that no longer. I know all about Mr. Corbin now.

CHAPTER ELEVEN

THE RAIN began around midnight, but everyone who had waited up to see what a typhoon looked like was disappointed. The storm was several hours late, and its reluctance to come ashore made some afraid it might not come at all and they would miss it. Those who went to peer outside before going to bed saw only straight unbroken strands of hanging rain. Later they listened in their sleep for the wind.

It began before dawn, slowly but with confidence. By morning the seamless drone on the metal roof began breaking with the gusts. The pilots lay curled beneath their covers, dozing in the luxury of a cool morning with nothing to do. Somewhere was a leak, and its steady *plop, plop, plop* broke time into tangible pieces.

A piercing, trailing scream awoke the hooch. Roark stepped across the hall. Dooley was sitting erect in his bunk making wheezing, whimpering sounds. "Dooley?" he said. McCawley and Baker emerged from their cubes. A gust peppered the roof with a loud volley.

"Okay," Dooley said, still out of breath. "Okay."

When he was dressed in fatigues and a flight jacket, its shoulders pale with dust, Roark began making coffee in the gangroom. Baker came out and nodded with a look indicating Dooley. The last thing before going to bed Dooley had told them about the day Ken Stoddard died.

A strong and sudden gust changed the tempo of the storm, announced it as a true storm, and laid a low moan across the camp. The doors rattled, and the rafters groaned like the beams of a ship at sea. There was a traveling sound of warping metal, then a loud crash against the hooch. A sheet of roofing struggled around the building, slammed into the next hooch, and finally sailed away. There were other sounds of flying things, impossible to hear without giving form—ponchos, beer cans, plywood, splintered lumber, pieces of aircraft, empty drums tumbling along. Anyone left outside was in real danger.

"They're supposed to leave tomorrow, aren't they?" Baker said, his voice low.

"The day after," Roark replied, handing him a cup. "We're about to become the oldest ones in the hooch."

"You mean *you* are. You've got four days on me." Baker had taken a few extra days of leave to be with his wife.

It was another stage, another level of development that every pilot looked forward to with a mixture of yearning and dread. Roark and Baker were new aircraft commanders, and now the two they depended on most, McCawley and Sharp—their teachers— were about to go back to the States. The only other ACs in the platoon, not counting Luper, were Barnes and Esch in the next hooch.

Dooley padded out of his cube in his undershorts, completely recovered from the dream. He said, "Damn, it's cold," and turned back. From the rear he looked like a skinned animal with his ribs showing, and no fat anywhere. His wide shoulders capped his narrow frame in a T. Roark and Baker watched him go, recalling the story, seeing it happen again.

It was only his third day in the air. Dooley had just begun to relax enough to see beyond the cockpit. Fred Luper was near enough to going home that he had begun saying, "Short," about every twenty minutes to remind himself, and to goad the others. When they left Blaze that day, the gunner, Stoddard, said, "Short," on the intercom to get him going, and Luper came right back with, "Shorter."

"I'm as short as a gnat's dick."

"I'm as short as *your* dick."

". . . as your memory."

". . . as your girlfriend's memory."

They followed the river toward Three Forks and were still

climbing when they felt the hits. Then the flame went out and the turbine sighed and quit. Luper dumped pitch so fast the swashplate bumped, and as the wind came up through the side windows he looked like he had himself pretty well together. He made a one-eighty and went right for a burned-off clearing on a shoulder half-way down the eastern slope. It looked okay, and everyone relaxed from the initial grip of gut-clenching fear. Dooley switched the radio to emergency and talked almost all the way down. It looked okay, then suddenly it did not look so good. When the sides of the canyon moved up around them, the perspective changed; what had looked flat from altitude was not flat at all, but it was too late to do anything else. There were stumps all over the clearing. Luper managed to put it down with only a little forward momentum, but the ground was rough, and the ship went up on the toes. When it rocked back, the right heel dropped into a hole, and the aircraft flopped over on its side. The blades disintegrated in chunks of honeycomb, and the Huey was swallowed by dust. The windshield popped out, and the pilots went out the front while Steve Kitchen climbed over the side and swung down from the skid.

"Where's Kenny?" Luper yelled, then they heard the scream. There was a muffled *whoof!* and black smoke erupted from the engine. "The battery!" Luper climbed back through the windshield to hit the forgotten switches, but it was too late. A round had severed a pressurized line, and JP-4 sprayed over the hot turbine. Other rounds had penetrated the fuel cell which seeped despite the self-sealing bottom. Flames rushed across the ship and up into Stoddard's well where he was blocked by a stump. Luper emptied an extinguisher, but it had no effect. The flames forced him back to the cockpit, then Dooley and Kitchen dragged him out. Stoddard screamed awhile longer, but had stopped long before the Huey exploded. An egg-shaped Cayuse scout flew slowly around the tree line, and high overhead was a Cobra, but it was a long time before the three men lying in the dirt knew they were there.

The wind was still building, but there were fewer sounds of flying trash. The moan deepened, and the windward side of the hooch rattled beneath driven pellets of rain. An invisible mist fell from the rafters.

Dooley came into the room fully dressed, said, "Good morning," then poured himself a cup and took the vacant rocker. He was only there a minute when Gil McCawley entered the room.

"Morning," they all said. McCawley was everyone's older brother. He had logged over twelve hundred combat hours and enjoyed respect throughout the battalion. The face that always seemed to carry some hint of humor looked tired and sober. He unbolted the door and opened it just enough to see. Everyone stacked their heads along the opening, then stood in awed silence. The rain was a hissing, horizontal slash, and whipping across the ground were writhing snakes of white vapor. An airborne guillotine of sheet metal sailed past like a piece of paper. When the door was closed, Dooley said, "You take the rocker, Gil."

"That's all right."

"No, really, take it. When I'm an old codger like you, ready to go home, I'm not going to want some newbie sitting in the short-timer's chair. You want some coffee?"

"Yeah." McCawley sat in one of the café chairs. When Dooley had delivered a steaming cup, he reluctantly resumed his position in the rocker.

A light came on in the cube beside the front door, and a few minutes later Turner Wilson came out. "You guys got no respect," he said.

"You figured that out awfully fast for an LT," said Baker.

Wilson smiled a quiet clown's smile and went to the bar for coffee. The only commissioned officer in the hooch, he caught a lot of flak from the warrants. He would engage in light banter in the hooch, but the moment he stepped outside in uniform he assumed a worried expression. He paid close attention to Phillip Crable and did what he could to make himself look good to the XO. No one held it against him; it seemed a reasonable way for a lieutenant to be. "Don't forget the inventory," he said, apparently to no one.

"Right," Roark said after a few seconds.

The light from the hanging bulb flickered and died. A moan went up, though no one expected the generator to last. Candles and matches were in place, and soon their dancing light turned the room into a cavern with gigantic, jerking shadows. "I need to piss," Dooley said.

"Do I look like your mother?" Baker asked.

"Her tits are bigger. So what are we supposed to do?"

"Here, sonny," Wilson said, cupping his hands. "Go ahead and tee-tee. Daddy will take care of it."

"Seriously," Dooley said.

"Cut the top off a beer can and toss your troubles to the wind," McCawley said, his eyes amused. Dooley looked like he thought he was the brunt of another joke, but he at last got a can from the small drum beside the bar, held it close to his chest, and opened it with the P-38 that hung with his dogtags. Then he disappeared toward his cubicle.

"Don't get none on you," Wilson called, and the others snickered. It reminded McCawley of a story.

"There was a warrant officer in a latrine taking a piss," he said, "when in walks a first lieutenant. They're standing there side by side, and when the warrant officer finishes, he zips up and starts to leave. 'Hey, aren't you going to wash your hands,' the lieutenant says. 'My mama taught me to wash my hands after I piss.' The warrant officer considered that a moment, then said, 'That's most commendable, Lieutenant, but *my* mama taught me not to piss on my hands.'"

Wilson sat with a chagrined look and shot the laughing warrant officers the finger. Dooley walked into the room, carefully holding the warm can. He opened the door enough to get his arm out, then flung the container into the gale. The wind grabbed it and slammed it against the next hooch. "Piss on you," he said, and closed the door.

The storm blew all day. The boys sat around telling stories, drinking sodas or instant coffee heated over Sterno, and tossing cans out the door. Occasionally some new piece of trash could be heard tumbling along; small things bounced off the building. Near noon Steve Sharp wandered into the room looking like he had just come out of hibernation, panting softly from the effort. His boots were unlaced as though he planned to not be in them long. "Get out of my chair," he said. Dooley stood without a word, dragged an ammo crate out of the corner, and sat with his back against the wall.

"You look like shit," said Allen Baker.

"Fuck you."

"Well, how does it feel to be short—one and a wake-up?" Dooley asked, trying to be friendly.

Sharp sat without expression, his eyes drifting toward the floor. His head shook and his mouth came open, but he seemed to change his mind. When McCawley handed him a cup he held it with both hands. "It doesn't feel any way at all," he said.

"Seems like you'd be glad to be getting out of here."

Sharp was coming around. "What are you talking about, Newbie? You don't want to leave."

"Sure I do."

"Bullshit. You're still gung ho."

It was true. Talking about going home was a game that everybody played. You said you wanted to go even if you wanted to stay, because that was considered normal. "Well, I'd like to be here long enough to feel I'd accomplished something," Dooley said.

"You better plan on staying over."

"I meant the year. I think when I'm short I'll be ready to leave."

"What is it you expect to accomplish?" Sharp asked.

Dooley glanced around and saw that he was on his own. "I'd like to win the war," he said boldly.

"Well, I'm sure your mama's proud, son, but don't get your hopes up."

"It may not happen while I'm here, but I think we'll win." ⹀

"We've already lost."

The statement was so final, so unexpected, Dooley could think of nothing for a rebuttal. Turner Wilson piped up to help him out. "One thing's for sure," he said brightly, "we got snookered. It's like that saying—young and dumb and full of come—I guess that's us, sitting here in a hurricane waiting for it to be over so we can go get killed while the people who arranged all this are home watching *Bonanza*."

"Welcome to Vietnam," Sharp said.

Dooley could not let such talk go unchallenged. "Look, I haven't been here as long as you guys," he said, "so I know I've got a lot to learn, but I still believe we're here for a good reason. I admit it's not quite so heroic as *thinking* about it was—it's not exactly the kind of part you'd expect to see John Wayne play—but I think it's worthwhile."

"Fuck John Wayne," Sharp said.

Dooley thought he was kidding. "Hey, man," he said with a tenuous smile, "you're talking about a great American patriot."

"That's right. He and Lyndon Johnson made a hell of a team—Johnny set our asses up, and Lyndy shipped us out."

"What are you talking about?" To Dooley, attacking John Wayne was in the same boat as denying Christ.

"Look, stupid. John Wayne is not even human—he's an institution. He's everybody's hero, and has no right to be. There's been a hundred thousand kids *slaughtered* trying to be John Wayne, and the only war he ever fought was in Hollywood. Then there's good ol' L.B.J., the bastard. He was a hell of a president, a hell of a politician. Not afraid to squeeze when he had a man by the nuts. A patriot? You bet. America all the way, by God. But at the heart of it all was a power-hungry old son of a bitch who didn't care who or how many he had to kill to prove a point."

Dooley was in utter shock. "You're in bad shape if you believe that," he said.

"You'll be in worse if you don't," Sharp replied, pointing a finger. "You listen to this, new guy. You can go out and kill all the slant-eyed little fucks you want to, and with my blessings, but don't ever delude yourself into believing you're doing it for your country. Your country is doing its level best to murder your ass."

Dooley was so angry and frustrated that tears came to his eyes. Sharp glared at him a moment, then the look seemed to soften to sympathy just before disappearing altogether. He stood and put his cup on the bar, then walked slowly toward the rear of the hooch, laces whispering along the floor.

"Don't worry about it," McCawley said. "You'll get it worked out. And if you don't, it won't matter."

"What do *you* think?" Dooley asked, genuinely confused.

"Well, it's not what I thought it was, but it's what it is. I guess I'm somewhere between. But the job's the same, and you're already here, so don't spend too much time thinking about it. You might end up like him."

"I'll *never* be like him," Dooley said, looking down the empty hall.

"Why not?" McCawley replied. "He used to be like you."

Late in the afternoon the wind slowed and finally stopped. The rain tapered off to a few fat drops plunking into the mud. After the hours of deafening noise, dripping sounds and boots on the hollow floor seemed harsh. The doors of the hooches were propped open to get air and to see what had been destroyed. Soon men began slopping around in the mud and shouting. Dooley was the first to go out. "Looks like it's over," he said.

"Half over," Sharp replied. "We're in the eye."

"Oh, yeah." Up high were broken clouds, wafer-flat and in many colors, patches of pale blue and apricot beyond. All around was depthless gray. "I've never been in the eye of a storm before," he said.

"You were born in one," Sharp declared, then walked out to the bunker to stand on the sandbags.

The camp seemed to have weathered the storm fairly well. The back was blown out of Alpha's hangar and a few curled pieces of corrugated steel shone blue-white where they had lodged between the hooches. Many of the sandbags on the roof had been leached of their contents and blown away. Pools of gelatinous mud filled low places while the high ground was littered with rough red pebbles. The clotheslines were down.

"Let's get to work while we've got daylight," Wilson said. They boosted Roark up to the roof, then tossed him new bags to distribute across the corrugated steel. Before coming down, he gazed all around the camp. Evans was almost an island. Instead of ten miles away, the Pacific Ocean now began at the flight line. All he could see to the east was water. Phong Dien was mostly submerged, the bamboo around it squashed.

The light was quickly failing, but the evening was pleasant and cool. It was McCawley's idea to bring the chairs out, and they sat in front of the hooch drinking half-cool beer and kicking at the puddled sand. Dooley was quiet and thoughtful, and after a while he got up and walked around with his hands in his pockets. He finally squatted alone at the edge of the bunker where he could look back and watch the others.

"Things are going to get worse from here on out," McCawley said. He was not talking about the storm, although it had returned in the night. From the opposite direction this time, it brought back all the junk that had been blown away. "This is when the season starts to change," he said. "It's pretty much the same as in the States—winter comes at the same time. It's not as cold, but the weather is worse. By the end of October you'll be getting more days of rain than sunshine, and a month after that it'll be almost all rain. You'll go weeks without seeing the sun. The weather is different down south. It rains some during the monsoon, but they don't get what we get up here. I Corps gets a real winter, and you'll be freezing your butts off."

"Freezing?" said Dooley.

"Not really, but you'll think so."

They were drinking hot cocoa that Dooley had made from water and dry mix over Sterno. A big change was about to occur in the life of the hooch, and the newer pilots were trying to glean everything they could from Gil McCawley. Sensing their feelings, certainly knowing a good deal of it himself, McCawley the teacher had done most of the talking for almost two hours. If the weather allowed, he and Steve Sharp were to leave the next morning.

"Well, one good thing about the monsoons," Dooley said, "we'll be out of the valley. That'll help some."

"No, it won't," McCawley said. "It'll be worse. You'll be on the Z most of the time, and the weather is going to take out a lot of folks. You need to start getting as much instrument practice as you can." The mood in the hooch became more solemn. The helicopters were much less stable than airplanes, and most of them vibrated to some degree. The resulting sloshing of the fluids of the inner ear made vertigo a real prospect. Vertigo, a confused state in which the inner ear becomes disoriented and sends erroneous information to the brain, was a condition feared by even the most seasoned pilots. It could happen to anyone. Typically, the sensation was one of turning when no horizon was visible other than that provided by the instruments. The pilot became convinced that the aircraft was rolling over to the side. The feeling was so strong that he would usually believe his instruments had malfunctioned. When he attempted to satisfy the sensations in his head, he unwittingly put the ship into a steep turn, became partially inverted, tried to pull out, and dived into the ground. "I mean it," McCawley said. "Whenever you fly at night, take turns on the instruments. Flareship is a good place to do it." One of the general support missions was to keep a standby Huey loaded with million-candlepower parachute flares. No one said anything for some time.

Finally Dooley said, in a voice that sounded like thinking aloud, "My mother said I'd come back a man."

"What made her think you were coming back?" said Sharp.

That hushed the room again. "You got your things packed, Steve?" McCawley asked, his eyes suddenly flint. Sharp made him wait for an answer.

"Nope," he said. "Not yet."

Turner Wilson turned to Roark. "Have you done the inventory?" he asked.

"No." He sighed. "But I guess this is as good a time as any." He took the keys from the bar and started down the hallway. Dooley went with him. A few minutes later, Roark returned holding a tablet. "Here's something everybody needs to hear," he said, then began to read. "'Dear Cindy, I have known from the first I would not be back. I wish we could have had more time. I go out each day thinking this is the one, for I know it is coming. I have not made friends with the guys in the hooch. I keep this letter with my things, so I know you will get it. I love you. I miss you. You will be my last thought. Andy.'"

Even the wind seemed silent. Everyone but Steve Sharp looked stunned. "I'm getting tired of sitting around," he said. "I'm going to go rest awhile." He left the room.

"I'm cooking lunch," McCawley announced. "We're having ARVN lurps."

"What's that?" Roark asked, blinking.

"Jesus Christ," Wilson said softly.

"Freeze-dried rice."

"I didn't know him at all," Dooley said.

"Who wants a beer?" Baker asked. "We need to drink it before it spoils."

"Neither did anyone else."

"I do."

"Me, too." Everyone was dry.

"Here's to Andy Ross. Whoever he was." When they banged cans, a few drops sloshed to the floor. McCawley went to his room and returned with the rice and three cans of chopped ham. His description of the meals for the ARVN and Cambodian reconnaissance teams was correct: simply a quart of rice in a clear plastic tube three feet long. He hung the bag from a nail, opened the cans, and began heating water.

"This sure explains a few things," Dooley said. McCawley chopped around in the cans with a knife and dumped the contents into the bag. He added salt and pepper and a generous dose of powdered garlic, then shook the bag to mix it all. He added hot water to the full mark, then sat with the others to wait for lunch to cook.

Something hit the hooch hard, then scurried away, and the storm seemed loud again. "I don't ever want to be an aircraft commander," Dooley blurted, surprising everyone. "I keep thinking about Ken Stoddard. Luper and I both forgot those switches, so it was half my fault he got killed. I don't ever want the day to come when it's *all* my fault."

"It was an accident, Dooley," McCawley said, "and you had just gotten here. Nobody can think when they first arrive."

"No, it wasn't an accident. It was a fuck-up, and I was so proud of myself for remembering to put out a Mayday. Then we hit the ground, and everything went to shit, and it was every man for himself. And Ken Stoddard's dead."

"You don't count it that way, Dooley. When a ship gets shot down in the mountains, and three men walk away, that's three miracles. Everybody was dead when the flame went out."

Dooley did not seem to hear. "There's something else," he said. There were tears in his eyes now. "All this talk about my mother is pure rot. I don't have a mother; she left when I was a year old. My old man is a good man, and all I've ever done is fight him and treat him like shit. I just wanted to say that."

"Good gosh, Dooley," Wilson said.

"Anyone want another beer?" Baker said, and he jumped up and ran to the refrigerator.

"Not me," Dooley said. "I've got a letter to write." He started out of the room.

"Hey, Dooley," Roark said. "Next time you decide to get emotional, how about waiting for the weather to clear so the rest of us can get the hell out of here."

Dooley laughed. "I'll do that."

The wind still blew and the rain still rattled against the hooch, but everyone could see that the worst of the storm was over. Soon the rice had soaked up the moisture; the fragrance of ham and garlic filled the hooch.

CHAPTER TWELVE

L IEUTENANT COLONEL Wilbur Blackburn, the MACV adviser to
the 1st ARVNs at Dong Ha, approached the Huey with a cardboard box in his hands. Strung out like ducks behind him were
fourteen ARVNs with identical loads. Some balanced the boxes on
their heads. "Looks like a safari," Dooley said. While there were
some good soldiers among the ARVNs, this bunch resembled care-
free kids in costume, going on a picnic. Caccini and Kitchen,
standing on opposite sides of the ship with their helmets still
plugged into the intercom, moved forward to direct the loading.
Colonel Blackburn lowered his box, then stepped up to the flat toe
of Roark's skid.

"Good morning," he said briskly, and poked his arm through the
window. Roark fumbled at his glove, then shook the colonel's
hand, feeling distinctly awkward.

"Morning, sir," he said. Roark saw immediately that something
about Colonel Blackburn was different, and was shocked when he
realized that the man was simply friendly. He had never heard of a
friendly colonel. Blackburn was lean and gray, a handsome man
in his mid-fifties who had a straight nose and stained teeth. His
eyes were gray, and he smelled of coffee. "I guess there's not much

we'll be able to do this morning, sir, with all this water," Roark said.

"To the contrary," the colonel proclaimed. "Our enemy is drowning out there. We need to take advantage of that." Bloody right, Roark thought. The man reminded him of the way Australian officers were portrayed in movies—bright, cheerful, enthusiastic, and apparently unaware they were in the business of death. "These are *Chieu Hoi* leaflets," Blackburn said. "Propaganda, if you will; PSYOPS. We need to get these out while those boys are miserable and wondering if what they're doing is really worthwhile." He drew a wrinkled section of map from a hip pocket and indicated the drop zone.

Roark marked his map, wondering about the colonel's words. *Boys?* He had a sudden vision of suffering kids, wet and huddled in a thicket with faces like those of the ARVNs. He had never allowed himself to think of the enemy as people who got hot and cold and sick and who missed someone back home. Then the vision changed; the kids became hardened NVA with malarial skin and bloodless eyes, gripping cold AKs in ambush for an American patrol. Fuck the bastards, he thought.

"Two men will go with you to do the drop," Blackburn said. "Just set up a pattern that will cover that area, then tell them when to begin." The ARVNs scattered up the hill like kids at recess while the two eldest squatted aboard the helicopter, smiling at each other. Dooley made the takeoff while Roark called artillery clearance and glanced at the map. It was a beautiful morning.

Even on a pretty day there was a certain bleakness to the lowlands near the DMZ. The A Shau, and even Khe Sanh, were handsome places, and sometimes that could be recognized. But after the mountains dropped down to become hills a few miles east of the Rockpile, the beauty of the land was suddenly lost. Roark gazed out Dooley's window toward Cam Lo, wondering if they would go there today. It was too far to see, but he thought he could make it out in the green smear of distance. Several specks of aircraft were silhouetted against the sky.

The drop zone was a rectangle, four kilometers by five, among the scrubby hills that rolled several miles southwest of Dong Ha. It was a vacant land where airmen often test-fired weapons, flushing pheasant, wild boars, or golden deer the size of dogs. Beneath tight cover along the creeks and ravines lay a network of trails leading toward Dong Ha and Quang Tri.

When they were positioned at a thousand feet, allowing for wind, Roark motioned for the ARVNs to begin. The leaflets were tiny pieces of newsprint, three inches by four, covered with a cryptic message. Each box contained 10,000—150,000 in all—seemingly sufficient to cover most of northern I Corps. But these were ARVNs. Mindlessly, they ripped open several boxes and began heaving double handfuls toward the door. Everyone shouted as paper replaced the air in a sudden maelstrom; the instrument panel and windshield disappeared.

When they landed at Dong Ha, the gunners stepped down and shook like dogs. There were leaflets inside their shirts and helmets. Roark and Dooley sat buried in the cockpit. Colonel Blackburn appeared at the top of the hill and immediately began to laugh. The closer he got, the more the situation seemed to seize him. Finally he began to lose his balance, and he sat on a stump beside the path. A bushel of paper fell out when Kitch opened Roark's door. He climbed down and stared. The machine guns and stabilizers were wrapped, bits of paper stuck everywhere.

"Go ahead and shut down," Blackburn said. "Throw the trash on the ground. I'll have the boys police it up when we're gone." Roark made a cut sign to Dooley, slashing a hand across his throat. "We're going to Cam Lo next," the colonel said. "The Kingbees inserted a company while you were making the drop. They'll just sit on their hands if I don't go get them started. I'll be back in twenty minutes."

He returned wearing a flak vest and steel pot, holding a flight helmet and a plastic-covered map. A .45 was strapped to his hip, but he carried no rifle. He climbed aboard the cranking Huey, switched helmets, and plugged a Y-cord into the intercom. An older ARVN carrying a PRC-25 radio came hurrying over the hill. A solemn little man with impenetrable eyes, he strapped himself in beside the colonel and waited rigidly for the flight to begin. Colonel Blackburn motioned upward with a thumb. *Chieu Hoi* leaflets scattered in every direction.

The sun was high enough now to make it clear that the coolness of the typhoon was an aberration. Roark followed Route 9, slightly to the right, wondering if he had done a very stupid thing assigning himself and his crew to the 1st ARVN mission simply to assuage his guilt about the death of Andy Ross. From what the gunner, Keisler, had said, Ross never had a chance. Every pilot had at one time escaped a situation when all it would have taken to spoil the day was a gook who knew how to shoot. Somewhere near Cam Lo were two who did.

They passed a long column of armored personnel carriers—APCs—parked on the paved highway. They seemed to be trying to decide what to do about the boggy ground. The land between the road and the DMZ was pocked with thousands of bomb and artillery craters, each filled level with muddy water. Watery paths through the grass glistened reflections of the sky like slug trails. "We're going to be landing near where that bird was shot down," Blackburn said. "It was one of yours, wasn't it?"

The crew acknowledged in unison. "One of the pilots lived in our hooch," Dooley said.

"Wiseman lived in mine," said Caccini.

"It was a terrible thing," the colonel said, his voice deep. "How about that young man who survived?"

There was a pause, then Steve Kitchen spoke. "He's back in the air, sir."

"That's unfortunate," Blackburn said, surprising them all. "It might have been better if he were slightly injured and sent home. He should quit flying."

"He's doing what he wants to do, sir," Kitchen said.

"Aren't we all," the gray gentleman replied, sounding nothing like the robust, laughing man of a short while ago. They were approaching the village of Cam Lo.

"Exactly where are the ARVNs, sir?" Roark asked.

The colonel glanced at his map, then toward the ground, and back at the map. "Seven klicks north-northwest," he said.

"Coming right."

"Clear right." The Huey banked, then leveled off facing the DMZ. The miles were short in a Huey, and in no place was that more apparent than just below the Z. From fifteen hundred feet, a point on the ground three miles ahead was easily visible low in the windshield. It would take less than two minutes to overfly it; for a standard landing, the descent should have already begun. The Dead Man Zone seemed very near. Roark braced the collective with his thigh, then switched hands on the cyclic to study the map and the terrain ahead. "Have them pop smoke, sir," he said, then he put the ship into a steep, descending turn. "Coming down."

"Clear down left," said Kitchen.

"Clear down right." Ahead was the flat of old paddies, and beyond were low brown hills at the edge of the DMZ. Past the hills was dark green scrub pocked with craters, and beyond that, the pale line of the Song Ben Hai.

The DMZ, created by the 1954 Geneva Conference as a temporary buffer between the two parts of Vietnam, was actually a protected sanctuary for the NVA. When the president made the decision to halt attacks into and north of the Z in November of '68, the land became, in effect, an extension of North Vietnam. Aggressive action by the U.S. military, including artillery and aerial bombardment, was prohibited. So instead of separating opposing forces, the demilitarized zone merely provided safe haven for one side, an invisible line their men could step across and become instantly beyond reach.

The bleak face of the Z was as real as anything in Vietnam. Roark suddenly discarded all romantic thoughts of giving fate a second chance; he decided to go in low level. Soon they were on the deck, racing northward. "Hold your fire unless you get a positive," he said. The gunners acknowledged, checked their weapons and braced for action. The Huey weaved along a series of shallow ravines, swapping sides through the curves, skimming the saddles by an arm's length. The drab green Huey matched the general color of the terrain, and the vegetation and curving surfaces of the earth absorbed its sound. Even if they passed directly over the enemy, by the time they were recognized as a target they would be lost from view.

When they reached the abandoned fields, the bare brown hills were ahead and very near. "There's where the ship went down," Kitchen said. The hills formed an L around the paddies on the west, and low on a flank that was mortared clean were a few twisted pieces of junk.

"Yellow smoke at two o'clock," Caccini said. The smoke grenade was spent, but a pale cloud lingered. Roark turned the ship directly through it; the scent of sulfur was strong.

"How do they look, Rico?"

"They're ARVNs," he said. They circled to the right, then landed at the edge of the paddies. The ARVNs were huddled in deep grass, waiting quietly, not looking much like soldiers. There was no perimeter set up, and most were just squatting on their haunches, their rifles pointed carelessly about, no one watching the brown hills.

"Wait for me," Blackburn said. "I'll only be a minute." Before Roark could answer, he had switched helmets and was out the door with the old ARVN.

"Well, *shit*," Roark said. A bird on the ground was a danger to everyone; it attracted the enemy and invited an attack. Roark brought the ship to a hover, swung the tail left so Kitchen would have a clear view of the hills, then settled back into the grass fully aware that if a .51 opened up, escape would be almost impossible. He held the collective raised to keep the ship light on the skids, ready to fly.

It was a genuine relief when the mortars began to fall. The first landed short, fifty yards off the left nose. Blackburn was at the edge of the paddy with the ARVN captain. The ARVN went belly down, but the colonel just hunched his shoulders a little, then turned around and waved the helicopter away. Roark had begun to hover toward him, but at the signal he quickly spun the ship about and hustled away to the south. As he turned, he saw a muddy volcano erupt from the paddy near the colonel. The old soldier flinched, then squatted down as if waiting out an inconvenient rain, his RTO at his side.

Ten minutes later the colonel called to say he was ready to be picked up. But when the helicopter landed, Blackburn was still chatting with the captain. They saluted, then the adviser turned and strode casually toward the ship, followed by the old ARVN. "Good God!" Roark said. "Come on!"

"I think the old coot's senile," Dooley declared. Colonel Blackburn stepped calmly into the ship. As soon as the ARVN was aboard, Roark yanked the Huey off the ground, spun about, and pulled in torque to the red line. The colonel, unprepared, was thrown roughly against the seat. Mortars slammed into the muddy ground behind them.

The clear skies lasted until noon, then all the moisture the sun had sucked up turned into clouds. A northeast wind pushed the soggy mass against the mountains, and very quickly it was raining in earnest. Blackburn wanted to go down to LZ Barbara, but it was socked-in and they had to turn back. The colonel had them shut down on the pad, then invited the crew to his bunker. The others declined, but Roark charged up the hill through the rain between Blackburn and Trung. The blades of the Huey seesawed and bumped in the rain-driven air.

Blackburn's bunker was not what Roark expected. It was a gopher's den, small and dusty with a low ceiling and dirt walls. Candles in C-ration cans, tucked into carved pockets, supplemented the light of a single bulb. The trapped air was dense with odors of mud and mildew. As his eyes adjusted, Roark was astonished to see that this was also where Blackburn lived. Between a table supporting radios at one end of the rectangular pit and a hanging closet draped with linen at the other were three canvas cots separated by various bags and ammo crates for personal gear. Blackburn said he shared the space with Trung—who spent the evening hours helping him with his Vietnamese—and an ARVN captain when he was not in the field. Roark sat on a cot and dried himself with the colonel's towel, drank the colonel's coffee, and wondered about this man who gave so much. They talked more than two hours while rain slapped at the tarpaulin door and a muddy puddle grew at the foot of the steps. Sergeant Trung crouched in a corner, and when he looked at Roark his eyes were flat and inscrutable.

Blackburn did most of the talking, saying with a bittersweet look that he would soon be leaving the service, retiring as a full bird at the completion of his tour. He had a wife named Ellen who had waited many years, and they were going to buy a trailer, do some fishing, and see some country.

Then the colonel switched subjects. He spent a long time asking about helicopters, their abilities, and how they could best be employed, surprising Roark more than once by asking his opinion—an unnerving experience for a warrant officer. Trung slowly began to acknowledge his presence.

When it became apparent the rain would continue the remainder of the day, Colonel Blackburn released the crew to return to Evans. They groped along the highway at a hundred feet and fifty knots with the spotlight aimed ahead so they might be seen. When Phong Dien appeared in the chin, they veered around the ARVN antenna and made a doglegged approach, unable to see Evans or the nest until they crossed the bunkers. Kitch and Caccini decided to stay with the ship and wait for a lull, and they stretched out and went to sleep. The pilots ran to the hangar, but were so drenched by then that when they left Operations they just walked and let the water pour over them.

A doorless jeep was parked in front of the hooch. Rain was pouring in, and the seats were pebbled wet. They found Steve Sharp in the gangroom, sitting in the rocker in chrome handcuffs, his cap gone, hair pasted to his head. The sight was such a shock, Roark and Dooley just stood with their mouths agape. "What in the world is going on?" Dooley finally asked.

"I got apprehended," Sharp said with a wan smile.

"For what?" Roark asked. "Where's McCawley?" There was a sound at the rear of the hooch.

"He's gone, I think. I took a walk this morning and missed my ride."

An MP sergeant wearing a black plastic helmet and a .45 appeared in the hall with Steve's bag. He nodded as he entered the gangroom. "You ready, sir?" he said to Sharp.

"What's going on?" Roark asked.

"Seems like Mr. Sharp has grown attached to this wonderful place, sir," the MP said. His pants and boots were soaked. "They want us to be sure he gets home."

"Well, he can't leave in this weather."

"No, but we're supposed to keep him company until he can,"

the sergeant said. He turned again to his prisoner. "You ready, sir?"

The CW2 stood, and as he started forward, Dooley grabbed his arm. "Nice knowing you," he said. Sharp's face folded like canvas, but the results could not be called a smile. He walked out with his arms against his chest, on his way back to the good ol' U.S. of A.

CHAPTER THIRTEEN

H ARLAN WILEY stood balanced before a gigantic grill, a butcher knife in each hand. He flipped a row of steaks with the blades, then dribbled a concoction from a whiskey bottle, using a thick thumb to regulate the flow. All around his makeshift grill, except a small area where he sometimes turned to spit, stood a thicket of men drinking beer and watching the meat. Nearby, kicked into submission, sat a gathering of camp dogs, drooling and licking their chops, shuffling about impatiently. "Okay," Wiley said, "let's get this animal eaten before the entire camp comes along." The men shouted their agreement and lunged into a scuffling line. Wiley began serving on paper plates, yelling, "More meat," over his shoulder. A warrant officer named Throckmorton who had ears like car doors brought a heaped tray from the table where three men were hacking at the big carcass of an elklike red deer.

A short distance away several pilots were sprawled in front of the hangar, sipping drinks and waiting for the enlisted men to be served. Roark, Baker, Dooley, and a new pilot named Forsythe who had been in the hooch a month sat in a loose circle with Jim Tyler from Alpha Company and Deiterman and Luskey from Delta. Kitchen and Caccini, claiming rights as the successful hunters, had

126

been at the head of the serving line, and they took a seat on the ground near Roark. Caccini held a slab of meat as large as a dinner plate in his hands. "How'd it go with the new CO?" he asked in a low voice.

"He said I'm reckless and irresponsible," Roark replied.

The other pilots exchanged glances. Luskey said, "You did take a hell of a chance, Roark."

No one knew that better than Billy Roark. His thoughts returned to the tense moments on the creek, the realization of danger now complete. But while it was happening, it was that danger that was so compelling.

They had jumped the herd taking water in a clear green stream late in the afternoon, low level between Evans and Nancy. Roark brought the nose up, made a modified hammerhead turn, and Caccini drilled a buck through the neck on a three-shot burst. The herd vanished into the brush. After a quick reconnaissance, Roark brought the helicopter to a hover, and Caccini and Kitchen jumped out. But they were unable to move the animal, even when Dooley climbed over the console to help. They had almost decided to leave the beast when Dooley thought of carrying it by the antlers. With Kitchen's harness securing the rack to the skid, they slipped into Evans low level, dropped their prize at the nearest revetment, then sneaked out. Roark called Motormouth and, after determining he was alone, had him contact Sergeant Wiley. An hour later, when they were released from their mission, Wiley was well on his way toward having the animal dressed.

"Is he going to do anything?" Baker asked, referring to the new commanding officer, Major Pax.

"I don't think so," Roark said. "He's okay. It was just his job to chew my butt. He said what we did was senseless and dangerous, and he's right."

"Did you tell him that fits what we do every day?"

It was almost November, and already the days of pleasant weather were outnumbered by days of rain. Units were still operating in the mountains, but access to the A Shau and the firebases was tentative. The past two days of sunshine had followed five consecutive days of unrelenting rain; the war was about to move to the lowlands.

The crowd began to thin as men got their fill, but others who had been late getting the word were still showing up. The 155s on the southern perimeter began firing north across the camp, forcing the ear to follow the shells tearing across the black sky. Roark went to the grill where Harlan Wiley still stood, his shirt soaked through at the shoulders and down the belly. "You've done a day's work in the last four hours," Roark said. "Like some relief?"

"No, I'm fine. Here, get some more of this meat. Take some to your boys over there." He prepared a fresh plate.

"I appreciate you doing this."

"You're talking nonsense," Wiley said. "I'm doing what I like. I like to see the men eat." He paused with his eyes in the fire, then said quietly, "You ever pull another stunt like this, you skinny shit, and I'll gut and quarter *you*."

Roark smiled. Each night when he completed scheduling, especially if he was off the following day, he sat and talked with Wiley on the bench inside the hangar.

At last Wiley had everyone served. Throckmorton cut the last of the good meat from the hindquarter, boned the scraps, then heaved it all toward the dogs. There was a brief but vicious fight.

When they had finished eating, the pilots stretched out and lit cigarettes—all but Tyler, who did not smoke. The light from the hangar hid most of the stars and made the sky seem shallow.

"I heard over at Battalion today that S-2 is saying we're supposed to get hit in the next few days," Luskey said.

"Has there ever been a time when they didn't say that?"

"Not really. But it sounded serious."

"It sounded serious when Uncle Ho died, but all we did was sit here on yellow alert for three days."

"That's true, but I can't get past the feeling that one of these days they're going to come. A handful of sappers could do a lot of damage, but a company could come through here like a lawn mower."

"They'd die."

"That's right, and we'd die with 'em." It was an endless subject, one which very quickly became pointless. The perimeter was weakly defended, easily penetrated, and there were no secondary defenses. Once inside, an enemy force would be extremely difficult to pin down and could cause damage far out of proportion to their numbers. It was true that most would die, but no one believed that was a deterrent. The NVA had just not yet decided to come. Every couple of weeks they would lob a few rockets into Evans or pepper the place with mortars, but it seemed to be more a reminder that they were there than a true effort to inflict damage.

"I could sure stand a shot of pussy," Forsythe said dreamily. He was new, so such a dumb statement was almost excusable.

"You won't have to worry about that much longer, new guy," Deiterman said. "After three months you'll lose all the feeling in your cods. After six they'll shrivel up, and you won't even be able to get a pee-hard. You'll spend your first two days of R and R with a little Thai doll jiggling your broken balloon and saying, 'You no likee me, GI? You no likee fuck-fuck? Wossamatta GI? Wossamatta you?'"

"Shit."

"You wait."

"That's right, Newbie. They don't call this the Limp Dick Division for nothing. That eagle's not screaming; he's groaning. This is the only outfit in Vietnam with regulations against fucking."

"Maybe the division commander's a eunuch."

"No, it's just a lot easier to dictate morality when you're so friggin' old your balls have atrophied."

"Speaking of which, Baker, I hear you've been checking out the nurses," Luskey said.

Allen Baker looked sharply at Luskey, then Roark. Roark had been absorbed in thoughts of his own future R&R, wondering how long he should wait before getting it scheduled, when Luskey spilled the beans. He turned and met Baker's gaze. "I just mentioned you'd seen one," he said lamely.

"That's all I've done, just seen one," Baker snapped, though there was more to it than that. Before the rains began, he had developed quite a tan, sunning behind the hooch on his days off just so he could catch a glimpse of her. Finally, she began to smile and speak. Her voice was a lot like Paula's.

"Well, tell us about her," Deiterman said. "I thought the doctors kept them all locked up."

"There's nothing to tell, I said." Baker stood and glared at Roark. He was starting to walk away when suddenly all hell broke loose, and he dived to the ground with the others.

It was an all-out attack on the ARVN compound across the highway. Mortar rounds were raining down all around the walls, then inside. Green and red tracers laced the corner guard boxes, and the ARVN .50 calibers boomed back. A few of the bunker guards beyond the flight line had opened up in reaction to the initial explosions, but they finally dribbled away and waited for something to shoot at.

"Let's get the guns, boys," Wiley yelled from the hangar, but everyone had had the same idea at once. They lugged the cans and weapons outside and set up a quick perimeter in the dark shadow on the north side of the hangar, then waited, tensely watching the show. The ARVNs were taking a beating. In addition to the mortars, RPG airbursts were erupting over the tiny fort. Tracers were thick as cobwebs. The main attacking force was just west of the highway, but the men on the flight line could see nothing more than the fireworks. About two hundred mortar rounds fell, and perhaps thirty B-40 rockets were fired. Then it was abruptly over. One of the ARVN .50 calibers continued to fire through the brush, seeking revenge, sending huge red tracers gyrating across the sky. Finally the man gave it up.

There was an empty moment when it was over; once the attack had shattered the night it seemed unnatural that it should end, leaving a weird sense of disappointment. The men waited for the attack to be resumed, or for it to be turned on Evans. Just a few hundred feet away, out there in the brush, were the invisible enemy. It felt strangely good *knowing* they were there instead of having to wonder. There were several parachute flares hanging beneath trails of smoke in the flickering amber-black sky, and an occasional *oof* as another was sent aloft. When at last they were allowed to burn out, the night was very black and still. The men put the machine guns back in the cage and walked slowly up the hill toward the hooches. Roark walked beside Tyler and asked about his family.

Phillip Crable awoke in that early morning wasteland where people sometimes have heart attacks, and sometimes go to the bathroom before returning to bedside to kill themselves. He lay staring into the darkness, consumed with doubt, thinking that maybe he had wasted it all. He thought about Rita and hoped briefly that the bitch was miserable, wherever she was.

She had left him in Germany, which seemed especially ironic since it had been her idea for him to put in for the transfer from Knox. But not really; Rita had never recovered from her sense of betrayal when, two years into their marriage, he had joined the Army without so much as discussing it. That irreversible tactic guaranteed that he would win the resulting battle, but he knew it was the only hope he had of defeating his wife.

From that point on, their life had become a contest for control as Phillip grew increasingly determined to no longer submit to her will. Once they were settled in Germany, it became quickly apparent that Rita, unaware that he had other reasons for what he called "the German concession," assumed that there she might somehow reclaim a portion of her old authority. Though Phillip had no intention of yielding control as in the early years of their marriage, it was too soon for him to understand that when that became apparent to Rita she would be out the door.

He was very happy when she left. A year later, the executive officer of a sister company became seriously ill and was forced to return to the States. Phillip transferred to replace him, and for the first few months things went well. Then his commanding officer received orders to Vietnam. The man who replaced him, a Major Barlowe, had spent half the previous year leading a battalion. Miffed at his apparent demotion, he directed his anger at his XO. Then the unit failed an IG inspection, and Phillip realized his future was in jeopardy. As his final months in Germany trickled away, so did the resolve and conviction that battling Rita had always kept in good supply. He began to doubt his ability to direct his own life. Long after she was gone, he began missing his ex-wife, and soon after that, almost hating her.

His primary concern was the looming situation in Vietnam. The conflict was the real reason he had agreed to go to Germany. While being a soldier had a definite masculine appeal, being a *real* soldier—a combatant—was another thing entirely. Somewhere between the two was the line dividing manliness from insanity—a line he never intended to cross. Surely three years would be a sufficient period to get things straightened out in Southeast Asia, and he would miss it altogether. But in 1965 the conflict became a war, growing in intensity with every month that passed. Soon it was obvious where Phillip's next assignment must be. In great confusion, he submitted the papers for helicopter flight school, realizing the move was a certain ticket to Vietnam, but feeling he had no other choice.

Now, lying in his bunk with all but four days of Vietnam behind, Germany seemed an eternity ago. At a time when he had expected to be elated, he was instead more depressed and discouraged than he had ever been. His combat tour was almost finished, which would be a credit to his record, but that was exactly all he had gained in the past year. His hope of commanding Charlie Company had been demolished when Major Andrews coolly announced on the day before his departure that another major would soon be arriving to replace him, and that Phillip would be in charge only a few days. The period of self-delusion was over. As he turned all his critical faculties inward, he found that he failed the inquisition. Never since joining the Army had he felt so out of his element, and the realization that he had no idea what his element was only left him feeling desolate and hopelessly lost.

V

There were about forty of us, sergeants and officers, on bleachers in a miniature jungle, and out of the jungle Sergeant Burdock suddenly appeared like something wild. He strode up before us and said, "Awright, motherfuckers, listen up!" That got our attention; at least half the group outranked him.

He was there to teach us about hand-to-hand combat, and he eventually got around to that—telling us how an entrenching tool could open a man's head like a gourd, how a heel stomp could crush a skull or rupture a kidney or even stop a heart, how a hooked finger could pluck out an eyeball so easily—but first he taught us something about Vietnam. "I guess you gentlemen thought you had outgrown the stage where a black man could call you motherfuckers motherfuckers," he said. "Well, welcome to the 'Nam." The oldest captain's expression caught his attention, and he aimed black, glassy eyes at him like looking through a gunsight. "You thinking about telling on me, Cap'n?" he asked. "Well, it won't do you any good—there's not a swinging dick in the division with balls enough to do anything about me. So forget it, Cap'n." He put his hands on his hips like Hercules and eyed

133

every one of us. "I've been here four years," he said, "and nobody outranks me." We were ready by then to believe him.

"Now you dumbfucks are in the One-oh-first," he announced, "and that means you're going north. The little men on the other side are not as chickenshit as you, and they'll be coming some night—with a satchel or a knife or their fingernails. We got artillery and jets and gunships and tanks and all kinds of shit to keep them away from you babies, but they're not gonna send an engraved announcement when they come. You're gonna maybe hear a sound and look up and see something in the dark, and he's gonna be on you, killing you, and you're gonna die right there."

Then he began going through all the ways to kill a man, and all the ways to get the advantage when he was killing you, right down to literally biting his balls off. He lectured us and threatened us and did everything he could to make us know that this was no game, and nothing like anything we had heard. Then he suddenly turned and disappeared into the jungle, leaving us to wonder what we'd seen.

For a long time I thought the man was crazy—before I knew the contradictions of commitment and survival. But insanity is a hell of a lot easier to explain, so later when I told the story I'd always begin by saying, "There was this crazy dude when I first got to Vietnam . . ."

CHAPTER FOURTEEN

MORNING ON a Huey flight line. Even through the bone-aching, eye-burning fatigue that was the normal condition of the crews, there was an excitement in it that could not be denied. Stumbling around in pitch-darkness, getting the birds ready, was sometimes almost an act of sleepwalking. No one said much of anything. But when the first ship began to crank, the sparking sound of the igniters traveling across the ravine seemed to ignite something in the men as well. As the turbine fans began to move and fuel was dumped into the chamber, a wave of energy moved through everyone. The spirits rose with the rising sound of the turbine, and by the time other engines joined the chorus there was the throbbing beat of blades to move the blood. Then the liquid blackness of the air seemed to fade to an amber tinge, or violet, and the flight line became a dim pool of flashing blades, colored like the sky. One by one the ships hovered and gathered in a line, and one by one flew away across the dark hills and glowing paddies, every man aboard pumped up and vital, prepared to do something fantastic.

*   *   *

"Two-six, flight's up," Allen Baker said.

"Roger, Two-niner," Wilson replied. "Two-five, call arty."

"Got it, Two-six," Roark said. "We're clear to Quiver Tit at fifteen hundred east of the highway."

"Two-six, roger." The three Hueys moved into a tight echelon. It was an Air Force joke that an Army flight formation was two helicopters headed in the same direction on the same day. Standard separation was one rotor disk, about forty feet, but often it was much less. Unlike fixed-wing craft, which fly by gliding through the air as opposed to beating it into submission, the helicopters had one important consideration the jets did not: If they collided, it was the tips of the fragile rotors which met, going at tremendous speeds in opposite directions. Unlike the rocket jockeys, the helicopter pilots never got to say, "Oops!" when they screwed up, and they didn't have the privilege of bailing out.

"Anybody checking out the ADF?" Baker asked.

"Affirmative," Roark replied. A moment passed as Turner Wilson tuned his radio. "Sho nuff," he said. The Animals were singing the most popular song of the war.

"We gotta get out of this place . . ."

"Two-six will be rocking left." The others acknowledged by breaking the radio squelch, depressing their mike buttons twice briefly. Wilson's ship swayed left and right with the music, the others following his lead. The three Hueys danced through the sky toward the DMZ, the crewmen singing.

". . . if it's the last thing we ever do."

No matter what the mission, regardless of the weather or what had happened yesterday, it was impossible to begin a day in a Huey in low spirits. Something about youth and energy, and what the sound and smell and feel of the aircraft could do to you; something about the power of the machinery, the focus of force, the camaraderie; something about being in a war and believing you were doing the right thing and were going to live forever despite all the evidence to the contrary. The twelve boys flying north prepared themselves for another nonexistent day across the Laotian border by singing and laughing.

At the CCN compound, a lieutenant no one knew came out and told them to shut down, explaining that he was filling in for Captain Davis who was down at Phu Bai covering for somebody on R&R. There were two teams to be extracted, he said, but neither was in position; Gossamer was out in an Oscar-Deuce trying to find them. The lieutenant, a sincere but green-looking soldier named Thurber, started to leave, but seemed to realize what he had said. He turned back and faced the group of three. "One of the teams is being pursued," he said. "They've got one with a leg wound, and they're trying to break contact. We don't know where the other team is; we haven't heard from them since late yesterday." Baker gave the cut signal to the ships; the dying whistle of the turbines hung in the morning air like a thread of pain.

The sun oozed up from the sea, and in only minutes the air was stifling. The gunners stretched out in the open Hueys, and the pilots went to the standby hooch to sip sodas with the gunnies and check their watches. "I was talking to Hood last night," Baker said, "and he said that he and the XO of Bravo flew down to Da Nang yesterday and ate hamburgers."

"Did he get laid?"

"He didn't mention it."

"Da Nang. That's something. Sixty miles that may as well be a thousand. Hamburgers and pussy."

"Least we don't have to worry about getting the clap."

"I believe I could handle it."

"I'll wait for mama."

"I hope your pecker works when you get there."

"If you've still got one." The pilots grinned. Getting shot in the groin never got very far from anybody's mind; landing in a hot LZ invariably made a man feel like the enemy could actually see his balls.

Two hours crept past. Some of the pilots tried a card game, but it petered out after only a few hands. Roark, Baker, and Dooley wandered outside to squat in the cool dirt on the shady side of the hooch and smoke cigarettes. Soon Thurber emerged from the Operations hooch. "Gossamer just called," he said. "He's at QT getting fuel, then he's going back out. The team's broken contact, but there's an enemy platoon beating the bush looking for them. It's still going to be a while."

"What about the other team?" Baker asked.

"Still nothing."

After another long hour an urgent call came from Gossamer saying to rig the birds with strings, to get cranked and across the border. The team had been discovered again and would not be able to reach a proper LZ. The pilots scrambled, yelling, and the crewmen jumped and swung the blades. Men raced out with green coils of nylon rope, and in the time it took to crank, the ships were rigged, three ropes each, strung through the series of rings imbedded in the cargo floor. The crewmen drew machetes from behind their seats and placed them within reach.

They made the usual crossing between Co Roc and Arrowhead, and when they were several miles past the known flak guns they turned north for another forty miles. The fresh green of elephant grass and long running hills soon gave way to dark jungle and progressively larger mountains. They held seven thousand feet, but no one believed that the altitude made any real difference; there were radar-guided SA-2 missiles there that would fly right up the pipe. Everybody kept checking the ground.

They linked up with Gossamer adjacent to the DMZ, fifteen miles inside Laos. The gray Cessna was flying lazy ovals in the sunshine against a background of clean white clouds. They followed him north across a beautiful valley that held a meandering blue stream, then between two steep and ominous peaks. Approaching a rounded mass at the edge of a jungled plateau, Gossamer dropped to low level and gave them a mark. "They've broken contact," he said, "but it won't last long. When they hear you, the gooks are going to come running."

Baker was flying lead, with Roark in Chalk Two and Wilson as chase. When the guns were in position, and while the others orbited to the south, Baker made his approach to the mark. There was little to distinguish the point from the surrounding jungle, but it was out of the main canopy. When he came to a hover far above the trees, Baker reported that he could not see the team, and he began to move the ship slowly around the area. Everyone became conscious of the passing seconds. Finally, two coils of rope dropped straight beneath the ship. A moment later a sniper began taking potshots at the team. Apparently he could not get an angle on the hovering Huey and contented himself with sending bullets slapping through the foliage around the men's heads while waiting for the rest of his platoon. An agonizing minute passed. Finally Baker announced he was coming out. Slowly the ship rose from the jungle with two men far below looking like tiny ants clinging to threads.

Roark made his approach as close behind Baker as he dared, but still overshot the men; he had to back up, following instructions from the gunners. Even directly beneath the ship, the three Rangers would have been impossible to see if they had not held a plastic fluorescent panel. Kitch and Caccini carefully dropped the three ropes, but one became entangled, had to be brought up and fed back down. The sniper was getting closer and more insistent. "Hold it steady," Caccini said. "They're having trouble. Hold it steady." Roark was doing the best he could, but hovering high above the trees left little reference for the pilot. He could not see the men, or even see beneath the ship; all he could do was gaze forward and through the chin bubble, trying to keep the patterns of vegetation from moving.

"We're drifting right a little," Kitchen said. "Move back to the left. The ropes are getting into the trees. Back to the left."

"What's the holdup?"

"They're having trouble getting one of the guys into the harness. And they're getting shot at." Roark could hear the sharp report of the rifle.

"All your instruments are green," Dooley said.

"Back up just a little, sir."

"Chalk Two, are you having problems?" Gossamer called. Roark ignored him.

"What's the holdup?" Roark asked, his voice rising.

"The ropes are caught in the trees. Back up a little." There were two quick shots from the sniper. "They're almost ready." There was a sudden *crack!* and the odor of burning plastic filled the cockpit as a bullet smashed through the chin bubble beyond Roark's feet.

"Goddamn it! Where'd it come from?"

"Off to the left," Dooley said. Both the gunners were down on their knees working with the ropes, trying to keep them out of the trees. "Caccini, get on Kitch's gun!"

When the sixty began firing into the jungle, the pilots in the circling gunships could hear the sound. "Chalk Two, are you taking fire?"

"What's the holdup, Chalk Two?"

"We've got a sniper working on us," Dooley answered. "We'll be out in a minute." He checked the instruments. "Still green," he said calmly to Roark.

"We're up. Come up slowly. Straight up. Hold it. Hold it! The ropes are hung. Come back down a little." Caccini was trying again to help with the ropes, and the sniper fired, but without hitting anything.

"Get back on the gun, Rico." The machinelike throb resumed. Roark pressed his mike switch to the second stop. "Three-four, can you put your minigun about fifty meters off our left?"

"You bet. Coming hot." The minigun must have been an unholy nightmare to the enemy; it was a bad dream even to the friendlies. The Cobra dived toward the jungle, and when it was quite low a vomiting sound like a buzz saw began, causing a band of jungle to disintegrate into green dust. Two thousand rounds per minute.

"Okay, come up again, slowly. We're still hung, but come on up. Hold it. We've got a man hung in the trees. Hold it, you're gonna break his neck!"

Sweat was streaming down Roark's face. Suddenly several AKs opened up, firing wildly through the trees toward the men in the ropes, raining shredded leaves and twigs around them. Rico swung toward the sound and fired a long burst, hesitated while he pulled some ammo free, then continued firing blindly down through jungle. "Taking fire! Lots of fire, off to the left!" The sound of the minigun began almost immediately, the Cobra passing very close this time, slower than before, and with a flat belly on his dive.

"Okay, we're free! Straight up! Bring her straight up! We're clear! Let's go!"

"Chalk Two's coming out," Dooley called. Roark raised the collective until the torquemeter read fifty pounds, then began taking deep, even breaths. Rico fired until there was no longer any point. The Huey moved away from the jungle, and as the Redskins moved aside the Griffins each unloaded four pairs of rockets into the trees.

"You take it," Roark said, exhausted. "Hold fifty knots until we find a place to put them down." Far below, three men hung in an uneven cluster. "Kitch, Rico, keep the blades ready." If the engine failed, the gunners would have the grim duty of cutting the ropes just before the men hit the ground.

It took twenty minutes for Gossamer to find a spot he was satisfied would be safe. Finally a slope of elephant grass far from cover was selected. The Griffins fired two pairs of beehive rockets, flechettes, to nail down anything in the area, and the men were lowered to the ground. They could barely walk, and the gunners had to help them aboard. As they climbed away with Roark again on the controls, one of the men crawled forward and grabbed him by the shoulder, jerking violently. The aircraft shuddered with the sloshing of the cyclic.

"What the . . ." Roark looked around and into the eyes of a madman. "You got it!" he yelled to Dooley, and prepared to defend himself. Then he realized he was not being attacked. It was difficult to turn in the armored seat, but he reached around with both hands and grasped the man's arms and held him, and the man shook his arms and stared mutely into his eyes. At last the shaking stopped. The man knelt against the console and finally sat on the floor, but one camouflaged hand held tight to Roark's seat until the twisting Xe Pon passed below.

CHAPTER FIFTEEN

BY MIDAFTERNOON it was clear that the missing recon team was probably lost for good. The crews had seen it before, but it was always the same. The men went out and just didn't come back.

Suddenly the birds were scrambled to Camp Eagle for what Thurber described as being almost a Prairie Fire, a tactical emergency. Captain Davis, in some trepidation, was waiting at the western log pad on Eagle's perimeter. He quickly briefed the huddle of aircraft commanders outside their running ships. A twenty-eight-man recon platoon south of the A Shau in Laos, he said, had encountered a company of NVA. Outnumbered at least four to one, with one dead and four wounded, they were withdrawing through heavy jungle. Gossamer—circling overhead, vectoring the grunts toward an old LZ—had reported the platoon would be ready for extraction as soon as the helicopters could arrive. Meanwhile, the enemy was maintaining contact, but making no attempt to stop the retreating column. The pilots exchanged glances. They rushed to their ships while Captain Davis called Group for more help.

The landing zone was a narrow shaft through dense jungle about a mile beyond the border where steep, choppy hills climbed up from the valley toward towering mountains. When Gossamer confirmed that the entire platoon had reached the LZ, the escorting Cobras established a pattern on the western side, made a couple of strafing runs with their miniguns, then announced high-and-dry for the extraction to begin.

Baker went first, approaching from the south. He loaded the KIA and wounded men and got out without drawing fire. Then it was Wilson's turn. He got in okay, but as soon as five men were aboard his ship the enemy opened up in force.

"Taking fire!" he yelled. "Godalmighty!" There was a red flash near the Huey's tail, then the dull thud of an explosion. The ship spun halfway about, miraculously missing the trees, moving upward through a swarm of tracers. "We're hit bad!" Wilson yelled. The ship was wobbling, trying to turn about. The doorgunners and the grunts aboard were returning fire. Then the craft was clear of the trees and moving forward, yawing left and right, the engine surging wildly. Behind them, the gunships were unloading on the hillside. To give them room, Roark aborted his approach, circling to the right. "We're not going to make it," Wilson said.

"Hold on, Two-six," Baker called, holding to the north. "There's a clearing just over the next hill."

"Roger," Wilson said. Though the ship was still yawing, the pilot had backed the throttle down to manual, giving a little better control. But they were losing altitude fast. They skimmed the top of the next ridge, then the meadow was before them and they were safely down. Immediately, Baker landed beside them, dropped off three grunts who had minor wounds, then picked up Turner and his crew. The remaining men on the ground gathered in a nearby bomb crater. When Roark landed, four grunts climbed from the crater while Kitchen retrieved the radios from Wilson's bird. "I saw movement," Caccini yelled. "Too high to reach!" The gun mount had vertical and lateral stops to limit the swing of the sixty.

"Okay." Roark looked toward the hill, then at the four men in the crater. One grenade was all it would take. "Tell them to get on board," he said. Caccini yelled and waved at the men. They seemed confused, but relieved.

"I don't think we can carry them all," Caccini said. Unlike the usual recon teams, these men carried heavy rucksacks. They jammed aboard the Huey. Kitchen brought two of the heavy radios, then ran back and returned with two more.

"We'll never get off the ground with this load," he said. Roark knew he was right. Dooley was already thumbing the switch on the collective head, beeping the RPM to maximum. The needles rose until Roark pulled in power, then immediately began to bleed. The ship would not budge.

"Tell them to dump the rucks," he said. Without hesitation, the men shucked the packs that held food and ammunition, personal items, photographs, and letters from home. The Huey would barely hover. The deep grass broke the cushion, and as they bumped along, trying to get more room to make a run, the tail rotor screamed through lashing grass. "Dump some ammo," Roark said. "A bunch." The gunners broke the links, heaved long belts to the ground, and stopped when the ship would maintain a one-foot hover.

A twenty-foot wall of saplings lined the meadow, and beyond lay another field. They nosed through the grass, the rotorwash mashing it down, then turned to start the run. When it began to look like a bad decision, it was too late to make a change; the slender trees loomed before them. The ship shuddered into translational and began to climb, but the treetops were coming straight for the windshield. Then Roark remembered something McCawley had taught him a long time ago; he pulled the nose back, leveled, jerked the collective sharply, then pushed the cyclic forward. The ship climbed a few feet, seemed to hesitate at the top, then eased across with the skids in the leaves, the low RPM warning squawking in the pilots' ears. The maneuver worked on borrowed energy that had to be paid back, and without the field beyond, they would not have made it. They dipped low across the meadow, swerved slightly to avoid a lone tree, and as the Huey regained the destroyed lift, climbed heavily away from the valley. Far off they heard the rattle of automatic weapons, but no one saw the flashes.

The predicament on the Laotian hill was officially declared a Prairie Fire, giving it emergency status. The men still in the LZ were pinned down while only a few feet away crouched the NVA, waiting for the helicopters. With the pronouncement of the Prairie Fire, help was quickly forthcoming. The Air Force sent sortie after sortie of prop-driven, Korean War–era Spads, Al-Es, which could work close in and deliver their bombs with precision. The Marines shuttled flights of Huey gunships from Da Nang, while a steady stream of Army Cobras, both ARA and regular fireteams with miniguns, grenade launchers, and rockets, raced back and forth between the hill and the rearming points at Camp Eagle. The sky above the hilltop swarmed with aircraft. Bombs and rockets and bullets pulverized the jungle around the tiny clearing. A pall of smoke and dust, gray and white and filthy red, draped the hill. Red-orange explosions lurched from the jungle, sending shock waves hissing through the trees. The GIs reported they were still surrounded; the NVA, completely enclosed by a wall of destruction, were now also trapped.

Back at the log pad, Roark and Baker had to wait only a few minutes for additional help. Allen Baker had called Phoenix Operations to report the situation and to get a maintenance bird sent out to rig the damaged craft for recovery. Another ship was to be sent from Evans for Wilson and his crew. Captain Davis reported that Group was diverting two more Hueys to help with the extraction, and soon a pair of birds from Alpha Company, led by Jim Tyler, rounded the perimeter. Following a rushed briefing, the four birds hurried away toward a flaring red sun and sawtooth mountains.

"What's going on out there, Lieutenant?" Major Edward Pax stood at the center of an anxious group in Phoenix Operations. He was a tall, heavy man with wavy blond hair. Wilson and his crew had just arrived.

"Bad news, sir," Wilson said. "There's eighteen men, surrounded. Before I left Eagle, Roark and Baker were headed back out with two birds from Alpha to try to get 'em out."

"I'd better get out there," the major said as if thinking aloud. "It's almost sunset, and if anything else goes wrong, we're going to be working in the dark. We'll need a command and control ship, and we can act as a chase, too. Captain Hood, who have we got on standby?"

"Sir!" Crable suddenly blurted. Major Pax looked curiously at the captain. "Sir, I could go in your place," Crable said. "I've been in that general area before, and Lieutenant Wilson could fly as AC."

"I think that's a bit much to ask," the major replied. "You only have a couple of days remaining on your tour, and Wilson has already been shot down once today."

"No, sir," Wilson said. "I'll go."

"You sure?"

"I'd like to see this thing completed, sir."

"Very well," said Pax. "You'd better get started. Captain Crable, you'll be in charge, at the direction of CCN, of course. I'll be here in Operations; keep me posted."

By the time the four Hueys crossed the border, the mission had taken on a grim aspect. All the bravado was gone, and in its place hung the ultimate circumstance of war, men locked into a situation with no alternatives. The hilltop was the sort of battlefield peculiar to Vietnam, a tiny island of devastation where the soldiers' only objective was to kill the enemy and remain alive.

As the first Huey began its approach, the gunships shifted their orbits west of the LZ and formed a long daisy chain, still pulverizing the hillside. Baker insisted on going first. The sun was a bright monk's cap on a distant ridge when the Huey came to a high hover and began to pivot. The rotor blades flashed dull red, then the ship disappeared into the jungle. An excruciating minute passed, then Baker said in a quiet but determined voice, "We're coming out." There was no sound of gunfire on the radio. Roark was ready, and he began his approach though he could not yet see Baker. Since Turner Wilson had drawn the RPG from the south side of the clearing, it had been decided to land from the north, and to depart in the same direction. When Roark's aircraft was on mid-final, Baker's appeared slowly from the trees. Streams of red and green tracers shot straight into the ship and up through the sky around it. Both doorguns were belching yellow flames. Baker's voice was still incredibly calm. "Two-five, we're taking lots of fire. You might want to change your path."

But by then Roark's bird was almost face-to-face with Baker's, and they could hear the enemy guns. He held his course. The helicopters passed very close where the mountain fell steeply away, and the shooting suddenly stopped. As the second bird hovered above the dim hole, turned and started down, a sudden volley rattled the belly of the ship. Two bullets tore through the left chin and up through the cockpit between Roark and Dooley. Kitchen returned fire while Caccini gave directions down through the trees. Then more guns were firing. Roark felt three distinct raps on the armor beneath his butt, then two bullets exploded through the floor between his legs. "I'm hit," he said.

Dooley was already on the controls, and he quickly pulled the Huey skyward. "My AC's been hit," he reported. "We're coming out." The Alpha birds held their orbit.

Roark was dumbfounded, afraid to look at his legs. He sat staring instead at the holes in the floor, each more than two inches across. Dooley was watching him, and Caccini came up to see if he could help. "How bad is it?" he asked.

"I don't know," Roark replied, then looked at his legs. There was a small amount of blood oozing from a wound on the inside of his left calf and stuck in the material of his pants was the ragged copper jacket of a bullet. He pulled it free and held it up. "I think I'm okay," he said. Another wound was on the back of his right leg above the knee, and he reached around and felt a tight lump. His glove came away bloody. "I'm all right," he said. "I'm all right." The floor had absorbed most of the energy from the rounds. The sun was down, and twelve men were still at the bottom of the hole. "We're going back in." He took the controls and turned the aircraft toward the hilltop. Caccini returned to his gun.

"Two-five, what's your status?" Gossamer called.

"I'm okay. We're going to try it again."

"Two-five, Two-niner. We got hit pretty hard coming out. We're dropping lots of fuel, and one of the grunts took a sucking chest wound. How about following me back to Eagle in case we don't make it," Baker said.

Before Roark could answer, Gossamer spoke up, sounding tired. "Two-five, abort your approach and go get yourself patched up. Chalk Three and Four, you go, too. We'll get more help, then come back and try it again." The Hueys turned toward Eagle while the gunships continued to fire their loads into the jungle. Streams of glowing tracers sprayed from the miniguns like red water.

When Phillip Crable and Turner Wilson arrived, the crews were standing around, looking at the holes in the two ships, Roark's legs, and the chest armor that Baker's gunner was wearing. The gunner had taken a round directly over his heart, and it had only knocked his breath out and slammed him against the firewall. Everyone by turn stuck a finger into the hole in the ceramic armor, felt around, then walked away mumbling. Wilson smiled quietly at the mess that had taken place in his absence; Crable was silent and pale but looked unusually determined. Soon a pair of Hueys from another outfit, the Comancheros, arrived at the pad, and the briefing began. Jim Tyler was flight lead now, and Roark and Baker gave detailed descriptions of the LZ, and their opinions on how best to get in and out. Tyler was doing very little talking, and Roark noticed that he looked ill. If it was fear, it was okay; any man going into that LZ who was not afraid had to be crazy. "There're several dead trees sticking up on the east side," Roark said. "Be real careful, Jim." Tyler glanced at him, but remained silent.

Darkness was beginning to settle in, and Davis announced that a flareship would be meeting them on station. Baker's ship was left to be retrieved the following day. The extra crew members climbed aboard Roark's perforated bird. Baker manned the controls with Dooley while the wounded Roark rode on the floor in back, gazing from the door as Jim Tyler and the others flew off on a bad mission to Laos.

CHAPTER SIXTEEN

I T WAS near noon when they brought in the boy. Small and lean with smooth brown skin, he shuffled happily along in the hospital slippers, gazing about in wide-eyed interest at the strange surroundings. At the end of his right arm was a thick ball of gauze, and protruding around it like purple nipples were the tips of his splayed fingers. "You be a good kid, Quan," the orderly said. He turned to Billy Roark. "He's up on morphine, feeling no pain. He'll come down in a bit, then he won't be so happy."

Roark lowered a paperback. The child appeared to be about ten. The boy turned with a wide smile and said, *"Chāo!"*

"Hello," Roark replied. He nodded toward the hand, and the kid began an explaining pantomime. He had been playing with a .50 caliber bullet, using the six-inch shell as a hammer when it discharged. Roark wondered if it was a .50 or a .51, but then he saw the onyx eyes, the bright and open innocence, and knew it didn't matter. The kid was only a kid, happy and cute, a breakable Asian doll who would soon be in a lot of pain.

The boy held up his injured hand. *"Môt, hai, ba, bôń, năm,"* he said, counting the fingertips.

"One, two, three, four, five," Roark replied. They went over it several times, learning to communicate. Then the drug began to wear off; the smile became delayed, then disappeared. Finally the boy rolled into a tight ball away from Roark and began to cry. The sound grew to a pitiful wail. A nurse came with a syringe, and a few minutes later the child was asleep.

After less than one full day in the hospital, Billy Roark was wanting out, wanting back in the air. Compounding his anxiety was the fact that so far he had heard nothing about what had happened in Laos. Jim Tyler's face had left him uneasy. There was something more there than just fear. Later, he napped and dreamed; they were at Eagle, and he and Baker were telling Tyler about the shape of the LZ, where the stumps were, and the trees to avoid. He saw Tyler's face, exactly as before, and when he awoke he knew what he had seen.

Toward evening, the shape of Harlan Wiley appeared in the double doorway. He stopped to spit in the dirt beside the walk. The sergeant grinned broadly enough for the tobacco to show. "You know, you could qualify for Wiley family membership with those wounds," he said as he eased up beside the bed. His face was more flushed than usual, and he was huffing softly. He smelled of tobacco.

"How's that?" Roark asked.

"We got a tradition clear back to the Civil War, maybe further. Wileys always get hit in the backside. There's no shortage of excuses, but somehow they always seem to be facing some direction other than the one from where the lead is coming." Wiley became serious. "I crawled under your ship and looked up through the biggest hole. That bullet was headed for your throat when it split up."

"You heard anything about what happened last night?"

"Only a little," Wiley said. "Alpha lost a pilot, and a couple of the grunts got killed. I don't know much, just what Donner said. Alpha's maintenance sergeant just DEROSed, so Donner went out with a recovery team to see about bringing in the bird, but it was too messed up. When they got the pilot out they burned it in place."

"The pilot?"

"He was stuck on a stump, and they couldn't get him out last night. They had to unbolt his seat. Then they got the radios and burned the wreck. It must have been a real mess, 'cause I saw Donner when he came in, and there was blood all over him."

Roark's stomach felt like he had swallowed a rock. "Do you know the pilot's name?"

"No, I don't," Wiley said. He looked around the ward, groping for another subject. "Your buddy Crable's going home in the morning," he said. "Fort Lost-in-the-woods, Missouri." Roark nodded, but his thoughts were somewhere else. "I guess I better be going."

"Sorry, Wiley. One of Alpha's pilots out there last night is a good friend."

"Maybe he's all right. How long you going to be here?"

"A week, they say."

"Tell you what, I'll see you when you get out. This is too far for a fat man to walk."

He was gone less than a minute when Major Pax flowed into the room. He was tall and moved smoothly, without effort. "Well, Mr. Roark, how are you getting along? Have they gotten you sewn up?"

"Fine, sir. They cut holes in my legs and took the junk out, but the doctor says the wounds need to stay open a few days to see if there's going to be an infection. Something about the gooks dipping their bullets in shit."

"I've heard that."

"He says I'll be grounded about two weeks."

The major winced. "Well, no matter. I just wanted to come by and award your Purple Heart, and see how you were doing." He produced a flat blue box from a hip pocket. "Here you go. You did a fine job out there yesterday."

"Sir . . . what happened last night?"

"Well, the bad guys apparently sneaked away right after dark. Both ships got in and out without taking fire, but one bird either had an engine failure or hit a tree. Two grunts and the AC were killed, and everybody else messed up. The platoon leader had a broken back, but he got on the radio and directed the other birds to the crash. Then a Medevac with a jungle penetrator was sent out to pull the people up, but when he got there everybody on the ground was unconscious. So then a ground team went out. They hacked their way in from the LZ. It was after midnight when they finally got everybody out, everybody except the pilot, and he was trapped. I forget his name, but I've seen him around the club."

That night, Roark had a disturbing dream, very vivid, very real. It was all darkness, with just a faint sound of someone breathing, then a weak and gurgling cough. Something moved; he strained to see. A shape took form, and a moment later he saw with horror that it was a pilot hanging upside down. His eyes seemed to adjust, and behind a black gout of blood he could see the face of Jim Tyler. He screamed when he saw the eyes. "You all right?" The night orderly was standing over him. Roark jerked upright in bed and looked wildly around the ward. Then he was awake, catching his breath. The orderly went quietly back to his station and picked up a paperback. A kid on the opposite side of the ward with an arm in an L-shaped cast and a bandage over his right ear raised himself high enough to see who had awakened him, then lay back and went to sleep. Roark walked stiffly out of the ward, and spent the remainder of the night padding slowly along the covered walk on unbending legs.

He had no visitors the next three days, days of almost ceaseless rain. He read two books, learned to hold his own at chess with a staff sergeant in the next bed, and developed a small vocabulary in Vietnamese before it occurred to him that something was wrong. His hooch was less than two hundred feet away, yet none of the people he lived with had been by to see him. The rain stopped that evening, but the clouds moved even lower. That night he decided to walk over and see what was happening at the hooch. He found the new guy, Forsythe, writing by candlelight, but left him undisturbed. In the gangroom, watching an old Dean Martin rerun, were Turner Wilson and Allen Baker. They seemed surprised to see him, especially Wilson who asked how Roark was getting along, then quickly said he had an errand to run and went out the front door. Baker was interested in the show. Dean Martin and Joey Heatherton were lying across a bed, singing a duet. Martin had been drinking from a water glass and persisted in reaching behind the starlet. She kept removing his hand, and he kept putting it back, both of them singing happily along and smiling. High entertainment in Vietnam.

"Where's Dooley?" Roark asked.

"Filling in for you on scheduling," Baker said without taking his eyes off the tube.

"I just came over to see if you had all been killed," Roark said, and he turned back down the hallway. All he heard behind him was Martin telling a joke about a bunch of soldiers stationed in Arabia with no women and just one camel.

The terrible dream returned that night, as it had every night since the first. By now Roark knew as he watched that it was a dream, but that made it no less real. He always screamed when he saw the eyes, and he always stayed awake the remainder of the night.

It was raining hard when he quit hoping for a break and slipped the poncho over his head. He poured half a cup of coffee, downed it, and started for the door. "Don't get none on you," Baker said, but Roark stepped out into the weather without looking back. Camp Evans resembled the bottom of an ocean, with rain hanging so straight and thick there seemed no space left for air. The clouds were a depthless mass looming somewhere just beyond reach, and in no direction could he see more than a hundred yards. A bare bulb beneath an eave beyond the bunker made the evening seem darker and more oppressive. He lowered his head and walked with dumb determination while a cascade poured off the hood past his face.

The metal hangar was a bright drum of sound when he mounted the mud-tracked stairs to Operations, moving gingerly on legs just one day free of stitches. The past two days of grounding weather had allowed the maintenance crews to catch up, and only a single bird sat in the hangar; step ladders stood on either side of the vertical fin, and two men were replacing the tail rotor gear box. Roark looked around, and when he spotted Sergeant Donner in his familiar pose near the coffee pot he was reminded how much Donner resembled a smaller version of Harlan Wiley. Then for no reason at all he was suddenly hit with an image of Donner, calmly sipping his coffee with dried blood on his hands, and more smeared across the belly of his fatigues. It was there all at once. Roark's stomach seemed to turn wrong side out, and as he leaned trembling against the handrail he heard Wiley's words in the hospital, saw the dream again, saw Turner Wilson's guilty face. He sat on the wet stairs until the sickness and rage were in balance, then stepped down into the hangar to speak to Sergeant Donner.

Turner Wilson was cleaning his cubicle. Already the monsoon was having an effect on the living quarters, leaving the floor perpetually damp and a faint scent of mildew clinging to everything. He was absorbed in herding mudballs and pebbles with the dilapidated broom, totally unprepared for Roark's attack. "You chickenshit scum . . ." Before there was any chance for defense, Roark had him by the lapels, slammed him hard against the wall.

"What. . . ?" Wilson was defeated with surprise.

"You cocksucking coward, you lowlife murdering gook shit," Roark said. Wilson stared mutely at the eyes of a maniac.

"Roark! Hold it, Roark!" Baker yelled.

Roark tightened his grip and slowly turned. Baker was in the door, and behind him were Dooley and Forsythe, both craning to see. Turner Wilson found his tongue. "It wasn't me," he said. "It wasn't my decision."

"Who?!"

"Crable."

"You were the aircraft commander!"

"And he was the air mission commander."

"That's right, Roark," Baker said.

"Well, let me tell you something, comehead—*all* you sorry comeheads—I've been dreaming about this every goddamned night, and I finally found out why. Donner came back covered with blood. He said there was a pile like a cow patty under Tyler's head, and he didn't see it and crawled right through it. *Red blood.* Eight hours after you bastards left him. Dead men don't bleed. Tyler was alive *all fucking night!*"

A look of horror and terrible pain swept Wilson's face. Tears flooded his eyes. "I didn't do it," he said. "They said he was almost dead, and there was no way to get him out that wouldn't kill him." Roark stared straight through the man, then finally turned him loose. With a face as still as stone he pushed past the others and went out into the rain.

There was dense fog the following morning, and the birds were late getting off. Then the rain began again, and one by one the birds returned. Allen Baker was the first to get back to the hooch, and he immediately sensed that something was different. He was entering his cube when he saw that Roark's was empty. He dumped his helmet and armor, then walked slowly down the hall until he found Billy Roark in Steve Sharp's place. "What are you doing back here?" he asked. Roark was lying on his back, staring into the rafters, but made no indication he had heard.

"Come on out with it," Baker said. "You got a hair up your ass, let's have it."

"You knew."

"Yeah, I knew. Lots of people did; it was no secret."

"Why didn't you do something? Why didn't you tell?"

"Because it was too late. Tyler was already dead."

"And you let Crable stroll out of here without a word . . ."

"Look, Tyler was your friend—he was my friend, too—and everybody knows how you feel about Crable, but there's one thing you're going to have to accept—all Crable did was make a common, everyday command decision. It might not have been the one that you or I would have made, but it was legit."

"Horseshit! You don't leave wounded men in the woods to die! If you can't get 'em out, you stay with 'em until you *can* get 'em out. And if that means you have to die with 'em, then you fucking die."

"I agree. But that's not the way higher sees it anymore. They're counting bodies, and Jim Tyler is just one, and anybody else who died out there trying to bring in a dying man would have only been that many more. So nobody is going to fault Crable. I'm real sorry about Tyler. I'm real sorry. Maybe he could have been gotten out. Maybe somebody got scared. Maybe somebody guessed wrong. I don't know, I wasn't there. But whatever happened, there's nothing that can be done about it now."

"So why were you protecting Crable?"

"I wasn't, pal. I was protecting you from Billy Roark, trying to give you time to think this thing through."

"I think it through every night."

Baker looked down the hall and sighed. "I'll help you move your stuff back. This cube's not near as nice as the one you had."

"Forget it," Roark said. "I'm staying where I am."

VI

White gulls were flying around the lagoon, looking pretty and clean. One blundered in front of us, and more or less on reflex I began to chase it. It seemed an interesting turn of events for the bird. He picked up speed and began showing us a few snappy maneuvers. But I had some of my own, and I stayed with him. It wasn't long before the bird was showing signs of fatigue, and began looking back with real fear. He weakened quickly then, and I had him. I hadn't meant to take it that far, but then I did. There was an explosion of feathers as the blade slashed through, and I was completely surprised when bright red blood splashed across my windshield.

CHAPTER SEVENTEEN

T HE PHOENIX Club had undergone a slow metamorphosis. There were stools now along the bar, an ice maker, and a long span of mirror. Plans to send someone to the Philippines for carpet and fixtures had been put on hold until the return of the dry season. Roark and Dooley acknowledged a few of the pilots, then sat at a table in the dark nook in front of the bar. They lit cigarettes from a candle in a C-ration can.

Now that the monsoons were in firm control of northern I Corps, the heavy downpours that marked the early season had given way to lighter, more constant precipitation. It had rained or drizzled every moment of the past seventeen days. Even on the better days the face of the nearby escarpment, normally lost in the foggy soup, was rarely more than a short wall, dull green and tilted beneath a sagging ceiling. But the change in climate only paralleled the greater change, a change in the war itself.

Since summer the troops of the 3d Marine Division had packed their bags and left for Okinawa and California, it having been decided somewhere that they had accomplished their purpose as a new and even more confusing phase of the war began—withdrawal. From a peak of well over 540,000 at the end of May, troop strength was now said to be 60,000 below that figure, and falling rapidly. A last-minute sweep to meet announced quotas before year's end had sent three men in Charlie Company home early, including Harlan Wiley. With the removal of the Marines and their helicopters stationed at Quang Tri, the remaining elements near the DMZ were considerably more vulnerable now to annihilation. It fell to the aviation outfits supporting the 1st of the 5th Mechanized Infantry to keep a platoon each of Hueys and Cobras stationed overnight at Quang Tri. Curiously, adequate billets could not be found for the transient pilots. Working in two-week shifts by platoon, Charlie Company spent a wet and miserable December in a makeshift shelter with a flapping blanket as a door, learning how truly cold a tropical winter can be. Roark and Dooley served their time during the first part of the month, and now were enjoying the luxury of sleeping in their own bunks.

Luskey, Deiterman, and a gunnie named Buck Morton rounded the corner to the bar. "You guys going down to Eagle to see Bob Hope?" Luskey asked.

"No, we're going to be killing gooks," Dooley announced.

"We're standing guard," Roark explained. "Manning the bunkers Christmas Eve."

"You're serious?"

"Sure. Why not? Maybe we'll get overrun."

"Heard you guys got into a little scrape today," said Deiterman.

"Good thing they couldn't shoot," Dooley said. "They fired about forty rounds at us. Put a bullet through Jerk-off's left pedal." Roark was smiling like it was his birthday.

"That's what we heard," said Luskey. "Drake was talking about it."

"Speak of the devil," Roark said. Drake, a scrappy gun pilot who had a broken nose and heavy black brows, marched up to the table.

"I want you to know I just took your ass-chewing," he said, pointing a finger. Roark stared, but said nothing. "That bunker we took out for you today was inside the DMZ. It could cause an international incident."

"Well, just where the fuck do you think we are?" Roark said. "And how could you tell, anyway? There's not a line on the ground up there, and you can't read a map in bare sand."

"We didn't have any trouble with the map work," Drake snapped, "but the coordinates were inside the Z."

"Well, anybody dumb enough to report they destroyed a bunker in the DMZ deserves an ass-chewing. Why didn't you tell them it was on this side of the line? Nobody's going to go out there and check it."

"Okay, big shot," Drake said. "Just don't call me the next time you get your ass in a sling."

"I didn't call you this time. I called for a gun pilot and got you instead."

Drake stood weighing things, then turned and stalked out of the bar. It was quiet when he was gone. "Actually, he did a good job," Roark said to no one. The table was silent. As they finished their drinks, each man made excuses and left. Even Dooley. "War's hell," Roark said to the empty table. He went to the bar to get a drink from Keeper, then ordered a pair to save himself a trip.

"Holy cow, Bill, you look like you're going to war," Baker said. In addition to the regular gear, Roark carried a grenade launcher Caccini had lifted one day from a pile of dead ARVNs, and around his neck was draped a bandolier of rounds for the weapon. A spare magazine was reversed and taped to the clip in his rifle. Besides other small items he had begun to routinely carry, in his hip pocket alongside his wallet was a large folding knife with a locking blade, a Christmas gift from his father. He gave Baker a look that resembled a smile, then stuffed two packs of filterless Camels into his jacket and went out the door.

Standing guard in the early evening was easy and interesting. The officers poked their heads out the slots and yelled at each other between the bunkers. It was after midnight, as novelty yielded to boredom and fatigue, that the real chore of guarding the perimeter began. The watch was broken into two-hour shifts, and Roark volunteered for the arduous two-to-four slot, a decision that had less to do with self-sacrifice than with not trusting Dooley. In an adjacent bunker, Allen Baker made the same arrangements with Forsythe.

Even then, Roark had a hard time falling asleep on the moldy cot behind Dooley. He lay beneath a poncho with his eyes wide open to darkness, afraid if he let them shut he might never use them again. It was after 0100 before he slept, his ears more finely tuned than ever. It seemed only a few seconds until Dooley was saying, "Your turn."

Roark closed one eye and flashed his lighter behind him so he could see the layout and arrange his weapons. Then he sat on the plank, checked the machine gun and ammo by feel, checked the detonators and flares, and bent with both eyes tightly closed to light a cigarette. "I've already called in," Dooley said, then pulled the poncho over his head and went immediately to sleep.

In twenty minutes Roark could see as far as he ever would,

about thirty feet. Beyond that the images grew indistinct, shapes without substance that appeared and moved and disappeared. The ground was soon alive with imagined enemy. He moved his head back and forth to erase the scene, then began to slowly map the area before him, concentrating off-center where he could see a little better. He wanted another cigarette, but was afraid he would damage his night vision. He stuck a Camel between his lips and cold-smoked it. To give his hands something to do, he withdrew the new knife and sat opening and closing it, polishing the internal parts of the hinge, beginning the essential task of breaking it in. He held it for more than an hour.

He was okay through the 0300 commo check, but less than a half hour later his head bobbed forward and he jerked upright in wide-eyed terror. His heart was pounding, and the cigarette was gone. He shook another from the pack, quickly scanned the wire, then bent to light it. He looked around but could not see Dooley's cot. He checked his watch and felt the cold steel of the machine gun, at once frightened and furious. How can you sit here, he silently raged, knowing gooks are out there, knowing they might be crawling toward you now, knowing you might wake up gurgling a fountain of blood? Wake up, you dumb son of a bitch! *Wake up!*

When the cigarette was gone he felt his face go slack. He dug his nails into his neck, but the pain was not enough. The days were too long, the nights too short between, and a few moments of sleep seemed all that mattered in this world. He checked his watch and realized he was not going to make it. "Well, hell," he said aloud, then bent over the machine gun, thumbed the selector, and squeezed the trigger. The gun bucked and roared, shattering the night with explosions and a stream of careening red tracers. At once all the adjacent bunkers were blasting away through the wire.

"Goddamn!" Dooley screamed, and scrambled to the slot with his rifle. Roark was still firing, and Dooley emptied a clip through the wire, loaded another, and fired again. "What in the hell are we shooting at?" he asked.

"Nothing," Roark said, laughing. He raked the wire with another long burst.

"Are you crazy?" A handflare shot into the air nearby, turning everything lime green for a moment before it disappeared. Slowly the shooting tapered off and finally stopped. Roark went outside with his rifle and saw Baker standing behind his bunker, firing another flare and laughing.

"I was thinking about doing the same thing," Baker said, then laughed again in a high giggle. "We're gonna catch hell for this."

"Not really," Roark replied. "They'll scream and piss and moan, but they won't do a thing. They need us too badly to fight their war." They could hear the landlines rattling, Battalion calling, wanting to know if the camp had been overrun. Other bunkers farther down the line in both directions were firing sporadically; bright starbursts flashed around the camp. "Merry fucking Christmas," Roark said, then went inside the bunker to talk to Battalion.

CHAPTER EIGHTEEN

BULLETS WERE screaming past, plowing through sand all around, plunking into the burning hulk of the Huey. The crew chief, Kitchen, was dead, and they were down in the DMZ with only one of the M-60s, Roark's rifle and launcher, and what little ammunition they could grab before the ship was covered with flames. Dooley dug frantically while Caccini worked with the gun, firing in short bursts, conserving ammunition. Roark fumbled at the launcher, finally got it loaded, and fired. The round went high, missing completely. Dooley shifted right, and the others moved with him, sliding deeper into the hollow. A sudden hail of fire pinned them all to the dirt, and Caccini twisted to his side and fired his machine gun blindly at a rush of men. Three fell, and as the others withdrew, Dooley caught two in the back with the rifle. Caccini finished off the ones on the ground. There was a lull, and Roark looked up at the circling Cobras, gliding beneath the clouds like patient sharks waiting for the kill. But they never turned and dived, and they never fired their rockets. Suddenly there was another flurry of fire, from the right and left, then more from the center. Beyond the low lumps of sand, the NVA were crawling

159

from the other bunkers, spreading out and setting up a cross fire. "I'm almost out of ammo," Caccini said.

Roark remembered his emergency radio, pulled it from a shin pocket, and screamed into it. "Fire, goddamn you! Fire!" When the Cobras rocked from side to side, then turned toward Quang Tri, he grabbed the rifle from Dooley and emptied a clip at the lead bird. He could not have missed, but the gunships flew away.

" 'Ey, GI, you gottee cigalette for me?" an Asian voice called. "One cigalette? I likee Veenston."

"Fuck you, you slant-eyed cocksucker!" Roark yelled, and when he rolled over to fire, remembered his weapon was empty. Caccini hammered out the last of the ammo in the sixty, then a stick grenade plunked into the sand between them.

Standing cold and naked in the gray light that slipped beneath the eave, he lived the dream again, saw the help they needed sail away, felt the gut-seizure of the grenade. The mosquito net hung in shreds around his bunk.

He dressed in the rancid flight suit he had worn four days, dwelling on the dreams that had become an extension of the war. The one this morning was new. So far, there were only two that kept coming back. There was the dream of the bamboo structure he had seen in the A Shau the day with Crable, nothing frightening about it, but with unnerving changes. The only true change was his vision, his ability to see what his mind had photographed. Each time it came, the dream was slower, the shape of the structure easier to see. But still it made no sense. The other dream was Jim Tyler, waiting in the jungle for help, bleeding to death one drop at a time. The dream itself never changed, but Roark could progressively see everything clearer, as if his eyes were adjusting to the darkness. It was always terrible and real, nothing dreamlike about it.

Each dream left him thinking about Phillip Crable. It was not long until Roark's thoughts had distilled the captain's final deed down to nothing less than murder. If anyone else had been running that mission, he reasoned, they would have remained on station until everybody was gotten out. Maybe Tyler wasn't hurt all that badly; maybe he would still be alive if Crable hadn't suddenly understood that the longer he flew above the black jaws of the jungle, the more likely it was that the beast would lunge and swallow him as well. Crable had done just enough to make one last try for a medal, then ran like hell for home.

Roark glanced at his watch. His bird had just completed periodic inspection; Kitch had guard duty, so he and Caccini planned to work on the aircraft. He strapped his revolver to his hips, felt for his big folding knife, donned his flight jacket, and stepped out into the drizzle carrying his poncho.

Caccini smiled and shook his head when he saw him walking down the flight line. The gunner was cleaning the gray quilted soundproofing that covered the bulkhead, squeezing a sponge into a soapy bucket.

"So what's so funny?" Roark said.

"Just you and all that junk you carry around. You look like Mr. Bojangles."

Roark stared down at his pants. The zippered pockets on both thighs and shins were sagging and lumpy, giving his clothing a life of its own when he walked. "If they issued survival vests like the Air Force, I wouldn't have to lug this stuff around," he said.

"Is that it—survival gear? I've been wondering."

"Go ahead and laugh."

"You really think you'll need it if we go down?"

"If I don't, it won't matter. Maybe it'll give you bums some incentive to save my butt."

"Fat chance. We go down in the jungle, you can forget it. We're dead."

"Maybe so," Roark said. "Everybody dies. But right up until the moment when the light clicks out, I'll still be believing that I'm gonna survive."

Caccini had everything prepared. Roark grabbed a towel and a plastic bottle of glass cleaner, then climbed into the left side of the cockpit and went to work on the radios and instruments.

"You really think you could make it in the bush?" Caccini asked, scrubbing at the jumpseat.

"It'd be hard, but yeah, I think so."

"You ever do anything like that?"

"Not completely. My dad's sort of a survivalist. Had me out in the woods as soon as I could walk, showing me how to live. He was always talking about it. Stuff like, 'The most important thing a man can learn is how to survive on his own.' And, 'It takes two things to stay alive, and the first is being ready.' That sort of thing. Anyway, I've gone a few days eating grubs and seeds and raw fish I've caught with my hands, but I've never tried it long-term. Dad and I talked about doing that someday. He's done it. Maybe we'll go when I get home."

"Is that what the knife is for?"

"I guess so," Roark said. "He sent it to me." He dabbed at the overhead panel, carefully cleaning the rows of breakers and switches.

"Does he know about that part?"

"What's that?" Roark asked. When Caccini didn't answer, he looked back to see the gunner walking out of the revetment with the water bucket. He swirled and dumped it, then headed toward the hangar for a refill. Roark went around to the right seat and was finishing with the cockpit when Caccini returned.

Suddenly the clouds ripped apart and an instant downpour began. Caccini ran the last few steps with the bucket, and the two leaped into the rear of the Huey, slid the doors shut, and watched the rain through the windows. Caccini lit a cigarette and sat casually mopping at the floor with the sponge. Roark pulled his knife and a small stone from his pockets and began sharpening the blade. Caccini turned at the scratch of sound, then stared out the window.

"When I was a new grunt," he said, "been here about a month— we were tramping around the north end of the A Shau and came up on a pair of gooks taking a crap." He rubbed a hole in the fog. "We had this Kit Carson scout with us, a VC that had switched sides, a tough little prick. He went to work on the gooks, had both of 'em trembling, but couldn't find out anything. So in a little while the lieutenant—a dildo if there ever was one—told me to take one of 'em for a walk. I wasn't too sure, so I looked at Roundman, and he just stood there like he didn't know my name. The whole platoon was looking at me. So I picked one, took him out in the bush. Put my knife in him, right here." Caccini reached back to a spot above his right kidney. Roark looked, then focused his eyes on the blade of his knife. "I had to put my foot on him and pull with both hands to get it out. When I went back, the other gook told us about that warehouse area north of Airborne." Caccini was still staring out at the rain. "He was just a kid," he said. "A hard-core NVA, but just a kid."

"You sorry?"

"No," Caccini said, his voice suddenly hard. "I'd do it again right now. But he was still just a dumbfuck kid." He looked at the knife in Roark's hand. "You think you could stick somebody with that?"

Roark stopped working the stone and stared at the blade. "Yes," he said. "I could. Used to, maybe not. Now I could."

"It's different than you think it is," Caccini said.

The rain had slowed, but a dense white wall was bearing down on the camp from the north. Roark eyed the clouds and said, "I think we've done enough." He returned the knife and stone to his pockets. They secured the Huey, then walked up the hill toward the hangar.

"What's the other thing your old man said?"
"Being willing to do whatever it takes."
"Like eating grub worms?"
"Or sticking a knife in a man's back."

Two platoons of the 2d of the 506th had been inserted into the foothills west of Camp Evans, the result of a brief contact by a pink team—a hunter/killer combination of a Cobra gunship and a Loach as scout. Skimming the brush along a trail that led from Phong Dien into the foothills, the tiny Loach had caught four Viet Cong in chest-high cover. He and the Cobra quickly dispatched them all.

It was decided that a sweep should be made in the jungled area farther up the trail. The lift involved eight Hueys, two sorties each into a pair of landing zones less than a kilometer apart and within sight of Evans. When the insertion was complete, and the other aircraft flew off on their day's assignments, Roark and his crew stayed behind as the support bird for the infantry. They had not even had time to report to the log pad when they were called back to pick up a dead GI. The LZ was cold, but as soon as the gunships left station, a sniper had fired a single round, killing a man who was leaning against a stump with his rifle at his side. It was a delaying tactic to give the enemy elements time to grab what they could and escape.

When the Huey landed in the clearing, the dead man, his rucksack, and his rifle were loaded by four solemn soldiers. Dooley turned in his seat and watched. The man was loaded face-down with his arms pulled upward to hold his head, the rear third of which was gone. When the Huey departed and made a wide arc to the southeast low above the trees, Dooley's lips were pale as paraffin.

Graves Registration—the morgue—was at Camp Eagle. Rather than following the safer route along the highway, Roark elected to fly low level along the base of the mountains.

Approaching the Song Bo at the gap in the escarpment, the gunners tightened and leaned forward. "Sampan!" they shouted at once, and Roark put the ship into a tight turn. He had also seen the boat, tucked beneath the jungle overhang at the southern bank, moving downstream. Once they were in position where they could see the craft and the two men paddling it, Roark began to fly a figure eight, gained a little altitude for the radio, and hastily called Operations for clearance to fire. The men in the sampan had stopped paddling and were clinging to tree limbs, staring at the helicopter and talking excitedly. They were obviously frightened, but made no move to establish themselves as civilians. Slowly they began to move downstream, no longer using their paddles, working hand over hand with the hanging limbs. Between them lay a large mound wrapped in a woven rice-straw mat.

Captain Hood answered the radio, asked Roark to wait, and a minute later came back saying that the area was under ARVN control, and that Battalion was trying to get clearance. The boat was still moving.

Roark was about to explode. The sampan had obviously just emerged from the mountains, probably carrying a load of rockets or mortars. If they had only spotted them while they were still beyond the gap, still within the mountains, then they could have blasted the boat out of the water without clearance of any kind. It was three miles to the nearest fields or village; armed or not, the men were Viet Cong. Finally, Hood came back on the radio. "Negative clearance, Two-five," he said. "Battalion was unable to raise the ARVN colonel, so they're saying your gooks might be civilians. You'll have to let them go." Roark did not answer. Just then, the boat reached a canopied side stream and slipped away to safety beneath the cover of jungle. "Two-five, did you copy?" Hood asked. Roark looked at the radio and almost broke the switch turning it off.

"God*damn* it!" he shouted loud enough for everyone to hear without the intercom. "I don't see anyone in the area," he said to the gunners. "Test fire your weapons." Both sixties began hammering away at the jungle, groping for the hidden stream. When they had fired several hundred rounds into the trees, Roark turned the ship toward Eagle to deliver the man whose war was over and who did not seem to mind the delay.

CHAPTER NINETEEN

I T WAS a perfect, breezeless day, a jewel for that time of year. Spans of mountains that had not been seen for weeks now lay exposed in marching repetition, adding green and blue depth, contributing their colors to the atmosphere. As the Huey climbed, turning northward toward the vacant sand flats, the muddy blue surface of the long lagoon could be seen. Beyond the white embankment at its distant shore the flat and sparkling sea stretched ahead to blue infinity.

Steve Kitchen, who had decided to extend his tour, was just back from R&R in Bangkok. He was still dreamy with the experience, tormenting himself and the others. "So when are you going on R and R, Mr. Roark?" he asked.

"Oh, I don't know. I think I'll save it 'til later."

Their destination was the hamlet of Phu Kinh which lay in the strip of paddies and farming communities that the French had named the Street Without Joy. Phu Kinh was Viet Cong. Each time the Americans went there they were sniped from the hedges, booby-trapped along the dikes, and sometimes mortared in bivouac at night.

A platoon of Rakkasans had been inserted near the village at dawn, but when it became apparent that the clear weather would hold, the men began to grumble about wasting such a day looking for gooks they would not be able to find. It was decided to choose a night defensive position early, to give the men time to dry their feet and catch some rays. A few hundred meters south of Phu Kinh, along a wide dike that once carried automobiles, was an acre of raised ground where the bombed-out remains of a villa lay crumbling beneath a few stately trees. It was a place that seemed to belong to no one, and the GIs had used it before for their NDP.

The old villa was a known position, an island in the paddies that was easy to find, but Roark called for smoke anyway. Soon a yellow cloud was rising in the sunlight, waiting for a breeze to lead it away. Dooley began the approach to the wide dike where a number of Vietnamese women in conical straw hats, white blouses, and black pants hurried past the GIs, some with balanced loads bouncing from shoulder poles. When they heard the approaching helicopter, the women stopped short or jogged to get out of the way—all except one grizzled old gal with a swinging load of new baskets who pretended she could neither see nor hear. She held her course with her eyes toward the ground, pacing herself deliberately, apparently certain that the Huey would abort the landing to avoid her. The soldiers grinned and watched the developing drama; the women looked fearful. "Well, damn it!" Dooley said, but just as he began to add power to initiate a go around, Roark seized the controls and said, "I've got it."

When the sound of the blades turned husky, the old woman probably knew she had misjudged, but she held her course. Roark cut it as close as he could, calculating the inches. The blast of wind from the blades stripped the load from the woman's shoulder and sent her baskets and hat tumbling across the dike and into the deep grass surrounding the villa. She was almost knocked down, but she braced herself against the wind and turned toward the ship, screaming her hatred and anger. Her mouth was a black pit, her teeth lost in the tar-black stains of betel leaf. The GIs laughed, and a couple of teenage girls cried as the old woman spewed forth her darkest poison on the invaders. She left her scattered baskets where they lay and stalked away in the direction she had come, still screaming, lunging with her words as if they were vomit.

It was good for a laugh, but the victory was small when four men in a helicopter whipped a basket-weaving granny, even if she was a VC. While the gunners and grunts unloaded the cargo, the pilots regarded the remains of the old villa that once had stood in the trees—everything gone now but a couple of stone and plaster corners and part of a low encircling fence. Ahead of the Huey were two squat posts of stone, and on one stood the bullet-scarred shell of an ornamental concrete urn. A black soldier in a helmet leaned against it with a new basket in his hands.

Their next run was a load of rations to a platoon gathered on a ridge beyond the escarpment near Firebase Rakkasan. The tiny clearing was an old LZ commanding high ground. Around its top was a ring of old foxholes with the openings enforced with sandbags. The patrolling platoon had just arrived; some were digging their holes deeper while others sat with their rifles, enjoying the sun. Several men moved around the clearing, policing trash that might be sucked into the rotor blades. The aircraft swung west, then turned back and began to descend. Roark was on the controls, flying with the mechanical boredom of a truck driver. He was familiar with the LZ and remembered there was only one clear spot where a ship could actually touch down clear of stumps. They were on mid-final when Dooley pointed to the sandbags—a large loose bale left behind by whoever had dug the foxholes; the rotorwash would peel them away like pages of a book, and some would circle back and come down through the blades. At that moment a man on the ground must have had the same idea, for he stepped over to the stack, stooped and lifted it.

The explosion was instantaneous and awful; a tall cone of red dirt shot from the ground, and through its center tumbled the pieces of the man. Roark's first instinct was to turn away, but he caught himself and made a tight circle. When he landed beside the knot of screaming men, there was no place to put the left skid, and he held it floating above the raw dirt crater. The man was on his back, wide-eyed and conscious, silent. His helmet was gone, his dark hair rumpled and full of soil. The bags had protected his body and face, but his hands and his legs from just below the buttocks were gone. A blond kid soaked in bright blood knelt in the dirt before him with both hands shoved into the spewing fountains, crying toward the sky like the day he was born. The cargo was swept out the door, and in one motion four men lifted the man into the Huey. Caccini straddled him and grabbed the stumps while Kitchen squeezed the gushing arms. The blond grunt jumped aboard to help Caccini, trying to clamp the slippery arteries with his fingers, screaming helplessly all the while. The Huey dived off the hill; the wind drew red patterns down its sides.

The 18th Surgical Hospital was only three minutes away, but that was too far for a man with no hands and no legs. When the body was lifted out to a stretcher, blood was lumped on the floor, and the men who had tried to save him were slick with it. The soldier who had stayed with his friend knelt down in a tight ball on the pad, and when the men had lowered the body to the slab inside the wide door, they returned and helped him into the building. The Huey sat for a time, dripping on the white pad, then rose and flew away toward the Song Bo.

They landed in the milky shallows on the gravel shoal and shut the engine down. The blades had almost stopped before anybody moved. Caccini was doubled over behind his unattended gun, making wrenching, moaning sounds like his breath had been knocked out. The others were chalky and silent. Suddenly Caccini leaped out with a roar and fell facedown in the water, thrashing around and yelling. Then Dooley and Kitchen stepped out and stood numbly in the river, not talking. Roark unbuckled and climbed over the console into the cargo bay, slipped and fell in the blood, then jumped out and stood beside Caccini. The gunner had stopped yelling, but was moaning again, sitting with his knees drawn up in the water. Roark turned around and looked at the blood. Then he saw that it was on his hands and pants, and he knelt and began to wash. Caccini was quiet now, and in a moment Roark reached out and took his helmet from his head and hung it over the grips of his machine gun. Kitch was washing, and Dooley was helping him, both of them still silent. Roark got his cap from the chin bubble and began dipping water from the river, splashing it across the cargo bay. Dooley stripped to his waist and used his T-shirt as a mop while Kitchen waded around to see about Caccini. A tapered swath of bloody water moved slowly away.

The helicopter turned as it reached Truong Tien bridge in Hue, still descending. On the wide Perfume River, a number of covered sampans, floating homes, lay anchored near shore before the ancient walled Citadel. A few motored quietly toward the market in the downtown district, spreading wide Vs across the glassy pool. The Huey slowed and gradually turned toward the south shore until it came to a hover in a vacant lot between the river and a busy morning street.

Beside a waiting jeep parked near the shaded avenue stood a captain and his interpreter. While the crew eyed the slender, delicate girls passing along the sidewalk or riding sidesaddle on backs of mopeds, the two men climbed aboard. Their mission for most of the day, the captain said, would involve a series of hops between ARVN compounds, bridge defenses, Vietnamese clinics, schools, and homes for orphans. It would be pleasant and boring. The captain slipped a pair of elasticized dummy sleeves over his bare arms so he would not have to spoil his starch. The Huey hovered at the river's edge, checked for traffic, then swung out low across the water, buzzing a sampan before climbing away to the east. Where the river passed the southeast corner of the Citadel, hundreds of covered sampans were jammed together around the tight knot of metal roofs at the market. The helicopter soon left the clutter of the city. At the edge of the hovels stood a grand and stately Catholic church with a red tile roof, unblemished, seemingly untouched by war.

Roark was still thinking about the girls. The flapping ao dais, revealing nothing, were distinctly alluring. The Vietnamese girls, he noted, were not nearly so ugly as they once had seemed.

Suddenly all he could see was the blood and screaming men of yesterday. His hands began to tremble. "You take it awhile," he said to Dooley, and he lit a cigarette and sat looking out the side window. Then a glimpse of something from the early morning came: As they were preparing the ship they heard the sound, and when they looked there were two Medevacs coming past, tails high. They passed low across the flight line, straining hard, headed north toward Phu Kinh.

The day was predictably dull, but relaxation never came to the crew. Each time they landed at the edge of a hamlet the gunners sat tautly behind their weapons, watching the people. They were a ship alone, far from help, and it would have been easy to knock them out with a single rocket. At lunchtime, a jeep was waiting for the captain and his ARVN at the pad, but the crew declined an invitation and ate a quiet meal beside the water. They took turns sleeping and watching the street.

The afternoon was tedious, and everyone felt a lift when they were finally given their last assignment—to deliver a thick manila envelope to the American adviser with the ARVN regiment based at Firebase Nancy, northwest of Evans. They departed toward the west and, after calling artillery clearance, dropped to low level and raced northward across the foothills. When they crossed the Song Bo, Roark made a tight turn and dropped near the water, still hoping to see the sampan again. The river was empty, so they continued toward Nancy low level. Nothing had been said, but everyone realized what they were doing. When they flashed suddenly across the streambed near the spot where the deer was killed, they all understood at once what was about to happen.

"Gooks!" Caccini yelled. Roark made a tight flaring turn, and in a short moment the Huey was hovering above two terrified boys, naked in the clear stream. Like the herd of deer, they had been surprised, enjoying a refreshing swim on a sunny afternoon. They appeared to be about twenty and apparently had left their weapons with their clothing. Roark pulled the ship to a high hover and, while Dooley found the coordinates on the map, called Operations for clearance. Meanwhile, the boys decided they had no choice and were dead anyway, and began climbing through the dirt and vines of the steep embankment. In a moment, Motormouth was back on the radio.

"Two-five, it may be a while, but I'm trying," he said.

"They're going to get away," Roark replied.

"Wait one, I'll see what I can do."

The south embankment was forty feet high where a curve in the stream had cut into a hill, and at the top was dense jungle. The two naked boys were scrambling straight up the bank, clawing toward the trees. "We're not going to get clearance," Roark said flatly. The leader had almost reached the safety of the trees. "Take the top one, Rico," he said, and the machine gun immediately roared. The bullets struck the Vietnamese in the side, the back, and the head. The dead kid crashed face first against the dirt, seemed to recoil, then tumbled backward down the slope past his companion and into the clear water where he immediately sank. The other boy stopped, looked down at his friend, then up at the hovering monster. The throbbing, screaming machine hung there a moment, then slowly turned on its axis so that it was facing the other way. "Kitch." The second boy's chest seemed to explode, his body shuddered with spasms. He was slammed against the ground, then began to slide, turning head down with his arms trailing. Just short of the water he became entangled in the vines and hung there with blood dripping from his head into the stream. A short distance away was the fleshy blur of the other. The Huey turned and faced its work, then rose slowly backward, turned and flew away.

After they delivered the papers to Nancy, after they went to POL to refuel, after they landed in the revetment at the nest, Motormouth called. "Hey, Two-five," he said, gazing down from the window, "you're gonna love this. I got that clearance you wanted. Those are Cong all right. You can go ahead and shoot 'em up out there." Roark turned the radios off.

"Got them motherfuckers," Kitchen said, the first that any of them had said about it. He unplugged his helmet and began getting things ready to go to the arms room.

"Dear Mom, guess what we did today?" Dooley said in a husky voice. When no one responded, he added, "Well, I guess that makes up a little for yesterday."

"No," Roark said. "Nothing makes up for that." He seemed to be gaining momentum. "A gook is nothing but a piece of dead meat, but a GI is one of us. We could kill a thousand and it would never make up for a thing."

"Okay," Dooley said, "take it easy."

"I'm taking nothing easy. This shit's permanent. They can send us home, but we're going to be fighting this war for the rest of our lives."

Dooley looked out the windshield, then at the instruments. The temperature was down, and he pressed the button and rolled the throttle off. The turbine sighed and whistled, the rumble of gears grew louder before fading away.

Motormouth was waiting when Roark walked through the door. "Sorry about that," he said. "I can't give you clearance until they give it to me." Roark swept his eyes around the empty room, laid his emergency radio and SOI on the counter, and turned to leave. "D'you hear about the Rakkasans?" He stopped and looked back. "They got fucked-over at first light this morning," Motormouth said. "Greased eight of 'em out at the villa. The gooks had a booby-trapped howitzer shell in a stone gate post. Hey, where you going?

"Hey!" Motormouth called to the empty door, realization in his tone. "What d'you do, waste them motherfuckers without clearance? You think this shit's a war or something? Hey, man, I'm talking to you!"

CHAPTER TWENTY

T HE BATTALION commander, a lean man with a curving back, paced the bunker, hands in his pockets. Word had just arrived from Delta Company confirming that yet another Redskin ship had disappeared, the third in seven days, lost to the weather. He lit a cigarette with a pocket-worn Zippo and continued pacing his cage. Across the dugout sat the RTO at his station, and next to him a duty officer from Bravo. A pudgy major who ran Battalion S-3 sat on the edge of a nearby desk, nervously flipping through a folder. Faintly in the distance came the unmistakable sound of a Huey beginning to crank.

"Tell all units they're not to launch another bird until daylight," the colonel said, "and not even then until they clear it with me." The young RTO nodded and began making the calls.

"What were their names?" the colonel asked.

"Captain Luskey and Warrant Officer Deiterman, sir," the major said. "Both were aircraft commanders."

"What were they doing flying together?"

"I'm not sure. Maybe switching out crews at Quang Tri."

There was a sudden rush of boots down the steps, and when Walters turned he saw a gaunt warrant officer with smudged and sunken eyes, breathing hard. "Sir, they said I had to have clearance from you to take a bird out," the young man said.

"Nobody's going out tonight," the old man replied.

"They're my friends, sir. I want to go look for them."

The two held each other's gaze. "There was an explosion," the colonel said. "Your friends are dead. Go on back to your hooch. There's nothing you can do."

"Sir, I'll hover every step of the way. I've got a good crew, and they're ready to go. The ship is already running."

"Go on, son. I've lost all the men tonight I'm going to lose. Tell your men to go back to their hooches."

"They're my friends, sir," Roark said, his eyes as dry as rocks. He looked around the bunker, stood dumbly vacant, then went up the stairs into the drizzling, miserable night.

When the Huey landed at the log pad of the 506th, the pilots were told that a platoon had encountered a few Viet Cong a short distance from Evans. The gooks had been pinned down, and a pair of Cobras were called in to finish them off. S-2 wanted the bodies. A cargo net was loaded aboard, and a separate length of rope attached to the cargo hook beneath the ship. The remainder of the coil was secured beside Caccini. A few minutes later the helicopter was hovering over the platoon in a swath of scorched jungle, waiting for the net to be loaded.

When the grunts signaled Caccini, he tossed down the loose end of the rope, and in short order the Huey climbed away from the jungle with its grisly pendulum swinging below. "There's pieces falling out," Caccini said.

When they got back to Evans, someone from S-2 was waiting with a camera. Roark set the ship down at the side of the pad and rolled the throttle back to flight idle. "I'll be back in a minute," he said as Kitchen opened his door. He reached for his camera and climbed down.

The men in the cargo net had been disassembled by the rockets and miniguns—arms, legs, torsos, and heads—and no single part complete. Roark used all his film, then walked back to the aircraft smiling. "You want to get out and go take a look?" he asked as he strapped himself to his seat.

"You need to go on R and R."

"Not me, buddy. That shit's for tourists. I don't have time for it."

After photographs were taken and the pockets searched by S-2, the crew was directed to deliver the butchered flesh to the pad across from the ARVN compound at the edge of Phong Dien. A jeep was waiting as they approached with the suspended net, and around it and moving out of the village along the highway were about sixty Vietnamese women, children, and infants. When the net was lowered, the Huey landed next to it to wait for it to be emptied. An ARVN untied and unfolded the net, and the people pressed forward. Waves of screeching agony surged through the crowd; families collapsed in hysterical heaps as each decapitated head was turned and recognized. Billy Roark watched with satisfaction, thinking it served the families right for being mothers and wives and children of his enemy.

Mortars were pounding across the camp, crushing footsteps toward the hooch. A mad scramble of bodies pushed for the door. Roark found himself carried in a blind, unreasoning panic, naked, without a weapon. Red explosions were flashing among the hooches, silhouetted debris sailing through the air, larger and larger, directly on line. The black maw of the bunker loomed before him, and there was just enough time.

All at once the night air moved—congealed into a sapper—no naked kid in a creek this time, but an armed and seasoned soldier, pumped and going about his work, every detail clear—the eyes, the jaw, the comfortable heaving of the flat hard chest, the hands on the cold AK, the shape of the feet, the way the knotted toes gripped the earth. Then the corded muscles moved, the barrel came around, and Roark looked straight down the tiny hole. It was all wrong and all right; nothing indistinct. The night exploded in a blast of fire.

"You want some coffee?"

"Huh?"

"Coffee. You want some?" Baker said from the hall. "I just made a pot."

Roark swung his feet to the floor, still breathing hard. "What time is it?"

"Oh-three-hundred."

"Okay. I'm up." The sound of boots moved down the hall. "Son of a bitch," he muttered. He lit a cigarette, then held the lighter beneath his fingers until pain was all he felt. The odor of singed hair filled the cube. "God, I'm tired," he whispered. "I'm so tired." Suddenly he saw a cloudy day, five men carrying a bloated black sailor up from the river, loading him aboard his ship. The dead man's skin sloughed away in the loaders' hands, the flesh hard and white and waxy underneath.

They went out front and sat on the sandbags. Above their heads the antlers Dooley had nailed to the gable reached like fingers for the sky. Roark carried his rifle and ignored Baker's gaze as he chambered a round and studied the bunker door, wanting very much to fire a clip down into the black hole. This was the first time he had died in a dream, but a certain clean quality made him understand that it would not be the last.

"You get zapped?"

"Right out there."

Baker was quiet a moment, then said, "Mine got me in my bunk about three weeks ago. I heard a sound, and when I raised up, a gook was in the hall. He swung his AK around slow and easy and just blew my shit away. I'm one dead son of a bitch, and there's no recovering the difference." He fumbled at his jacket for another cigarette.

Suddenly Roark saw his own Huey flying back and forth through a marijuana cloud above a burning field, all of them laughing until they got the call: a Loach pilot and his gunner shot down somewhere in the Z and surrounded. They were still trying to find them when a new voice came on the radio, the gunner. "My pilot's dead," he said. "I'm out of bullets. They're coming in."

It was going to be one of those days, he could tell. The flashes were worse than the dreams, and both were worse than the war. Though the dreams invaded his sleep, they were only filling available space, making the war a constant event. That somehow seemed natural. But the flashes—the waking dreams that weren't dreams at all, real moments replayed without warning—supplied an extra layer to the war, lent it smashing weight.

He glanced at the bunker again, then leaned his rifle at his side and withdrew the hunting knife from his hip pocket. The blade was much looser now; he had spent hours working graphite into the hinge and had learned to flick it open with just one hand. He stood idly practicing the move. "What were you doing up?" he asked.

"I don't know," Baker said, glancing at the knife. "I don't sleep much anymore. Or maybe I sleep all the time. I was thinking about going home—what it's going to be like. It's not much longer, you know."

Roark had made a conscious effort to *not* know, and he avoided it now. "What ever happened to the nurse?"

"Nothing. Nothing at all. She's gone home, I think. I was going over to see you one night when you were laid up, and ran into her instead. We talked maybe thirty seconds, and I knew how damn stupid I was. Nobody could be Paula, least of all in a place like this."

"Did she really look like her?"

Baker smiled. "She had brown hair," he said.

Roark thought a moment about the nurse. Women came sometimes in the night—never so real as other dreams, but real enough to leave a mess, and later an ache much deeper than before. Sometimes it happened without a dream—just pumping, pulsing life, launching itself on a mission that could only end in death.

He saw Dooley, Caccini, Kitchen, and himself flying down the Song Bo on a sunny day, murdering crocodiles with machine guns just to have something to kill. He saw the Cong they killed in the creek, then a river, bank to bank with blood.

Baker watched a thin layer of scud moving in from the east and, far above, a layer of broken clouds. "So what are you going to do when you get home?"

"I don't know. Bum around. Maybe go pay a little call on Captain Crable." He flicked the knife harder. It made a sound like a switchblade.

"Jesus. I hope you're kidding about that."

"Sure. I'm just kidding."

"Really, Roark. You can't carry that around. You got to leave it here."

"That's where it is."

"You interested in going to the mess hall? They're probably cooking by now." Roark declined, then watched Baker walk away with his hands in his pockets, a few loose strands of hair standing against the hangar lights.

He saw the A Shau—BG, Hamburger, Currahee, Tiger Mountain—and the flights of troops that soon would take it again until the monsoon wanted it back. He saw the abandoned trenches of Khe Sanh, the white membrane of parachute flares rotting in the trees. He saw funnels of blue-white smoke when the Marines burned Vandegrift and left the rest behind. He saw the ARVNs, dressed for combat along the DMZ, glancing back over their shoulders. He saw a pink and eager kid who wanted to be a hero, staring down with sweaty palms at a scattered galaxy called Saigon.

The duty officer wandered past, another brand-new new guy, studying his clipboard in the blinding beam of a flashlight, turning his head dumbly at all the hooches. Roark watched without offering to help. There were sounds inside, and a light came on. Men were moving beneath a yellow bulb down by the latrine. Somewhere someone sneezed.

He went back inside and poured another cup. Behind the bar

hung a cluttered collage—irregular bits of paper spreading outward from a penciled sign of peace. An atomic mushroom, the massacre at My Lai, Nixon with his arms extended in a V; a military grave-yard; a baby New Year with amputated legs, Henry Kissinger smil-ing; Agnew with a finger in his nose, a B-52 dropping its load, a field of white daisies, one of Lyndon Johnson's ears. There were pictures of dead friends, piles of gooks, piles of GIs, tiny sections of the *Stars and Stripes* obituary. There was a photo of a mangled dead Cong with a caption that read, "$55,000 won't buy what it used to."

Dooley was awake. He came dragging down the hall, his boots unlaced, still getting dressed. He fell into a chair and said, "We were babes when we came over here, now we're weirdos, killers, and queers."

He saw Dooley—who never outgrew the habit of referring to the mother he didn't have—laughing one day as he told about seeing an ARVN walk into a tail rotor. He sat there a minute when he was finished, then said, "Mama said I'd be different when I came back from war. I wonder what the fuck she meant?"

Roark went to his room. Try as he might, he could not imagine a day when he would pack his things and leave Vietnam. There was nobody waiting but his parents, and he felt no more connected to them than a seed might feel, cast some considerable distance from the pod.

He opened his diary and was surprised to see that the last entry was two months old. But there was less and less he wanted to tell, and no longer anyone he wanted to tell it to. He began adding names to the list across from the Gahan Wilson cartoon: Miller, Craft, Drake, Briarly, Berman, Luskey, Deiterman. He had stopped even trying to keep track of his classmates. He read through the column, wondering why his name was not among the others; it seemed that it should have been. At last he flipped back to the final entry, noted the date and wrote: "I am going to extend my tour of Vietnam."

"No you're not," Major Pax said. "You're going to serve your time here, then you're going back to the States."

"I want to stay, sir."

"Why?"

"I don't know, sir. I just don't want to leave. It doesn't seem like that much has been accomplished. I'm a good pilot, there's not a thing I can't handle."

178

"Oh, you're right about that," Pax said. "I hate to lose you—but you're going."

"Why's that, sir?"

"I don't need any hunters."

"That was a long time ago."

"I'm not talking about deer."

"They were gooks, sir."

"If I weren't absolutely certain of that, you'd have already been court-martialed."

"May I see the battalion commander, sir?"

"Not a chance."

"Leaving just makes it all a waste."

"And one other thing: I've just discovered that you never put in for R and R. Why not?"

"I've been doing other things, sir."

"You go pack your bag, fella. I don't know where you're going—it depends on what's available—but you *are* going, and you're going *today*. So go get packed."

"Yes, sir." Roark saluted and started to leave.

"Do you have a preference, in case there's a choice?"

"No, sir."

"My jeep will be at your hooch in forty-five minutes."

"Sir, I can't just walk out of here and call it done."

"You can and you will. Have a good time on R and R. Forget this crap. You've got your whole life ahead of you."

"Sir, I'm twenty-one. Half the friends I ever had are dead and they died right here. I don't want to go home."

"Good day, Mr. Roark."

"Dead, goddamn it!"

"That will be all, Mr. Roark."

VII

On the way to Sydney I learned there really are tiny dots of islands stranded out to sea with nothing but a single palm to assign them purpose. We crossed leafless spits of sand a thousand miles out, and I saw myself there, awaiting rescue or a rising tide.

Sydney only showed me how far Vietnam was from the rest of the earth, how deeply immersed in the war I had become. The city was buoyant, pleasant, unreal. I wandered around like a person on drugs, knowing that soon the hallucination would end. The dreams I had that year are more vivid than the memory of that brief moment in Australia.

I still see myself at the hotel, standing before a mirror in a blue rented suit, a rented shirt and rented shoes; I was going out on the town my first night there. I checked myself in the mirror, and everything looked fine until I saw the eyes. Then I undressed and threw the clothes in a pile, and sat naked on the bed and drank whiskey straight from a bottle until I was blind.

I slept late the next day, and when I went out I wore shorts and a T-shirt, unconcerned that I was pale as a mushroom. I saw girls and frightened them with my eyes. I walked up to Kings Cross, then back down to the quay and rode a hydrofoil across the bay. I *watched the surfers and got sunburned, then bought a black opal pendant for fifty bucks, with no idea who to give it to. I spent another wasted night in my room.*

The next day I almost met a girl. She offered to share her cab, and by accident we got out at the same stop—I to go down to photograph some sailboats, and she to walk up to her flat. I looked back as she crossed a wide lawn beyond a bending boulevard and saw that she had been watching me. But I was afraid I would scare her with my strangeness, so I went on down to the boats, still full of the way she smelled, the way her legs looked beneath her skirt as she sat beside me.

The next morning I waited where I was sure she would see, but turned in such a way so she could ignore me if she chose. But she walked right up and began talking like we were old friends. I was choked with embarrassment and fear, but she kept asking questions until I gradually was able to speak. I'm sure she was sent to help me; I could have never found her on my own.

Her name was Celia, and she had golden brown hair to her shoulders. Her skin was softer than anything I have ever known, the tone of her words a healing poultice. We spent that night, the next day, and one more night together. We ate dinner in a dungeon and walked along the bay and saw the moon. We lay on a sunny lawn and watched bits of rainbow form and disappear in the whiskered, cloudy fringe. Then it was time to be over, for her to return to school, for me to go back to war. We made love that morning the last time, then I gave her the opal, and we vanished from each other's lives. Even then I knew she would be the hardest part to remember, the dream within the dream. At times I think she almost made a difference.

I had hoped to glimpse the naked isles once more, but the light was gone. The window tried to hold me in its plastic stare, but I heard sliding waves on coral sand, felt the black persistent nudge against my chest.

CHAPTER TWENTY-ONE

"**H**OW LONG'S it been, *Chief?*"

"Forty-seven hours and twenty-three minutes," Roark said, smiling. He and Allen Baker were to be promoted to CW2 that evening, and Dooley was missing no chance to display the appropriate obeisance, using *chief* at every opportunity. He had also tried, without success, to get the details of R&R.

R&R was just beginning to catch up with Billy Roark; he saw colors again, and for the first time knew how many days remained until DEROS. The rocketing trip across the dimensions of reality had begun to take hold, and now it seemed that the fantastic potentials of life beyond Vietnam might actually once again exist. He entertained thoughts of returning to Australia someday; maybe he would dig for opals at Coober Pedy; maybe he would meet Celia once more. A red speck penetrated his thoughts, and the vision vanished; suspended in the haze beyond the river was the NVA flag, an irritating chigger.

Colonel Blackburn's ARVNs were above Cam Lo again. In a long afternoon engagement, followed by a predawn ambush of a retaliating force, the South Vietnamese had all but destroyed an enemy battalion. The morning was moist and clear, and as the rising sun turned the sea to molten metal, the weary ARVNs finished their work among the berms and craters.

It had been good to see the colonel again. The projection of energy and humor in his lively gray eyes cemented Roark in a happy mood. He had grown fond of the unconventional commander and, despite their disparate ranks, considered him a friend.

Suddenly Cam Lo was just ahead. Dooley initiated the approach. Roark checked the instruments, announced them all green, and thought how good it felt to be back in the air.

The first three sorties involved bringing back weapons, and it was a good and unusual sign that well over two thirds of the small arms were those of the NVA—two entire Huey loads of dirty, splintered, blood-spattered AKs, SKSs, and RPG tubes. The ARVNs were exhausted, but they were proud. They loaded the enemy weapons first, glancing up at the faces of the crew. The rifles rattled into a stack, each a man dead somewhere among the craters. The crewmen smiled and jerked their thumbs at the soldiers. Men were still working the slopes east of the brown hills, strands of gray smoke immobile above their heads. One in a sweeping line stopped and fired three quick rounds into a hole before moving on. The air smelled of fresh earth and burned powder. "Some of these guns are brand-new," Caccini said when they were en route toward Dong Ha.

Roark turned and smiled at the stack of firearms, so much more reassuring than a pile of enemy bodies. "Pick out a couple if you want," he said. "They'll never miss them." The gunners extracted two AKs—their stocks still bright with varnish—wrapped them in a poncho and tucked them beneath Caccini's seat. When they had finished unloading at the pad and were about to head back to Cam Lo, Caccini jumped out and put the stolen goods in the aft compartment.

When the final load of firearms, mostly M-16s, had been deposited at Dong Ha, a smiling Colonel Blackburn in steel pot and flak vest came down to the pad with Sergeant Trung. "They've found a one-forty!" he announced as they climbed aboard. "Take me to Cam Lo." While Dooley brought the ship to a hover, turned and departed, Blackburn connected his helmet to the Y-cord.

"What are you going to do, sir?" Roark asked.

"Shoot the son of a bitch back at them!" he declared. Roark was stunned. He stared at the colonel a moment, considering the possibilities of firing an enemy rocket into North Vietnam. It was a tremendous idea. He and Dooley exchanged glances, but could say nothing.

The rocket was a finless tube of rusty steel, thick and ugly as a fat man's cigar, lying flat in a patch of trampled grass circled by ARVNs. Colonel Blackburn gave instructions to hold to the south and wait for his call, then leaped out with Trung behind him. He immediately began rattling at the Vietnamese as he unreeled a length of wire from a detonator. The sun was high in the east, blazing happily in the overlap of seasons, and when the colonel pointed from the rocket to an embankment, flecks of perspiration sparkled in the dark hair along his arm. The grass around him whipped and silvered in the wind, changing colors as the Huey moved away.

In less than two minutes the rocket was in position and on its way. The men in the Huey talked about the possibility of prompting a return bombardment, maybe making the national news. Then there was a bright spark, and the projectile climbed swiftly into the sky. After a thousand feet there was a tremendous acceleration, and the rocket vanished with speed. Everyone watched for the impact, but they never saw it.

Blackburn was smiling at Roark, striding comfortably through the grass with the brown hills behind him when his face gave a slight twitch and a burst of red erupted from his vest. His motion continued, but without his feet, and he went over facedown, his arms loose at his side.

"Oh, no. God, please no."

Roark grabbed the controls from Dooley and jerked the ship off the ground, sliding over and across the colonel and the ARVN kneeling beside him. Kitchen sprayed the hills with lead. Most of the ARVNs went to their knees and began peppering the hillside, glancing back to see if the colonel was going to rise. "You got it!" Roark yelled, then he was over the console and out in the grass. Trung had already turned the man over, and the colonel's face was gray and slack and old. Blood was in his mouth and on one cheek. Trung gazed across at Billy Roark, his eyes deep with pain. Caccini was yelling about mortars, and the ARVN captain appeared. The pop and rattle of rifles rose and fell while Kitchen hammered away with his machine gun. Then they loaded Colonel Blackburn on his back. An ARVN kid who looked confused reached down for the steel pot and handed it up to Caccini. Trung squatted beside his dead friend, cushioned his head with one hand, then the Huey rose and flew gracefully away. The ARVNs looked at one another. The delicate grass trembled in the retreating beat of sound.

Roark and Baker sat at a table in the dazzling splendor of the Phoenix Club. It was complete now—the run to the Philippines had been made. The floor was cushioned with red-and-black shag, and along the walls hung cut-glass lamps, casting crescents on gaudy gold paper patterned in clipped red fuzz. It looked like a whorehouse. "The NVA are going to love this someday," Roark said.

Baker pulled hard on a stubby cigarette, started to throw it to the floor, then used the glass ashtray. "Well, I always wanted to know what it felt like to be a CW2," he said, lighting another smoke. "It's pretty fucking impressive, wouldn't you say?" Roark just glanced at him. The alcohol was beginning to hit, and he knew it wouldn't be much longer.

The ritual of promotion involved downing a large mug containing a near-lethal dose of various types of spirits. Shining at the bottom of the glass was the brown-and-brass bar of a CW2. The two pilots had emptied their drinks to chants and laughter, then with their new bars pinned to their collars were left alone at a table to share their last sober moments. Major Pax, who had been there to make the ceremony official, had slipped quietly out of the club, but not before Roark made one more effort to extend. "Sir," was all he said. The major simply shook his head, then walked around him and out the door.

Sitting at the table with his head beginning to droop, Roark's thoughts were vague and wandering. Sydney was far away. Wilbur Blackburn was dead. Jim Tyler was hanging upside down with ants in his mouth. Phillip Crable was somewhere running free.

Dimly, he could see the shine of new insignia at the lower edge of vision. It meant something, but he could no longer say exactly what. Not what it should; not what he thought it would. That made him think about manhood, and he remembered a thing Dooley had said, trying to joke his way back from the brink the day after they bloodied the Song Bo, the evening they killed the two guys in the creek. "Am I a man yet, Daddy?" he quipped. "Am I a man? Will you tell me when I've done this shit long enough to be a man?"

Am I a man? Roark wondered. If you're a man when you stop feeling like a kid, I guess I've made it. Maybe you know it's happened when the meaning's gone. He felt his gyro wobble then, and it was time to try to make it to the hooch. He and Baker helped each other stand, then they stumbled out the door, down the steps, and up the gentle rise. Halfway there, Roark knelt and vomited with an agonized cry, heaving again and again as if being torn in two.

* * *

Word came from Division two days in advance, saying that the entire battalion was to be involved in a special mission under the command of a general. Television crews from the three national networks were to be on hand. Details were slow to trickle down, but when they finally did, the helicopter crews just looked at one another, shook their heads, and made sad, hysterical little smiles. Nothing surprised them anymore.

The mission was to be filmed; three Hueys were assigned for the exclusive use of the media, their flight paths carefully coordinated so as to yield the best possible coverage for the folks back home. Keep it tight, the platoon leaders said, we're gonna be on TV.

A battalion of GIs was waiting beside the oiled airstrip at LZ Sally. The great swarm of birds landed by groups in formation, took on their loads of living cargo, and headed northwest. Meanwhile, a fifteen-minute artillery barrage was preparing four broad landing zones in the empty hills east of Mai Loc. As the bombardment of the targets ended, eight rocket-laden Cobras swooped down and attacked the smoldering fields. Moments later, tiny scout helicopters darted through the smoke, checking for living debris. Then eight more Cobras came, bearing flechette rockets this time, each loaded with beehive rounds to insure that no living thing remained. Then the ponderous formations of Hueys came down from the sky, quickly deposited some five hundred combat troops, and flew off with a great orderly thrashing against the ominous backdrop of the DMZ.

When it was done, the general extended his personal congratulations to each of the unit commanders, smiling with appropriate reserve, nodding his august head. This portion of the day was not filmed; the journalists had long ago been whisked away. In fact, they completely missed seeing the battalion of helicopters circle to pick up the battalion of soldiers from the ruined hills; they also missed it when those same aircraft returned those same men to LZ Sally a short while later. The newsmen had no way of knowing that what they had witnessed was not real. They did, however, get some excellent footage of the war in Vietnam.

The new light colonel was pleasant and brisk, about as starchy as most, and probably a fine man. But he was not Colonel Blackburn. Very quickly Roark regretted the assignment he had given himself for his last day at the controls of a Huey. You can't go back, he thought. You can't ever make things like they were.

A company of ARVNs had been inserted that morning on a razorback ridge just north of the Rockpile. Hardly an hour had passed before they were in trouble. An American RTO who was with them radioed that they had been hit with mortars, machine-gun fire, and RPGs. They needed ammunition and had a number of casualties to evacuate.

The ridge was quiet when they reached it, but Roark came in from beneath, climbed the steep slope of the southern face, then popped suddenly into the open on top. The ARVNs were huddled close to the bald earth, completely exposed in exactly the same spot where they had been dropped. While Kitch and Caccini shoved at the cases, Roark held the ship at a low hover and stared ahead, feeling hollow. The ridge formed a V with another to the north, and less than three hundred feet across the scrubby ravine was the enemy position. For the first time ever, he honestly believed he was about to die. "Watch for an RPG," was all he said. Dooley did not reply. Several wounded ARVNs had been carried and helped toward the helicopter, and they began to come aboard.

The first three mortar rounds passed over the ship, exploding harmlessly down the slope beyond the tail, but the next two struck to the east along the ridge. "Let's go!" Roark yelled.

"Not yet," Caccini said. "Okay, we're up!" The ship moved backward, pivoted, and dived down the face of the mountain.

"One of these dudes isn't wounded," Kitchen said.

Roark looked back and saw a Vietnamese kid wearing several clean wraps of gauze around a forearm, smiling tentatively. "Okay, we're going back," he announced. "You know what to do."

"Roger on that," Kitchen replied. A hysterical laugh swept the crew.

They did the pop-up approach again, but the hover was much higher this time. Kitch and Caccini moved without warning, and in an instant the ARVN was sailing through the air, thrashing and screaming, doing his best to fly. He slammed facedown into the rocky ground, unconscious and truly injured. The Huey turned and flew away.

Roark's thoughts were drifting, thinking about the right and wrong of going and staying. Suddenly he caught a flash of the bamboo dream, the dream that had grown in progression from a glimpse of structure in the jungle. It carried terror with vacant simplicity, worse each time it came, with no hint of reason. Then it jelled in final form, three nights in a row, finely focused and real, everything clear: crisscrossed pieces of bamboo flat against the earth, and from the black vapor beyond, two clenched and withered hands gripping the prison bars. Overlaying the scene was the disappearing sound of a Huey. *His* Huey. Again and again he heard it fly away.

"We might need to speed it up a little," Caccini said. "One of these guys is pretty bad. I can see his brains."

The ARVN was sitting erect, slack-jawed and staring. A slab of flesh and bone had been gouged from the base of his head, the wound white and unbleeding. Roark looked at the man without feeling a thing. He nosed the ship over, intending to go to a hundred, but settled for ninety instead. Before they passed Mai Loc he was drifting again. The airspeed slipped toward eighty, but nobody bothered to tell him.

BOOK II

VIII

It was a blustering day with cold clouds tight against the mountains outside Tacoma. A weak cheer rolled through the Stretch-8 when the tires screeched against concrete, and another, less certain, when the hatch was opened to rolling stairs. Everybody looked around for an attitude. We were a load of strangers, tumbling down the stairs like so many spent shells. Nobody kissed the tarmac.

I ended up alone in a cab, headed toward Sea-Tac, and all I saw of the state of Washington was four lanes of new asphalt and new stripes, racing down an alley through a forest. The driver and I didn't talk. At the tiny terminal, choked with traveling people, it seemed I became invisible. I was wearing jungle fatigues and a flight jacket—violating regulations, and not giving a damn—and I recall people being both intensely aware of me and ignoring me, the way we treated blacks when I was a kid. I went to the latrine, and after I washed my hands I realized there were no paper towels. A fat man positioned nearby smiled and said welcome home soldier, then offered me a towel for fifty cents.

191

CHAPTER TWENTY-TWO

THE CANYON was quiet. For two hours he watched, shivering in the morning chill while a bleaching sheet of sunlight crept along sheer ocher parapets, crossed wrinkled slopes of clay and scree, and finally touched the trembling tops of cottonwoods. When the fiery eye broke the rim, he turned and burned his vision red, blinking images of green.

From the brushy point he could see a quarter mile upstream where the winding river rolled and turned beneath a flat elliptic wall. A blue haze in the shadowed bend made the water seem to flow from solid stone. Through the grass across the meadow lay the curving void of a trail.

"There are no gooks," he whispered.

It was his first time in the canyon without his father. Over the years they had fished all forty-three miles from the headwaters to the highway. Now the man who had taught him survival—life itself—was left behind. There was no other way.

Home wasn't home anymore. His parents looked older, less confident, uncomfortable. Even their joy at having him back seemed tentative and confused. Those first few days, he was a person on the verge of unconsciousness, a stranger with amnesia sitting

192

quietly in the house where Billy Roark grew up, responding to his name, assuming his family and memories as they appeared. He slept on a firm bed with clean sheets, took two showers every day, and walked barefoot on the carpet. In the afternoon he sipped beer in the shade of a giant elm. It was a drifting, edgeless time where nothing was demanded, a recurring dream more familiar each day, but never so familiar as to make it anything but a dream, one not particularly desirable. His parents were pleasant and patient, and he pretended to not notice the effort.

On the fifth day he put on jeans and combat boots and walked into town. It took only a few blocks to realize that he was a ghost. The town was like a house put up, musty and old, a yellowed scene where even the light seemed to have lingered too long. Uncertain where to begin, he bought a roll of stamps from Mr. Oathan. The man was worried and old, and either didn't recognize him or never knew or cared that he'd been gone. He left without telling him who he was.

The only person he recognized at the grocery where he and Jay had worked was a saggy old checker he could never abide. Hook-nosed and humpbacked, when idle she hitched her butt against the counter and hung like a buzzard waiting for a meal. She gave a ghastly smile when she saw him, but did not speak. A sackboy named Godfrey had made assistant manager, and he charged out of the office and past Billy Roark as if he had some place important to go, a big wad of keys jingling on his hip. Another one of those 4F motherfuckers.

The street beside the store had always been his favorite because it led past a number of old houses, large in their day, with swings on painted porches and wide lawns of clover. Many times he had walked four extra blocks to school just to begin his day on that street. But now he stopped. The pretty neighborhood was the same—the white, upright houses on horizontal green, the sweet scent of clover, the sound of a working mower—but the soothing magic now stopped rudely at the curb. He walked away to the scrape of pebbles caught between hard soles and unyielding city streets.

Sam's Barbecue was next. There had been a brief period when he and Jay had tended fires around Sam's place. Sam had a daughter named Melinda who was kind to them both, and never seemed to mind that they were younger. The arrangement fell apart when she went off to Tech. Sam began letting the boys eat all the burned ribs they wanted, and they gulped them down like passing hounds, suddenly aware of the smoke and suffocating heat.

Sam looked up from a brisket as if he had been caught scratching too long. He wiped his hands on the greasy bulge of the apron, then rubbed them through a towel and reached across to shake hands. The corners of his smile were twitchy. It was lunchtime and they were holding up the line. "Good to see you," Sam said, but didn't call him by name. Roark took his sandwich and a fistful of green onions and sat in a corner booth facing a brick wall.

That evening he fired up the Ford and went up to the Mixer. His father had driven the pickup on weekends, and it roared to life on the first crank. The straight pipes were loud.

When Patti came out she said, "Hi," and her eyes immediately turned to mist. She leaned through the window and kissed him lightly on the lips. Someone howled. "You hear about Jay?" she said.

"Dad wrote me."

The cruisers were beginning the endless procession down Main. He recognized two of the cars, but new faces were behind the wheels. Out near the curb, two boys sat cross-legged on the hood of a pickup. "You still at your mama's?"

"Yeah," Patti said. "We're still there."

"Think she can baby-sit?"

"That's what she's doing now."

"I'm headed to the circle. I'll see you later."

"I get off at ten. Make it ten-fifteen."

They drove out to the sandbar, let the tailgate down, and backed into the lake. There was enough moon to make a line of splinters across the water, bits of light playing in the shadows along the shore. They sat on a quilt in the bed of the truck with their shoes off and jeans rolled up and drank beer and talked quietly about Jay and the old times. They brought him briefly back to say good-bye, then let him go.

"How'd it go yesterday," his dad asked. "See anybody you know?"

"No," he said. It was late afternoon, and they were in the shop behind the house where his father was building cabinets for a job just down the street. "You know, I didn't expect a parade, but it would sure be nice to find one son of a bitch who would look me in the eye."

His dad looked straight at him. "Nobody knew it was going to be like this, son," he said. The blue tattoos on his arms were blurred with age.

"I guess not," Roark said. He looked across the yard at a mimosa tree beginning to fold.

"Why don't I take a few days off, let's go to the mountains, back to the canyon? Catch a trout or two."

"No," he said. "I'm going alone." He went out, backed his truck to the garage, and began to load his gear. "Tell Mom bye," he said. "I'll be back in a week or two." He turned away from the eyes and let his father watch him go.

He had tried to sleep at the trailhead, curled in the seat beneath a quilt, waiting for the sun. But it was no use. He remembered the canyon; he walked the grassy meadows, crouched and stalked the green river, cast toward rings on polished pools. It was the place of completeness, beginning and end. He saw it again the first time.

They had discovered it on one of their wandering, antlike trips when he was fifteen. From a bald mountain at the upper end of the wilderness, the canyon was merely a sunken shape coursing through timbered folds. It didn't look that far. With fly rods in metal cases, canteens, and one small pouch, they left the truck and gear and began the long descent.

The canyon was steeper, deeper, the distance much greater than it appeared, but neither would acknowledge the misjudgment. Once the wide grassland was crossed and the forest began, they encountered a succession of transverse ravines, each deeper and more difficult than the last. The rugged terrain which appeared so smooth from afar should have been a warning. They walked without talking.

Finally yielding to a narrow gulch, the way was soon blocked when it plunged a hundred feet in a dry and rocky fall. Billy moved ahead, inching across a face of loose dirt and scrub, groping for a safe way down. Suddenly a wide sheet of earth sloughed loose, and the two fell like ants into a trap—spinning, twirling, tumbling—crashing through clawing brush. When at last they stopped in a choking cloud and found that neither was injured, they laughed the rich and reckless laughter of men who are strong and happy. What the hell, they were in the canyon; never mind how they were going to get out—it was time for some serious fishing. They loosened their pants and shook down the dirt, then emptied their boots. Grinning through filthy faces, they passed golden red trunks of ponderosas and entered a meadow of whispering grass.

The river was small, remote and lovely with curving green pools, protected pockets, room for a backcast—the kind of water to make a man forget most anything, particularly that he later had to leave. They leapfrogged the pools upstream to the willows, then walked back down a mile and started over. The midday sun was full upon the water, but they coaxed the dozing natives from beneath the cut with imitation hoppers and tiny hare's ear nymphs. They released thirty or more. As the sun approached the western rim, they cleaned four beautiful brooks in the river and built a fire.

"It's decision time," his father said, relaxed among the boulders. He held a roasting trout above the driftwood fire, skewered on a green willow branch. The speckled skin was beginning to blacken and curl, and apricot flesh showed through. "We can stay the night if you want."

Billy sighed and said nothing, glancing around the canyon. From anyone else it would have seemed a wild remark, miles from the truck with no food or bedding, and only light jackets. Even in summer, nights in the mountains were cold. He looked at the strange man beyond the fire and wondered if he had been tricked. "What about tonight?" he asked.

"Tonight's no problem. It's tomorrow."

"There's plenty of fish."

"Fish won't get us up that mountain."

Now he knew, and he tried to prevent the smile by gazing along the gently roiling water. It didn't work. "You finally got me, didn't you?" he said quietly.

"It's time," his father said.

Yes, maybe it is time, he thought, and inwardly cringed at what that meant. It could be avoided by simply starting back toward the truck, delaying passage for another year, perhaps forever. He drew his trout from the flames, blew it cool, and carefully tasted the delicate flesh.

The evening hatch was late and frenzied, and for twenty minutes the violet water churned with feeding fish. It was dark in the canyon when it was done. A blushing purple sky held a pale gray cloud of mating flies in dancing silhouette.

They stayed four days. At night they slept back to back in a willow nest deep in a shelter beneath a cliff, feeding a tiny fire against the chill. The essence of an ancient people was in the dust and on the blackened stone around, and there was approval. During the day they fished, explored the canyon, and grazed on things they found. By the time they walked out of the wilderness, Billy was eating wood grubs raw, tossing them far back in his throat, chasing them with a small sip of water. He was proud, but it was secret, manly pride he could not have found words to explain. He never told his mother, or anyone at school. Not even Jay.

Recalling the courage it took for a teenager to eat a worm, Billy Roark slipped into the straps of his pack, stood and buckled the belt, and gazed down from the knoll. The meadow was still empty. The sun had begun to turn the grass to creamy beige and green that changed and flowed with a silent breeze. Across the canyon, far from the water, stood tall cottonwoods, and between them and the river was a dense screen of willows. He moved down the slope quietly, using cover as he made for the trees. His eyes moved everywhere. When he reached the bend at the cliff he felt better, but he watched from the willows a long time before crossing, then quickly abandoned the trail.

He heard voices once, and hid and watched a young couple moving downstream. When they were gone he felt strange and lonely. He continued into the wilderness.

It was warm at midday. His shirt was wet across the shoulders, and he stopped to rest. The flesh beneath the straps was indented, pliable, and numb, the load heavier than he thought.

When he had walked a few more miles, and it was afternoon, he came to some gray cliffs that he remembered. There was a sandy nook behind some trees where the riverbed had been, and along the base were several tiny caves. He lowered the pack and sat a while with his damp shirt cool against the stone. He knew now what to do. With sudden energy he stood and began to gather boulders. From the rucksack he removed his fly rod and a small pouch with a shoulder strap. When he had packed a few small things, he checked a hole, shoved the ruck inside, and closed the door with the stones. Then he continued on his way, forgetting all about a need to hide.

The sound was faint, almost natural—a pebble turning over where the soil had given way, or the slip of a careless foot. Without a detectable motion he eased farther back into the cleft of rock, deeper into the growth of poison oak beside the spring. The hand that held the flint-tipped spear drifted slowly back.

This was his third attempt in as many days, each more desperate, more willing to pay. Yesterday's decision to hide in the shrub was a major step—already, lines of agonizing welts coursed along his arms and bare upper body—but the lovely green growth completely covered the best and only logical place of ambush.

Today's decision was the elk dung, and it seemed quite natural once it occurred to him. He found the mound still steaming, buzzing with several blue-tailed flies, as he fished the river for breakfast. He knelt beside it, and immediately his eyes climbed the barren wall to the lip of a high ravine and the vertical streak of dampness that oozed beneath it. Far back, almost out of sight, he could see the green tops of cottonwoods which fed upon the spring. He covered the mound with moist sand and marked it for the afternoon.

Now he crouched in a bed of poison oak with dung smeared over his body, on his boots, britches, and face, in his hair, and beneath his arms. The flies had found him, but they worked quietly so long as he did not move. A trickle of water dripping from a curling vine into the pool seemed loud.

The doe appeared with no sound at all, just eyes and nose and one slowly turning ear in a small opening in the greenery. When she looked behind with a slow, fluid motion, Roark lowered his lids until they were almost closed and let his mouth come open. The doe moved into the space where the trail came down to the water, tested the air, and searched every inch of the tiny clearing. Again she looked around.

There was a soft rustle and a movement of leafy branches, and a spotted fawn stepped gingerly past and into the open. Wanting hopelessly to be other than what it was, the tender one gawked with wet, protruding eyes, snorted softly, spread spindly legs, and dipped its head.

There was an exploding rush of sound—a roar, a bleat, a snort, and the frantic beat of hooves quickly gone. Then all was quiet but Roark's labored breath, the buzz of outraged flies, and a wheezing squeak from the fawn.

He quickly cut the creature's throat, then dragged it toward the ledge beyond the pool and dressed it out. With cord from the pouch he rigged a strap between the legs, then hoisted the little carcass across his back. He had forgotten all about the doe. As he started up the low ridge that he had to cross to get back down to the canyon, he felt the eyes upon him. The mother stood in the open among the trees, staring blankly at the empty package on his back. They held each other's gaze, then the killer walked away, using the butt of his weapon as a staff.

CHAPTER TWENTY-THREE

THE SIGHT of Gil McCawley was like an oasis after a thirsty walk. He was ambling along the hall with a student at his side, one arm through the chin strap of his helmet, using both hands to explain some flight maneuver. He stopped and smiled when he saw Roark, and they shook hands while the student walked ahead to the briefing room. McCawley looked the same, a little darker perhaps, but still lean and bowlegged. His face was still friendly, but the eyes had gone weary. "Hello, stranger," he said. "You in B-1?"

"As of today."

"Well, it's a good flight, you'll like it." They moved down the hallway. "So how's it been going? Glad to see you got out okay."

"All right, I guess," Roark said. "I had a tough time with instructor training. Couldn't concentrate. Who else is here? I haven't seen a soul I know since I got to Wolters."

"Nobody in this flight. You didn't know Harper—he was instructing in Matel Messerschmitts, but they've already sent him back for another tour. Jeb Brady's a classroom instructor—fat like

199

you wouldn't believe—and Fred Luper is a Tac officer in Preflight. You haven't seen anybody, huh?"

"Nobody at all," Roark replied. "Baker was supposed to be here right behind me, but I think he may have gotten his orders changed." They had reached the briefing room.

"I bumped into Turner Wilson at the PX a couple of days ago," McCawley said. "He'd just gotten here. Said he'd been assigned to Headquarters, School Brigade." He paused. "Listen, I've got to debrief. You need to fill out some papers. It'll only take a few minutes, then we're through for the day. We'll go get a soft drink."

Beyond McCawley, Roark could see the young faces in the briefing room. This was the WOCs' last working day there; the next stop was Fort Rucker, Alabama, for instrument training and Huey transition. "Did you say 'through'?"

"That's right. This is flatdick city. Come on, I'll introduce you to Eddleton."

Captain Eddleton, the flight commander, was a perspiring man with round cheeks and a matching belly, thoroughly unpretentious and likable. McCawley quickly slipped away, and after a few minutes of orientation and introductions, Roark was left to himself in a corner to fill out forms. The bustle in the room gradually diminished. A short time later McCawley returned from across the hall. Something suddenly made Roark realize that he had said nothing about Steve Sharp.

They got sodas and found a table in the break room. Most of McCawley's good humor was gone by then, and none at all was in his eyes. "So what happened to Steve?" Roark asked.

"Steve's dead."

"How?"

"It was just the direction of things; I think he lost interest in the entire program. Maybe he sobered up and didn't like what he saw. Anyway, he was here about six weeks. One day he called, and I went and found him." McCawley studied his hands. "Sometimes I get the feeling that everybody who ever went to Vietnam got killed," he said. "It just takes longer for some to comprehend."

They were silent for a long time. "Did you know about Tyler?" Roark asked.

"Not 'til I talked to Turner."

"Did he tell you how it happened?"

"He told me."

"Crable got scared and left him."

"It didn't sound that simple."

"Like hell it wasn't."

"Well, I'm real sorry," McCawley said, "but it's done, just like everything else. Nothing's going to change any of it. You may as well bury it now." Roark was angry and would not meet his eyes.

"There's something else," McCawley said, his voice hard and unrelenting. The tone turned Roark's head.

"There always is."

"Baker and Dooley were killed in a midair about two hours after you left. It was Baker's last day to fly."

He did not react at all—not a flinch, not a blink, not anything for anyone to see. He looked around the room. A pilot walked in and bought a sandwich from one of the machines, opened the cellophane, peeled the bread back, and said, "Motherfucker," then dropped it in the trash and stalked out.

"Everybody dies," Roark said. He looked at McCawley, his face drawn and vacant. "That was Steve's line, wasn't it? Everybody dies."

IX

I began feeling good about being home the moment I knew I was going back to Vietnam. Before that I just wallowed around, trying to convince myself that I didn't need to be there, that everybody was right and in a little while I'd feel great and life would be just fine.

Then one day Gil McCawley went back without a word. We fished together, and I never knew. It was a double shock because he had a wife, and they seemed to get along. The next thing I knew he was gone to Fort Rucker for Cobra transition, and from there straight on across without taking leave. I finally got where I laughed every time I thought about it. I guess there wasn't as much of Gil McCawley left as he thought.

For my part, the war was still happening, and it was happening without me. I might as well have been there; I was living it— flashes every day, dreams at night, a cordless closed-circuit TV. The flashes were the worst, especially when it rained, but it was a dream that made the difference—the one about Jim Tyler, hanging upside down, blinking his eyes and waiting.

I began to call Phillip Crable every time I dreamed that dream, passing it on, sharing the good times. Then one night Crable became a part of the dream, a scene at the end where I tracked him down and used my knife. That was a shock to me at first, but it wasn't that much longer until I began to accept the definite satisfaction.

Finally, one weekend I drove up to Fort Leonard Wood to see what would happen. When I got back, all the decisions made, I put in for reassignment to Vietnam. I never dreamed again about Jim Tyler. And I never dreamed that the entire affair was anything but over.

CHAPTER TWENTY-FOUR

FIVE THOUSAND feet below the Caribou transport a wide plain of bleached bamboo and brush lay stretched between parallel ranges of jungled mountains. Breaking the flats were clumps of dark green hills, standing alone or projecting from the heights in diminishing spurs. A narrow blue river moved lazily southward, making a long, uncertain run before twisting through snakelike contortions, then tapering into the hazy distance. Roark studied the terrain, beginning a mental map of his new area of operation, momentarily forgetting the worrisome gnaw of Nha Trang.

Nha Trang was Pearl Harbor on Sunday morning; it was a drowsy sergeant in a tilted chair, a sweating fat man who had no idea if the command had a scout unit operating at An Khe or not.

"What do they fly?" he asked.

"OH-58s, Jetrangers, Kiowas," Roark said. Upon departing Wolters he had spent two weeks at Fort Rucker transitioning to the smaller, single-pilot craft.

"Oh, yeah, those little new ones," the sergeant said. "I guess you can catch a shuttle up there tomorrow and see. If they're not there, I can put you right here flying VIPs around."

204

"I'll find them," Roark said, making no effort to hide his contempt for the man.

Riding an empty airborne bus on the return lap from Pleiku, Nha Trang seemed like a warning. It looked like the war was over, and nothing Roark had seen so far had challenged that impression. The only other passengers—a Special Forces medic who sat as far forward as he could and didn't look at anyone, and a black grunt who had found help somewhere and sat staring as if through the window of a deep-water submarine—got out at Pleiku. There weren't even any corpses to carry. Roark strained to see ahead through the dirty window, trying to get a glimpse of his new home.

The Army compound at An Khe took its name from the adjacent village which lay astride Route 19, the paved highway connecting the coastal city of Qui Nhon to Pleiku in the Central Highlands. The plateau of An Khe was an intermediate terrace some twenty miles wide, roughly fifteen hundred feet above the coastal lowlands, bracketed by two distinct groups of mountains. The terrain and vegetation ranged from broad stands of dense dryland bamboo to fields of elephant grass near the river, ancient canopied forests to the north and east, and heavily jungled hills and mountains to the south. The slow and shallow Song Ba drained the valley southward, passing beside the camp.

When the airstrip was almost directly below, the twin-engine C-7 banked and began a twisting series of turns, plummeting from the sky in a tactical approach suggestive of a field under siege. Sunbeams swept through the windows like searchlights. Suddenly the aircraft leveled, flared, and bumped, and after a short roll came to an abrupt halt. It pivoted, taxied quickly to a Quonset hut, dumped its single passenger with his gear, and promptly flew away.

Roark watched the airplane climb steeply into the sky, wondering about the tactical maneuvers amid the surrounding silence. There was not a single helicopter in the air at An Khe, and nothing was moving on the ground. He shouldered his duffel and walked toward the tubular shack, his helmet bag dangling from his other hand.

"You tell me where Delta Troop, First of the Tenth is?" An Air Force sergeant gazed across a paperback with his head tilting off his neck. He had heavy lips and coarse black hair flecked with chunks of scalp. His face was peppered with blackheads. "No," he said, and returned to his reading.

Roark stared at him blankly, then said, "Fuck you, Jack," and lugged his bag outside, stood it in the shade at the end of the building, and walked up the taxiway with his helmet.

An Khe looked like a place that had a working agreement with the enemy, something left behind, a sleepy garrison. The dominant feature of the camp was a boxy, two-story house of French design. The stucco walls were cracked and peeling, and the once pea-green paint was faded almost white. At one corner of the flat roof a red-and-white checkered air traffic control box had been emplaced, its kinked antennae pointing vaguely toward the sky. On top of the box was a silhouette, familiar, yet out of place, the tower operator sunbathing on a cot. A thin strand of rock music floated on the air.

In front of the house, a large opening let off the middle of the airstrip, forming a flight line beyond a grassy depression. Placed around the oiled surface were a half-dozen steel-and-dirt revetments where sat the sleeping forms of a pair each of Cobras, Hueys, and Kiowas. On the open ramp were four more birds, also tied and abandoned. Beyond the helicopters stood a gray building identified by a white sign on a false front: TASK FORCE 19. Near the taxiway, off to itself, sat a squat green hooch sprouting a cluster of antennae. In front was a small lawn with a flagpole bearing a bleached Stars and Stripes and a limp yellow unit flag.

From the northeast, across the Deo Mang Pass, came a sound so ordinary that he did not notice until the aircraft penetrated his vision. It was an OH-58 making an oblique approach, low level with no semblance of a pattern. Like those on the ramp, all four doors had been removed. The aircraft shot past Billy Roark, flared suddenly, and came to a hover beside the cot atop the control tower. A paperback fanned, then sailed away, and the reclining figure, who Roark now could see was naked, stood in a bewildered crouch. A poncho liner, two towels, and a pair of fatigue shorts took flight in the rotorwash, then the canvas cot, tumbling like a stringless kite toward a tangle of concertina wire. The man saluted, then backed matter-of-factly down the ladder, clutching his radio. The 58 swooped across the clearing, executed another sloppy flare, then began to pivot, coming in sideways toward the lawn. The pilot overshot his mark and had to tilt the rotor hard to fight the momentum. The blades dipped toward the ground, then the ship responded, lunging toward the flagpole. The pilot overcorrected again, moved the helicopter the other way, wobbled, and came crashing down in a swirl of grass.

"Damn," Roark said through his teeth. He looked back toward the tower. The operator was inside now and had his bare butt pressed against the window, looking remarkably like a fat man's face. Roark laughed and walked slowly toward the ship, holding a hand over his cap and lowering his head against the rush of debris. When he looked up, the pilot was standing outside the running aircraft, his back turned, tightening the friction on the controls. When the major turned around, Roark was so dumbfounded he almost forgot to salute.

"Morning, sir," he said. The jet exhaust smelled good, like coffee or alcohol after a long abstinence. Someday it would be discovered the fumes were physically addictive.

"Afternoon," the major said, eyeing him as he jerked a cap onto his head. Roark returned the inspection; nobody who was that rotten a pilot deserved too much respect. The major looked like a man with something to prove—long in the arms, short in the legs, and with a hard, protruding belly. The eyes were oiled and sheltered, matching the rust of his hair before it began to whiten. The left cheek was pinched, the nose badly broken. The lower lip had been stitched near the center, and beneath a sweeping white mustache was a silver tooth shining like some outrageous mirror. Something in the set of the head, the way his arms hung at his side, said this was precisely the way the major wanted to look.

The turtle eyes flicked from Roark's collar to his first-tour patch. "I hope you're looking for Delta Troop," he said. On his right shoulder was a tattered patch Roark did not recognize. Stitched to his left shirt pocket was a unit patch matching the yellow flag, bearing a black man-figure with a rifle and conical hat; around were the words LIGHT SCOUTS, D TRP 1/10 AIR CAV, VIET CONG HUNTING CLUB.

"That's right, sir, I am."

"Well, you've found it," the major declared, removing a glove from a rough hand. "I'm George McLeod, the CO." He pumped Roark's hand and body. "Good to see you, son. Let's go inside." He turned and walked briskly away. Roark looked back at the unmanned, running ship, then reluctantly followed the major.

Standing in the doorway of Delta Operations, smiling toward the control tower, was a short captain who had large square teeth and a round head, almost bald. A brown band of hair above his ears was no more than a shadow. His nametag said Dunning. Behind him stood a skinny spec 4 named Acres who wore black-framed glasses and had white, nearly hairless skin.

"I see you've got your helmet," the major said, handing Dunning some papers. "Where's your gear?"

"Down at the shack, sir."

"Let's go get it. I'll show you around the AO." They left the captain in the doorway. When they reached the ship Roark looked back in time to catch Dunning's derisive smile just before the man turned and disappeared inside.

"Is Gil McCawley still in this outfit?" Roark asked.

"Sure is. One of my gun pilots. You serve together?"

"Camp Evans and Wolters. He wrote me about Delta Troop."

"He didn't say anything about you coming."

"He doesn't know." Roark smiled.

By the time they cleared the perimeter, any thoughts of attributing the major's flying technique to anger were completely dispelled. McLeod was rough, with no trace of a control touch; it was plain he had no idea what the term meant. He jerked the controls around the cockpit and stomped the pedals as if he were driving a bulldozer. The little bird skimmed the metal roofs of An Khe before slogging into the sky, redlined and out of trim. Roark was truly frightened; there were no controls on the left side that he could grab in an emergency, which was what this seemed to be. He fumbled for a cigarette, then had a hard time lighting it.

"Used to smoke those things," the major yelled into the intercom. "Finally broke myself. Nasty habit," he said, then he folded his mouthpiece back and spat a syrupy bullet into the jetstream. Only a little splattered against the firewall; some made it overboard, and the rest streaked along the ship.

They flew south at altitude across the top of Four-Mile Mountain and into the jungled hills beyond. The major seemed pleased that Roark was there and rambled along about Delta Troop and its mission. Delta was the aviation element of the 1st Squadron, 10th Cavalry, which consisted of three additional troops of armor. Like the 9th Cav, the 10th had its beginnings in the 1860s as a regiment of buffalo soldiers—black cavalrymen led by white officers—fighting Indians in the American West. The outfit arrived in Vietnam in 1966 and was the reconnaissance unit for the 4th Infantry Division until the 4th went home. The 1/10th was left behind essentially as a road guard, assigned to I (Eye) Field Force Vietnam and Task Force 19, charged with keeping the highway open between the two passes. Secondary responsibilities included reconnaissance of a specified area north and south of the highway, providing aerial cover for supply convoys en route to Pleiku, and the insertion and extraction of recon teams of a Ranger platoon attached to the task force. Delta Troop had recently moved from An Khe to Lane Army Heliport at An Son nearly fifty miles east, not far from Qui Nhon. They still worked the territory, but only a handful of aircraft remained on the plateau overnight. The majority flew back to Lane each evening, returning to war the following day like first-shift commuters.

The troop was a company-sized element consisting of a platoon each of Cobras, Hueys, scouts, and infantry. It was an arrangement designed for aerial as well as limited ground reconnaissance, very effective when used in conjunction with a large reactive force. However, in a region that had once been the base for an entire airmobile division, tiny Delta Troop was now the only aviation unit in operation. The nearest infantry battalions and the helicopters required to transport them were at least an hour away, two counting assembly time, leaving Delta with a lot of potential for getting into trouble and limited resources for getting out.

The redistribution of combat units to accommodate the continuing withdrawal had required considerable juggling of responsibilities and commands. While it was logistically practical to concentrate the aviation units, the move of Delta Troop to An Son presented particular difficulties for Major McLeod. Not only did he have two commanders—administrative and tactical—but Delta Operations, where all the missions were controlled, remained at An Khe a full fifty miles from George McLeod's desk.

Roark listened carefully to the major, feeling better now that they were at altitude, but still wishing he had chest armor, a weapon, and a set of controls. He divided his attention between the ground and the instruments. The rolling terrain was covered with double-canopy jungle, chopped apart by hundreds of random openings, slash-and-burn fields of only an acre or two, some bearing sparse crops of corn. Green, irregular indentions marked abandoned fields overgrown with vines and grass and palms, giving the same deceptive look of many areas in Laos; at its thinnest part, the growth was deep enough to hide an army standing erect.

"There're Montagnards here," the major said. "One of the problems we have to work with. They were supposed to come in for resettlement. Some did, some didn't. Anyway, the official policy is that they don't exist, probably because the Vietnamese government would just as soon we killed them all off. They say they used to be on our side, but that's not true anymore. We know some of them are Cong, maybe some aren't. They're scattered all over these hills, and at the very least they're the major food source for the enemy. There're lots of VC camps around. Then here lately we've been running across more regular NVA, never very many at a time, but enough to know that there's a big nest of 'em out here somewhere. My guess is it's a regiment. I've reported it all to higher . . ." His words trailed off, then he spat again and became silent. Roark watched the land, regularly returning his attention to the cockpit and the neglected gauges.

"I can tell you right now things have changed a lot since your last tour," the major growled. "You'll find out soon enough. Anyway, things are real quiet around here, especially compared to what they could be. The gooks are leaving us alone. They fight when we go out and find them, but An Khe hasn't been hit with a ground attack in more than six months. I think they're trying to make it look like the war's over, just waiting for us to go on home. They're sitting up in those hills, training recruits and piling up supplies, getting ready. And Command is going right along with it. Maybe rightfully so, who knows? Anyway, when we're gone the North Vietnamese will march through here in a single day. The country will be cut in two, and that precious highway we're taking such good care of will look like a freeway from Cambodia to the coast." There was deep frustration in his tone. "We're losing this war by default," he said. "Just giving up."

Surprised at the major's candor, Roark kept his thoughts to himself. They made a large loop and crossed the river several miles below the coils called the Mouse Ears, then turned northwest toward Mang Yang Pass, crossing a wide area of short green grass dotted with tall and individual trees.

"They say there's a blond-headed Frenchman out here, a survivor of the Mang Yang massacre, wandering these hills with nothing more than a knife," McLeod said. "One of the Ranger teams claimed to have seen him a couple of months ago, but from a long way off."

"You believe it?"

"I don't know. I guess not. Hell, it's been seventeen years." The major smiled; the tooth shined behind the mike. "Boy, don't you know he'd be one loony son of a bitch by now!? No, I'd like to believe he's there—I *hope* he's there. Sometimes at night I think about him slipping around in the dark, letting the juice out of some pukey little slope, putting pure terror in the ones he misses. But they couldn't stand that very long, they'd have to find him. He'd have to move around a lot and be smart as hell to last any time at all. So, yes, I'd like to believe he's out there, but no, I don't. Not really."

Roark gazed toward the mountains, imagining a ghostly, silent maniac crouching in the foliage with a knife. It made him remember his own knife, made him feel it against his hip. The major was right; the thought had a lot of appeal.

"Whether he's still alive or not," McLeod said, "he developed quite a reputation. Hell, I even heard about him on my last tour down at Lai Khe. In fact, an S-2 type named Robbies or Robbins or something like that told me there was a green-eyed Montagnard kid in the refugee camp here whose mother claimed to have been raped by the Frenchman. That was a real rip. It was when she still lived in the hills, and the story was that she was out collecting turnip greens for supper. She had this secret place she went to look for them, and one day when she was bent over, the Frenchman launched his attack. Well, she was a fairly young gal, but she was married to this older fellow who couldn't get it up anymore. So, after a while she became pregnant. Well, he knew the baby wasn't his, of course, but he couldn't very well tell everybody that, so he decided to stick it out and play the proud father. But after a few months he gave it up and divorced her anyway."

"When the baby came?"

"No, before that."

"What happened?"

"Said he got goddamned sick of turnip greens."

Roark laughed until tears streaked his face. It just kept coming. He would think he had control, then he'd see a bare brown rump protruding from a turnip patch, and off he'd go. McLeod rumbled along with him like a bear character in a cartoon. They probably don't even have turnips in Vietnam, Roark thought, then he laughed again.

"So what are you doing back over here?" McLeod asked abruptly. "You had to volunteer to come this late a second time. So what's your story, Billy Roark?"

Roark took his time choosing an answer, and when he spoke he kept his eyes out the door. "I came back because it isn't over," he said.

The major was silent a long time. "What d'you fly?"

"Hueys."

"Where?"

"The A Shau and the Z, some across the line."

"What do you want to do now?"

"Scout," Roark said, still gazing out the door. "I want to go out and find the bastards."

McLeod nodded slightly as if some unasked question had been answered. He checked the instruments for the first time since leaving the ground. "You may have come to the right place," he said in a hard, quiet voice. "Are you a good hunter?"

Roark understood what was being asked. He turned and leveled his eyes on his new commander. "Yes, sir," he said. "I am."

"Well, scouting is nothing more than hunting men. Hunting them and making them dead." He spat out the door. "They're short a man now—Batman's going home. But they're a real tight bunch. I can get you in, but staying'll be up to you."

"I don't anticipate a problem," Roark said, studying the ground beneath them. They flew the rest of the way to Mang Yang Pass in silence. The Mang Yang, where the highway made the final climb to the main plateau of the Central Highlands, marked the western limit of Delta Troop's area of operation. Responsibility for the land from there to Pleiku was now in the hands of the ARVNS, McLeod explained, which meant it was largely undisturbed, a true NVA sanctuary. VC Valley, just beyond the pass and to the south, was a prime example. Easily accessible from the highway and with few areas of dense jungle for cover, the narrow valley was now regarded as a place to be completely avoided by aircraft.

"This Vietnamization shit ain't working," the major said. They turned back then, passing two small firebases along the highway, one near the approach to the Mang Yang and the other midway to An Khe. "That's our fireworks," McLeod said. "A battery of one-oh-fives at Alpha Two, one-fifty-fives at Schueller and at An Khe. It's that or airstrikes."

Roark had become increasingly serious during the flight. As they approached An Khe, his attention was drawn to the shape of Hong Kong Hill rising in a solitary cone from flat ground beside the highway. Spreading north and east were the remains of what looked like a leveled city. "That's Camp Radcliff," McLeod said, "where the First Cav used to be. Named after a major shot down over the Mang Yang." Roark studied the place in silence. It was huge. The buildings were gone, and all that was left were rotting sandbags, rusting coils of wire, and blue-black sections of steel plating grown through with brush and weeds. It lacked the hazy mystique, the aura of loneliness and isolation that belonged to Khe Sanh, but it had the same sad look of a place that had been abandoned. The 1st Cav, the fabled outfit that had blazed a bloody path through the I Drang and the A Shau, the unit that produced the scarred and limping young officers of Preflight. Their old camp looked like a graveyard.

As they passed An Khe, his attention shifted to the helicopters still parked on the ramp. He wanted to ask about them, but the major read his thoughts. "They're on standby," he said. "That's mostly what we do around here—stand by. We usually do a recon in the morning, then later we'll cover a convoy coming up from Qui Nhon. Sometimes something extra comes along, but that's about it. Just before sunset we do a last-light mission with a pink team—a scout and a Cobra—just to check things out close to the perimeter and up in the nearest hills. The rest of the time we sit around at the Doghouse like a bunch of goddamned vultures."

They followed the highway past the village, then northward before dropping to low level, cutting east through the Deo Mang— the pass the pilots called An Khe—and descending into the lowlands while the major talked. The weather at An Khe, he said, would be very different from what Roark was accustomed to. It had been a determining factor in the selection of the location for Camp Radcliff. Situated between the northern and southern wind patterns, the plateau sometimes caught the overlap of seasons, but had no true monsoon of its own. Compared to Hue, which received more than ninety inches of rain in the five months of September through January alone, An Khe had almost no weather at all.

Roark was trying to listen, but kept drifting off, so much so he even forgot McLeod's flying. It had been a day crowded with events that would take time to interpret. He wondered about this strange major. "So we're out here on our own," he said. They were skimming along the Song Da Mang, catching the afternoon bathers squatting naked on wide stone steps that let down to the water, hundred-knot glimpses of breasts and bush.

"We may as well be," McLeod said.

A silent minute passed. "So do we look for them, or not?"

"Oh, yeah, we look. And find them eventually. That's our job. It's our obligation."

"And then?"

"We get our asses blown away if we're not careful."

CHAPTER TWENTY-FIVE

GEORGE MCLEOD dropped a dripping ammo can of ice on a crate, tossed his cap, and flipped the switch on a fan. The sun had disappeared beyond the elbow crook of hills; fluorescent amber feathered the shadows. He sat heavily on the edge of his bunk and began to free his aching feet. When he shucked the boots and peeled the damp socks, a matched set of carbuncles glowed brightly on the sides of his big toes. He wiggled his toes, then turned to a reclining position and placed them directly before the fan. Soon the lines of his face relaxed. When he had slept ten minutes he sat up and began building a drink. He held the first sip of Scotch in his mouth and breathed the fumes until the energy began to return.

Maybe coming back wasn't a mistake after all, he thought. As if there had ever been a choice; besides, it seemed a fitting way to wrap things up. He raised the drink and held it, then scooped more ice to make another, shaking his head as he poured. He had never dreamed there would come a day when he would be forced to leave the Army. But then, in the beginning, he never had any idea he would ever want to stay.

The beginning was Korea, though unintentionally. He had never admitted that to anyone, but the first he heard of the conflict was on the bus en route to Basic. He quickly learned to say that he had joined because he had been too young and missed out on the last war. In an Army filled with boys eager to unleash the fanaticism of wartime childhood, it was an explanation which no one questioned. It was also a lie. While it was true he had been too young to be involved in the war with Germany and Japan, even his brother Edward, four years his senior and strong as a buffalo, had not been required to participate in the national inconvenience. The sweep of Uncle Sam's arm missed a few nooks in Montana just like every other place where it bounced across a large enough mound of money.

The suggestion of patriotic zeal was another lie, though George decided he was probably as patriotic as most. It was just that he had never thought about it. He had grown up unconcerned with what was happening in the rest of the country—or the rest of the world, for that matter—an easy thing to do on the Red Cloud where he never listened to the radio and rarely saw a newspaper, or wanted to. So long as he could avoid his father, work outdoors, and get laid now and then, there seemed no call to be concerned about what might be happening miles away. Once Coomie came along, he probably would not have noticed if there had been another world war.

Coomie was a Kutenai from Whitefish who one day found herself at the end of a motorcycle ride in Big Timber and wound up waiting tables. Henry McLeod didn't have much to say when he learned his younger son was seeing the Indian girl, but he was completely blindsided when George brought her onto the ranch three months later and introduced her as his wife. Standing in the blowing dirt in front of the bunkhouse, the old man and the young woman locked eyes. Nothing untoward was said, but bolts of fire fairly flew, mortal enemies to the end.

The end was two rocky years in coming. When she finally disappeared, two days after an early blizzard, George learned about being alone in the wintertime after being with someone. It took a year to convince him he was fortunate she was gone, and a half-dozen women after that to begin to believe it. He had always thought it was funny the way some things stuck while others passed you by unnoticed. He got over her, but he never stopped wanting her. What later surprised him was that as the years went by she aged within his memory. He had no delusions about what she would be like now—fat and saggy from having kids, a tongue still sharp as a bullwhip, and the same black fire still burning in moist, weathered eyes. He knew he'd never see her again even if he did go back to

Montana, but her memory had left him feeling he might someday like to bed an old fat Indian woman who had once been wild.

Coomie had broken the pattern, and by the time she left, things were forever changed. Just as his brother Edward had done, George had been obliged to work the ranch as a hand. This apprenticeship was to have ended at twenty-one when, like Edward, he was to have gone off to Missoula to study animal husbandry and modern ranch management. With more than 42,000 acres under fence and another 20,000 leased from the government, Henry McLeod had plans for both his boys. But Coomie was the spoiler. On top of that, George discovered he liked being a hand and did not give a whit about running the place, especially alongside the obedient Edward.

His father was tolerant for a full year after the girl left, then began to apply pressure. By the time another year had passed, there were open and sometimes public confrontations between them. The situation came to a head one day when Henry invoked the imagined wishes of his dead wife. "It's what your mama would have wanted," he declared in that grandiose tone he used to issue proclamations to the peasants. They were talking about the university again.

"You keep her out of this," George said. He was twenty-three and powerfully built from years of hard work.

"Son, there's things you don't know about your mama."

Quick as a snake, George's left hand leaped out and seized his daddy's throat. The older McLeod did not move, but stared steadily at his son, trying to maintain dignity as he passed toward unconsciousness. George released him to fall choking to the ground, then stalked to the bunkhouse for his gear.

Gertie McLeod had died when George was fourteen, killed by a bolt of lightning which shot from a clear sky before a band of August showers. The field was set ablaze, and Gertie was discovered burned naked when several hands went out to fight the fire. Later, when the sheriff, Jake Arns, was called to see if he knew the whereabouts of Hank McLeod, he said no, then drove out to the place on the Sweet Grass and honked his horn until Henry walked up from the creek. They talked a minute, then Jake put on his dark glasses and drove the postmaster's wife back to her car while the man who owned the biggest ranch in Sweet Grass County raced off in the opposite direction.

George knew the story, though his daddy didn't know he did, just as he knew why his mother had taken to walking evenings in the fields after the week with her sister in Thermopolis. He had never had any doubt who was to blame for his mother's death. It would be years before he understood that the direction of his life had been dictated by a desire to get even with godalmighty Hank McLeod in some way short of killing the son of a bitch.

Korea was where the direction began a life of its own. George quickly made sergeant as a tank driver. Then one desperate afternoon near Inchon when his outfit was caught in a trap and it seemed that all was lost, he got frantic and crazy and earned the Distinguished Service Cross. Back stateside at Camp Hood, that translated to a direct commission to second lieutenant.

He met a blonde named Carletta who, he discovered too late, was known all over post simply as Colonel Johnson's daughter, and it was his misfortune to be the first fool to dance with her on the evening she decided to change her life. She was the sweetest, lovingest, most accommodating female he had ever met, and he was suddenly and totally in love. They were soon married, and as quickly as possible after that she became pregnant. Soon George was a daddy, but not before he realized there would be problems.

Once it was certain she was pregnant, the hook deeply embedded, Carletta's loving sweetness and all the rest of the bullshit came to an abrupt halt, reminding George of something his father was fond of saying, that even the warmest womb could have jaws of cold steel. He began to think he'd be lucky to escape with anything more than a bloody nub. Meanwhile, he had his career to think about. Quite unexpectedly, the Army had become just that—a career. He discovered he liked the machine and decided to stay. He devoted himself to his work, thinking that would save him. But Carletta was not to be ignored, though George did try. First were the manufactured battles in front of a crying child, then later the sideways glances he caught from other men. When it reached the stage where she was no longer trying to hide it, he decided it was time to make a move; he proposed divorce. Carletta took it calmly without committing herself, but two days later George was called to an interview with Colonel Johnson who explained that his daughter was happily married. He decided to hang on.

One October when their son was four, George was sent to Fort Bragg for a month of training. Upon his return, as they drove to the store for milk on Sunday, young Michael confided about the new uncle who sometimes had breakfast at their house. He even knew where he lived and proudly showed his daddy how well he remembered. "You did real good, son," George said, smiling. "Let's not mention this to Mama." He dropped the boy off at home, then said he had forgotten to get cigarettes.

The man who answered the door was an olive-skinned, dark-haired sergeant with Cupid lips and a pretty-boy smile. George introduced himself, then led the fellow outside by the throat where he rattled his face against the concrete corner of the porch until the sergeant could see his own smile without a mirror. Then he stopped at a pay phone to give Carletta a head start.

He felt certain he would pay at the hands of Colonel Johnson, but apparently the man knew his daughter pretty well; besides, the incident served to warn the enlisted men about the perils of officers' wives. George was sent to Germany to join the NATO forces. He also got his divorce, but it was Carletta who landed the killing blow. While he was overseas, she moved away with his son to parts unknown. Then, just to be sure, she changed their names. He tried for months to find them.

He was a captain by then. He made major on sheer momentum when Vietnam came along, but things were no longer the same. A man can train for war, but he can never prepare himself for a Carletta. The realization of the disproportionate power that a ruthless and calculating female can wield was a bitter surprise in his life. After Carletta, Vietnam and the way it was turning out seemed almost a reasonable development. As the years went by, he tried to pretend he didn't have a son, but he *did* have one, out there somewhere. There was never a day he didn't remember that, and never a night he didn't ache. Compounding the pain was the fact that he had no idea what his son looked like now—he might see him someday and not even know it. Sometimes he tried to conjure a face for the boy, but even the strongest image was vague. Green eyes was all that was certain; maybe the hair was still blond.

All along, George had displayed an abrupt, tactless style in his military performance. Montana style was how he thought of it: cut the crap and get the job done. It worked fine as a sergeant and was even tolerated through the rank of captain, though it did begin to be increasingly reflected in his efficiency reports. But tolerance diminished sharply with the rank of major; nonconformity at that stage could only be accepted with an academy background and during a world conflict. Vietnam didn't help. It became increasingly apparent that he was viewed by his superiors as a man who should have remained a sergeant. It was finally explained to him that it seemed unlikely he would ever make lieutenant colonel, and he might want to consider the alternatives. When the suggestion was not taken, he was told more forcefully that he should soon elect to retire. With no real choice, he agreed. He asked for helicopter school and reassignment to Southeast Asia before he left. By the time he got to Vietnam, he no longer cared what anybody thought about his style.

What he did care about was the Army. The power and integrity

that had first attracted him to the massive force had slowly withered away with Vietnam, had been bled out of it by politicians
trying to be generals, and by generals trying to become politicians.
It tore him apart to see what the fools had done to his Army. Even
had he been able, he knew it was too late to repair the damage. It
would take an entirely new generation to even begin, a fresh batch
of young men who had not yet learned how really bad it could get.
And, of course, a fresh batch of politicians who had not yet forgotten the true function of the military.

He downed his drink in a gulp and seined the can for more ice.
He was on his way out of the Army, and Delta Troop was a daily
reminder. With his own Operations beyond range of direct radio
contact and technically under control of a bird colonel, the little
air cavalry outfit seemed custom-made for a man in his position.
Just like the Army and his career, the war was slowly falling apart.
There was nothing he could do to stop it, but for the first time in
months he felt encouraged that it might still be a long way from
being over.

CHAPTER TWENTY-SIX

I T WAS almost 0900 when a scruffy little dog named B.M. walked up to the tent carrying a cap. She laid it carefully on the ground, looked up at Billy Roark, then ambled away toward the mess hall. The morning sky had already passed the moment of deepest blue, beginning now to fade as the sun climbed above the paddies. Though the sides of the big tent were rolled and tied all around, the air beneath the dark canvas was becoming unbearable. Roark put aside the map he had been studying, then walked out and examined the cap. It was damp and smelled of urine. Across the back stitched in black was *Batterman*. The famous Batman. He dropped the cap, wiped his hand against his pants, then brought the map and a metal chair outside.

Batterman was the only other occupant of the tent, a scout shorttimer Roark had not yet seen. His unmade bunk, now gritty with sand, had been vacant all night, and it was empty when the duty officer came around before sunrise trying to find him. Batman, he said, had last been seen at the officers' club when he went outside to take a leak. Roark decided that if the stranger did not show by the time the sun was high enough to do damage, he would backtrack the dog until he found the body.

220

Up the hill on the sunny side of a long building which housed the pilots, the squatting hoochmaids were doing the morning laundry. Through the sound of their screeching, birdlike voices came the steady, stammering *whack!* as they slapped flat sticks against wet clothing. The sunlight made blue-white flares on the black silk across their rumps. Roark studied them several minutes, his eyes narrowed against the glare of the sun and his own prejudice.

The moment the Vietnamese women arrived in a deuce-and-a-half, a sharp-eyed old nag had hurried toward him in a hipless shuffle, squawking back over her shoulder. She was too ugly for even the morning light to soften, sort of an Asiatic, female version of Phillip Crable. Roark was shocked at the thought; already Crable and the trip to Missouri seemed part of something far in the past. He looked beyond the woman toward the others, all of them younger, some almost comely in their black silk pants. He wondered if he had a choice in the matter. It turned out he did not. "You my GI," the woman said in an irritating rasp. The bones of her legs showed sharply through the cloth like the skeleton of a malnourished animal. "I come back ti-ti. Was' clos', shi' boo's. You mi' now. You no talkee otha gull," she said, shaking a warning finger from side to side. "I come back ti-ti. You wai' fo' me." So much for boom-boom with the hoochmaid, he thought.

The hoochmaids were only one of the surprises at Lane. Lying seven miles northwest of the coastal city of Qui Nhon, the camp also sported an officers' club where mini-skirted Vietnamese girls served T-bone steaks and French fries. Just inside the front gate of the heliport was a sheet-metal concession, operated by Vietnamese civilians, that featured a bar with an adjacent massage-and-shower facility known as the Blowbath. Not exactly Camp Evans, and it did not stop there. Not only was the water supply almost unlimited, allowing for showers every day, but USO and other groups came to the club at least once a month, sometimes with strippers from the Philippines and Bangkok. The hoochmaids were there to wash and fold the clothing, clean the rooms, and even do spitshines for a few extra piasters. The women were as virtuous as most, but a few who considered themselves in love had been known to do more, though they were forever ruined after that. Such a blunder by a GI seemed unnecessary, however; Roark had heard that there were sometimes whores in the troop area at night. It all was just a little too incredible. As each astounding amenity became known, his anger grew greater. It was the good-news, bad-news drill; everything they didn't have up north was here, but much too late for what it might once have meant. He glared up the hill toward the girls. It was the boys up north who needed the whores, he thought, not this congregation of flatdick cherries who didn't even know there was a war on. He was suddenly disgusted with the entire scene and with himself, knowing that *he* would enjoy the steaks and showers and girls as much as anyone. But it would at the same time be a constant, unending insult, an affront to everything that had gone before.

Delta's troop area was draped across the eastern end of the low hill of Lane Army Heliport. Most of the living quarters were along the high ground where the men could catch the evening breeze and possibly fight off a night attack if one ever came. But the overflow tent that Roark shared with the unseen Batterman was low in a pocket of dead air between Supply and the foot of the hill. If there was any wind at all, it always came from the direction of the officers' four-holer. It seemed odd that despite all the conveniences, no one had come up with an alternative to crapping in a can. Inside the lovely facility, he had discovered the standard graffito: *Here I sit all brokenhearted, thought I'd shit, but only farted.* Beneath which another wit had penciled: *Don't be so sad at heart—someday you'll shit when you thought you'd fart.*

Around the curve of the hill a capless figure appeared, moving slowly and carefully on legs wide apart, head down and bedraggled. Roark looked up as the man came near. He was a CW2 dressed in stained and rumpled fatigues, damp with sandy orange mud across the back, salt-ringed in front. He was very thin with dark and unkempt hair. His face was red and swollen.

"Morning," Roark said quietly. The figure turned and looked at him, seemed to nod, then shuffled on past in silence. He covered the hundred feet to the bathhouse, fumbled a moment with the screened door, then showered fully dressed. When he came out he shook his head like a wet dog, sending a bright disk of droplets into orbit. He used his fingers and thumbs like pliers to pry his eyelids open, blinked several times, stroked the sides of his head, and walked toward the tent. His hair looked like wet feathers.

"They musta pissed on me all night," he croaked. He sat on the lip of the pallet floor at the edge of the tent. "I fell off the piss point," he added, trying to make things clear. Remembering he was talking to a new arrival, he took a deep breath and slowly explained. When Lane was first constructed, the hilltop was sharply pointed, with three skinny ridges running off in different directions. The Engineers had flattened the hill into a multilevel arrangement of terraces. The club, at the west end of the highest tier, stood only a short distance from the raw edge of the terrace where erosion had made several deep and vertical cuts into the soil. The rest room in the club was inadequate, so the men had taken to walking outside on busy nights, sometimes standing shoulder-to-shoulder, pissing into the black void of one of the eroded cracks, hawking up and spitting, tossing cigarettes. Batterman had lost his balance and fallen into the hole unnoticed. It was ten feet to the bottom, and he was knocked unconscious. So there he spent the remainder of the night in a jointless heap, oblivious to the occasional shower.

"Batterman," he said, extending a damp hand. Water still dripped from his fatigues, leaving freckles in the dust.

"Billy Roark."

"I heard about you," Batterman said. "Some guys up at the club were talking." He glanced at the 101st patch. "Why'd you come back? They said you volunteered."

"I got bored," Roark said dryly.

"Well, if that's the case, you came to the wrong place. They said you want to be a scout. You met Blue yet?"

"A black guy?"

"Yeah."

"More or less," Roark replied.

Batterman looked embarrassed, like he knew something he was not saying. "We flew together," he said. "He extended. He'll make you a good gunner if you don't kill each other." He offered no explanation for the remark, and Roark was in no mood to ask. Following the events of last night, then Blue's stormy entrance in the early morning, he was liking this place and the people in it less all the time.

It had been before sunup when Blue passed through the tent, stomping loudly along the pallet floor. Roark had pulled his cot back inside and was lying on it, listening to the barking cadence of Major McLeod doing calisthenics. The intruder stopped at the end of the bunk and glared at Roark with his hands on his hips. He was dressed in a flight suit and cap, wearing chest armor and carrying a helmet. Roark watched him without moving. It was too dark beneath the tent to see more than the shape and tilt of the head and the whites of the eyes, but the belligerent attitude and the seething anger were unmistakable. He waited without blinking, coiled for defense, thinking that here was another someone come from nowhere just to be his enemy, not even requiring his participation. So be it, he decided. Then the man who was going to be his gunner, whom he would soon be flying with almost every day, and with whom he would share a mutual life dependency, had stomped furiously from the tent without a word.

"They told me you're short," Roark said.

"Yeah, three days," Batterman replied. "And a wake-up."

"So what are you doing in the tent?"

"That's the major's idea. He says that if a man ain't working he doesn't deserve a cush life. I stopped flying twelve days ago—twelve? yeah, that's right—and as soon as the old man figured out what I was doing, he moved me in here. But it's not so bad. I'd sleep in a foxhole now to keep from going back out."

"I thought you said it was boring."

"Mostly it is. We sit an awful lot, but for about two hours each day—at least for whoever has recon—it's real. I went a long time without thinking about it, but when I did I decided it'd be a damned shame if I was to get killed here." He looked up, his face serious. "I don't know who you are, or what you're doing here, but it's a mistake and a waste."

Roark groped for some way to change the subject. "The CDO was by here earlier looking for you."

"Yeah," Batterman said. "Probably got some shit detail for me from the CO." It seemed there was something he wanted to say, but was not sure about. Then he went on. "I wouldn't judge everybody just by last night," he said. Roark looked at him sharply, realizing that there must have been considerable discussion at the club. "The scouts are a bunch of assholes," Batterman continued, "but once you're in, you're in. It's the most dangerous flying there is, and it's all volunteer. When you're out there on a mission, your ass is on the line every second. It's total. It's four men, and there's nothing else, and those four have to be committed to one another more than brothers. It's not like slicks or guns or any other kind of flying. It's recon, pure and simple. That's why the scouts are the way they are. They have to be."

"Makes sense to me," Roark said flatly.

"And right now you're fucking up their system, threatening their lives, by their way of thinking. Keep that in mind."

"I'll do my best."

"Things are fairly screwed up around here anyway. I read a story once about this real bloody game that had replaced football in the future, and every time the guys went out to play, the rules had been changed just a little bit more, always giving them another disadvantage, less of a chance to survive. That's what's happening here. It's a little better since McLeod came, but it's changing in spite of him. It's nothing like it was a year ago." He paused, then a light began to grow. "But I'll tell you something," he said, "it's the only place to be, being a scout. Right in the middle of it all." The light suddenly snapped off. "But that's finished for me . . . I'm going home . . ." He drifted a moment, then looked briefly at

Roark before turning away. "I understand you're going out on a mission tomorrow," he said.

"That's right."

"Well, keep your eyes wide open," Batterman said quietly, gazing up the hill toward the hooches. Then he turned. "I gotta go. If they come looking for me again, just say you saw me but don't know where I went. That'll be the truth." He grabbed his cap from the dirt, stopped by the shower to rinse it, then disappeared beyond Supply.

Roark stared after him until he was gone. It was still the same old thing: one arriving, another going home.

He had not missed Batterman's warning, but after last night it was completely unnecessary. At dusk McLeod had led him up the hill to the officers' hooches. The buildings had recently housed a medical company, gone now as part of the withdrawal. The buildings had generally the same lateral dimensions as a standard hooch, but were more than a hundred feet long, each adjoining another end to end by a continuous roof. Inside were private rooms with ceilings, concrete floors, and painted walls. Most had furniture left behind by previous occupants, as well as electrical outlets and recessed fluorescent fixtures. No stateside opulence like some enjoyed, but certainly plush by Army standards. Air conditioners projected from a few of the windows.

The scout pilots occupied the eastern end of a building near the highest part of the hill. A stone retaining wall lined a pathway in front and wrapped around a wide terrace at the side which contained a sand-filled volleyball court, a wooden sun deck with outdoor furniture, and a round umbrellaed table. The flight line, the front gate, and a fourth of the camp could be seen from that elevation, as well as the Korean compound to the south. East in the flat darkness of the paddies, dim specks of light floated on a single plain like lanterned boats at sea. Qui Nhon seemed very near.

The major led the way down the hall and stopped before a white door on which was painted THE RECTUM in large brown letters. Above was a generous rendition, a brown-rayed sun in eclipse. The surface of the door buzzed with the beat of drums. When McLeod's first knock went unanswered, he bashed at the door with a hammered fist until the hinges rattled. "Yeah," a voice yelled, then the music was lowered. "Yeah?"

McLeod tried the knob, but the door was bolted from the inside. "Open the goddamned door," he growled. Somebody slid the bolt back, and the music stopped. The major turned the knob and stepped into swirling red darkness.

In addition to being the quarters of two scout pilots, the Rectum was a gathering place due to its size and air conditioner. A wall had been removed to combine two rooms, and the rectangular space divided into sleeping quarters, a central living room, and a small bar and kitchenette. The air was icy. Red figures tumbled in the revolving sweep of a rotating beacon mounted on the wall, the only light in the room. No one spoke. After groping for a moment, the major found the switch and flipped on the lights, revealing four squinting, blinded men, all in T-shirts, holding cigarettes and drinks. He gave them a few seconds for their eyes to adjust, then announced, "This here is Billy Roark. He's second tour, and he's joining the scouts." Roark thought the introduction was rather abrupt, and the scouts seemed to agree. None of them said a word. McLeod pointed a finger at each of the men and called their names. "Talley, Cook, Jarvis, and Gladewater."

Roark followed his aim and nodded stiffly at each. Cook and Jarvis returned the greeting. "Lieutenant Jarvis is the scout platoon leader," McLeod added. Roark looked at Jarvis and nodded again, this time with a puzzled frown. McLeod was not following form.

"Are you asking or telling?" It was Victor Talley, a blond kid who looked nineteen and wore a distinctly snotty expression. His hair was cut close on top, greased and swept back on the sides, and his lips were curled in a sneer. He was sprawled on a bunk to the right, slumped against the wall with a cigarette hanging from his lips.

The major's head turned slowly around like the clanking turret of a tank. "Telling," he said.

There was a long silence. On the other bunk was Charlie Cook who looked about a year older. He had a wide face, straight brown hair, and a heavy mustache. He moved his eyes around the room as if he were amused. Jarvis and Gladewater sat in cushioned chairs with hard, implacable faces. Jarvis stirred his drink with a finger, and the ice made a clear tinkling in the room. "Scouts choose the scouts," Talley said.

"I know that," the major said in a surprisingly mellow tone, "but Roark's got experience—not scouting, but up north—and we're short one. He'll take Batman's place."

"Not likely," Talley fired back.

That was when McLeod earned a nickname. "Look, you little peckerhead," he said, "unless you want your face to look like mine when you grow up, start calling me sir, goddamn it."

Talley blanched at the insult and the physical threat behind it. McLeod was the only mature man in the room, and the difference that could make in a scrap was not wasted on anyone. But scouting did little to develop social discretion. Talley steamed ahead. "Well, I sure wouldn't want that, *Sir Goddamnit.*"

"That's the way it's always been, sir," Charlie Cook said quickly. His voice was smooth and quiet, respectful but firm. "That's the way it has to be."

"That's right," Jarvis, the senior scout, said. "He has to be approved by us." Up until that point he had seemed content just to watch. Gladewater, the newest in the group, sipped his drink and said nothing.

McLeod looked around the room, considering the young men. They were intelligent, alert, aggressive, insubordinate, and moderate-to-complete buttholes—just like him, exactly what scouting produced and required. "He's got a lot of hours, a lot of experience," he said. "He's spent a year getting shot at, and he came back over here to be a scout. I don't think there'll be a problem."

The four looked at Roark as if he were defective merchandise. "Okay, Major," Talley said. "We can check him out for you, take him out and see how he does. Not tomorrow, 'cause we've got that bunch out at No-Name to work over, but the day after. He can be my gunner." He turned to Roark. "Can you handle a sixty?" he asked.

Roark recalled the time so long ago when Gil McCawley had asked a similar question. "I'm sure it'll be tough," he said, "but I'll do my best to manage." He gave each of the scouts a glance, then opened the door and stepped out into the hallway. A moment later, McLeod joined him.

"You've kind of got a short fuse," McLeod said.

"I didn't come back to play."

"Don't let it get you," the major said. "It's just the way they are. You won't have any trouble."

"I never expected to," Roark replied, more sharply than he intended. McLeod was quiet as they walked down the hill. " 'Night, sir," Roark said when they reached the tent, his anger gone. He stood and watched the wide shoulders move away.

The night was quiet and empty, the air completely still. A billion perfect specks of stars pierced the heavens. He dragged his cot outside and lay a long time smoking, watching for circling satellites. When at last he spotted one he threw smoke rings around it until it disappeared on its endless journey to nowhere. He felt comfortable about the days ahead, knowing now for certain that coming back was right. He thought about the Frenchman then, the man in the Gahan Wilson cartoon. Sometime in the night he heard the dog named B.M. curl up in the dirt beneath his cot.

* * *

Toward sunset, Gil McCawley appeared along the path leading up from the flight line. When he glanced over and saw Roark sitting outside the tent, he stopped dead still, stared, then began to shake his head. When he walked over, a quiet smile was spread across his face, his head still moving like he couldn't believe it.

"Serves you right for not telling me you were leaving," Roark said.

"I didn't want to be a bad influence," McCawley replied. They shook hands warmly, then McCawley sat down. "You might have picked a better place, though." He produced his pack, and they both lit up.

"From what I hear, it's all gone to hell. Wish the facilities had been like this up north."

"No kidding. Say, what did you do to your arm?"

Along the outside of Roark's left forearm was a fresh pink scar two inches long. He looked at it thoughtfully. "Snagged it on a barbed-wire fence," he said. He gazed around the camp, then, with his eyes on the mountains to the south, said, "I don't have to ask why you came back, but what made you leave Wolters?"

"It just wasn't the same," McCawley said. He suddenly looked very tired. "I decided I didn't want to teach anymore."

"What made you pick guns?"

"Well, I knew I didn't want to fly slicks or VIPs, and I sure didn't want to be a scout. Guns seemed to make the most sense. What are you flying?"

"Scouts."

"I should have known that," McCawley said. "You always were the hunting type, always trying to find the war."

"So how do you like flying guns?"

"I like it," McCawley said. "More than I thought I would. It grows on you. When I was flying slicks there was always the question of how you were going to explain it all. Just flying around, stupid, waiting for somebody to blow you away. There's something real satisfying about thumbing that red button, watching the rockets reach down. Something happens now, at least I'll have an answer."

Roark was watching the mountains, darkening far to the south. High in the pockets of high ravines, haze was beginning to form, unreasonably blue from the evening fires of the men on the other side. He smiled with quiet understanding, thinking that McCawley had summed it up as well as anyone possibly could.

CHAPTER TWENTY-SEVEN

MASCULINE MUSIC rolled from the ramp—the metered tick of igniters, the lusty heart-timing beat of blades, the thin steel voices of the turbine song. Though outwardly calm, projecting workaday boredom, Roark was charged with excitement, only slightly tempered by another encounter with Spec 5 Blue. He checked himself and his equipment, then buckled the belt in a loose loop, steadied the machine gun dangling from the door frame, and leaned out and cleared the left side of the ship. He made a thumbs-up signal. Victor Talley acknowledged, but waited for the four other birds to call ready.

The sun was well above the green mountains, already empty of golden morning tone. Along the oiled ramp, gouts of clear burned air tumbled from the ships, distorting images as through a mirage. The heavy Cobras, or Snakes, which had parked in the open, were the first to move, rising slowly, nose low—ponderous, meditating beasts, muscle-bound and dumb. Inside the blue canopies, tandem faceless shapes of visored helmets turned like mechanical parts, revealing nothing human. Behind the turrets, painted shark's teeth snarled in a bloody maw.

The quicker 58s, the Little Boys, waited until the guns had

taken the taxiway, then rose nimbly from the revetments, darted past the Cobras, and took the active at a run. By turn, each of the gunships hovered inches above the strip, eased slowly forward, scraped and bumped, then struggled into the air, explosive anvils hung from spinning blades. Thin as wafers from the rear, they gathered speed and climbed away toward the southern sky. Last came the chase ship, the rescue bird in case anything went wrong. The Huey rose carefully from the corner of the ramp, moved down the taxiway at a standard three-foot hover, made a precise pedal turn onto the active runway, then executed a textbook takeoff. When it had cleared the wire and was climbing to altitude, its pilot called the air mission commander in the lead gun to say that his flight of five was safely off.

The warm air turned cool, churning through the open cockpit, drying the nervous moisture beneath Roark's helmet. He had a sudden, reassuring sense of being back where he belonged. The machine gun in his hands said it all. He flexed his arms and held its weight and smiled, then gave a tug on the ammo belt feeding from a can behind the seat. He checked the linkage, cleared the bolt, opened the breech, then clamped the cover down firmly across the first round. He flipped the selector, flexed his arms again, and gazed toward the ground, calculating how much he would have to lead a target. He was ready now, the strain of the morning past.

It had begun rather clumsily, unacquainted with procedure, not knowing how things were arranged or done. He was familiar with the M-60; he had fired it many times during his first tour and had spent almost an hour of the previous afternoon on the western perimeter at Lane, firing John Wayne style toward the surrounding hills. Though the rocky faces near the top were a thousand feet away, he discovered he could see the bullets splatter and could aim quite effectively from the hip. It made him realize how easy it would be to shoot a helicopter down. It also brought to mind another cold fact: The mysterious people in Research and Development, who must not have comprehended exactly what it was that scout ships did, had decided that the little birds didn't need armor beneath their seats; the Hueys and gunships did, but not the scouts. Roark remembered a bloody Loach he had seen parked outside 18th Surg at Evans—six rounds through the left seat—and he still could feel the bump of bullets against his own precious butt that bitter afternoon in Laos. Being a scout meant literally putting your ass on the line. It made him wonder how the dollars saved stacked up against the asses lost.

Talley's regular gunner, an eighteen-year-old named Grouper, had walked down to the flight line in the dim predawn to help out, passing up a chance to sleep in on his unexpected day off. But he knew that the first sergeant had a habit of sometimes walking through the hooches before morning mess, grabbing idle men for details. Grouper was short and thin and had oily red hair, acne, and a perpetual smile. Unlike Clayton Blue, who maintained his distance, avoiding even looking in his direction, Grouper seemed to think nothing was unusual about a pilot going out for a day as a doorgunner. He showed Roark how to rig the gun and ammo can, where to hang the smoke grenades, the black concussions, and the numerous pink incendiaries. "Things happen real fast out there," he said casually, clipping the gun to a D-ring and bungee attached to the door frame. The weapon was the same version as those used in the field, with a pistol grip and a plastic forestock. The barrel had been hacksawed flush with the gas cylinder to make it lighter and easier to handle. The modification made it less accurate, but at close range that was not necessarily a disadvantage. "The best thing you can do in any situation is just start shooting. Squeeze this little thing here," he said, grinning, indicating the trigger, "and everything will be fine."

On the opposite side of the ship, Victor Talley was just completing the preflight. He strapped himself in to the right seat and began the start-up procedure, glancing now and then toward Roark to show that his attitude had softened.

"What's all the stuff in your pockets?" Grouper asked.

"Survival gear," Roark replied. Grouper made a face like he didn't think it would matter, then showed him how to feed the ammo so it wouldn't bind. He stood beside the revetment, squinting and holding his cap against the wind until they were gone, then waved good luck before heading up the hill to find a cool place to hide.

The briefing at An Khe was short and informal. The pilots gathered before a plasticized map where a block of grids fifteen klicks north of the highway were bordered in black crayon. Talley protested the instant he entered the room. "Bullshit," he said. "We're not going up there." Several men suppressed smiles.

"And why not?" Farrell Dunning asked, his voice indignant and condescending, edged with exasperation. The operations officer had been in the unit only a month, but already had made known his opinion that warrant officers and scouting produced the most unmilitary combination.

"There's nothing there," Talley replied. "And even if there were, we couldn't find it."

"And how do you know if you don't go look?"

"We've been there," Charlie Cook said. "There's a few camps

around, but not many, and they're too hard to find." Though Cook and Talley were both lead scouts, they had doubled-up today instead of allowing a less experienced man to fly wing off Talley, a fact that Roark had not overlooked.

"All the more reason to check it out," Dunning replied. The chase pilot, a second-tour CW2 named Corbish, stood in the doorway catching the breeze. He shook his head slightly, but said nothing.

"Not so," Talley said. "It's triple-canopy jungle, and not even near the river. There's no fields at all, which means there's no food, and there's no major trails between here and there. We've got more dinks west and south than we've got napalm to bake, more than we've got time to find. That's where we need to be working."

"Well, I disagree."

"He's really right," McCawley said. "They've got to move too slow to find anything, and if one of 'em was to go down, we'd never get 'em out. It's just too thick."

"Smoke won't even make it through the trees," said his frontseater, Shadrach.

"There's just not much we can do up there," said Kirby Hockett, the gun wing. "If higher wants to know what's there, they need to either defoliate or put in some ground teams."

"Both of which are going out of style," Dunning said.

"Look, Captain," Talley said, more conciliatory now. "They've got us restricted to one recon per day, two hours of mission time. Every time we go out we find at least one base camp, sometimes more, right? And where are they? You keep track of them. They're west and south where there's access to the road, the village, and the food supply. I'm sure there're dinks to the north—we've found some of 'em—but we can go up there and spend our entire two hours and come back with nothing. Now if they'll let us go back to doing two missions a day, okay, but as it is I think it's a waste. It just doesn't pay. Besides, I've got a new doorgunner today, and I want to be sure we find something, break him in right." Several of the men snickered, and they all looked at Roark. He smiled tightly, unembarrassed, dwelling on Talley's words.

"Okay," Dunning said, "we'll change it. But I still think we need to do some visual recon missions up north."

"I agree," Talley said. "Just get 'em to let us fly more missions, and I'll be all for it."

"We both know that's not going to happen. So where do you want to go?"

"Here." Talley outlined a section of map about six miles south of An Khe. "We haven't worked that area in eight weeks. There'll be something there for sure."

Everyone but the scouts marked their maps, then the covey of pilots funneled through the door. Somebody broke wind tremendously. "Taking fire!"

"Secondary!"

"Rolling in hot." Shadrach lifted a leg and ripped another. The others gave him room, and the group gradually dispersed as they moved toward the ramp. Roark walked between McCawley and Hockett. Both had been off yesterday and had accompanied him to the firing range. Ahead he could see Blue moving between the two Kiowas.

"You sure you know what you're doing?" Hockett asked. He was a warrant officer, short and lean with dense black hair prematurely sprinkled gray. Tangled black brows shielded his eyes.

"Maybe you should try it," Roark said, smiling. "You seem the gung-ho type."

"But I'm not crazy. I want to blast some gooks, but from a distance, thank you."

"No kidding, Roark," McCawley said. "I wouldn't do what you're doing for anything."

"It's better than being strapped into one of those tandem coffins like you guys fly."

"They say people like us come back because we left something here," McCawley said, "but has it occurred to you that maybe you left something extra?"

"Could be," Roark said, eyeing the hills. "Could be."

Approaching the ships, the thrashing shadow of a twin-rotored Chinook skittered across the ground like a frantic animal. Everyone turned their eyes toward the sun as the pilots split apart. "Kill a Commie for Christ," Hockett called.

"Fucking-A," Roark said with a grin. He untied the rotor, then walked up the left side of the ship. Four incendiary grenades were missing from the piano wire strung along the jamb. While Talley strapped himself in, Roark checked everything else, then walked to the next revetment where Blue and Charlie Cook were getting cranked. Without a word or glance he removed four grenades from Blue's stock.

"What th' fuck!" Blue yelled, but made no move to stop him. The spec 5 had high cheekbones, a flat, square forehead, heavy brow bones, and darkly venomous eyes. His anger and hatred emitted a force like an electrical field. "Motherfucker!" he spat, only partly under his breath.

Roark returned to his ship and got himself ready, ignoring Talley's questioning look. He wondered about Blue, who had bumped Cook's regular gunner just to be on this flight. Things seemed likely to get a lot worse between them before they got better. That thought amused Roark; he was beginning to look forward to flying with Blue. He glanced around, cleared the ship again, and turned his thoughts to hunting gooks. In a few moments the flight was off, the mountains outside his door, the wind all around, and he was part of a mission going out to kill the enemy. Quite a switch from a galleried duck in the A Shau. He hefted the gun and smiled stiffly into the wind, careful not to let Talley see.

While the rest of the flight climbed to altitude, the scouts crossed the Song Ba low level, then skimmed along the western bank. When they test-fired the sixties in the low scrub just short of the Mouse Ears, the powerful gun felt fantastic in Roark's hands, bucking and snorting, blazing ragged gouts of yellow fire into the wind. He swept the weapon around with enthusiasm, only to hear Talley yell when the ejection angle sent a stream of red-hot shells bouncing off his helmet. The aircraft wobbled as Talley dug a couple of cartridges from between his legs, then the two Little Boys climbed out to five hundred feet in wing right, crossed the river, and headed south. High above, keeping a watchful eye, were the gunships, and higher still, the chase.

The area Talley had selected was beyond the southern slopes of Four-Mile Mountain. It was an irregular block of low jungle bounded on the east by a shallow stream nearly hidden by trees, and on the west by a low and branching ridge line running north toward Four-Mile. The tangled canopy on the higher slopes was gapped like missing teeth by fields of stumps and growing corn. Farther down, the terrain smoothed to rolling jungle, cut occasionally by ravines deepening eastward, all buried beneath a tangle of dense bamboo, broadleaf trees, palms, and blanketing vines.

The flight approached obliquely from the west, avoiding overflight until Talley had the entire zone in sight. He studied it carefully to make a firm mental image that would guide him once they were among the trees. Then the two Little Boys turned their backs on the area and began a steep descent. When they were on the deck, they turned back sharply, skimming the treetops, using ridges and ravines to screen their approach. From that point, direction of the mission switched to the lead scout, with overall command still resting with the air mission commander, McCawley. He ordered radio silence on the UHF, the doorgunners slipped halfway out of the ships with their left feet on the skids, their right inside, and the reconnaissance work began.

An abandoned field near the top of the ridge gave an upper tree-line an unobstructed view of much of the area, so the scouts checked that first, sweeping across it low and fast to draw fire, then again much slower for a better look. A .51 could have done a lot of damage from there, booming down from above, so they checked it once again, very carefully. The wing scout, called Al-phie, maintained a covering position forty-five degrees off lead's right, adjusting separation with speed so his gunner was always in position to place effective fire. All turns were made to the left, keeping the gunners in visual contact with the jungle. Communi-cations were on UHF with both doorgunners put on line so that everything they said was heard by the entire flight.

When he was satisfied the field was clean, Talley made a wide descending sweep to the creek bottom, flew a single pass along its length at fifty knots, then moved back to high ground. He knew from the beginning where he wanted most to search—an almost flat area of mixed bamboo and trees halfway between the sloped fields and stream—but there was more preparation to be done. Methodically, but quickly, they worked the high ground, sweep-ing back and forth across the slopes, moving lower with each pass. The gunners reported an occasional footpath, but nothing more.

At last Talley broke from the pattern, skipped a sloped band of thirty-foot scrub, and moved into the bamboo. He circled the area at fifty knots, glanced around to do an assessment, picked his route, and slowed his airspeed to twenty knots. The two birds moved along just clear of the growth, fanning it with rotorwash. "I got hooches," Blue said. Roark had seen nothing. Talley sig-naled a quick left turn, and they crossed the area again, slightly faster.

"Yeah, I got 'em," Talley said. Roark looked quickly around, completely baffled. Where? he wondered. The surface of the bam-boo formed an impenetrable mat. He leaned far out on the skid, straining to see.

"Coming left," Talley said. As they came around, the bamboo swayed, an opening appeared, and Roark saw deeply into the complex—thatched hooches, bare swept earth, scattered baskets. He jumped as a brown chicken darted across a clear space and almost blasted it. Then the bamboo window slammed shut, and the base camp vanished. He tugged gently at the ammo belt, then leaned farther out, his eyes wide. He could feel his body tightening.

When they had made four passes without drawing fire or seeing anyone, Talley turned a tight circle over the complex, said, "Go high, Alphie," and brought the ship to a near-stationary hover. Cook commenced a slow circling pattern, slightly higher and at a distance that would provide covering fire and allow enough room for Talley to move in a hurry. The downward force of the rotorwash took complete effect, and the hooch complex was suddenly opened for their inspection. Leaning far out the door and peering straight down, Roark began to report. "Four, five hooches, looks like more to the east, a few chickens. Got a mess kit, a khaki rucksack, pieces of clothing, khaki shirt, black pants. Can't tell what's in the hooches." Talley let the ship drift slowly forward. "More hooches," Roark said. "Looks like eight or nine. *Goddamn.*"

"What?"

"Got a bunker. Two-by-two opening. Move forward, it's looking straight at us. There's another one at ten o'clock." Suddenly the war took on an entirely different dimension for Roark; it was no longer flying above it in relative safety; it was not even dashing into a hot LZ with the heroic excuse of delivering ammunition or trying to pull someone out; it was instead the bloody, suicidal, everyday insanity of trying to kill someone who was trying to kill him. Never before had it seemed so much like a thrilling, horrific game.

Suddenly he could see himself and the little helicopter from the deep shadows of a bunker, hear the hovering devils, the thrash of bamboo, feel the occasional puff of air against his face. Across the square of light was the silhouette of an AK, cool in his sweaty hands, ready. Then he was in the bird again looking past his boot, the machine gun poised, his eyes jerking all around. A frantic wave swept through him. He could feel the indecision of the enemy, the crouching body crushed between helplessness and strength, awaiting the imbalance when hiding in a hole would be no longer acceptable.

The energy of fear was suddenly loose like concentrated light. His left leg began to tremble, then his boot was tapping hard against the skid. He had a sudden vision of his balls dangling beneath the ship, sacred jewels, fragile as Christmas tree ornaments. Then all at once it was okay; nothing else existed but him and his enemy, life complete. Soon the man would appear, and one of them would kill the other; there was no longer any fear or thrill or doubt. "Did you hear me?" Talley said. "I said start burning the hooches."

"Right." Without releasing his weapon, he grabbed an incendiary grenade with his left hand, snagged the ring on the door pin, let the spoon pop, then held it sputtering at arm's length until it was thoroughly ignited. The Thermite grenades, designed to destroy such things as motor blocks, armored vehicles, and cannon, performed adequately on a dry thatched hooch. Roark dropped the grenade and watched as the rotorwash fanned the flames, igniting an adjacent roof with blowing sparks. He guided Talley toward others. In less than a minute the complex was ablaze, sending tall torches above the bamboo.

"We're coming out, Two-three, but we're going to stay close," Talley said. Cook assumed the wing position as the Little Boys gathered speed. They established a slow orbit around the burning complex at a distance safe from secondaries, watching for movement. The camp quickly became an inferno. As the blazing hooches developed into fiery onions, the surrounding bamboo withered to naked stalks, leaving all the area open to the sky. In only minutes the flames had dwindled to flicking tongues, and the thin black smoke drifting across the jungle changed to smoldering blue. From high in the gunships or perhaps from a distant mountain, the smoke was a curved and angling finger pointing across the hills toward a speck of devastation.

"We're going back in, Two-three," Talley said.

"Roger, One-four, gotcha covered. Be advised we've only got three-zero minutes left on station."

"One-four, roger." The complex was an oblong swath of charred earth and blackened posts. Two more bunkers that no one had seen were plainly visible now. Nothing moved. After swinging wide, the two birds turned back and flew quickly past the camp several times. "Two-three, we'll be reconning by fire," Talley said, then on the intercom to Roark, "Go ahead and put some lead in those holes." Roark fired a long burst on the next pass and managed to put a number of rounds into two of the openings. Beyond his vision, he could hear Blue's gun hammering away, but the fire went unanswered. "That's good," Talley said. Blue fired a few seconds longer.

"Slowing," Talley called, and they moved past again, watchfully, but still perfect targets to anyone waiting in the depths of the bunkers. Nothing. They slowed still more, then turned and moved along the opposite length of the burn.

Now it was different for Roark. He stood far out from the ship with his right leg crooked inside, leaning confidently against the belt, sweeping around in search of movement, knowing that if that scrawny chicken made another appearance there wouldn't be enough left for soup. He felt especially fine, though he was still trembling. The ships slowed and moved across the complex, then back again. "Go high," Talley said. Alphie went into orbit. "See anything else?" he asked.

"Not yet," Roark replied, looking all around, moving the gun barrel with his eyes. He glanced up then as Alphie came around and caught a glimpse of Blue looking back at him, smiling strangely. Quickly he shifted his eyes back to the ground, to the remains of a hooch. Smoke and ashes, fanned by the blades, swirled through the cockpit.

Suddenly a burst from a machine gun splintered a bamboo post beneath Roark's skid, sending shards in every direction. He fired reflexively, drawing the weapon quickly in the direction of the bunkers, teeth gritted, eyes intense, his left hand mechanically working the belt of ammo. The earth erupted with the impact of bullets, and tracers careened as the ship nosed sharply downward. "Taking fire!" Talley yelled, pulling in everything he had. High overhead, McCawley was just coming around; he rolled in on target and waited for the Little Boys.

The scouts had hardly moved when it came together for Billy Roark—calmly in a separate part of his brain—the angle of fire, the sound of the weapon, the smile on the angry face. Cook's bird was at eight o'clock, Blue firing toward some trees upslope. Roark swung his weapon toward Blue, still firing, sending a stream of tracers hurtling beneath him. With the amputated barrel, he dared not shoot as close as he wished, but it was enough when Blue looked up and into the belching flame, the look of terror as he scrambled backward. Then Cook's bird was around on the opposite side, and the two ships were hurrying across the jungle. Pausing only an instant, Roark brought the weapon forward until the angle was correct, then fired a long burst into the vacant growth. "Goddamn it! Cease fire! *Cease fire!*" Talley screamed as the stream of debris peppered his head. He howled as two hot shells went down his collar and lodged against his armor. Roark released the trigger and turned his eyes back toward the complex. Two pairs of seventeen-pounders slammed into the base camp, four quick bursts of flashing red, sending up lunging waves of orange earth, spreading clouds of gray and tan. Heavy, staccato thuds rattled the ship. A red cloud was beginning to rise from a smoke grenade that Blue had thrown, and the jerking motion of the air ragged the edges. Then came the vomiting sound of the minigun as the Snakes traded places, and the barrage of rockets resumed. When McCawley rolled out, a dirty, bloody cloud moved slowly away, low against the jungle. Talley fished the shells out of his shirt and threw them across the cockpit and out Roark's door.

"One-four, you guys okay down there?" McCawley said.

"We're okay. You, One-eight?"

Charlie Cook made a wheezing noise that sounded like a sucking chest wound, but it soon developed into a weird, hissing laughter. "Yeah, we're okay," he finally said.

"Okay, One-four, we're high and dry if you want to take a quick look," McCawley said. "Then we gotta head back."

"Roger, Two-three," Talley said.

Blue finally found his voice. "That motherfucker tried to shoot me," he yelled, his words high and breaking. "He tried—" Cook apparently flipped his gunner's selector to intercom; nothing else was heard from Blue.

"What d'you do?" Talley asked as they circled back.

"Nothing," Roark said. "Just returned fire."

What had been a lovely shaded camp was now a dusty, smoking scar of splinters, ash, and black-charred earth. It smelled of sulfer, cordite, and plowed ground. There was nothing left to do. The scouts made two slow passes, then the flight turned toward An Khe.

After the engines had cooled and been shut down, after the blades had coasted almost to a halt, Blue strode forcefully around the revetment, then stood pointing a finger at Roark, looking at Talley. "He tried to shoot me!" he yelled. Roark's helmet was off, his armor turned wet-side-out against the seat. Giving Blue only a glance, he fished his folded cap from a shin pocket and pulled it firmly over his head. "What the fuck are you trying to do?" Blue demanded, his fists on his hips, madness in his eyes.

Roark folded the excess ammunition back into the can, leaving the end hanging over the seat, then began transferring the remaining incendiaries from the piano wire to the outside lip of the can. He straightened and looked calmly at Blue. "Just returning fire," he said. Talley was out of the ship now, standing nearby with Charlie Cook.

"Like hell! You were shooting at me!"

"No, I was shooting at that gook. You didn't see the gook?"

"There wasn't any dink out there," Blue said.

"Then what were you shooting at?"

Blue hesitated. "I heard fire," he said.

"So did I," Roark said. "I wasn't shooting at you, Blue." He reached over to pat him on the shoulder, but Blue jerked away. "Why would I want to kill my own doorgunner?"

Blue's eyes flared; he stalked back to his ship to the sound of Charlie Cook's breathless, squeaking laugh. Victor Talley unbuttoned his shirt, revealing two red marks on a hairless chest.

"Damn," he said, his chin pushed downward. "Other than this, you did all right out there." Charlie Cook laughed harder, and his voice finally got involved. The sound was thin and airy.

"Fucking-A," Roark said in a low voice. He was smiling absently, gazing toward a place beyond the top of Four-Mile Mountain.

X

I was in a bar between tours and met this dude named Pinkleton. He looked like a lawyer, but said he had been in the infantry. He named some place and outfit I'd never heard of, but there were lots of those.

He had a wife named Patsy who reminded me of the telephone operators at Rucker. In Phase II of flight school if you wanted to call home you had to go down to the phone room about a mile from our company area. Like most of Fort Rucker, the building was a pre-war cinder box painted military cream. The operators sat before switchboards behind a partition of wood and glass; the rest of the room was nothing but phone booths lining the walls. I asked an older lady at a window what to do, then found an empty booth and waited.

Finally Operator 17 came on the line, and about ten seconds after that I knew I was in love. Her voice was a beautifully played clarinet, high and lilting one moment, low and throaty the next, playing a sensual performance just for me. She poured herself into my ear and swam all through me. She was friendly and chatted a lot more than her job required, and I had sudden visions of doing great havoc inside her panties. I was lonely, but it was more than that. She was everything female and I was everything male; I was going off to war to get killed in a few weeks, and she was somehow part of the reason, maybe all of it. Everything seemed complete.

When my call was finished she came on the line again and we talked some more. Then she had to go and so did I. I took off my flight jacket and carried it in front of me to hide the wet place, then walked slowly past the windows looking for Operator 17. She was watching for me, and she turned in her swivel chair and smiled and fluttered her fingers and said something to the girl beside her. I glanced around the room. There were eight of the little dumplings there, the best part of a metric ton.

When I got in my car I stuffed a couple of Whataburger napkins down inside my underwear and drove on back to the barracks frustrated and disillusioned, incomplete again, going to war for no reason at all.

All this to say that Pinkleton's wife was fat. But she was a sweetie. She said she had been a go-go dancer two years before when they met, thin with a tight little ass. They both told me that several times. By then I was trying to figure out how to get gracefully out of there, but every time I made a move to leave, Pinkleton would grab my arm and buy another round and insist I stay. He was getting smug, storytelling drunk, and kept talking about the war. I looked around the room, hoping he'd shut up or change the subject. Then something set me off.

"Sorry, fellas," he said, smiling, holding his glass high, toasting the ghosts of the thousands he must have killed. "It was nothing personal."

I turned around, feeling like a napalm canister on the way down, tumbling end over end. "Well, it was goddamn sure personal to me," I said. "I'd like nothing better than to go back and kill every fucking gook in Vietnam and I guarangoddamntee you every time I pulled the trigger I'd mean it. That's personal, motherfucker!"

It was okay for me to leave then. Later I remembered the way Pinkleton's wife looked at me, not shocked or dismayed, but suddenly knowing that her war hero had killed no one, equally certain he had never seen a buddy die.

For a long time I was embarrassed about that night, thinking maybe I was wrong. Finally I understood that my only mistake was talking. The fact is that at the bottom rung where the killing takes place, war is as personal as it ever gets.

CHAPTER TWENTY-EIGHT

THE DOGHOUSE at An Khe was littered with men. Four pilots bent over a wooden table, mechanically playing spades, while a lazy breeze shifted between two doorways and a gaping hole in the west wall where some dreamer once had planned a fireplace. Slumped at an adjacent table was a dozing pilot, his arms and feet crossed, a crushed cap draped across his face. Opposite sat another, forehead on his arm, trailing saliva.

It was just past noon. Outside on a patio lay several men in varying stages of undress, working on their tans. Nearby, in the shade of an ancient eucalyptus, Billy Roark sat fully dressed on a weathered crate, waiting for a mission. Pressed into a wallowed cavity at his feet like gobs of mud lay three mongrel mutts named Yardcrap, Downdamnit, and Cunt.

"It could be worse," Hockett called, raising his head from a cot. "You could be getting your ass shot off." Sweat glistened on the flat of his belly, burned purple-brown. Roark gave him a look, then shook his head. He checked his watch, wiped the moisture from his face, and leaned back against the building, studying the mountains beyond the Greenhouse. Yardcrap opened one yellow eye, then closed it dreamily.

After two months, everything new about An Khe was old. Roark kept thinking about the 101st—how the men passed out from fatigue instead of hangovers, how the average day was seven hours in the air, how the aircraft and men were pushed until they literally fell from the sky, how the night was part of the day, and the day was war, and nothing existed but that and being tired. He kept remembering his friends, and how they had died. Amid the constructed stagnation that was the war effort at An Khe, it was impossible to avoid a smoldering anger.

Part of the reason was My Lai. More than two years after the massacre of civilians, the full impact was now being felt in the lower ranks. As career terror rippled through places like An Khe, the GIs were repaying the debt. Rarely did a month go by without some new adjustment in the rules of engagement, some restated directive making their job more difficult.

Scouting had at first been exciting for Roark, giving him at last an opportunity to *do* something in this war, to move toward getting it finished. The need for reconnaissance was tremendous; each day at least one new base camp was discovered, and on one busy day the Little Boys found and destroyed five, drawing fire from two and producing a number of impressive secondaries from another beyond the Ears. It was apparent that the Viet Cong in the area roughly equaled, or possibly outnumbered, the Americans at An Khe, and that was without considering the still undiscovered NVA. He was convinced more than ever that they were there. He could feel their hostile energy in the hills. But only he and McLeod seemed to believe it. They had discussed it at night many times. "You'll find 'em," McLeod said. "Sooner or later. I may not be much help—I'm sort of caretaker here—but there're ways of getting things done. You'll figure it out; you'll know what to do." But I don't, Roark thought, I don't have any idea. Tomorrow he would be flying lead ahead of Jarvis—they were staying overnight for the mission that had been planned for today—and he looked forward to it with eagerness and doubt.

The others leads, he had learned, were very proficient. Talley, with his quick wit and rebellious attitude, was perhaps the best, pursuing the enemy with the malicious glee of a devilish child. Cook's style was quieter, more methodical, but he was persistent as a bloodhound and *never* returned without having discovered and destroyed a target. Jarvis had less natural hunting instinct, but made up for it with a problematic approach aimed more at achievement than a desire to punish the enemy. The results, however, were the same, and he had developed an impressive record. The only thing missing in the three men, Roark thought, was personal, vindictive involvement.

As in most of Vietnam, the war at An Khe was in suspension. The scouts went out as usual, sometimes returning with holes in their aircraft, but it had been months since there had been any serious contact. One visual recon mission each day, one convoy cover—occasionally two—a five-man Ranger team inserted into the mountains about once a week, and a rare combat assault by the grunt platoon into a base camp or bunker complex if it appeared the situation could be controlled. If there was contact at all, the enemy fired a clip or two, then disappeared into the jungle. What made it so frustrating was that while the war was being allowed to dwindle away, the hills were full of enemy. Just this morning the daily reconnaissance mission had been canceled by Task Force S-3 with the lame excuse of needing to preserve aircraft time. Roark was still fuming about it. He thumped his cigarette into a clump of dry grass, hoping it would start a fire. But even that was expecting too much. He glared at the Greenhouse as if it were a traitor. Through the years the structure had been occupied by the French who had built it, then the Japanese, the French again, the Viet Minh, the South Vietnamese, and now the Americans. Soon the ARVNs would have it back, and a short time after that—there could be no doubt—the NVA. The Greenhouse was an old and willing whore, servicing whoever wanted her most.

The landline in the standby room made a motoring croak, and the pilots jerked in reaction to the sound. Steel chairs screeched against the concrete floor. Cris Jarvis looked up from his recliner and returned Roark's parting wave. "Convoy cover," someone said. McCawley trotted out of the Doghouse as Roark gave a shrill whistle toward the birds. Far down the ramp a reclining silhouette rose beneath a 58, made a motion as if to lie back, then crawled sullenly into the sunlight. Blue moved along the tail boom to untie the blade. Roark jogged into the revetment, slipped into his armor, and glanced up to see the blade swing free; nothing could be taken for granted with Blue. He fastened the belts, ran his hands quickly across the switches, set the throttle, yelled, "Clear!" and punched the starter, watching the turbine outlet gauge. The needle jumped to the red line, wavered there, then slowly descended and stabilized. Down the ramp, the blades of the Cobra were already drumming along at operational speed. "You up, One-two?" said McCawley.

"Roger, Two-three." Actually, they weren't. Blue was taking his time, creeping through his usual routine, not yet inside the aircraft.

"An Khe Tower, Shamrock Two-three." No response. "An Khe, Shamrock Two-three, flight of two on the ramp for hover departure." Still nothing. "One-two, I think the sucker's asleep again. Let's go ahead and taxi."

"Roger, Two-three." Blue's helmet was on and plugged in, but he was still standing outside the door. Deliberately, he turned and edged into the seat. When his butt had barely touched nylon, the aircraft leaped three feet straight up. Blue was caught unprepared, forced to grab at the seat to keep from falling out, but he gave no indication that anything unusual had occurred. He calmly buckled the belt around him, braced a foot against the doorjamb, and lightly gripped the suspended machine gun so it could not swing. The birds moved down the taxiway.

"An Khe Tower, Shamrock Two-three."

"An Khe, go ahead."

"Well, hello, An Khe. Sorry to be such a bother, but we need departure instructions. Flight of two on the taxiway right out your window."

"Roger, Shamrock Two-three, gotcha in sight, current altimeter two-niner-niner-six, winds one-five-zero at one-five, we've got no reported traffic in the An Khe area, you're clear to take the active and clear yourself for a south departure."

"Roger, An Khe, understand we're clear to clear *ourselves* for departure?"

"Uh, that's affirmative, Two-three. You're on your own out there."

While the Cobra moved gingerly into position on the hard surface, Roark held the Kiowa at a hover above the taxiway, playing at flying. He allowed the ship to push downward through the cushion and nudge the penaprimed surface with a skid. It left a short black mark. The substantial weight of the ammunition, grenades, machine gun, and gunner—all on the left—made the 58 hang nose low in that direction. In a series of tiny sideways hops, he made a straight row of marks, then pulled up to examine his work. "That's plumb fuckin' amazing," Blue said. Roark ignored him. He had a thought that made him smile: Who needs a Corvette when you've got one of these? The Cobra moved past like a wide spoon turned on edge, tail up and determined. Smoothly it took to the air. The scout checked again for traffic, then sailed away low level, breaking sharply right along the highway.

Flying was the only thing that had not changed for Roark. Every bit of the thrill of simply being in the air, every sparkle of the fabulous accomplishment, was there exactly as in the beginning. He recalled a day in flight school, just after he soloed, doing hover work on a grassy lane at Bien Hoa stagefield. As he turned left and right, moved forward and back, then tried to hold the Hiller stationary, he was suddenly overwhelmed with the magic of the feat—the utter, complete impossibility of what he was doing, floating suspended above the earth. It was the most fantastic dream come to life. Look, Mom, no hands! He began to laugh so loud that soon he had to force himself to stop for fear that someone would hear him above the tractor roar of the OH-23. Now, after everything, that alone was unchanged.

He had also discovered that flying the Kiowa was a more personal experience than the time he had spent in the Huey. The diminutive size, the compactness of the cockpit, made the pilot even more at one with his aircraft, more finely conveying the sense of his actually *being* a helicopter. He believed it helped develop the gutsy reputation of the scouts. While the pilot of a larger ship could never stop thinking that some tiny part might fail, and that he would then be strapped to a falling piece of junk, the sense of intimacy with the smaller craft produced an attitude one step closer to true flight; like a real bird, the pilot feared falling, but the possibility was accepted as a bird might accept it—death as part of life, and not something to be constantly regarded.

The tail of the convoy of ten 5,000-gallon tankers was just passing Firebase Schueller, moving into the Rome-plowed strip of elephant grass leading westward toward the Mang Yang. A hundred meters or more separated each of the tractor-trailers. Guarding them in front, behind, and spaced between were four black and sinister guntrucks—open-topped, five-ton armored rigs bristling with .50 caliber weapons and men in combat gear, painstakingly polished and painted with names like Widowmaker, Death Angel, and Doctor Doom. At the head of the convoy, antlike against the vastness of the countryside, a jeep bearing three men and an M-60 on a pedestal moved earnestly toward the pass. Another brought up the rear. Almost imperceptibly the terrain began to rise, exposing the sweep of the valley behind. They crossed one last screening rise, then the funnel lay ahead for the drivers to contemplate. The dark thread of asphalt and the brighter outline of cut earth beside it rose quickly in a twisting line toward the V of the pass. The scout ship skimmed along the ground beside the highway, buzzing each of the guntrucks by turn, catching some of the men unaware, drawing waves and smiles and voiceless shouts. High overhead, off to one side, cruised the predatory Cobra.

Quickly the scout ranged ahead, staying low along the highway, studying the shoulders carefully for traces of wire, footprints, or disturbed earth, watching for signs of passage in the grass. When he had gone a mile or more, he turned back, swept the length of the convoy in a series of meandering turns, then dashed up to check the high ground and the slopes beyond for mortar and machine-gun positions. He moved like a hummingbird, darting here and there, pausing now and then to check a spot closer, trying to be everywhere at once, moving unpredictably. Sometimes he returned for a second look at likely place. As the convoy moved into cleared ground, the scout swept farther ahead. He rounded threatening knobs, skimmed low along creekbeds, dipped suddenly through meadows, examined the length of broken ridges.

Because a pink team—a scout and a Cobra—was such an effective combination, the enemy had given up attacking covered convoys in the Mang Yang. For that reason, many of the pilots had grown bored with the routine, passing along the short missions to anyone willing to take them. Roark flew them as often as he could. He never stopped believing that the enemy was there, and that he would eventually find him. It was the difference, he felt, between a hunter and a person who merely likes to shoot.

Soon the convoy—moving much slower now, bunching slightly at the front—entered the tapered throat of Mang Yang Pass. Very quickly the lead tanker was struggling along at a little more than a walk, slow enough that each lug nut could be followed with the eye. The pass had been defoliated years ago, and tall bleached trunks stood along a dry streambed and were scattered up the steep slopes. Above the road, a second growth of palms and smaller trees and vines caped a rising succession of bluffs. Here and there stood stone outcroppings, deeply cracked, gray and dangerous. The little helicopter moved carefully along the wall above the convoy.

The road weaved uncertainly, clinging to a steepening ledge, then coiled sharply through an alleyed crack where each truck momentarily lost sight of all the others. The drivers yelled, then laughed when into that tense moment the scout helicopter burst between the walls at eye level, blades flashing past.

The jeep finally topped the pass, then started down the short slope beyond with obvious restraint. Then came the first guntruck, moving even slower, keeping the first tanker in sight, then charging suddenly ahead with a gush of black smoke. This was the difficult moment, as a portion of the convoy gathered speed, wanting so much to run full blast to release the tension, while those behind were still held captive by the pass. Since the crest of the Mang Yang marked the boundary between U.S. and ARVN responsibility, in the event of an ambush of the lead element, neither aircraft could fire their weapons without specific clearance from ARVN command.

As the last guntruck topped the pass, the men in back waved at the scout ship and held up soft drinks. Matching their speed, Roark brought the bird down until Blue was able to grasp the ice-cold cans. Everybody waved good-bye and thanks, then the convoy was off on its own across the bloodred soil of the Central Highlands. "Two-three, you want a drink?"

"You're crazy," McCawley said. He and his front-seater, Tom Shadrach, had shaken their heads throughout the exchange.

"You in any hurry to get back?"

"Not really, One-two. We could stand the flight time."

"Okay, I just want to check something out."

"Roger. We've gotcha covered." Above the Mang Yang stood a lovely group of green hills. One long ridge ran parallel with the pass, overlooking it, while to the north and east the ground rolled steeply yet softly away in random mounds with rounded tops and wrinkled, rounded flanks like the skin of a silky green creature. It was open terrain save for a few wooded ravines stabbing upward, thinly covered by a pale green carpet of knee-deep grass. A narrow roadway of dirt, washed in places and sprouting green shrubs, turned off the highway at the top of the pass, then climbed a weaving course across the folded face of the ridge until it reached the tip. There it turned sharply back along the top, dividing several times, finally fading in the grass. Besides the slash of the roadway, which was necessary, there was only one thing that spoiled the natural perfection of the place. Over every bit of it, even the steepest parts, lay row upon row of countless freckles, ordered indentions in bounding succession until it seemed that all the face of the earth must be marked in such a way. A planted crop that didn't produce; a pox upon the land. The hilly platform above the Mang Yang was a cemetery for four thousand sons of another empire, buried, it was said, erect and facing France in eternal homage to those who sent them there.

Hovering close above the ground, the little scout moved slowly across the hills, leaving a trail of rumpled grass. The two men eyed the graves in silence. On the rounded point of one of the knolls lay a ring of softened foxholes edged with sun-bleached bags in tatters, bleeding orange dirt downhill. Inside the ring was one of the unmarked graves, while all around lay others. Roark hovered a scant foot above the disturbed soil, considering the skeleton army standing slumped beneath the grass. He had always heard that Dien Bien Phu had ended the First Indochina War. Unfortunately for several thousand soldiers still fighting for France, that was not true.

McLeod had told him the story. During the ten weeks following the loss of Dien Bien Phu, while French diplomats honed out the delicate details of defeat, their army was being slaughtered in the Central Highlands. Mobile Group 100, the equivalent of a task force, was massacred from ambush along Highway 19 as they withdrew from An Khe toward Pleiku. Only six days before the signing at Geneva—the war by this time acknowledged as lost and all but officially over—France committed yet another task force to a doomed offensive south of Pleiku, those men also to be slaughtered.

No wonder the Frenchman took to the hills, he thought. He pressed a pedal until the ship faced the opposite side of the valley, twenty miles away. The air was unusually clear. Around the far mountains the reflected colors of jungle and sky each seemed to work upon the other. With a gentle nudge of the cyclic, he let the aircraft follow the land, eventually falling forward into the canyon, accelerating down the wall at terrific speed. During this time Blue had said nothing, but now he stomped his foot switch. "Batman was twice the pilot on half the experience," he said.

Another time, Roark might have laughed, but the remark came too close to the mood of the graves. He steered the bird low past Alpha Two. McCawley reported he had him in sight, and the bait-and-bullet pair flew back toward An Khe. Roark sipped the soda, then trapped the can between his legs.

It had never changed between him and Blue, and he knew now it never would. But it did not matter. He had quickly realized that, son of a bitch or not, Blue was an excellent gunner. Most of the pilots and gunners were very close; each day they depended on one another for their lives, and it was hard to avoid feeling any other way. But Blue had continued to campaign relentlessly. When he was younger, Roark might have said the words or made the moves to try to bring the daily confrontations to an end, but that part of him was gone. Wrestling with Blue had become one of those grisly forms of amusement that soldiers find, like laughing at the dried contortions of the dead.

Approaching No-Name Mountain just north of the highway, he radioed McCawley, then veered slightly toward a course that would take him around the far side of the jungled knob. They passed the charred remains of the large complex that Talley had naped, empty now and open to the sky, no longer worth a second look. North of No-Name lay a flat plain of dense bamboo, miles across, an area interwoven with countless trails and dotted with base camps, productive though difficult to work. Roark moved along the edge of the thicket, low above the flashing tips of bamboo. Selecting the moment, he braced the collective firmly with his thigh, then casually lifted the soda to his lips with his left hand, delicately working the cyclic, taking aim. Blue was sitting with his left foot just barely inside the door, looking purposely bored.

CRACK!!! With a sound identical to a gunshot, a spear of bamboo disintegrated across the strut mere inches from Blue's foot, sending him flying upward almost to the limit of his belt. He screamed and looked wildly at Roark, then just as quickly turned away, completely insane with sudden adrenaline.

"One-two, you taking fire down there?" McCawley said.

"Negatory, Two-three." Blue didn't look around again, but his right hand was trembling on the weapon. A convulsive shudder ran through him. "You know, Blue, I think you're right," Roark drawled, grasping the collective again. "I don't believe I'll ever get the hang of flying this thing." He fought it for some time, but a wide smile soon crept across his face. Finally he laughed out loud, and the sound was rolling and derisive, rising again and again in taunting repetition. Blue sat staring out the door, his face completely blank except for a dancing tic beneath one eye.

CHAPTER TWENTY-NINE

G EORGE McLEOD paused beneath a bulb to give his feet a break. The carbuncle on his right foot had ruptured, and his toes were damp with the juice of it. Down the long hall the doorway was framed by a light he couldn't see. Glancing behind, he spat on the rough concrete floor, then limped along on the edges of his feet. Through the wall he heard a muffled male voice, then the musical tinkle of a girl's laughter.

Over the weeks he had made a point of befriending Billy Roark, stopping by his room to visit and see how things were going, checking his progress and thoughts about the NVA. He was certain now that his assessment had been correct. It would take time for Roark to put the pieces together, but sooner or later he would locate the regiment. There was a difference in him, a single-mindedness that left no room for failure. In the first few minutes after returning from a recon, when he had not quite made it back from the hunt, there was a total isolation there, an utter aloneness. The other scouts were quick to exclaim about their finds, to expand and speculate in retelling while wire-tight nerves uncoiled a single cell at a time. But not Roark. His radioed reports were straightfor-

252

ward and dry, and though he willingly answered every question in debriefing, there was always a sense of things unsaid.

McLeod paused at the door. He had come the long way around, not certain he was coming at all. His feet were paying for a need to talk being manifested as a need to walk. No motives tonight, he thought. Just visiting.

Roark answered his knock with an absent look, dressed in an olive T-shirt, his flight pants loose at the bottom with Velcro ankles flapping at Ho Chi Minh sandals. Over one ear was a short pencil, and in his hand an open map. The room was fluorescent with smoke. "Evening, sir," he said, immediately folding the map. "Come on in."

"Don't stop what you're doing on account of me," McLeod said. He reached for his spit can on the top of the wardrobe, hit it with a squirt that rang like a wet rubber dart, then squashed down heavily into his accustomed chair. Without asking, Roark produced a new bottle of Scotch and a plastic cup, then flicked open his big knife and cut the seal. "That's not necessary," McLeod said, but he was already reaching. "You tracking 'em down?" he asked, nodding at the map.

"Just doing a little homework," Roark said.

"Let's have a look."

"There's really nothing to see," he replied. "I'm getting nowhere, sir." He folded the map once more, then zipped it into the calf pocket of his pants. "I've been looking at contour lines so long my eyeballs are calibrated."

"Got any ideas?"

"Yes, sir. We need a battalion on call."

"Don't hold your breath."

"Another thing, if we do run into this outfit, we're going to have to be real quick and real together to have even half a hope. They're either going to murder us, or get clean away. Maybe both."

"Could be," McLeod said. He made a little smile.

"Was Korea anything like Vietnam?"

"Only when it was over."

Roark crossed the room, tilted the fan against the wall, then got a beer from the fridge. The fragrance of the brew mixed with the odors of smoke and sweat and wet tobacco. "Is that what happened to your face?"

"No, I already had that. It's the reason I joined the Army," McLeod said. "Sort of." He sipped Scotch through the side of his mouth opposite the wad of tobacco.

"What are you going to do when you get out?"

"I don't know. Sometimes I think I'd like to have some chickens." McLeod looked up, then laughed at the words. "I don't know what I'm going to do."

"You going back?"

"Where's that?" When Roark just smiled, the major said, "What makes you ask?"

"You look like a man with Montana on his mind."

"Perceptive."

"Keeps me alive. You going?"

"I don't know. I've considered it."

"So what's in the way?"

Good question, McLeod thought. Nothing but Daddy Hank and the Red Cloud Curtain, and twenty years of being gone. That and everything a person had to eat to be his son. But the pull of the land was still there. It was only in recent months, as it grew again in his thoughts, that he understood how much he missed it. "A fence," he said. "Twelve feet high, fourteen miles long, hog wire and cable and drill pipe."

"Some fence. Was it built to keep things in or out?"

"Depends on where you happened to be standing."

Roark smiled and began to look more relaxed. "Sounds like a story to me," he said. He poured a golden stream into the major's cup, lit a cigarette, and leaned back in his chair.

With retirement an imminent fact, George McLeod had found himself increasingly immersed in memories of Montana. Roark, who said he fished flies and had learned to tie on his daddy's knee, always seemed interested in hearing all about it, said he hoped to spend time there someday. McLeod had told him many stories of the early years, of hunting trips into the Crazies, the fierceness of the winters, and things that had happened on the ranch. It was a way of going back, maybe a way of getting ready. Maybe that was what made the meandering, limping walk up the hill, and the inevitable stumbling return, worth it. He trapped the edge of the can with his thumb, lifted it from the floor, and spat into it, then took a long, burning, soothing sip of Scotch. He waited for the glow to reach bottom.

McLeod told the story of the fence, a barrier that had been built because of a feud with a neighbor, the same neighbor who had hired young George after he left the ranch. Late that summer he fell beneath a steer, but it was the fence and all the other fences that he and his father had erected between them that finally caused George to join the Army.

When the story had been told, McLeod sat for a time in contemplation, then looked up as if it were suddenly morning. Roark was watching him like a cat. "You think leaving was a mistake?" Roark asked.

"I don't know. Maybe. Maybe not."

"It won't be the same when you go back."

"Never is," McLeod said. He reached down quickly to spit once more into the can, then pushed himself to his feet. He was wobbly from sitting and from the sudden pain.

"You need some help?" Roark asked, reaching.

McLeod gave him an indignant look. "It'll be a while before I need help down a hill," he said. "Thanks just the same, sonny." His tone was falsely belligerent, expecting something equally sharp in return. But Roark misread it; his eyes went suddenly reptilian, a look that was there for only an instant.

"Good night, sir," he said.

"'Night," McLeod mumbled, but not until he was already in the hall.

The scouts and guns had joined forces against the slicks, and were giving them a thorough thrashing. A cloud of dust gathered twenty feet above the churning boots, then eased toward the paddies in a pale and dissipating smear. The score was 20–12, and the point volley had turned into a desperate struggle marked by suicidal dives and bloody elbows, all-out effort, total war. After several long arcs across the net, the ball became trapped between the front lines, batting back and forth in quick succession. With a net-lowering assist by Talley, McCawley jumped high and slammed the ball toward center court. Corbish went horizontal to make a spectacular save, scooping a mouthful of sand and burning a raw patch on his chin. But the effort failed when Hockett shoved a standard, whipping the net upward to block the shot. A roar of victory and protest went out from the hill. "Jungle rules," Talley said, his eyes bright as buttons.

"What are jungle rules?" a lieutenant asked.

"You'll learn."

"That's not fair. You didn't say anything about that in the beginning."

"So who said anything about fair? This here's the 'Nam."

"And that don't mean Clemson, Looie."

The lieutenant lingered on the court, seeming to think justice would prevail, but the others drifted away, slapping at their pants and brushing damp sand from their arms. Most queued up to an ice chest, while some wandered off to take showers. "What's Clemson?" said a nineteen-year-old pilot.

Corbish, who had a mulish face and yellowed teeth, was still spitting sand. Specks of blood dotted his chin. When someone handed him a beer, he sloshed the first mouthful, then sent a jet of foam spewing toward the dirt. Nearby, in a gook hammock suspended from the eaves, Billy Roark was slumped with a beer, a cigarette, and a disgruntled look.

It was the first of July. A USO group was scheduled that night in the officers' club, so Delta Troop had been released from An Khe when the last convoy cleared the pass. The club was to be open to the enlisted men for the event, and the anticipation could be felt throughout the camp. Among the Delta crews, however, the spirit was somewhat dampened.

"How'd it go with the old man?" McCawley asked, breathing hard, his white T-shirt wet and transparent. Beside him Talley flopped back on the sun deck and smiled at the sky. Roark opened his mouth to speak, but only shook his head. He glanced toward the sun balanced on top of the ridge, then looked away. "So what did he say?"

"He said we're fucked."

"We knew that," said Talley.

"No help at all, huh?" Hockett sat on the edge of the deck among the others, unlacing his boots. Bent over, the black bristle of his brow made a line that hid his eyes.

"He said Colonel Calvert chewed his ass when he went over there. Said he needed to lose weight and get a haircut."

"Knowing that old bastard, I'd say G.D. did some gnawing of his own," said Talley.

"It's not quite the same, is it?" McCawley said.

"I mean, what are we doing, risking our lives to find the sonsabitches, if they're just going to let them go?"

Talley rolled over on an elbow, held an imaginary microphone to his lips, and said in a mincing voice meant to imitate Dunning, "'Okay, boys, we got the enemy location marked on the map now, thanks a lot, be sure and call us next time you find something, y'all be careful out there now, you hear?'"

"Be sure," Roark said.

"That's an idea," said McCawley. He caught Roark's eyes for only a second, but long enough.

"No," Roark replied flatly. "Used to, but not anymore."

Cris Jarvis shook his head. He had a sharp nose and a pointed chin. "They're looking to catch somebody screwing up," he said. "It's their only way left of making points. It's 'cover your ass' for us, but for higher it's 'salvage your career.' Better a hundred dead GIs than one wounded civilian. Easier to explain." With only a few weeks remaining on his tour, Jarvis had returned to flying wing, giving the others more experience at lead. It was he and Roark who had discovered the camp.

"What are you guys talking about?" John Huckabee asked. He was a twenty-year-old Huey pilot from a village four hours out of Denver, the son of a taxidermist and hunting guide. New in the outfit, he had made it known that he was 58 qualified and wanted to become a scout. He was going about it right, hanging around, listening. No one bothered to answer him.

"Those aren't civilians," Roark growled, "and those today sure weren't Montagnards."

"Has it occurred to you that you might be wrong?" said a quiet but abrasive voice. "That instead of a base camp, what you found today might be a village?" The speaker was a warrant named Glenn Castle—tall with light brown hair needing a barber, a thin mustache hiding his mouth. He sat in the sand, leaning against the deck on both elbows.

"That's exactly what I think every time I get my chin bubble shot out," Roark said. He moved his right leg across the hammock.

"Right on," Talley piped.

"Well, what do you expect?" Castle said. "They're out there minding their own business, and we come along, burn down their houses, kill their livestock, and then for good measure blow whatever's left to kingdom come. Hell, I'd shoot at us, too. That doesn't prove they're Cong—just that they got their bellies full of us, that's all."

Castle was the newest scout, and already Roark didn't like him. He had a laid-back style common among the newer troops, but there was something more—almost an aggressive pacifism, some score to settle that only he seemed to know. Reflecting the confusing blend of life in the States, he was quickly popular. He talked of growing grass back home, played the spoons like nobody's business, and was a virtual Louis Armstrong on the kazoo.

"So what are you doing in scouts?"

"Same as you, I want to find the enemy."

"You just think you do," Roark said. He made his eyes smile. "Follow me around. Someday I'll show them to you."

There was a sudden, explosive tension. "Come on, Bill," Mc-Cawley said. "Let's go on up to the club. Everybody's flush, and a game's starting." Roark kept his eyes on Castle.

"Castle's okay," Talley said, standing beside McCawley.

"That's right," said Hockett. "Come on, fellas, let's get cleaned up and go on up to the club. Shadrach's saving us tables."

"Go sniff some of that Filipino pussy," Talley said, grinning.

"That'll make you forget your problems." Everyone stood but Roark and McCawley. Talley began to sing as he walked away. *"My husband's a colonel, a colonel, a colonel, a very fine colonel is he . . ."* Corbish and Hockett joined in. *"All day he chews ass, he chews ass, he chews ass, and at night he comes home and chews me. Oh, sing a little bit, fuck a little bit, follow the Cav . . ."*

When they were gone, McCawley said, "The kids are different now, Bill. They haven't been where we've been, and they didn't start where we started. Things aren't so clearly drawn, and they've heard a *ton* of crap back home that you and I never heard. They're coming over with lots of doubt."

Roark reached for a beer and opened it. When he looked at McCawley, he seemed drained and tired. "He thinks this is make-believe," he said. "He doesn't have any idea."

"No, but he's got to learn it himself, just like we did. He's got to come up with his own definition." Hockett was walking back toward them. "You coming?" McCawley asked.

"I'll be along in a little while. Save me a seat."

"This thing's going to end someday," McCawley said. "Don't forget that." He crossed the deck.

"Hey, Gil." The CW2 turned around, looking too small for his flight suit, two vertical lines in his face adding to an impression that he had once been larger. "Nothing."

"Be cool, Kilroy. See you there."

Roark nodded. The sun was gone, the crest of the gloomy ridge fuzzed with gold. Toward Qui Nhon the upper parts of the mountains were still golden green. Out to sea a string of salmon thunderheads lined the purple edge like mushrooms.

For a month he had been flying lead. He had discovered that the job was at once exhilarating and agonizing. Each day the teams went out, found another cluster of thatched hooches hidden in the jungle, counted them, set them afire, perhaps got shot at, then returned to An Khe to sit and wait. There were NVA rucksacks, pith helmets, and empty satchels lying about the encampments, and sometimes meals being cooked over smokeless charcoal fires. But almost never did they see the enemy. Searching day after day, hovering along trails with muscles coiled and gloves soaked through, peering into the jungle with time ticking away, waiting for the cockpit to explode; combing the bamboo thickets, burning a few empty shelters, spending the energy a day at a time, all the while knowing the NVA were watching, waiting for whatever it was they were waiting for.

Then along came a day like today. For weeks Captain Dunning

had been calling for more missions to the north. The scouts finally agreed to spend an entire week in the northern AO. Dunning immediately became more pleasant.

On the way out that morning, the scouts had paused at the cone-shaped top of Hong Kong Hill to remove a bunker, the last remaining structure of the 1st Cav's radio relay station. Someone had suggested that a Super-C would probably do the job. A Super-C consisted of a concussion grenade wrapped in a number of sticks of C-4 explosive, bound together with green hundred-knot tape. It was a scary-looking thing. Jarvis's gunner lobbed the bomb through the bunker door, then the scouts dived off the hill. When they went back, twenty thousand pounds of material had vanished; the rock was swept clean.

The northern forests were slow work, but at last a camp was discovered tucked beneath the canopy near a tributary of the Song Ba. The cover was too dense for the gunships to be effective, so an airstrike was called. Soon a pair of A-1E Spads arrived, piloted by Vietnamese, loaded with 250- and 500-pound bombs. Only one of the pilots spoke any English, but when a Snake fired a pair of marking rounds into the trees, the bombing proceeded in competent fashion.

Observing an airstrike by fastmovers normally consisted of the scouts marking the target with smoke, then moving aside and waiting for it to disintegrate. But the propeller-driven Spads flew an old-timey war, and with Vietnamese pilots that was especially true. The camp was in a basin of jungled mountains which kept the shining airplanes low to the greenery. They banked and turned with wingtips mere feet above the trees, then swooped gracefully down, practically hand-delivering each bomb before pulling out with the engine roar drowning the helicopter sound. Theirs was a more personal war than that of the jets; they were low and slow enough to see what they were shooting at, and to be seen in the cockpit from the ground. The bombs huffed gray-brown and red, and the big trees broke and fell until there was only a tangled, burning hole in the jungle. "We go now . . ." the pilot said happily, and the airplanes flew away like something borrowed through a fold in time.

Returning with a little mission time to squander, the scouts swung west from the river, past the fields of elephant grass, toward a narrow north-south creek which bordered the wide plain of bamboo. They checked the creekbed, but found nothing there but trails. "What about those trees to the west," Roark asked Jarvis on the UHF. "You ever checked them?"

"No," he replied. "It always looked too obvious." Far out in the bamboo stood a mound, an island of trees no larger than an acre. Roark moved the flight in that direction, and on the first pass both doorgunners at once said they had sighted hooches. It was a clean and well-worn complex, with eight large hooches and eight bunkers, more than the usual number. There was no undergrowth at all, and once the scouts were at a near hover they could see everything quite clearly. There was the feel of the enemy there, unmistakable and strong; the direct approach without the usual sweeping search had not allowed time for escape; the bunkers were occupied.

Insufficient mission time remained to work the complex, so it was decided to call back to Operations for clearance to drop some concussion grenades down the throats of the bunkers, then empty both gunships on the target. There was a delay, then Dunning came back on the radio. "Negative clearance," he said. "Do not fire on the camp. Take note of what is there, but do not disturb anything."

"Why not?" Roark asked.

"Orders from higher." It was a baffling message. Perhaps there was some explanation, a reason, a plan. They left the base camp unmolested. When the flight landed at An Khe, the pilots quickly gathered in Operations. Dunning's expression was detached, as if he were beyond reach of what was happening; it was not his life that was on the line every day. He placed a sheet of paper before them without a word. It was a new directive from Colonel Calvert, stating that effective immediately any contact with the enemy would be strictly on a return-fire basis throughout the AO. "Specifically," it said, "this includes armed and uniformed NVA troops. DO NOT FIRE UNLESS FIRED UPON." It went on to warn that violation of the order would result in prosecution under the Uniform Code of Military Justice.

"Jesus."

Jarvis said it better. "In other words, when we get shot down we can return fire right up to the point we slam into the ground and explode."

"I guess that's right," Dunning said, smiling nervously, ready to laugh if anyone else did. The room looked at him.

"That fucker's watched too many episodes of *Gunsmoke*," Hockett said.

"No problem," Roark declared. "We'll go out tomorrow and see if we can't get them to shoot at us."

"'Fraid not," Dunning replied. "The colonel says he wants that camp left alone."

CHAPTER THIRTY

THE LANE Army Heliport officers' club was spacious and plush by Army standards. On the left, see-through partitions and a freestanding wall separated a section where stood a long bar facing the only windows, a draped line of Plexiglas commanding a view of paddies and mountains. In one corner stood an octagonal craps table, complete with green felt and a ledge for drinks, surrounded two-deep by jostling men with red faces. There was a momentary hush as the bones rattled and fell, then a burst of shouts and curses. An elbow knocked a beer to the floor, and the chugging can was kicked a couple of times beneath the table before someone picked it up.

With the floor show still an hour away, Delta Troop was warming up. Victor Talley led the cheers and gritty songs, while limericks rotated around the table.

A barmaid named Lin sashayed past with a tray, and Roark caught her arm. She turned with a haughty look. "Wha choo wan', GI?" she said. "I busy now." She was tiny and very pretty with glossy black hair hanging straight down her back to her waist. Her skin was almost white, a feature she carefully protected by avoiding the sun. She wore a tight emerald dress that barely covered her

261

bottom, deeply scooped in front where a pinching bra produced an illusion of breasts.

"I need beer for my friends," Roark said, pointing toward the rowdy table. He slipped a twenty between the empty cans.

"You frien's numbah ten," she said, her eyes flashing.

"Of course," he said. He watched her walk away, his eyes caressing her bobbing butt. She was as cute as somebody's kid sister, old enough but not really. Like most of the girls, she plowed along through the shag carpet on cork-bottomed elevator shoes, impractical but apparently worth the struggle.

"Roark!" Talley called. He started toward the table. "Hey, Roarko, you through being pissed at the world?" Charlie Cook handed him an unopened beer.

"All but one small part," Roark replied with embarrassment. "A toast," he said, and when the others stood, he suddenly went blank. Lin arrived with a loaded tray, waiting impatiently. Talley sneaked a hand toward her bottom, and she jumped back with a dark look, spitting something in Vietnamese. Roark caught Castle's eyes and said, "Fuck the war." That seemed as good as anything. They banged cans and smiled, and the echoed shout filled the room. "Fuck the war!"

The Cav esprit was not universally shared, but fed upon itself like drunkenness, unappreciated by spectators. Men who were trying to have a peaceful drink cast venomous looks, but subtleties were lost on Delta Troop. An occasional beer can, almost empty, arced across the room like a dud round.

"Mr. Roark!"

"Yo!" He looked around. Grouper and several other enlisted men had captured most of the chairs in front of the low platform.

"I'm saving you a place," he said, indicating a vacant chair. His hair was freshly oiled, and the red blotches of several angry pimples shone vividly on his face. Roark did not see Blue.

"'Preciate it," he said, smiling. "I'll be up there after a while. How was R and R?" Grouper had been back several days, but they had not had an opportunity to talk.

"Oh, it was all right while I was there," he said vaguely. "Tell you about it later."

Slowly at first, then more rapidly as show time approached, the club became choked with men and smoke. The chants and songs and limericks finally ran out, snuffed by the crush of the crowd. Beyond the stage, behind a screening plywood wall, stood an open door which led to the troupe's dressing trailer. The sticky scent of layered perfume moved into the room on a sigh. The voice of the club grew louder.

A skinny Filipino kid walked out carrying brushes and sticks and moved quickly to his roost among the drums without making eye contact with anyone. He worked his way through a soft series of rolls, rhythms, and rim shots, loosening up everything but his face. Next came a slightly older boy sucking a reed, carrying a badly scratched trumpet and guiding a sax on a lanyard. Immediately on his heels came two more with guitars. All were cut from the same lean cloth, none older than twenty, with straight black hair in a modish style, pointed sideburns. In size and features they resembled the people the audience was accustomed to killing. They wore black, tightly tailored slacks with legs no larger than a GI's arm, and had white, long-sleeved shirts opened to the navel, exposing chests that were flat and featureless. They made last-minute arrangements on stage and commenced warming up.

The drummer suddenly began a long roll, followed by a sweeping musical flourish from the others. Then four girls burst from behind the wall, bouncing in ostrich feathers of red, yellow, purple, and green, dazzling smiles, G-strings, bras, and heels. The club roared, and the group opened up with an Asian version of "In a Godda De Vida." The girls sang, then, during the instrumental portions, whacked at tambourines and danced around the stage, showing the men what they came to see. The lead girl, who wore purple, fancied herself an artiste and kept going up on her toes, holding her arms out like wings while managing to maintain a bodily rhythm that had nothing to do with ballet. No one noticed she was ugly. After the song, she took the mike and began the introductions. Roark commenced a visual recon of her pubic zone. "Where's Blue?" he said.

"He's not coming. He's not too big on officers."

"No kidding." When Blue heard that Colonel Calvert had altered the rules of engagement, his single remark had been that the man needed to be fragged.

"I hear y'all got screwed over today," Grouper said.

"More or less."

"What are you going to do? We can't just fly around out there waiting to be blown out of the sky."

"That's right, we can't."

The group started into "Purple Haze," and a great shout went up. Later, things slowed down with "Galveston." The Filipinos, who spoke English mostly by rote, became confused in the middle of a song, got lost, and had to go back to the beginning to start over. At intermission, Roark was again going to ask Grouper about his R&R, but the gunner disappeared in the rush to the piss point and did not return until the band had started again. "So how was it?" Roark asked, his mouth almost against the spec 4's ear. By this time Grouper had downed several beers, and his face changed emotions instantly.

"I got a small problem," he said, yelling. "I picked up a weird kind of clap in Taiwan. I'm bleeding. I gotta wear a rubber all the time to catch it. I got it taped to my balls to keep it from falling off. See." Roark looked involuntarily. Grouper was leaning back in his chair, and had unzipped his pants. Like most men in the tropics, he wore no underwear, and he simply reached in and pulled out his penis. Apparently he had just changed or cleaned the rubber, but the reservoir tip was already half filled with blood. Astonished, Roark looked up at the horrified face of the girl in red less than five feet away. She broke stride, almost screamed, then ran to the opposite end of the stage where she stayed for the remainder of the show, still singing and dancing, but not nearly so well. It seemed an excellent time to leave.

The spray of spotlights around the club made the sky seem black and opaque. Roark stood between two men he didn't know and urinated into the black pit. He thought of Batterman down there in the dark and grimaced and fought a smile. He wondered what the civilian Batman was doing now. Probably growing hair. He sighed and began the walk toward his room.

Not everyone had gone to the show. The fragrance of burning marijuana oozed so thickly from some of the hooches that it seemed a man could get high just by hanging around outside. It was such a bizarre situation, a world turned wrong side out. So much had changed so quickly. With the 101st, Roark had seen marijuana exactly once—hollowed-out and reloaded 100s, surreptitiously offered beneath the T-shirt of a ten-year-old on the Song Bo. Never had he caught the insuppressible scent at Evans, not even on the perimeter at night. There was a need to remain alert. But fifty years could have passed since then. Though the men at Lane did not smoke in the open, the officers pretended to have no sense of smell, passing through a hazy enlisted hooch without missing a step. Marijuana was viewed as the hopeful alternative; out on the perimeter it was impossible to make the rounds without hearing the crunch of tiny plastic vials called caps—containers for the pure heroin that the guards were snorting.

Roark was filled with a feeling of loneliness and deep futility. So much was wrong, so little right. Up at the club the men were shouting and drooling, most of them too drunk to use a gun; in the hooches they were sitting glazed and dreamy, lolling their heads about and saying "Oh, wow . . ."; out on the perimeter they were either asleep or doped out of their minds, while the few who still had their senses were sprawled with their pants around their boots, screwing another whore who had just come through the wire in front of their machine guns. Fifty miles away in An Khe was a man giving orders to be sure to let the enemy shoot first. No wonder the gooks didn't attack; they were sitting up in the mountains laughing their asses off.

He leaned against the sandbags outside his hooch and lit a cigarette. It was darker there, and in the faint light of stars and a crescent splinter of moon he could see the shape of crowning clouds on the mountains to the south. Far away across the paddies, beyond the reach of sound, a helicopter moved, the silent pulse of its beacon painting a red ellipsis on the night. Thin, throbbing strains of music came down from the club. *We gotta get out of this place, if it's the last thing we ever do* . . . It was the same old song, the song everybody had been singing all along, everybody wanting to be someplace else because they couldn't think of any reason for being where they were. *Girl, there's a better life for me and you* . . .

Let the enemy shoot first. Goddamn right.

There was a sound in the sand, and a shadow moved, homing in on the glow of his cigarette. "'Lo, GI," a girl's voice said. "W'at choo do, watch the ni'?" She came slowly, a vague shape in the darkness.

"Yeah," Roark said. "I'm watching it rot."

"No savvy word ro'"

"Rot. Corrode, wither, die."

"Ah," she said. "I savvy die. I watch wi' you, okay?" She leaned against the bags beside him. In the faint light she was little more than an ivory shadow, grayish where a sleeveless shift hung to midthigh. Her hair and eyes were black voids.

"It's a free country," he said, then shook his head at the irony. He caught the female scent of her and felt a gripping pressure beneath his chest. The girl was an intruder; he hadn't wanted her there, hadn't asked her to be there, and wished now that she would leave. He looked out across the sprinkle of lights of the lower camp. "You want a cigarette?" he offered gruffly.

"No, t'ank you," she said.

His had begun to bite sharply at his tongue, so he lit another from the glowing butt, then flicked the orange spark wobbling off the hill beyond the retaining wall. He felt clumsy and uncomfortable, caught between his needs. "So what are you doing up here?" he asked brusquely. Normally, the girls stuck pretty close to the enlisted hooches—the officers having to maintain appearances.

"You talk you'self," she said. "I t'ink you maybe lonely."

"Talking to myself?"

"I hear," she replied gently. "Is hokay. I do, too, sometime I need frien'."

A whore needing a friend? That's a new one, he thought, and was immediately ashamed. It occurred to him that being a whore might be one of the loneliest conditions in the world, as lonely as being a soldier—whores and soldiers so much alike. "So what's your name," he asked, less defensive now.

"My name Sakrung."

"Sock Run?"

"No. Sakrung, like fat Amelican gull put in tea."

"Saccharin? You mean like sugar?"

"Bettah," she said with a sly smile that showed in the dark. "No make fat."

Roark chuckled, then laughed at her joke. "Where'd you get your name, Saccharin?"

"Frien' long time gi' me."

"Is your friend here?"

"No. He go home now," she said. "We no talk 'bou' him. Talk 'bou' you. W'at name you, GI?"

"Billy Roark."

"Bi' Ro'?"

"That's close enough," Roark said. "Be-Ro."

"Glad to meet choo, Be-Ro," she said, facing him and extending a hand. He was surprised, but he took her hand in his and shook it, too hard at first, then more gently. It felt so fragile, easily injured. The knot in his chest returned, tighter than before, and around it was an emptiness. He felt his testicles move.

The music from the club grew louder, voices massed together in the traditional song of good-bye. He pictured the men lined up like chorus girls, their arms across their shoulders, doing a side-to-side step and grunting *oooh!* with each kick, linked together, all part of the same thing, part of one another. Even through the blurry levels of intoxication it was a moment apart. "I guess you need to get back on down the hill," he said. "They'll be coming soon."

"No," Saccharin said. "This no good ni'. Too much whiskey. Sakrung no like. Maybe I stay wi' you toni'? Maybe?"

"I'm not interested," he lied. Just go the hell away, he thought. I'm standing here crying about all the changes, and you're the biggest one of all.

"You do' know Sakrung. I diffah othah gull. I good fo' you, be frien' all time. You need, I show, you see."

He looked in the direction of the club. Hundreds of men would be pouring out now, spreading across the camp in weaving lines like so many ants. Soon the troop area would be filled with drunks, singing, shouting, vomiting in celebration. "You're not going?" he asked.

"No," she replied. "I talk wi' you."

"Well, let's go inside then. But just to talk and have a drink. Okay?"

"Hokay by me, Be-Ro," she said pertly. Roark frowned, then led the way around the end of the building, quickly through the light beneath the gable. The hall was empty. His room was just inside the doorway, and he quickly removed a padlock and hustled the girl inside. He switched on a box fan, then opened the small window high on the opposite wall. When the stuffy air was expelled, he closed the door and bolted it with a large screwdriver, then turned the fan around. Saccharin stood watching quietly, surveying the little room. "You make clean room," she said.

It was small but comfortable. A bunk with an Air Force mattress stood in a corner, freshly made with clean white sheets, a thick pillow, and a poncho liner. Beneath were polished boots, a flak vest and steel pot, a case of cola, and two cases of beer. A matched pair of steel-and-vinyl cushioned chairs, a large plywood armoir, and a small refrigerator filled the remaining space. There was a fluorescent light in the ceiling, and at one end, a small hole guarded by geckos. Roark looked around like he had never seen it before, checking Saccharin very quickly as he did. She was less than five feet, no more than ninety pounds, and wore her hair banged in front and cut squarely across the shoulders. She appeared a smart nineteen, cute but not pretty, and wore no makeup. "You want a drink?"

"You have Coke?"

"Sure," he said, then remembered his manners. "Go ahead and sit down." He turned quickly away and stooped before the refrigerator, feeling himself begin to blush. This is ridiculous, he thought, she's a whore. But when he turned around, he saw only an ordinary Oriental girl, sitting with her legs crossed, her hands folded in her lap, looking up at him with chipmunk eyes. No come-on looks, no gawdy makeup, no clothes she couldn't afford; only a cheap dress, plastic sandals, and a faint scent of perfume. Just a girl. He frowned as he opened her drink, and when he handed it to her he noticed her legs were pale and blotchy.

"T'ank you," she said.

You're welcome, he almost replied.

"You nevah have gull here befo'."

"No," he said before he realized it was not a question.

"Why you no have gull?"

"I don't know. I guess it just doesn't fit my image of war. Not right here in the hooch." He looked away.

"Viet Cong have gull."

"They're smarter than we are."

"How old you, Be-Ro?"

"Twenty-two."

"You need gull all time," she said. She sipped her soda and looked at him very frankly. "Sakrung good fo' you."

"I can't imagine you being bad," he said, then looked at the beer can as if it were responsible. He saw her smile.

There were voices in the hall. "Roark! Roarko!" Talley yelled, banging hard against the door. "Open up, I know you're in there." Roark reached over and turned out the lights. "Hey!" Talley roared. "What gives, man?"

Another voice, lower, said, "Maybe the hard-ass broke down and got him a whore. Let's leave him be, he needs it."

"No kidding." Talley shouted Roark's name again, converting it to a hound-dog howl as he moved down the hallway, banging walls.

The rectangle of the screened window showed faintly, but Roark was still night blind. He heard Saccharin moving. He struck a paper match and touched it to a candle on the refrigerator. When he turned, the sheets were pulled back, the girl lying naked on his bed. She rolled over on her side toward the wall and drew her legs up until her rear made a heart. He downed the beer and began to undress. When he got into bed and curled around her, his flesh began to quiver. He lay as still as he could, feeling her softness from his chest to his thighs, and within the wrap of his arms. Her hair was beneath his face, and he breathed her scent. He held her as long as he could, the muscles of his stomach and chest jerking in spasms, his entire body shuddering with anticipation.

CHAPTER THIRTY-ONE

"**R**OARK!"

Phillip Crable heard the shout, but it took a while to register. He was slumped at the bar, turning a highball glass between his fingers, enjoying a rare evening at the club. The word echoed through his head, and when it finally reached him, it caused a weak reflective smile. Another Roark, he thought, but surely not another *Billy* Roark. It had never occurred to him he would feel this way, but now he was actually thankful that the disturbed warrant had come along to terrorize him. And terror it had certainly been, in one clean move rescuing him from Missouri and sending him hurtling back to Vietnam. Already that awful evening seemed long ago.

The telephone rang thirty-six times before it finally stopped. In the following silence, Phillip could hear the sound of the distant interstate pouring down from the sky, an audible rush of people getting out of Missouri. From a convenience store at the corner, a trail of leftover neon made a dusty green smear across his car. He

269

lifted a sack of groceries from the porch and went inside, latching the storm door, then carefully locking the new dead bolt. The phone began to ring.

"That's one bloodless individual," he said, crossing the living room of the duplex to the nook that formed the kitchen. He had everything put away before the caller gave up. He removed the phone from the hook, then went to the bedroom to change out of his uniform. When he returned, dressed in an old pair of soft khakis and a long-sleeved shirt of blue flannel, he smothered the dial tone with a pillow, then relaxed with a book in a deep chair. But he had read only a few pages when he found himself staring into space, following a trail of thoughts past the many hopeless features of his life, something he had done a lot lately. Regardless of where he began, or which direction he took, the trail inevitably led back to Rita.

He had missed her long enough now to stop hating her, long enough to concede that he needed her in his life. Shortly after arriving at Fort Leonard Wood he had tried to write her at her mother's home in Charlotte. When a month had passed, he wrote again, but neither letter had been answered.

It had been only recently that Phillip had been able to admit that his life—his career—had gone nowhere but downhill since the day Rita walked out. His careful, long-term calculations had wasted too much time, and now he was trapped in Missouri, facing the prospect that soon the duty stations would stabilize, possibly leaving him there for years. Then August came, dealing the shattering blow, so obvious now, so unexpected when it came: He was passed over for promotion.

It was easy now to see; no command time, the glut of officers who were his competition, men who had already completed two and sometimes three combat tours, the lack of vacancies among the higher ranks, and the looming reduction in the standing Army as the war ground inexorably to a conclusion. It was the dawn of a new era in the Army; the days of easy promotion were suddenly past.

But regardless of circumstances, being passed over bore the telling weight of failure. He began to question every decision he had ever made, and especially those he would make in the future. After the initial shock, he tried to be positive, to plan measures that would insure his name would be on the next advancement list. It took six weeks to admit it was useless; the spark, the energy, the hope that makes a person get out of bed each day, was gone. He performed his duties without interest, and at the end of the day went home to sit and read and eventually fall asleep. For the first time in his life he was plagued with headaches. The simple act of walking across the room could cause his heartbeat to surge as if he had run a great distance. Sudden movements made him feel faint. Even then, he was slow to realize what was happening.

"I wish to God I were dead," he said one morning, slumped on the side of his bed. The shock of hearing that statement, coupled with the knowledge that he meant it, jarred him suddenly awake. "I don't mean that," he said quickly, fearing that God might hear and take him at his word. But a moment later the first voice was back. "Yes, I do," he said with resignation. "I sincerely do." He waited a minute, and when nothing happened, he got out of bed and began getting dressed.

It was different after that. Some barrier had been broken, punched through with a hole not easily repaired. From then on, escape was always available, a lethal capsule sewn into his flesh that he had only to reach over and crush. Life was now equipped with an ejection button, a built-in last resort.

There was still one possibility that he thought might save him, one which until now would have seemed completely insane: He could ask to return to Vietnam. It was clear that the war would not last much longer, and a second combat tour on his record could make all the difference. In recent months the casualty count had dropped sharply, the danger factor accordingly reduced. He might even be able to pick up a company command, he reasoned, and from there possibly a decoration or two. And if the maniac on the phone was real, it would solve that problem as well. The idea had a lot of merit, but he wanted to think about it a little longer.

The calls had been coming for weeks, but intermittently, impossible to predict. A tracer was out of the question since it would have involved the Army. Besides, he told himself, it was probably a prank. Gradually, the image of a jokester evolved to that of a lunatic.

"Crable," the voice said.

"Yes?"

"Phillip Crable?"

"That's correct," he replied with hesitation. It was early morning, and he could not imagine who would be calling.

"I've been looking for you a long time," the man said. "I just want you to know that you're not going to get away with killing Jim Tyler." Then the line went dead.

Phillip felt as if something heavy were smashing his chest. He tried a small laugh, then fear overwhelmed him. "I didn't kill anybody," he shrieked, then looked up with alarm, afraid that his neighbor might have heard through the wall. He stood trembling, thoroughly shaken. "I didn't kill anybody," he whispered, still grasping the phone.

Three weeks passed before the next call, again in the morning. "I know where you are now, Crable," the voice said.

"Who are you?" Phillip demanded. "I don't have any idea what you're talking about!" But the line was dead. He could taste the steaming rot of acid in his throat. He rushed to the kitchen for milk, almost heaved when it hit his stomach, then sat pale and drained for several minutes.

Slowly, the calls grew more ominous. "Some night you're gonna maybe hear a sound and look up and see something in the dark, and I'm gonna be there . . ."

Then, this morning, with an awful difference. "I drove past your little duplex a while ago, Crable . . ."

Not once all day did Phillip have any thoughts about wanting to be dead. His other problems seemed suddenly manageable if he could somehow get the lunatic to go away. Maybe even he can be managed, he thought. Maybe, if I am careful, maybe I can talk to him, find out who he is, at least find out what he's talking about. He considered a moment, then lifted the pillow and put the receiver back on the hook. Then he went to the kitchen. He had a bottle of antacid at his lips when the telephone began to ring. He flinched, then drank the cooling liquid. Finally, he walked toward the phone.

"I'd like to talk to you," he said calmly when he answered.

"You've got exactly five minutes, Crable," the voice said. "Then I'm coming."

He was totally unable to breathe, and for a moment it seemed he would faint. Then a rasping, convulsive breath filled his lungs, and his chest began to heave, giving out a helpless wailing moan. The phone fell from his hand, and he looked blankly around the apartment, unable to form any thought. I've got to get out of here, it finally came, but the mechanism for action seemed severed. Suddenly he lurched to the bedroom for his jacket, remembered his boots when he slipped on the floor, and managed to tie them half unlaced. Then he dashed to the front door, flipped on the porch light, and checked the peephole. Nothing in sight. He unlatched the bolt and slowly opened the door, peeked around to one side and then the other. Something close was there, and he backed away to focus. Then he screamed an animal scream and fell backward to the floor. Fresh red blood was sliding slowly down the glass.

It had all worked out amazingly well. Upon his arrival in Vietnam, Phillip was assigned as the adjutant of the 7/17th Air Cavalry stationed at Lane. Though not the command he had hoped for, the position put him in daily contact with the squadron commander, Lieutenant Colonel Westin. Westin was a man he immediately felt a kinship to, their views dovetailing neatly. It became clear that the colonel was thoroughly satisfied with his performance, often commenting on his talent for meticulous organization and attention to detail. Doing something that suited his capabilities, performing a job well, and receiving credit, Phillip felt his career was again on track. Surely some better thing awaited him in the months ahead. Thanks to Billy Roark.

It had taken almost a full week—locked in a Waynesville motel—to finally arrive at the conclusion that the harassing calls and the bloody nocturnal visit had been the work of Billy Roark. It occurred to him that he may never have seen this person, may never have known him at all; he had heard stories of officers being killed by such men bearing misplaced grudges. Then there was the name, Jim Tyler, the man he was accused of killing. Try as he might, he could not be sure he had ever known anyone by that name. In only one year, the details of Vietnam had already been erased from his memory like one of those children's perpetual drawing games where you lift the sheet of plastic and everything disappears but a tangle of indecipherable impressions.

He listed every man in Vietnam whose name he could recall, and Tyler's seemed to belong among those, but he wondered if that was only because he had recently repeated it so many times. He read the list over and paused when he came to Turner Wilson. He had written Wilson in Vietnam when the full impact of Fort Leonard Wood began to hit, telling him how wonderful a place it was, so full of opportunities, suggesting that he also try for an assignment there. But Wilson—a captain now—had replied that although he had applied for assignment to Fort Lewis, Washington, he was instead on orders to Wolters. A few months later another letter from Wilson arrived, bearing the depressing news that he was now happily ensconced in Texas, very pleased with everything. Phillip never answered that letter, but he did save Wilson's address and number. He decided to call.

Turner Wilson seemed surprised and glad to hear from him. As Phillip listened to the young officer go on at length about how marvelous things were, he could not help but picture an excited puppy. It made him feel old. He waited patiently, then directed the conversation to Vietnam. Wilson gave him a complete update on who had made it out and who had been killed.

"Oh, say, I ran into a fellow a few days ago who asked if I knew a Jim Tyler," Crable said. "Said he was stationed at Evans. The name sounded familiar, but I couldn't place him. Do you recall?"

"Yes, I do," Wilson said, his voice instantly flat. "Tyler was the one we left in Laos that night."

The sudden memory sent a wrench of fear twisting through Phillip. He stayed on the line long enough to not be obvious, then made his excuses and hung up. He immediately put on his coat and hat and walked to the corner store for a bottle of antacid. Now that he remembered Jim Tyler, he remembered him much too clearly; he could see his face.

The next day, during spare moments at his desk, he studied the list again, shortening it to include only those who he was certain were acquainted with Tyler. Then he narrowed it to men who might have been his friends, removing six that Wilson had said were killed. That brought it down to only five, but by then the answer seemed obvious: Billy Roark. Crable had not thought of him for some time, but Roark was a memory that grew more bitter with every repetition of his name. Foremost was the humiliating experience the night they landed on Hamburger Hill, the belligerent self-righteousness, the scathing remarks in front of the enlisted men; then later, the principled rebuke about the decorations. Roark the hero, Roark the snot-nosed kid who was going to win the war or be blown to bits. Oh, yes, he remembered him very clearly now: Roark of the dormant insanity that had only been waiting for war. Suddenly he had almost no doubt that the madman of the night was Billy Roark.

Turner Wilson had mentioned that Roark was at Fort Wolters. Under the pretense of being an old buddy, Crable placed a call to Wolters's Personnel. The officer he spoke with was most helpful, producing not only the name of Roark's outfit, but also the name and phone number of his flight commander. Phillip composed his lines, then made the next call.

"Captain Eddleton, I am an old friend of Billy Roark. He came by to see me last weekend, but I was out of town and missed him . . ."

"Oh, you must be in New Mexico."

"Yes, that's correct."

"Well, he's out giving instruction right now. Should be back in here in a little while. You want me to have him give you a call?"

"No, that's okay. I'll catch him later at home." Crable got off the phone before the man thought to ask his name.

So it was definitely Roark, creeping around in the dark, trying to blame his devils on somebody else. But that was not especially surprising; there were thousands of kids just like him who went to war looking for excitement and glory, and wound up instead with their friends dead and parts of their own bodies chopped off. Then they spent their time searching the black hallways for someone to blame for their bitter disappointment that their one-way journey had ended at some unexpected destination. War was glorious, all right, but only for a piddling few.

There was still a bit of hopeful complacency in Phillip, a feeling that if he did nothing at all, something would eventually happen to make things work out. He was abdicating responsibility for the direction of his life, and when he realized that, it scared him almost as badly as the threat of Billy Roark. Unwittingly, he had allowed the return of the insidious moral laziness he once thought he had so soundly defeated. He set about taking positive steps to regain control. He first called post housing, asking that he be assigned bachelor quarters. That done, he stood to make the next crucial move. Was he absolutely certain? Yes, he decided. Absolutely. He walked out to the desk clerk, asked for four copies of Form 483, Officer's Assignment Preference Statement. When the clerk gave him a questioning look, he did not even notice. A convincing, explanatory letter would have to accompany the request, and he was already writing it in his head. He returned to his desk to initiate the procedure for getting orders to Vietnam.

It had all gone so smoothly. It felt great to be back in control. The two months it took to receive orders passed very quickly, then he was suddenly on his way, leaving Missouri and Billy Roark and all his troubles behind.

"Mr. Roark!"

Crable's pale eyes went wide. *Mister?* Did he say *mister?* The word sent a spear of terror shooting through his chest, exploding upward to his head. *Mister Roark.* It couldn't be. *It could not be.* The superficial part of his mind was saying the words, but the rest seemed to know the truth; a wave of nausea swept over him. He almost dropped his glass. "You wan' anotha?" the girl asked, but he didn't hear. Slowly he pushed himself off the stool. Mr. Roark, he thought. Mr. Billy Roark, of course. He moved to the end of the bar where he could see through the latticework and stood studying the men along the tables, row after row. When he finally came to Roark enough time had passed to reduce the shock, to know that the obvious was true. Of course Billy Roark was there; of course he had followed him back to Vietnam. Of course.

Crable was almost physically ill. Unable now to form any coherent thought, any explanation other than that he was being hunted by a determined killer, he turned his stricken face aside and hurried for the door.

What was it like, they asked. I told the simple truth and said it wasn't like anything.

Down at the tables the women worried with the midday meal, capable hands cooking for a hundred, talking of births and deaths and ailments, passing the record through the daughters. I remembered those magnificent women from when I was small, their backsides balanced around the stoves like so many blue uprooted stumps, a formidable wall of flowered rumps between me and the pans of cobbler.

Away from the tables, in the pollened breeze moving off the fields, the menfolk sat in council, stroking their faces with fingers bent like roots in rocky ground, telling the stories one more time. In my adolescence I sat outside that ring, watching as much as listening, learning how to load a cheek with tobacco, how to work a bleeding hangnail with a pocketknife, how to make a chain from a stick of mesquite, and how a cowboy can look dressed up just by wetting his hair and buttoning his shirt to the top.

I had arrived after midnight. In the morning, after the hugs and handshakes, the howdies and I declares, I retreated to my cot to *sip coffee, to watch the reunion turn, to await the right moment to step forward. But I was slow, and it wasn't long until friendly lawn chairs clacked into place beside me.*

No, really, they said, what was it like?

Others began to walk over. Naturally, rightfully, the teenagers came. I was a hero to them, and when I saw that, I wanted desperately to disappear. Some older ones came, though none with experience. Some brought an honest ignorance, wanting to understand; others had answers they were satisfied with, but came to study me with assumed wisdom, to stand silent with folded arms so I would see.

I cared for the adults, but the best among them were beyond importance. It was the boys now, the ones so near my own age. I saw their eager eyes and slipped a little, not so far from four-hour nights, listening for incoming or the step of a sapper; not so far from living like some grotesque jack-in-the-box, wondering how long before my head would slam through the roof and I'd be left weaving, grinning and glassy-eyed for the interpreters.

I couldn't talk to my people; we no longer shared a language. I could have horrified them, I could have made them hate me, but I couldn't talk to them. I could have told them about Burdock and Blackburn and Andy Ross, about Deiterman and Luskey coming down from the Z, about Baker and Dooley and Sharp and Jim Tyler. I could have told them how I hated it and loved it and missed it, and how I felt so many things that never were given words, and how there was a part so way down deep that wished I had died with my friends. I could have told them all the things I'd learned and everything I'd seen in the lifetime of a year, but I couldn't do it without saying so much less than it would take to truly explain, and so much more than anybody ever wanted to hear.

So one summer day some people I call family, sitting in lawn chairs and sipping iced tea, asked me to say the words that would make them know the essence of war. I forced my face into a smile and mumbled the ancient permissible lies until the questions stopped and the intimate strangers all wandered away.

CHAPTER THIRTY-TWO

B Y THE end of summer the dusty inertia of An Khe was the same that now blanketed most of the American troops in Vietnam. Vietnamization was the word. That and going home. The 1st Marine Division and most of the 1st Cav departed in April, the 173d Airborne Brigade in August. Most frightening of all, the 1/5th Mech was withdrawn from the edge of the DMZ, turning defense of the area completely over to the ARVNs. The responsibility of fighting the war was being suddenly transferred to the South Vietnamese. That the task should have been theirs all along seemed irrelevant since they still were incapable of handling it. For the GIs who were fortunate enough to have arrived late and thus did not become deeply involved in the losing effort, it was perceived as a brutal joke—*nice knowing you, Nguyen, you're a dead motherfucker.* But for those who were on their second or third or fourth tour, still trying to win the war, it was another thing entirely.

An ARVN firebase near Cambodia was overrun and completely wiped out, the artillery captured; a column of NVA was spotted on the outskirts of Pleiku by a pilot in a Bird Dog; and there was talk that something big was brewing again in the I Drang. But such stories in An Khe had become sleepy hocus-pocus. The scouts

scoured the countryside each day, and though the accumulated results were impressive, none of the individual finds was important.
On the occasional day when a bird returned from the boonies shot
through with a few holes, the event was discussed with the distance and hazy objectivity of a rumor.

All summer Roark hunted with dogged determination. He
quickly realized that scouting was natural for him; it was, after all,
simply hunting men, and men were much easier prey than most
animals. They were lazier, dumber, and burdened with egos. The
elements of survival were essentially the same—food, water, and
shelter—but there were many factors less obvious. Drinking water
must be moving, moving water makes noise, and a man will walk
only so far to reach it each day. Men like sunlight, they like a
breeze to drive away the insects and the odor of their waste, they
like to be dry. When they are hunted they like high ground to defend, with a way to escape. But what separates them most from the
animals is that they like a permanent camp. And a permanent
camp, no matter how well hidden, can always eventually be found.
All this Roark knew. He only overlooked the obvious, that when
men gather in camps the level of comfort they demand grows in
direct proportion to their numbers.

As the season changed and II Corps began to catch the fringe of
the northern monsoon, the mornings were sometimes laced with
fog, the Deo Mang—An Khe Pass—socked in. Soon, Roark
thought, there would come a night when Pleiku and Lane would be
struck at the same moment, and An Khe would be on its own. An
Khe would be lost, and even if the enemy did not push for the
coast, they would then control the Highlands; even if they did not
try to destroy Pleiku outright, the highway would be closed, the
plateau captured. The ARVNs would not have the conviction to
take it back, and the Americans would say it was no longer their
fight. Roark reasoned it through again and again, always arriving at
the same conclusion, always making the same mistake, forgetting
that the enemy was less desperate than he.

There were two encouraging events early in September. One
morning, on a preliminary sweep, Pete Gladewater and his new
wingman, Huckabee, who came aboard when Jarvis went home,
surprised a squad of NVA crossing a shallow stream. Huckabee's
gunner, Sergeant Altman, who had flown with Jarvis and was now
in his twelfth month, cut loose instantly, putting two men facedown in the water. The gunships rolled in with rockets, but overshot from lack of a good mark. When the scouts curled back for
another look and to drop a white smoke on the gloomy stream, a
soldier on the bank hit Gladewater's bird with an abbreviated burst

to the belly. Altman cut him down with rounds through both legs. The Cobras came in again with rockets, then shredded the jungle with miniguns. The skirmish was over. The bloody drag of the dying man stained the bank, and the bodies in the stream bobbed against some rocks. Altman fired a burst into each of the corpses, sending pink geysers through the trees.

Altman's quick response displayed what the scouts had decided to do about the adjusted rules of engagement. It was too much to send men out to hover among the branches as clay pigeons, airborne reporters. Regulations were made in offices; rules were made in the jungle, and in the jungle there were only two: survive, and take care of each other. Nobody but an idiot ever let the other man shoot first. A few days later, Roark and Blue took it the next logical step.

The wingman's machine gun jammed badly that morning during test fire, so while Alphie returned to An Khe for a replacement weapon, Roark spent the minutes flying fast and low along either side of the Song Ba west of the Ears. The gunships, led by Gil McCawley, flew casually overhead, keeping an eye on the scout, enjoying the scenery. Down the long valley toward Cheo Reo, tall cumulus columns stood softly rigid, platinum posts against a cirrus-streaked and steel-blue sky. Along the east side of the river where it curved back southward, the lower hills were covered with dense scrub, but across the water lay a flat plain appointed with slender trees in short green grass and clover, a parkland that seemed to belong on the plains of Africa. The land rose gently to the west until it began to be broken by rounded hills in thin forest, finally bumping into a timbered wall of mountains guarding VC Valley. Though numerous paths weaved across the plain, it was too open to expect to find anything there. The scout skimmed playfully through the trees, killing time.

Roark and Blue saw the men at the same instant; they passed less than ten feet above the prostrate forms. "We got gooks in the open," Roark announced, and he climbed in a tight turn and circled back, expecting a barrage of fire.

"Gotcha covered, One-two," McCawley said. "Be careful."

The eight men were NVA in khakis and pith helmets, camouflaged with fresh cuttings of bamboo. Each was armed with an AK and wore a small khaki rucksack, their pants wet to the knees. As the helicopter circled, one by one they raised their faces. "You want me to waste 'em?" Blue said.

"Wait a minute," Roark snapped. The reactive instant was past; it would have been much easier if Blue had simply cut loose like

Altman. The NVA began to ease their weapons around. "Two-three, be ready with nails."

"Got 'em dialed in."

"Let me know when you're coming around."

"Okay, One-two. Five seconds," McCawley said.

"You ready, Blue?"

"Right on."

Roark tightened his turn to flatten the arch and dropped to within twenty feet of the ground. Approaching an enfilade, he slowed, leveled the ship, and said, "Do it," then immediately yelled, "TAKING FIRE!" By then that was true. Three of the gooks never fired a shot, but the others spun through the spray of dirt, five guns blazing back at Blue, then four. The ship shuddered with several hits, and the cockpit was filled with a clattering, flashing swarm of ejected shells. Two rounds zipped past Blue and exited through Roark's windshield, and another bit off the pitot tube. Then they were away and peeling right, and the flechettes were screaming down, dispersing high above the ground with their peculiar double pop and crackling hiss. The remaining men were instantly dead, drilled through with a thousand steel darts—nailed to the ground, as the pilots said.

There were vague rumblings in Operations that afternoon. Captain Dunning seemed to know what had happened, but no one could argue with the bullet holes.

The two incidents made it seem that An Khe was again involved in a tiny war. Even then the situation might have returned to doldrums were it not for Billy Roark. He began to spend every spare moment studying his map, reading it like an absorbing book. For hours he would sit cross-legged against a revetment, map in hand, raising his head occasionally to gaze toward the mountains. Immersed in his imagination, the squiggly brown contour lines, the rambling blue threads of streams, the shaded tones of vegetation became jungled terrain—mountains, cliffs, and canyons—as if he were passing slowly above on a timeless mission. He visualized each detail, and what he saw was real. Then one day he remembered the Frenchman, and as he thought about him, moving cautiously through the jungle on his eternal search, Roark assumed his place. He discovered then that he could see beneath the trees, see the ground where the Frenchman walked. It was an important difference that made him know it would be only a matter of time until he tracked the regiment down.

A few miles southeast of An Khe, beyond the grassy saddle called Elephant Gap, the eastern slope of the Dak Pokor rose steeply along a tumbling brook to a rounded triangular shelf. From there the climb resumed in a gradual ascent before surging suddenly upward, forming a half basin with walls of five hundred feet. It was a natural fortress, unassailable except from the air. Merely by studying the map and imagining himself on the ground, Roark became certain a base camp was there. The next day, a mission proved him correct; it was a company-size element, larger than what they normally found, but not what he was looking for. They leveled the site with the help of Phantoms and called in artillery along the likely avenues of escape, but the massive display of firepower produced not a single confirmed KIA. As usual, the enemy elected not to fight, simply vanishing into the jungle.

Then, in October, they stumbled onto the NVA regiment.

He already had reason to believe it was going to be a bad day, but seeing Captain Dunning dressed in a flight suit instead of his usual fatigues felt like a written guarantee. The first words out of Dunning's mouth confirmed it.

"There won't be a recon mission today," he said. "We're pulling the Ranger platoon out of the woods a day early. Scouts, we'll need you to provide close air cover while they're moving to a pickup zone. After that, we'll come back here to wait for convoy cover."

"Why no recon?" Roark said. A mumble of agreement rose among the pilots.

"We need to save air time."

"For what?"

"We've been through this so many times."

"That's right, and I still say we need to be more concerned with saving our asses than air time. They sent these helicopters here to be flown."

"Roger on that," someone said.

"You're walking a thin line, Mr. Roark."

"So who isn't?"

"Are you through?" Dunning said. "If you're through, I'd like to continue with the briefing."

"Just one more thing. Sir. When are we going to hit that base camp out in the bamboo flats?"

"And we've been through that, too." Dunning's frustration was suddenly anger. "That's quite enough out of you, Mr. Roark. One more word and you're pulled from the mission."

Roark clamped his lips and gazed coolly at the captain, but he could not prevent the color rising in his cheeks. He leaned against the counter and mechanically lit a cigarette. One thing about the Army, he thought, when you run out of brains you can always fall back on your rank. Or your ass. He waited until Dunning had indicated the location of the platoon, then left the briefing room.

Blue was slouched in the back seat of the Kiowa, one foot propped on the ammo can. Roark paused a few feet away, and the two men exchanged silent paragraphs. When it was done, Roark moved to the tail boom, untied the blade, then gave the tail rotor a once-over as he circled the ship. The cotter pins were still in place.

Blue's most recent stunt had rattled Roark because it affected the aircraft. Though Blue had stopped in time, it seemed solid evidence of how far this thing might go.

That morning, Blue had waited until they were almost ready to lift off from Lane, then he keyed his mike. "You forgot to check the tail rotor," he said. Feeling like the coyote in the cartoons, Roark shut the engine down. His preflight had been hasty, and he had failed to observe that two cotter pins had been removed from the tail rotor assembly.

But no matter, Roark thought, there's always paybacks.

Soon the other pilots emerged from Operations. As Roark feared, Captain Dunning came with them; Shamrock Three would be flying as the right-seat pilot in the chase slick. As the ranking officer, he also assumed the position of air mission commander.

The mission was boring and simple and went off without a hitch. The Ranger platoon was moving through low cover along the narrow crest of a ridge, so the scouts moved ahead and around them, checking casually for ambushes, generally killing them until the troops reached the PZ. When they were finally assembled for extraction and the first Huey was beginning its approach, the scouts pulled out to wait in orbit to the south in case they were needed again. Still chafing because his anticipated reconnaissance had been canceled, Roark gave Castle instructions to remain on station, then peeled off to the south to have a look around.

When Roark groped for a cigarette, suddenly realizing he had left his pack on the counter in Ops, Blue noticed the move. He clipped the D-rings together, suspending the weapon from the jamb, then slowly produced his own pack from a shin pocket. Taking his time, he lipped a cigarette, then casually returned the pack to his pants. Roark stiffened at the scent of smoke, considering just how badly he wanted a cigarette.

The two men had never even come close to a truce. It was customary for the scout crews to strike a balance between the two ships, matching the more experienced pilot with the less experienced gunner in the lead ship, then reversing the arrangement at wing. By rights, now that Roark was experienced, Blue should have been gunning at wing, but he had stubbornly refused to change.

Tasting the traces of smoke, aware he was rebreathing Blue's breath, Roark eyed the mountains ahead and below. Occasionally he hung his head out the door to look straight down at the jungle. Delta's area of operation was completely surrounded by territory supposedly controlled by the ARVNs, actually controlled by the NVA. Since the ARVNs were in charge of those places, their sovereignty had to be observed. But so did their incompetence. It had to be considered that if the ARVNs ever went on patrol, they might blunder across the boundary. For that reason, the edges of Delta's AO were deliberately neglected.

Approaching the southeast corner, Roark began to turn back. He had gone much farther than he had intended—the other aircraft were small in the distance—but it was exciting to fly over new terrain. He increased airspeed to rejoin the flight, then gazed again toward the jungle, straight into the center of the regimental base camp. Immediately he keyed his mike. "We've got gooks *everywhere* down here," he said. Blue straightened from his slump, thumped his cigarette away, and grabbed his machine gun. Far beneath them, through gaps in the trees on a flat shoulder of mountain, figures in tan and black were scrambling for cover, clearly visible against patches of packed earth.

"One-two, where are you?" McCawley said.

"Uh, well, I drifted a little south. Just come this way, you'll see me."

"One-two, this is Three. That'll be a negative on anyone coming south. You're supposed to be here with the rest of us."

"Roger, Three. Any chance of getting some fastmovers out here ASAP? This is the big one. I can see about six acres of packed dirt through the trees even from this altitude. I can see rows of hooches."

"That'll be a negative, One-two. Return to the flight immediately."

"You mean you're just going to let them go?"

"We'll see about it tomorrow," Dunning said. "We've used up our mission time for today. Now get back on up here."

Where the hell is McLeod? Roark fumed. Blue laid his weapon across his lap, fumbled at his pants, and produced another cigarette. When it was lit, Roark turned and glared at him. "You got a cigarette you could spare, *goddamn it*!?" Blue turned black eyes on him, but the tip of the cigarette was unsteady. He removed the Tareyton from his mouth and slowly held it out. Roark stared at the wet filter, then took it without a word.

That evening, as all the other men who were not remaining overnight at An Khe made preparations to leave, Roark deliberately lingered in the Doghouse. All the other birds were gone when he made his way toward the ship. Blue was there, waiting beside the aircraft, looking unconcerned. Roark walked right past him. "We going back to Lane?" Blue asked in a carefully sullen tone.

Roark turned and glanced at his watch. "Yeah, in about a half hour. I've got to go see Acres about some maps." He walked away toward Operations.

"Just great," Blue said. He turned and stomped off in the direction of the Doghouse.

Operations was empty, but a light was burning beyond the drapes in the back of the hooch where Acres lived. He heard Roark come through the door. "Hello," he said. "Can I help you with something, sir?"

"No, just killing time," Roark said. "I'll only be here a minute." He stepped into the shadows behind the counter and watched until Blue disappeared at the far side of the ramp. He waited another minute before walking quickly back to the aircraft. Payback time, Blue.

As soon as the turbine whine began, Blue came jogging past the Greenhouse, then slowed to an indifferent walk when he knew that he could be seen. Roark went casually through the cockpit procedure. There was plenty of time. Then, when he was ready, he made his takeoff directly from the revetment, leaving Blue to bum a place to spend the night.

CHAPTER THIRTY-THREE

George McLeod sipped his evening Scotch, then leaned back in his new rocker and let his eyelids fall, listening to the traveling sound on the wooden floor. The chair cupped his body like a soothing hand, a consoling place to rest. He smiled at the image he must have made, but immediately rejected it. I'm not that old, he thought.

He had found the chair at a woodworking shop in Qui Nhon. Built oversize from tree limbs and strips of bamboo laced together without nails, the chair was designed for the shape of a man likely to enjoy it most. The woven bottom of bamboo ribbons was wide and ample, and the back was tall to support the head. The surfaces of the runners, as well as the arms, had been planed and carefully sanded, and across the toes was a narrow footrest which, when used, made the rocker tilt far back on generous heels. It was a chair where a man could meditate or sleep without considering the difference.

Deep in the comfort of the rocker, McLeod was unsure if it made him relax, or if it merely provided the excuse. For the first time in his life he was beginning to feel tired, or lazy, and to acknowledge that he felt that way.

The major's room commanded a long view of the pathway between the flight line and the hooches, and as he looked out now he saw Billy Roark slowly ascending the slope. Watching him, feeling more than a twinge of guilt, McLeod forgot to breathe. He was making it up with a chest-lifting sigh when Roark paused, then abruptly turned in his direction. "Well, have you seen the Frenchman yet?" McLeod called.

Roark said nothing until he opened the screened door. He looked drawn and strange, an old man with a bad facelift. "No, sir, I haven't," he said, "but he's out there."

"How do you know?"

"Because he *needs* to be."

The major smiled uncomfortably and sipped his drink. "The Frenchman was crazy," he said.

"No," Roark replied. "He was merely determined."

McLeod hesitated, then smiled again. "You want a drink?"

"No, thank you."

"Captain Dunning has been complaining about you."

"He's an amateur."

"He's also a captain."

"I can come back some other time, sir."

"No," McLeod said sharply. "Let's go ahead and get this done." He directed his eyes through the screen, and when he spoke again his voice was smoother. "You're going to have to soften a bit," he said. "There're ways of doing the job without making enemies."

"I'm not believing what I'm hearing."

"Your point," McLeod acknowledged. "Sit down. But I'm right. I'd like to see you stay in the Army. There's still time to get you a direct commission."

"So I can be like you someday?" Roark said, still standing. He waited for a reaction, but McLeod accepted the blow in silence. "Besides that, I won't be a lieutenant. That's a demotion from CW2."

"You'd be captain in a year."

"Not interested. What I want is to extend."

"Why?"

"I want to make certain I don't have to leave until I've accomplished something. I made that mistake before."

The major shifted in his chair. "So how are you and Blue getting along?" he asked.

Roark looked puzzled and annoyed. "Good enough," he said.

"You ever find out his story?"

"It never really made a damn."

"He had a brother, a grunt in the 101st. Got killed at Hue in '68 when a Huey pilot refused to bring in ammo."

"So this is a place of sad stories."

"To him you're probably that pilot. If he hasn't backed off by now, he's not going to, meaning he's going the other way. Don't take anything for granted."

"That sounds like excellent advice."

"What?"

"Why weren't you there today, sir?"

"I knew the regiment would be gone."

"So why weren't you there *yesterday* when we found them?"

"Losing interest, I suppose."

"You mean *quitting*."

"Maybe. Maybe I am. But there comes a time to call a waste a waste, a time to give up the game and stop pretending. We're losing, Billy, fighting too many things at once."

"You're losing, Major, I'm not. You're sitting here on your butt in that rocking chair, thinking about old times, waiting to go home and start over. Just like the whole goddamned Army, reduced to excuses."

"Easy, boy!" McLeod's big hands gripped the chair like the edges of a catapult. Roark didn't budge.

"You baited me every step of the way," he said. "From the first day we met. You recognized what I am the minute you saw me, and you figured I could find your regiment, get your war started again, and let you retire vindicated. So it's been you and me and Don Quixote, chasing an enemy that doesn't exist. But he *does* exist, and I found him, and now I'm out there by myfuckingself and you're here on your ass, halfway home, letting that pisshead you call an Operations officer run the show. *You* should have been there, and *you* should have gotten me some firepower *yesterday* when we needed it."

"Now you hold it right there . . ."

"I'm holding nothing! There was housing on that mountain today for six hundred men. Rows of hooches bigger than this one. A sapper school with real concertina wire. Hand-dug caves in the slopes behind. So we bring in Fox-fours and napalm and burn it all down, and we get lucky and get some secondaries from the caves. But we didn't kill one gook. Not one. They evacuated the place yesterday, naturally. So now the regiment's gone, but I guarantee you I'm going to find them again, and next time it's going to be different. *You* are the only one who's been pretending!"

"Sit down, Billy . . ."

"Fuck you, old man!"

When he slammed the door, a panel of dust shot from the screen, swirling furiously in a sunlit storm before the energy relaxed and died. The major sat motionless in his chair, watching the golden pieces fall. A glob of sweat broke loose and raced glistening down a burnished cheek.

The padlock was off, the door bolted from inside. He tapped a soft pattern, and a moment later a naked Saccharin slipped the screwdriver back and let him into the darkened room. The sight of her nakedness gave him a lift. "'Lo, Be-Ro," she said, then threw a quick hug around his middle and darted to the bed where she covered herself with a sheet. "Where you been?"

"Up at the club."

"I see you t'ings, know you heah. You An Khe las' ni'?"

"Yeah."

"I sleep heah las' ni'. Wai' fo' you. I don' know, maybe you come."

Roark gave a tired smile. "Sorry I didn't call," he said.

"Call?"

"Never mind." Since giving her the key, Saccharin came often to the room late at night, even when he wasn't there. Each morning before dawn she would slip down the hill to spend the daylight hours with the other girls in the Whoretel, the narrow secret room the enlisted men had built. Lately, as his efforts at locating the regiment had intensified, he had been spending more nights at An Khe. Though he never allowed himself to think of her as anything but a rather cute whore, it gave him a certain comfort knowing she might be sleeping in his bed while he was away. "You want to take a shower?"

"Sounds good to me."

He peeled away his smelly clothing, changed into shorts and sandals, and wrapped Saccharin in his terry-cloth robe. With his gunbelt around his hips, carrying his shower kit and a flashlight, he led the way down the hill, carefully watching the trail for deadly bamboo vipers. They passed Kirby Hockett coming up from the four-holer. "Hey, Roark," he mumbled as they passed, but made no indication he saw the girl.

They washed each other in the darkness, black silhouettes against the amber light from Supply, then Saccharin carefully shaved him in the beam of the flashlight. The night air felt chill as they climbed the trail. All the camp seemed asleep, but somewhere someone watched—maybe a new guard his first night on the perimeter, maybe a lonely, homesick soldier smoking deep in some dark corner, maybe the major sitting quietly in his chair.

The bed was built of two-by-fours, with four-bys for posts, nailed to the wall, telegraphing the struggle. While the fan hummed and cooled their bodies, the candle dancing wildly, Saccharin wanted to talk. "Eh, Be-Ro, w'at choo do w'en wah ovah fo' you?"

"It's not going to be over for me until it's *over*. I'm extending."

"You stay?"

"That's right. I'm staying 'til it's over."

"Maybe long time."

"Maybe."

"Then you fini' Army?"

"Yes."

"Maybe you stay Vietnam?"

"Stay? Why would anybody stay?"

"Vietnam beau'iful."

"I thought all the girls wanted to go to the States."

"No' me. I wan' mally GI, stay heah."

"That's one I haven't heard."

"Maybe you stay wi' me, have beaucoup baby-san."

He suddenly realized what she was saying. Marry a Vietnamese girl? he thought. A whore, yet? Stay in Vietnam after the war? Not likely. The war was going to be over very soon, the GIs gone. He got a sudden glimpse of what that would mean for Vietnam, what it would be like for Saccharin and the others. When the Americans were safely gone, the big attack would come. Some of the ARVNs would stand and fight, but Vietnam would fall. Then what would conditions be? He saw himself standing on a hill somewhere, looking out across the countryside, the last GI in Vietnam. It was a lonely feeling, but not all that different from the way it had felt for a long time. "When the war is over," he said carefully, "you will probably change your mind. A GI here would be out of place, and all the people will think he's ugly. His children will be ugly, and no one will want them. It will be much better for you if you fall in love with a Vietnamese man." He felt her stiffen at his side.

"Nevah happen," she said. "Sakrung love nobo'y. Maybe mally, maybe have baby, two baby, fo' baby, bu' Sakrung no love. No love nobo'y, *nevah*. Evahbo'y die. Sakrung no love."

When she was asleep, he pulled on shorts and went outside to lean against the sandbags and smoke. Soon the black surface of the night was painted with images of the day, the orderly rows of NVA barracks, the newly thatched roofs of banana leaves, the boiling, flaming mushrooms of the secondaries. The biggest find on the An

Khe plateau in years was a complete and total waste. The enemy simply walked away and left it, realizing that the Americans would not even consider inserting troops. Maybe they never left, but only pulled back a safe distance into the jungle where they could watch and wait. Roark saw it all as if he were one of them, looking down from the slopes across the canyon: the two helicopters, so small above the vast complex, hovering around in complete impotence, while nearby in the trees lay hundreds of NVA who ached to blow them away. The image was suddenly replaced with that of a dark-eyed girl asleep in his bed, a girl who still believed that the power and presence of the United States would eventually win the war.

Phillip Crable sat with his back to the corner, flicking his eyes between the cool red disk of the descending sun and the fading magenta patch it made on a steel cabinet. When the color was gone he opened the cabinet and took out an envelope, pausing to study a photograph taped inside the door, an old one of him and Rita that had been torn into four pieces and crumpled, then taped together. She had not yet cut her hair, and it puddled around her shoulders.

The letter from Rita had arrived more than a month ago. Though he had not yet opened it, the envelope was softened now with tiny wrinkles. He often sat and held it in the evenings, not yet ready to yield the possibilities.

The door of the hooch burst open, and Davy Pach strode in with his usual exuberance. He was a red-faced, excited young captain who worked in S-1 and doubled as the squadron Arms Control Officer. "Off your ass," he shouted. "Let's get up to the club. I'll buy you a T-bone."

"No, thanks," Phillip said with a polite smile. "I've already eaten."

"Well, come on anyway. Brown and Klepper are going, too. *Come on!* Get up off your dead butt and let's go! All you ever do is work or sit here holed up in the hooch."

"Thank you for the offer, Dave, but I'm tired. I've got a letter to write, then I think I'll turn in early."

"You always turn in early, you know that?" Pach said gently. "At least you say you do. I think you need to get checked, Phillip. You haven't looked good for a long time. You need some red meat. Come on, go with us."

"Thanks, really, but I'm okay. I'm just tired."

"Suit yourself. You're missing out." Pach disappeared into his

room. They shared the end of the hooch, and though a wall separated their quarters, it stopped short of complete privacy to allow
both spaces to be served by a common outside door. Brown and
Klepper had similar arrangements on the opposite side of the building. Pach rummaged around in his room a moment, then appeared
again in the doorway. "Last chance," he said. "Oh, say, did you
hear about the weapons?" That got Phillip's complete attention.
"They're taking them up," Pach said. "The whole camp is going to
have to turn them in every night, through the rank of captain.
They'll be locked up in a CONEX container."

"But what if there's an attack? What if sappers come?"

"Everybody's going to have to stand in line and wait to be issued
a weapon."

"Oh, my . . ."

"Yeah, it'll be murder. But we knew it was coming."

"I suppose . . ."

"Catch you later," Pach said, and dashed out the door and down
the side of the hooch, shouting for Brown and Klepper.

Phillip was thoroughly shaken by the news, although, as Pach
said, it was expected. The measure was the result of a recent sharp
rise in violent incidents at Lane, two in only the past week. On
Sunday, a captain in the 129th was fragged in his bunk. Addled and
seriously wounded, he still managed to find his revolver in the rub-
ble and kill the first man who came to his aid. Just three days later
there was a small war over at the 803d.

Fragging incidents—the tossing of fragmentation grenades
through a door or knife-slit screen to kill a sleeping man—were on
the rise. Though troop strength was now less than half the peak
reached in 1969, the rate of fraggings had nearly tripled, with one
new case occurring somewhere in Vietnam almost every day. Just
since Crable's arrival, there had been four such incidents at Lane
Army Heliport, plus two drunken exchanges of gunfire. In the
most recent, a squabble between sister grunt platoons had erupted
into a genuine firefight that put the camp on red alert and set the
sirens wailing; four men dead, a dozen sent to the hospital.

He reached for his holster where it hung at the head of his bed
and withdrew the .38. The pistol was filthy and neglected; flecks of
rust frosted the barrel. He fumbled with the locking mechanism
until he got the cylinder open, glanced at the bullets, then gingerly
pressed it shut. He had always been uncomfortable with the
weapon, but not nearly so much as he now would be without it.

His ears were ringing like thin-voiced cicadas, each in a different
tone, sometimes wavering as if traveling across a windy distance.
It was dark now. Through the side screen he could see a short dis-

tance between the hooches. A floodlight sent a harsh white spray sliding along the ground, drawing black slashes behind each tiny stone. He reached high to light a candle frozen in a puddle of wax atop the cabinet, then returned to his chair. All the room began to tremble in the fluttering light except his corner, hidden in darkness. He had always enjoyed candles for their soothing privacy, the smallness of their universe, the almost motherly reassurance of the flame. He held that thought as long as he could.

Since his discovery of Billy Roark, Phillip had almost convinced himself that the man's appearance at Lane Army Heliport was merely a coincidence. The warrant officer was clearly disturbed, and it was very common for such men to ask for reassignment to Vietnam. With the available number of units steadily decreasing, the likelihood of sharing the same camp had grown considerably. Besides, Phillip had discovered that Roark was now flying Kiowas, which meant that he had taken a transition course after leaving Wolters—not the kind of move a man bent on murder was likely to make. It all made perfect sense, he assured himself; Roark was there by accident.

Even if he could have believed that, Phillip still was faced with the problem that Roark *was* there; he was a threat whether trailing him or not. The best approach was to avoid contact as long as possible. He poured himself into his work and spent the remainder of his hours reading in his hooch. His stomach problems returned with flaming intensity, enough to knock eight pounds off his already bony frame, but he dared not see a doctor; not only would the diagnosis of an ulcer permanently ground a pilot, such a condition was an unacceptable sign of weakness in a society of men. Nothing less than vomiting blood would do.

Sitting in comparative isolation night after night, absorbed in consideration of his worries, it became very difficult for Phillip to control his imagination. Just as he had built himself up enough to risk another trip to the club, he would look out the screened side of the hooch and think he saw Billy Roark disappearing around a corner. Simple paranoia, he told himself now, and then remembered that his pistol was about to be taken away. Then what will I do, he wondered.

Eventually, just as he did every evening, he began to contemplate the newest problem in his life, perhaps the only one that truly mattered: He had begun to wonder if it was really worth the struggle. It seemed an eternity ago since he had been happy. The idea that began with a simple statement one bleak morning in Missouri, the one he thought was gone forever, had sneaked back home undetected. In the early morning hours now, and sometimes when he awakened at night, wrenching whispers involuntarily issued from his lips, cries from his unprotected soul. Later, thoroughly frightened, he would interpret for himself: "I wish this situation were resolved; I wish I were somewhere else with my troubles gone; I wish I could be happy again." That was what I meant, he said. *That* was what I meant. But he could never convince the infected part of his mind; the whispers did not change, and they did not go away. "I wish I were dead," they said. "I wish my life were over. I wish somebody would kill me. God, I wish I were dead." In the afternoon he would soberly deny that any of it was true, but he began to dread those desolate first moments of dawn.

It seemed he should have been prepared, but he was genuinely surprised one morning when he found himself sitting on the side of his bunk with his revolver to his head. It wasn't serious, of course—he hadn't even cocked it, though the Smith & Wesson was a double-action. Later, he regarded it more as a game, a deadly toy that yielded pleasure in its threat, a manly thing, really, caressing the ultimate danger, holding up a great long finger for all creation to take in the backside. He smiled now, remembering the giddy sensation of abandon, the power, the knowledge of unrepealable freedom. But it was only a mental escape, a harmless game of pretend to help him cope until things got better.

The candle was short, but the cabinet was steel and couldn't burn. With his back to the wall, Phillip finally fell asleep in his chair, still clutching the unopened letter.

CHAPTER THIRTY-FOUR

T HE LIEUTENANT crossed the ramp carrying a borrowed flight helmet and a plastic-coated map, walking stiffly and self-consciously as if in a one-man parade. Roark observed his approach with more than a trace of disgust. The young officer appeared fresh off the production line, the perfect American soldier—lean and forthright, perhaps even honest. Such a countenance had no place in Vietnam; it marked a man as a new arrival, a hopeful lifer, or simply an idiot.

"Afternoon," the lieutenant said. His voice was vigorous, but his smile was bashful.

"Afternoon," Roark replied. He helped the man with the belt and harness, then showed him where to plug in the jack.

"Brian Dailey," the lieutenant said, turning in the close quarters to extend a hand. Roark anticipated a strong handshake and got it.

"Roark," he replied, smiling in spite of himself. "So what's the mission, Lieutenant?" He was peeved at his assignment. Each day, Delta Troop was required to provide an unarmed scout bird for the administrative convenience of the task force—mostly mail and shuttle runs along the highway—reducing the permitted air time for reconnaissance.

"Registration," Dailey said. "Schueller just got a self-propelled eight-inch and a one-seven-five from Pleiku. We need to establish a few registration points in the northern AO."

"They shut down a firebase?"

"Sort of. These are leftovers from the Fifty-second."

"They want to get those guns a little farther from Cambodia so the gooks won't get 'em and turn 'em around."

"I really don't know," Dailey replied.

"Well, let's get to it," Roark said. He called the tower for clearance. For once, the operator was at his post; the sky was littered with clouds.

They flew first to Schueller where the lieutenant visited while Roark flew orbits. Despite the milky mission, he was enjoying flying without Blue. A cumulus fleet sailed slowly overhead, stacking far to the south, feeding a deep blue storm. Half a rainbow stood on end among the hills. Slowly he lengthened the circles into oblongs, swinging farther out across the boonies on each successive lap, scouting compulsively. He glanced toward the speckled hills above the Mang Yang, thought of the ghostly Frenchman and wished him well.

When the lieutenant waved, the Kiowa made a quick descent. While the forward observer strapped himself in, Roark eyed the eight-inch gun. It was a thick-barreled, evil-looking thing which seemed it might explode at any moment.

Dailey wanted to register the Long John first, so they climbed to altitude beneath the clouds and headed north. As they crossed the wide sea of bamboo, Roark stared toward the wooded mound where the VC camp was hidden. The lump of greenery had become an irritating blister for him, and he never flew near the place anymore. He had tried repeatedly to gain permission to attack the complex, and each time was denied. He had subsequently gone from thinking that the colonel was protecting the place, to wondering if the man had even had a hand in denying its destruction. There was no way of learning that other than by going directly to the colonel, bypassing the chain of command. But such impudence would guarantee disappointment; he would be out of line, and a smile and a nod today would eventually ripple down as resentment from more than one level. The logjam of the chain of command served many purposes. It was an impenetrable barrier, with each succeeding tier snuggled so tightly into the next it was said that a career officer who turned his head too quickly would break his nose.

"I wanted to fly . . ." Dailey said.

Roark had forgotten his passenger. "So why didn't you?"

"My wife is scared of flying."

"What's she got to do with it?"

"When I asked myself that question it was too late."

"You can still put in for it."

"Yeah, I guess so," Dailey said, but he sounded uncertain. "I'd have to stay in longer if I did that now."

"Three years after training."

"Yeah, well, we've been planning on me getting out before that. Her dad's got a Chevrolet dealership in Nebraska, and I've sort of got a job lined up."

"Where are you from?"

"Minnesota."

Roark was accustomed to talking to a voice rather than a face when he was flying, but now he looked at Dailey. "Sounds like true love to me," he said, then wished he had kept his mouth shut. "If we had a set of controls on your side, I'd give you a quick lesson."

That broke the lieutenant's embarrassment, and his face brightened. "That'd be great," he replied. "That would really be great."

There was an ache in his voice that Roark could understand. "I'll do it anyway," he said. For the next ten minutes he gave an orientation lesson, demonstrating the use and coordination of the controls, explaining each of the instruments, what they did and what a malfunction could mean. The words and movements flowed easily, making him aware of himself and how far he had come in three years. Dailey shifted anxiously in his seat, shuffled his feet around and moved his hands; it was clear he itched to feel the life of the machine himself. "You really ought to consider it," Roark said. "Tell her old man to kiss your ass, you want to fly."

"Really." Dailey smiled with unabashed excitement. As the idea soaked in, he added, "No kidding."

Without warning, Roark dumped the collective and nosed the bird into a curving dive toward the jungle, flaring just above the treetops. They were past the bamboo now, and into the forested hills approaching the winding Song Ba. The clouds were more widely spaced there, and in the sunlit portions the boughs and leaves of the jungle canopy stood out in startling clarity. A flowing flock of Indian Loriquets swept past, metallic sparklers flashing color across the jungle like a worried school of green and chartreuse fish. Brian Dailey laughed the laugh of a small boy.

When they climbed again to altitude and checked the map, they were in the northern extremes of the AO, an area where Roark had never been. The land was hilly there, but much flatter than the lateral reaches of the valley. The terrain was more open, dominated by tall trees and natural meadows.

The purpose of the registration mission was to establish a few known points from which quick adjustment could be made on future area targets. Dailey selected an intersection of two streams, marked the location on his map, then called the coordinates and mission orders back to Schueller. Roark held well to the east in a figure-eight pattern which kept them constantly in view of the impact zone. Both men peered expectantly toward the target. The first round struck amid an area of dense palms, cutting a large opening and sending up a splash of reddish dirt, leaving a suspended plume of gray-white smoke. Dailey called the adjustment, and in seconds another round was coursing through the sky. The second round fell much closer, though still long and to the left. The third was short and right, the fourth long and on line, and the fifth exploded in the treetops within twenty meters of the target, lopping off graceful gray limbs as thick as a man's body. Registration point one complete.

They moved west, then south to establish two more points, chatting between fire missions and rounds. Dailey said he had been in-country three months, and in that time had served three different assignments in the fumbling juggle of withdrawal. It had been a puzzling period; he had experienced no ground attacks and had not once seen the enemy, alive or dead. His only war experience was a halfhearted rocket attack at Pleiku. Still, he felt he was getting valuable experience. He had gotten married during his first and only year of college. He confided to Roark that he did not miss his wife as much as he thought he would.

When the third registration point was established, they moved toward the highway to begin working the eight-inch gun. Roark was enjoying the flight with Dailey. The lieutenant's eager outlook, his sense of wonder about helicopters, and his constant stream of questions were refreshing. Soon the little ship was again above the bamboo plains, with Dailey searching for a landmark to fix their location. Roark was struck with a sudden awareness. "Can you shoot anywhere out here you want to?" he asked.

"Sure," Dailey said. "All the northern AO is a free-fire zone for this mission." Something in Roark's question turned his head, and he saw a wide smile. "Why, what have you got?"

"A VC base camp," Roark said, his eyes bright and hard.

"No kidding? Where?"

"There." He pointed toward the distant mound of green. "In that clump of trees. Eight hooches, ten by twelve; eight bunkers." He switched hands on the cyclic and drew his map from his pants leg. "At the red X," he said.

Dailey made a similar mark on his own map and handed Roark's back. "How do you know about it?" he asked.

"That's my job."

"Has it been hit before?"

"It's never been touched."

Dailey blinked and looked at the trees. The ship was east of the target now, turning back toward it on the FO's side. "Well, let's blast those suckers," he said. Without seeming to do so, he glanced down at the tiny stream east of the camp, confirming Roark's coordinates, then called the fire mission to Schueller. "King Edward Three-alpha, King Edward Two-six. Fire mission, eight-inch, over."

"Two-six, Three-alpha, fire mission, go."

"Three-alpha, Two-six. Bravo Romeo three-four-six-four-nine-one, enemy base camp, eight hooches in heavy cover, eight sod bunkers. Destruction. HE and delay in effect, adjust fire, over."

"Two-six, Three-alpha, roger grid three-four-six-four-nine-one. Destruction. HE and delay in effect, over."

"This is Two-six, affirmative."

"Two-six, Three-alpha, shot, over."

"Three-alpha, Two-six, shot, out."

Roark positioned the ship so that Dailey had a clear view out his door, then began counting the seconds, peering past the lieutenant toward the complex. Somewhere through the sky roared a 200-pound surprise. Seven, eight, nine . . . The initial round landed with rare accuracy; a huge footprint appeared in the bamboo, on line and just fifty meters short of the trees. Three seconds later a heavy, huffing *BaBOOOOM!* rolled through and past the ship like a shuddering wave. "Three-alpha, Two-six, add five-zero, fire for effect, over."

"Two-six, Three-alpha, roger add five-zero, fire for effect, out."

The second round was exactly on target, exploding in the tree-tops, cutting a great swath in the leafy dome and sending a lethal shower of shrapnel slashing through the complex. The next round, equipped with a delayed fuse to allow it to penetrate the trees and become embedded in the earth before exploding, fell just short of dead center and sent a great dusty breath shooting outward from all sides of the grove. Roark guided the ship calmly back and forth, steady and quiet now that the killing had begun. He realized that something would certainly be said, but he had stumbled upon a tiny opening in the tangle of restrictions. Somebody had forgotten to lock the gate; it was time for settling old grudges.

They dropped fourteen shells on the little camp—twenty-eight hundred pounds of steel and TNT—and only two besides the first were clean misses, falling long and laying broad clearings in the bamboo. "You do good work, Lieutenant," Roark said, smiling. Even from a distance, the group of trees looked thoroughly pulverized. Dailey turned and extended his hand.

"Brian," he said. "Call me Brian. I get awfully sick of being called 'lieutenant.'"

"Bill," Roark said, and he switched the cyclic to his left hand. They did a standard handshake, then deftly changed positions to the friendlier grip that the dappers used. Both were smiling happily, for different reasons. Roark's eyes fell upon the fuel gauge. "We're just about out of time," he said.

"Can we take a look at the damage?" Dailey asked. "I'd like to be able to tell the guys at Schueller what they did. They don't ever get to see any of this."

"I suppose we can make a quick pass at three hundred feet or so, but we can't do a proper BDA. When we get back, if you'll initiate it at headquarters, maybe they'll let me come back out with a team."

"Good enough." They swept across the ruined grove, each man hanging his head out the side, looking straight down as they passed. Amid the tangle of shredded limbs, bare ground and destroyed hooches were clearly visible.

"Looks like we did a total job," Roark said. Dailey turned and smiled in agreement. Suddenly there was a double thump of rounds striking the ship, and something flew through the cockpit. Dailey's smile froze and changed into a question, and for what seemed like a long moment he and Roark stared at each other. Then they heard the rap of the machine gun, and in that same instant blood spewed through the cockpit. Dailey looked dumbly downward, and the spray of blood covered his face. He groped in mute, blind terror at a wound between his legs.

In seconds Roark had the ship low level, screaming across the flats toward An Khe. All the cockpit was laced with blood and red vapor. He glanced at Dailey. "Hang on," he said. "We'll be there in a minute." Dailey said nothing. He was leaning slightly forward, his entire body trembling. His hands clutched the inside of his thigh just below his groin, but they were slippery, and not enough to stop the pressured torrent. The floor beneath was soon a solid pool that spilled forward past his feet and into the chin bubble. The wind caught what slipped out the side and painted the length of the ship.

"Hang on, babe," Roark said. "Hang on. We're almost there." That was a lie. The ship was redlined, doing all it could do, but it had never seemed to move so slowly. The shape of Hong Kong Hill was not growing nearly fast enough. He glanced at the radios. They were covered with blood, and he didn't trust himself to try to change frequencies. A Mayday call would have been useless. Finally, he switched his selector to FM and called Schueller. The signal was weak, but readable, and the artillerymen radioed ahead to alert the medics at An Khe.

It took only a few minutes, but when they reached the ghost town the 1st Cav left behind, Brian Dailey was humped over in his seat to the limit of his harness. His hands were still between his legs, but only because they were trapped. The limbs were loose. The blood on his face was almost dry, and his skin was waxy pale.

The helicopter skimmed the roof of Task Force headquarters, then went into a wild flare across the revetments and aircraft and staring faces. Men were moving out from everywhere toward the medical tent beyond the Greenhouse. When Roark did a pedal turn to slow the ship, the FO's upper body rolled in the seat and flopped out the doorway where it hung with arms extended.

People were all around, curses and cries and shouted questions. Roark sat stunned and silent, his eyes fixed on Dailey's boots and on the blood that covered the floor. There was a brief commotion, and the boots slipped out of the scene, dragging twin trails. Then it was just the blood, and a voice he couldn't seem to understand.

"Mr. Roark!"

He jerked and looked into the face of Captain Dunning framed in the doorway where Dailey had just been. Then he glanced down at the seat, and through it to the jagged holes beneath, then back to the punctured nylon weave. The green material was deep burgundy. "What happened?" Dunning shouted. Roark stared at him blankly, then blinked and focused. All at once Dunning understood. His face flowed through shock, rage, revulsion, hatred, and sadness. Even traces of sympathy for Billy Roark. "Jesus Christ," he said.

Suddenly Roark rolled the throttle full open. As Dunning stepped back, the ship rose vertically twenty feet, then whirled around and moved toward the revetments. Most of the blood that would still flow had already dripped into the grass. Only a few misty drops speckled the pale and upturned face of the captain.

XII

I rode front seat with McCawley one day, convoy cover above Glenn Castle. The unaccustomed altitude reminded me how far away war usually is for a pilot until tiny bits start zipping through and gravity reels you down from the fantasy you thought was free. I missed being down there among the trees, eye to eye with the explanation.

The convoy was ten tankers, four guntrucks, and two jeeps headed up the Mang Yang toward Pleiku. By the time the last truck topped the pass, the first had almost made it to Dead Man's Curve.

After the highway cleared the pass, it ran straight as an arrow for several miles before becoming trapped between a narrow ravine of old paddies and a low protruding finger of a hill. The road ran around the point of the hill and back through the subsequent hollow in a double hairpin arrangement which put the sloshing loads of fuel at a crawl and momentarily isolated each tanker from the guntrucks. It could have all been changed with a few cases of C-4 and a bulldozer.

In order to hit a convoy there, and then escape, the enemy had to cross two hundred yards of completely open ground. No American would have taken such a damned-fool chance, but to the gooks it only meant they had to run like hell. Dead Man's Curve didn't get its name from a song.

When the column of smoke stood up like a black, hooded snake, uncoiling from the number-two tanker, McCawley instantly called Base for clearance to use the guns. Then the convoy leader was on the radio.

"Shamrock Two-three, Packer Three Bravo, we've been hit! We've got dinks in the open! If you hurry you can get every one of them!"

Gil told him we had to wait for clearance, then asked if he needed Dustoff.

"No, I don't need Dustoff, I need gun support, goddamn you! They're getting away!"

Then Dunning called to tell us to forget it, saying he couldn't get clearance for us to fire in ARVN territory, not even to defend our own men. Three Bravo called again, his voice breaking, telling us to go fuck ourselves and the horse we rode in on.

Long before smoke stopped boiling from the ruptured truck, McCawley and I were back at the Doghouse, looking at each other, wanting to kill somebody, and not necessarily a gook. Out in the revetment our fancy machine was cooling, while up on the next plateau a stranded convoy was making out as well as they could on their own.

CHAPTER THIRTY-FIVE

THE SCENT of Saccharin was gone from the room. Standing outside the hooch after four days at An Khe, he could feel the vacancy. It was evening, and down on the perimeter, guards sat outside the bunkers on the sandbagged slopes, their black sixteens angled across their knees, smoking as they surveyed the darkening coils of wire. A pair of Hueys rounded the camp, then banked steeply toward POL, their blades clapping loudly against the sky. The landing lights flashed through the turn, then the blade sound went throaty with descent, changing again as each bird lost lift and pulled in power to hover. An unseen jeep moved quickly across the camp, dragging a rising wedge of dust that stood above the rooftops. Down the side of the hooch, huddled around the table on the deck, four men drank beer and talked in the company of a couple of dozing mutts. When they stood and walked in the direction of the club, the dogs started to follow, but one had to stop to scratch. The other flopped down in the dirt to wait, but when the scratching was done they just looked at each other and decided to stay.

"Mr. Roark." Grouper appeared around the corner dressed in a blue T-shirt, knee-frayed jeans, and tennis shoes. A bead of lymph oozed from a freshly squeezed pimple on his nose. Grouper was one of the few unaffected by talk of Brian Dailey's death. During the two weeks since the incident, a chilliness had developed toward Roark, even among the scouts and guns. Dailey was the first American to be killed on the An Khe plateau in more than six months, and the first KIA that most of the men had seen. The consensus was that Roark's bending of the rules had gotten the man killed. Roark agreed, but it seemed that the forty-five thousand other Brian Daileys had been forgotten.

"What's happening, Group?"

"Just came by to see if you'd heard about the girls."

"No, I haven't," Roark said. He extended his cigarettes. Grouper took the Camel without hesitation.

"They carried 'em out of here the other day in four deuce-and-a-halfs," he said. "Turns out the girls down at the Blowbath have been digging tobacco out of cigarettes, lacing it with heroin, and reloading 'em. Been handing 'em out to try to turn everybody into scag freaks. What that's got to do with the freelance whores, no one seems to know, but they shut down the Blowbath, and then the MPs cleaned out the entire camp. Sack wanted me to tell you she'll be back as soon as she can."

"Thanks for coming up."

"Wanted to be sure you got the word. You flying tomorrow?"

"No, I'm off. Think I'll go to Qui Nhon for beer and cigarettes if I can find a jeep. You need any?"

"Got some today. It wouldn't matter, anyway. They made a new rule: If you get more than one case of beer, every other case has to be Black Label. So everybody today was buying just one case of Bud or Schlitz, carrying it outside, then going back for another. So they made another rule: only one case per man per day *unless* you buy Black Label. All that did was make a traffic jam, everybody having to go down there for just one case of beer."

"It's been stacked out there twelve feet high on pallets, boiling in the sun as long as I've been here," Roark said.

"Longer. It's been there for years. I mean *years*. The cardboard wrappers have rotted, the paint on the cans has faded off, and there're streaks of rust all over from the strapping. They've got it on at a dollar a case and can't get rid of it."

"Maybe we could use it for grenades."

"It'd probably work . . ." Blue suddenly appeared around the corner of the building and walked past without speaking. Both men stopped talking. When he was out of range, Grouper said quietly, "I don't know how you stand it with him."

Roark smiled. Truth was, the game with Blue was beginning to wear thin. As the search for the regiment increasingly occupied his thoughts, it seemed he had less energy to devote to Blue. He knew that could be a bad sign. "I'd rather have him with me than on my wing," he said. "He'd still like to get even for the day I flew door-gunner."

"It's more than that. You know about his brother?"

"I heard."

"Sometimes at night when he's been smoking, he talks to him like he's right there. It's creepy as hell. And when he's drunk or high he says things about you." Grouper looked away as he spoke.

"I sleep with a loaded knife," Roark said. Turning in the weapons at night was a blow worse than leaving a base camp undisturbed, worse than being ordered to let the enemy shoot first, worse than almost anything. It made him realize that what he feared most in Vietnam was the United States.

"That might not be enough," Grouper said, missing the joke. He shifted positions. "You think there's a chance of ever finding those dinks?"

"We'll find them."

"I sure hope so. I hope I'm there."

"Might not be a fun day."

"Maybe not." Grouper stuffed his hands into his hip pockets and slumped his shoulders. He was lean as a wild rabbit, but his posture made his belly poke out. He looked all around the camp. "Still want to be there," he said. He scuffed a shoe in the dirt and said, "Well, there's a card game waiting on me," but he didn't move.

"Good night, Group."

" 'Night, sir," he said. When he was walking away he added without looking back, "I'm not kidding about Blue."

When he was gone, Roark drew his knife from his hip pocket, flicked it open a few times for practice, then put it back. He knew Grouper was probably right; if Blue ever decided to come, there would be little chance for defense. He went inside, and had just turned on his fan when he looked up and saw Glenn Castle. "May I come in?" Castle said.

"Sure," Roark replied, reaching for two beers. He was surprised by the visit; they flew missions together often enough, but though Castle was developing better than Roark had expected, there still was a gap in their philosophy.

"I owe you an apology," Castle said, taking a seat. "Some of the guys blame you for that LT getting killed, but it could have been anybody. The thing is, that was the complex I said was civilian. I just wanted to say I was wrong."

"You weren't wrong," Roark said. "You weren't right, but you weren't wrong." He told Castle about a day when he and Huckabee had caught some Montagnards in the open—a bent old man, a fat old woman, and a plump younger woman—all brown as tobacco. The women were wrapped at the waist in lengths of brown-and-black material that fell below their knees. The younger one clutched a large clay jar between her breasts. The old man held a tall walking stick and a rusty bushhook, and on his back was a deep basket covered with rough cloth and held in place by woven straps. When they realized they were spotted, the three moved slowly into a burned field where they squatted with their eyes toward the ground. "We let them go," Roark said. "Dunning radioed for us to hold them until a slick could pick them up, but I told him they got away. Later, we found their camp inside the Mouse Ears, and there were pigs and chickens everywhere. Little woven nests with doors and carrying handles, laundry on a line, fish traps down in the river. Domestic as hell, and not a bunker in sight. Then I got a sudden bad feeling. After we fired the hooches, we held off to the west, and in about two minutes that place went up like an ammo dump."

"I've got an uncle," Castle said, "who flew B-17s out of England. He was in on the firestorming of Dresden. Do you know about firestorms?"

"I've heard the term somewhere," Roark said, puzzled at the apparent change in subject.

"Firestorming is what they did to wipe out the major cities in Germany. Also Tokyo and some others in Japan. A raid involved hundreds of bombers loaded with HE to break things up and incendiaries to set it afire. The first bombers started at the center of the zone to get the air moving inward and upward, then each succeeding wave moved out in rings so that all the fires fed, and were fed by, the wind toward the center. And the rings got larger until most of the city was involved. Then the wind took over, coming in from all sides at more than a hundred miles an hour, going straight up from the middle, sending flames thousands of feet into the sky. People jumped into the canals and were boiled. Trees caught fire from the heat, then were ripped from the ground. A hurricane of fire instead of rain. They had to wait three days for the earth to cool enough for anybody to go in and see what was left.

"My uncle said it didn't bother him for the first fifteen years. Every city in Germany with a population over a hundred thousand was bombed, with the main objective being to kill civilians. And Tokyo? More civilians were killed in the firestorm there than by the atomic bomb we dropped on Hiroshima. The Allies decided that the way to end the war was to remove the enemy's will to fight, so they incinerated the families, torched the women and kids and old men.

"Then there was Hiroshima and Nagasaki, but everybody said they deserved it because of Pearl Harbor. Maybe they did, I don't know. But the thing that baffles me is how the ones who did all that could put us in the middle of a mess like this where we don't know which side anybody is on, and then somehow come to the conclusion that *we* are a generation of baby killers."

Roark could think of nothing to say. He hadn't known the details, but it was old news as far as he was concerned. Castle looked ill. "How're we supposed to know?" he asked. "How're we supposed to do right, and still survive?"

"I can't tell you that," Roark said. "Every day's a judgment call, and in a year of days maybe there's going to be some mistakes. But things are going to get a whole lot simpler real soon."

"You mean the NVA?"

"Correct."

"You realize you might die when you find them?"

"That's not something I worry about."

"You shouldn't have come back here."

"I should have never left."

Castle stood and started to leave, looking unhappy. He stopped at the door. "How many guys have you known that have been killed here?" he asked.

Roark's eyes settled toward the floor, and in a moment the hair stood up on his arms. "About sixty, I guess," he said, and tried to smile. There was mild amazement in his voice as if he had discovered an astonishing fact he had somehow overlooked. "That must be about right," he said. "'Bout sixty."

"Why you sit back heah?"

"I just wanted to get you in a dark place."

"You *diên caí dâú!*" Lin was wearing a tight black mini-shirt, a knitted burgundy blouse, and dangling black earrings that made her look like a little girl who had gotten into Mommy's jewelry. She was so cute, and such a little snot.

Roark was sitting alone at the edge of a darkened section of tables, while across the room several pilots, including some from Delta Troop, were finishing supper and having drinks. Kirby Hockett turned and waved. Roark returned the greeting, but stayed in his seat. He ordered a T-bone, medium rare, and when Lin prissed away it made him think of Saccharin. He hoped she would be back soon. Recently he had been spending even more time at An

Khe, staying at least two consecutive nights, trading out with other pilots who were glad to make the switch. It meant he saw less of Saccharin than he wanted, but he knew that if anything important was going to happen, An Khe—isolated and vulnerable—would be the place.

When the meal came, he slopped Worcestershire on the steak, catsup on the French fries, and shamelessly enjoyed the mess. Through the latticework he watched a half-dozen men, including McCawley, leaning around the craps table. He listened to them curse and laugh.

When he finished, he walked over, nodded at McCawley, then slid in behind the man who held the dice, a Pacific Architect & Engineers civilian who had gray hair and false teeth that failed to fill out his face. Roark watched the bets and waited for the dice, and when they circled the table he dropped a ten inside the wall. The old man covered it before anyone else had a chance, then complained because there was not more. When Roark rolled a five, the civilian dropped fifteen more dollars on the table, offering three to two. His voice had the irritating rasp of a man selling baseball throws at lead bottles. Roark declined the bet, and two pilots from the 129th came up with five apiece to match. He got his fiver on the next roll. "Goddamn it to hell!" the old man said, and threw a twenty-dollar bill on the table though it was not his bet. Roark picked up the ten he'd won and left ten on the felt. "Ain't you gonna let it ride?"

"No, I'm not," Roark said without looking at him. The civilian grumbled, replaced the twenty with a ten, then made two five-dollar side bets with the same guys. Roark rolled a seven.

"Sombitch is unconscious," the old man said to no one. Roark picked up the bills and slowly turned, but the old fellow pretended he was counting his money. Gil McCawley grinned across the table and said, "Do it." Roark grinned back and put down a ten. The old man covered and bitched, then covered the two Bulldogs who had decided they wanted ten apiece. Roark rolled another seven, and the old man cursed.

He held the dice for six passes without losing, doubling on the fourth, pulling half on the fifth and sixth. That gave him ninety dollars, all from the civilian. He folded the money and passed the dice. "What are you doing!?" the old man screamed, his voice high and brittle.

"I'm through playing," Roark said.

"You're not going to give me a chance to win that back?"

"Not tonight."

"Well, that ain't the way it's done where I come from," the civilian snarled, and he pushed back from the table and plunged his right hand into his pocket. Maybe he was bluffing; maybe it was one of those moves that a man sometimes makes, thinking he can laugh his way out of it if things go wrong. Roark didn't wait to find out. With a flash and a click his knife was out and open, leveled at the old man's skinny gut, sharp edge up. Then almost as quickly he folded the blade between his hands and slipped it out of sight. The civilian could not believe what he had seen. He stood frozen with his hand in his pocket, then pulled it out empty. "A fucking switchblade," he said, then pointed an accusing finger, black under the nail. "He's got a fucking switchblade!" The bar went quiet, and everyone looked around. Roark held his hands up with the palms open, then turned and quickly left.

"Gotcha covered," McCawley said. Roark shook a thumb over his shoulder just before he hit the door.

The room was too empty to sleep. The moist weight of the night air that oozed through the tiny screen and beneath the door made the fan sound rise and fall. It sometimes struck a resonant beat—packed sheaves of sound colliding between the walls, surging suddenly toward escape, then lapsing to a drone that seemed like silence. He turned in the soggy bed and searched the pillow for traces of Saccharin, but all that was there was the scent of his own oil and the sour smell of damp feathers. He checked the glowing hands of his watch and saw it was past 0100. He opened the wardrobe, slipped his knife into his flight suit, and dressed without a light. Out the window, deep weeds and a rubber cistern sat in darkness beyond the golden V from the gable bulbs. He left the fan running and padlocked the door.

It was a moonless night. When he was away from the buildings he stepped up on the stone wall, opened his pants, and sent a determined stream arching into the darkness. Piss on you, Vietnam. He shook away the last drops, remembering the joke about the lieutenant in the latrine washing his hands. But before he could smile, the lieutenant's face became Brian Dailey's, the piss turned into blood, and the night went red. He closed his eyes and cupped his hands to light a cigarette, then sat on the wall feeling numb. Far down the hill in the black pool of the flight line he imagined he could see the ships in the revetments. He saw a Huey on a bright morning, carrying Victor Talley on his DEROS flight. The aircraft rose from the pad and climbed alongside the hill, passing the hooches of Delta Troop in final review. And there in the wide cargo door was Talley, paying his respects with his pants around his knees, shooting the moon to the camp. Roark had laughed and waved, but the smile collapsed as the ship turned toward Qui Nhon. From the very beginning it had seemed like somebody was always leaving. He had talked to Talley the night before, sitting on the sun deck in the dark.

"I hear you've got to piss in a bottle now to get out of here," Talley said, "and they've got this pervert who sits and looks at your dick until you do. How's a guy supposed to piss?" Talley was an expert scout. He knew how to lead a mission, how to find the enemy and flush them out, how to direct gunships and airstrikes and artillery; how to get a convoy safely through a treacherous pass, and how to keep himself and his crew alive while doing it; how it feels to kill, and to almost be killed, again and again; how it feels to hang there on the edge, waiting for the rush that would carry him up and out and later lie stagnant in his veins; how it feels at the end. In three days he would be out of Vietnam, out of the Army and turned loose in the United States, and as he groped around for the old feeling, he found, like so many others, that the yeast of the dream had died. He was twenty years old, and his life had passed the pinnacle. "What am I going to be after this?" he said with a cigarette shuddering between his lips. "What's anybody going to be after this?"

Roark did not have an answer for him then, and didn't have one for himself now. A puff of air touched his face, and he looked up and saw a vacant space in the sky, a layer of clouds sliding between him and heaven like a lid. He looked across the inky paddies and the specks of light, and wondered if Saccharin was there somewhere. Through her, he could feel some part of himself beginning to grow. He missed her. He thought again about Talley going home, and he tried to put himself in his place, but there was nothing waiting there in his imagination. Then he remembered what Saccharin had said about staying after the war and was surprised by the rush of ideas that thought released. On the western slopes of the mountains north of the Deo Mang stood a forest of magnificent trees—mahoganies? teak? it didn't matter—and he imagined a logging operation there. Gazing down on the vision as if from a helicopter, he saw trucks winding along fresh orange roads toward slopes where yellow equipment worked. He heard the growl of two-man chain saws, watched the broccoli heads of trees lean slowly away from the pack, their slanting flanks brown and green with moss, heard the crunching thud, smelled the fumes and dirt and the liquored scent of fresh-cut wood. Four trucks to carry the logs from just one tree, they moved along the paths, and the dust stood up behind the tires so that by afternoon an orange fog hovered in the jungle. Here and there were fires, leaning posts of pale blue smoke turning gray against the sky. Across the crooked pass and down the long highway were the loading docks at Qui Nhon, and freighters from Australia and Japan waited there. From a great height he looked down, and it all was his.

And every bit bullshit, he thought, suddenly angry at himself for permitting the childish dream. He stared down the gentle S of the trail leading directly past the major's hooch. Enough time had passed since the blowup for him to realize he missed McLeod, missed his visits and interesting stories. He thought he understood now what had happened, what had changed the major's mind.

One night McLeod had been drinking, and at three in the morning he bashed his fist against Roark's door, a steady beat like mortars coming in. Saccharin was there, but Roark pulled on shorts and let him in. The major flipped on the overhead light, then glanced at the tiny form pressed beneath the sheets. Some black hair showed. He said nothing, but walked over and sat in the chair within an arm's length of the bed. Roark sat across from him, bleary-eyed and wondering about the occasion. McLeod did not make him wait. "Today's Mikee's birthday," he said.

Roark blinked and stared. "Who's Mikee?" he asked, suddenly certain he knew.

"My boy," McLeod said. "Michael. Mike. He was. Still is, maybe." Roark was awake now, and he lit a cigarette. Something looked strange about the major; the cheek that was normally round and shiny with tobacco now hung loose and gray. The fluorescent light made the damaged parts of his face stand out, made the white hair in his mustache and sideburns shine. It was hard to believe the man was not older. In all the time they had spent talking, McLeod had never mentioned anything about a life between Korea and Vietnam, so Roark listened closely to the story about Carletta and the boy. He leaned back in his chair and watched the geckos come out from their hole in the ceiling. Their hearts showed pink through translucent flesh, and their eyes bulged black and vacant like the eyes of embryos. "He's eighteen," McLeod said. "I don't know where he is, I don't even know what his name is now. But he's eighteen, and today's his birthday." One of the geckos jerked its head, then crushed a mosquito in its jaws. Its mate looked around excitedly and shuffled its suction-cupped feet, then resumed a motionless stance beside the hole. McLeod was silent, and when Roark lowered his eyes he knew he had never told that story before.

"I hope you find him someday," he said. He wanted to reach out and take hold of the major's shoulder, or shake his hand, or something. He did not know what to do so he did nothing. McLeod stood, and when he reached the door he turned and studied the motionless form of the girl in the bed. Then he had stepped out into the hallway, and from the hallway into the black empty morning.

I'm not your Mikee, Roark thought, walking slowly down the hill. As he passed the screened enclosure of McLeod's hooch he heard the rocker working the floor. He kept his eyes on the dark ground ahead.

The flight line was almost completely dark. The stars were covered now, and the only light was the faint collection from other portions of the camp. He walked slowly, counting the revetments until he found his ship, then circled it and finally lay across the back seat with one leg drawn up and the other dangling out the side. A breeze began to tumble across the hills to the north, and the sticky air of the camp with its burden of odors was pushed away toward the mountains. He reached into his pocket and gripped the folded knife in his hand, then with his arms across his stomach went immediately to sleep.

He was aware of the lightning long before the rain began, aware the explosions were merely thunder. There was a certain comfort in that. Soon the flashes were quite clear in his sleep, but he did not awake until he felt the rain. He turned and folded himself between the bulkheads on the downwind side and gazed at the sudden downpour. A blue bolt of lightning crashed somewhere and caught a million blue beads in flight, a photograph that lingered in the thundering darkness. A gust of wind shook the ship and lashed a sheet of water through, completely drenching him. His cap sailed away, and rain stung his cheek. He realized that the sensible thing to do was to run to the hooch, then dry himself and get in bed. But it had somehow become a contest; he was determined to stay. He curled around with his back to the wind, wrapped his arms around his legs, closed his eyes and waited.

Suddenly he was facedown in an inch of water with pebbles cutting into his cheek and no memory of getting there, just the fading echo of a blast. He'd been asleep; he rolled around and listened, still pressed tightly against the ground, his eyes wide and confused. Outgoing? No way. Incoming? He didn't think so. A sapper? Maybe. He listened to the memory of the sound, and it was short and flat and ugly with no tail. A grenade—a bamboo viper, a midair, a round through the head—a grenade. He jumped to his feet in a crouch, and when he dashed around the end of the revetment, saw a glow from high on the hill. A hooch was on fire; somebody else had been fragged. He stood and began walking, feeling suddenly sick, wondering who it was and who had done it. It was a terrible time when cowards prevailed . . . He looked up the hill again, but the view was blocked by the roof of headquarters. He began to walk faster. The wind had stopped, but the rain was still coming down. He was thinking it would help with the fire when he reached a position where he could see the hooches, then he began to run.

The flames were out when he got there, doused by the rain and a bucket brigade from the nearby cistern. He stood outside the knot of half-dressed men gasping for air, then sat on the wall and watched the white smoke rise from the shattered ruins of his room. Part of the outside wall had been blown out, and the corner of the roof slanted down at a sharp angle, resting its sagging weight on the sandbag wall. The corrugated steel had curled loose from the charred rafters, and it hissed in a sprinkle of rain. Some men were trying to kick through the splintered door from the hallway, and others were peering into the smoke through the hole in the side wall with flashlights. A faraway siren wailed.

"ROARK! God Almighty, Billy!" It was George McLeod, grabbing him, shaking him, his eyes gone wild. The others turned around and stared. Something seemed to move across the major, and he was suddenly still and in control. "We thought you were dead, son," he said quietly, his voice hoarse and trembling. He looked toward the room, then back at Roark. "Your door is bolted from the inside."

CHAPTER THIRTY-SIX

"SO YOU'RE saying you saw Clayton Blue outside his hooch just a few minutes before the grenade went off?"

"That's right, sir," Roark said.

"What was he doing?"

"Taking a piss. He was barefoot and in skivvies. He couldn't have done it." McLeod gave him a penetrating look, but Roark sat with his face slack, his eyes drawn and empty. His legs were crossed, and he scratched a fingernail along the laces of one boot.

"That does it then, sir," the MP named Cory said. He stood at the corner of the desk at parade rest, his black helmet tucked neatly beneath one arm. "We'll release Specialist Blue and continue the investigation."

McLeod was still looking at Roark. "Very well, Lieutenant. Would you ask Spec 5 Blue to report here?"

"Yes, sir." Cory came to attention, gave a confident salute, and closed the door as he left. Roark looked around the room as if nothing in the world concerned him.

"We've just got a few months to go, Billy," the major said. "Maybe weeks. It's looking like the Highlands will be turned over to the ARVNs by the end of the year, and when that happens they

317

won't need us at An Khe. We've got an even shot at being out of here as a unit by Christmas." Roark stuck a finger in his mouth, scraped the nail along his teeth, looked at it, then wiped the yellowish crud on the protruding seam of his pants. His eyes wandered around the room. "I'm going back, Billy," McLeod said. "It's what I've decided. If you come up in July, we can fish the Yellowstone. I've got a friend named Norris—guess he's still living—got a cabin on Sixteenmile. He'd be an old man now. Lost three fingers in a saw when he was young, and started tying flies. I don't know how he does it—just a little finger and a thumb and some nubs on his right hand—but he's as good as there is. I'm sure he can show you a lot. We can take him with us; I met him on the river. Later on, if you don't have other plans, you could maybe stay. I can show you what you need to know. I've been away a long time, but it's still mine. It'd be a good place to start a life." Roark's eyes shifted around, and when they finally met McLeod's he was looking at a stranger. "*Goddamn it*, Bill! Do you realize what you're doing!?" McLeod brought a big fist crashing down on the desk. "Don't waste it!"

Roark jerked with the impact of the fist, and suddenly the shield was down. "Sounds good," he said. "Sounds real good." But nothing in his voice suggested he meant it. Then he said he was tired and wanted to get some rest. When he stood to salute, the shield was up again, as distant as the far side of a mountain.

"I'm real sorry about the girl," McLeod said, but Roark made no indication he had heard.

When he was gone, the major sat looking at a picture on the far wall, a watercolor print of a fly fisherman standing waist deep in a gray-green morning river hushed with fog. The converging lines pulled him into the scene, and he could feel the chill weight of the water wrinkling the waders against his legs, hear the soft slurp of a trout somewhere downstream. He tried to see as far as he could along the sliding surface, but the fog and the roiled reflection held him back. A spent gray dun lay dead in the film, and he watched it until it spun away on the curl against his waders. His vision went deeper, and he saw the sagging lines of a sad and aging face staring back from a pearl sky.

He didn't know exactly when it came, but somewhere the focus had changed. With more than twenty years in the Army and retirement soon to come, it would have been easy to call it resignation. But it was more than that; it was the growing certainty, in the ending days of a war, that nothing whatsoever would be altered by the killing of another hundred, or five hundred, or a million.

Roark had been right, of course, about being used, and about him changing his mind. Many times he had recalled the day they met, and how he had unconsciously called him "son." Far back somewhere there had to be a voice saying, "Maybe this is what Mikee is like." For a long time, locked in the hopeful fixation that even if the war could not be won it might still be possible to leave his mark upon it, he had kept that voice confined to a subconscious chamber. But that had begun to change long before the evening that Roark came to his hooch to express his rage. Billy Roark was right about that, too, though he didn't know it; he had overcompensated for his guilt.

It had been easy enough to neutralize the effort to track down the regiment; Dunning's peculiar brand of incompetence could be counted on for that. All McLeod had to do was spend more time at Lane. He had quickly realized that the captain was one of the countless paper combatants whose war was a matter of statistics— find the enemy and write it down. *Ha! I know where you are! You can't hide from me!* He was certain that Dunning himself did not realize it, but one of the rules of that game was that bloodshed was best avoided lest it suddenly turn and end with him the loser. *Find the enemy and write it down.* Without acknowledging to himself what he was doing—which would have required an admission of fear—Dunning could be relied upon to screw things up just enough to defuse any situation. Like always wanting to do VRs in areas where he knew there would be no enemy, and like the VC camp that Calvert was supposed to be protecting. It had taken a while for that story to reach him, but Spec 4 Acres, probably fearing that knowledge meant complicity, finally let it slip. As McLeod knew, the initial denial did come from Task Force S-3, with Colonel Calvert later backing them up. But the *continued* denial was Dunning's fabrication. Roark had assumed the blame, but Dunning had played an important part in getting the lieutenant killed. And, as Roark had pointed out, it was Dunning who later saw to it that the regiment was given the time it needed to escape.

Just as it had been wrong to send Roark out to track down the NVA simply to make himself look good and to end his career on an upbeat, he knew it had been an equal mistake to abandon the boy in the midst of the effort. Unconsciously, he had duplicated Dunning's weakness, backing off when it was time to forge ahead. And what if Roark was right? What if the regiment fooled everyone? What if they really did decide one night that it was time to end the idleness, time to go ahead and sweep An Khe clean? Even if the war might end tomorrow, today it was still a long way from being over.

Clayton Blue gave the ammo belt a tug and locked it into his sixty as they crossed the muddy Song Ba. He lowered his clear visor and inched a little closer to the wind, scanning the north base of Hong Kong Hill. Ahead at ten-thirty he could see Huckabee on the controls at lead, and beyond him, Grouper. Larry Lockhart, Huck's regular gunner now that Sergeant Altman had DEROSed, was on sick call with diarrhea, and Grouper was filling in. Blue watched them a moment, checking their ship from the unaccustomed wing position. Since the day the regiment had gotten away, Roark had been reluctant to give up his slot at lead except for brief periods for training. He never said so, but it was clear he felt there was a better chance of locating the NVA if he were leading the flight. But this morning, as they backed out of the revetments, he had abruptly ordered Huckabee ahead.

"So why'd you lie?" Blue said, his back to Roark, shielding his mouthpiece from the wind.

A half minute passed, then Roark said, "Scouts take care of their own," his voice deep and flat, yielding nothing. It was the first time either man had spoken to the other all morning. Blue did not respond.

The scouts waited until they had cleared the deserted Camp Radcliff before testing their weapons in a grassy ravine rimmed with brush. The abandoned base was uninhabited, but Vietnamese civilians, and even ARVNs with trucks, occasionally wandered through, collecting bits of the lst Cav's junk, sometimes peeling up pieces of the old PSP matting. When he fired, Blue leaned out and back so that the ejected shells fell overboard. Just as the gunships called to say they were up and overhead, a tiny barking deer was flushed from its hiding place in a clump of shrub. Grouper killed it, then the recon flight moved west.

It was a gray, quiet day with none of the joking chatter between aircraft that commonly preceded a mission. It had rained in the night, and a high layer of clouds, flat gray and motionless, cut the available light in half, making a reconnaissance of deep forest out of the question. Even in the flatlands the sameness of the light was a concern; the shadows were muddy, the bright definition gone, everything blurred to a single dimension. The warships moved with grim confidence across the bamboo flats, the beat of their blades pounding a warning like footsteps through the sky. They passed a short distance from the shattered grove where Brian Dailey had been killed—the smoked and splintered trunks, a few singed leaves that still refused to fall. Everyone looked, but no one had a thing to say.

Twice in the past week, foot patrols operating from Firebase Schueller had encountered trail watchers north of the low hills where the bamboo became dominant. The troops found pathways tunneling into the thicket with walls that were almost impenetrable. Each time, they had turned back to avoid what likely would have been an ambush. It was decided to let the scouts take a look.

"One-two, any particular way you want to work this," Huckabee called. Scouting bamboo was more nerve-racking than other types of terrain. A much slower flight speed was required, and it was very easy to pass directly over a base camp without catching even a glimpse of it. If the enemy wanted to fight he was only a few feet away, with all the advantages his.

"Just take your time, watch for wire, anything fake," Roark said. "When I go high, keep my position in mind in case you have to get out. You know the rest." He resumed his silence on the radio, restricting his communications to double clicks of the mike switch.

Though Huckabee was not yet a designated lead, he had flown the position several times ahead of other pilots and had shown a definite aptitude for the work. He too had learned from his father; he too was a hunter. He took control of the flight without hesitation and set about the task of finding dinks, beginning with a high-speed sweep at three hundred feet, ranging almost to the foothills of the Mang Yang before turning back and dropping to the deck. He flew the entire perimeter of the area, looking for some clue that might give him a chance of success, calling out instructions to his wing and to the orbiting gunships with confidence unusual for his experience. The terrain was not so level as farther east, rising perceptibly toward the mountains, rolling in vague undulations north and south. Far in the center of the zone, between two of the deeper draws, stood the top of a tree struggling to survive the voracious competition. The bamboo seemed taller there, and it gave Huckabee an idea. He turned directly toward the tree and announced his intentions.

The moment the aircraft slowed, the bamboo erupted with tracers. "Taking fire!" Huckabee yelled, and he lowered the nose and pulled pitch. Grouper stood far out on the skid, spraying lead beneath him.

High overhead, a Cobra was in a dive, already punching off rockets. Then McCawley screamed, "Get out, Alphie. Get out! GET OUT! *GET OUT!!*"

When the shooting began, Roark had done a strange thing, an

insane thing. Instead of pulling pitch and following lead, he had calmly held back, sliding sideways, holding Blue toward the tracers. Only the dense vegetation kept them from taking rounds. Roark did this even as McCawley yelled, knowing that the rockets were already on their way, calculating the timing. Then he turned the ship and pulled in power at the last possible moment. The rockets impacted very close behind them, causing the ship to tremble with concussion.

When they were clear, turning to rejoin lead while the gunships worked, Blue looked at Roark. "What the fuck do you call that?" he asked. His lips were dead flesh.

"Laying down suppressive fire," Roark said without looking at him.

"Damn near got us killed."

When the gunships had made a pass apiece, they called high and dry. By then, McCawley had gathered his senses, and he was furious. "Alphie, I guess you know I almost shot you down just then!" His voice was unsteady, several octaves higher than normal.

"Sorry about that," Roark said. "We had a little trouble getting out." The explanation made no sense, but nothing else was offered.

The target was still hot when the scouts went back for another look. Roark pulled the same tactic, turning Blue to the fire, sliding out sideways, not waiting quite so long this time. A pair of slugs sailed past Blue's head and up through the roof, severing a hydraulic line and terminating the mission. Both Cobras emptied their loads on the target, then followed the Little Boys back to An Khe.

Unlike the Huey, a Kiowa with the hydraulics out could be manhandled and made to hover, though with some difficulty, something like steering a power-equipped automobile with the engine off. After executing a running landing, Roark guided the ship through a wallowing hover to the ramp where he set it down with a jolt to await maintenance. Reddish fluid still dripped through the holes in the ceiling a few inches from his head. Blue was out of the ship immediately, unloading his gear in a fury, hauling it over to one of the revetments where he dropped each load with a resounding crash. When the blades had stopped, and he saw that Roark was out of the aircraft, he walked around and stood in front of him. "I want to change birds," he said.

"No, Blue," Roark replied. "You're flying with me, ol' buddy, ol' pal."

The two men looked hard at each other for a moment, then Blue said, "I didn't waste your woman." Roark was standing with his weight on one hip, head back, eyes opaque and lidded. He gazed steadily at the gunner, then gave a gradual smile. When he walked away, the sound of his laughter rattled across the ramp like dry rocks.

"Fuckyou!"

The voice was high-pitched and clear, a gay creature of the night, calling from somewhere beyond the black hole in the wall of the Doghouse. The men seated around the tables stopped their card games and looked at one another in wonder.

"Fuckyou!"

The pilots turned and stared toward the hole, quizzical smiles beginning to spread. "You gotta be kidding," said Glenn Castle.

"Fuck you, too," Kirby Hockett said in a shrill voice, cutting his eyes around, then back at his cards.

"Fuckyou!"

"Man, that's creepy," said Corbish. Few men in the room had not heard tales of the Fuckyou lizard, but for most of them the stories had remained in the realm of fantastic mythology, part of the battlefield baloney that an army passes along to sustain any remaining shred of life amazement.

"Fuckyou!"

The voice was strong and almost human, making it difficult to believe it came from a lovesick reptile. "God! They've even got the animals on their side," said Shadrach. "We may as well go home."

"Wish someone had thought of that a few years ago."

"That's no kidding about the animals," Castle said. "We were out south of Alpha Two the other day, and this monkey screaming his guts out comes hooking ass past my door about sixty miles an hour. Scared the *crap* out of me!"

"That was a gibbon," said McCawley.

Billy Roark walked into the room from the dark patio, apparently looking for the source of the call. He was fully dressed, and in his left hand he carried a poncho liner tied as a bedroll. He appeared exhausted beneath his cap. His pants were bunched at the waist, sagging and swaying from things in the pockets. He did not acknowledge anyone in the room.

"Hey, Roark, how's it hanging?" Hockett said.

"Okay," he replied.

"Fuckyou!"

Roark turned toward the sound. He stood still a moment as if listening or thinking, and the others watched. Then he walked slowly toward the hole in the wall. Just before he stepped out into the darkness he drew his knife from his pocket and flicked it open, letting it hang straight down at his side. Then he disappeared in the deep grass.

"Jesus Christ," somebody whispered.

"That dude is some kind of weird," a new guy named Matthews said in a low voice.

"Well, tell me you wouldn't be, dipshit, with your girl murdered in your own bed," McCawley said.

"He didn't mean anything," said Hockett.

"No one ever does."

"You've got to admit he's been strange," said Corbish.

"Like I said, who wouldn't be."

"Did you see his arms?" said Castle. "His left one is nearly shaved bare from testing that knife. That sucker's sharp as a razor, but he still sits around sliding the edge across that Arkansas fine."

"Just leave him alone," McCawley said.

"That's not hard to do," Corbish replied gently. "Have you noticed where he sleeps now? He moves around. Sometimes under a helicopter, sometimes in the open top of a revetment, sometimes sitting on the front porch of the Greenhouse so you can't tell if he's asleep. But *never* inside. At Lane, he wanders all over the camp, at all hours."

"And talks to himself," Matthews said. "I've heard him."

"There's nothing wrong with him that wouldn't be wrong with anybody, put in his place," McCawley said. "He'll be fine in a few days if everybody will just leave him be. It's a plain fact that somebody tried to kill him, and they're still around. Besides, he was pretty attached to that girl."

"A whore?" said Matthews.

"That's right," McCawley replied, cocking an eyebrow. "If somebody didn't fall for the whores, this world would be packed with old maids. Just where do you think they all go when we're through with them?"

There was silence at the tables as the boys reflected on this new idea. It seemed a perfect moment for the lizard to have his final say, but he was hiding now in the dark, keeping quiet. The card games resumed, but the atmosphere was altered. Occasionally someone checked the vacant hole as if they expected Roark to emerge with a swinging, headless lizard in one hand.

CHAPTER THIRTY-SEVEN

T HE CAPTAIN could hear nothing but the terrifying sound of
nighttime silence—that and a thread of music riding a breathing wind, barely louder than the ghostly violins inside his head.
The hooch was empty. Three dancers from Taiwan were performing at the club, and Pach and his buddies had gone to see the skin.
Normally Phillip would have been pleased at being alone, but the
value of privacy, his last refuge, had vanished the moment Billy
Roark discovered his hooch.

For three days he had been almost completely alone, resting in
his bunk or in his corner chair, all on doctor's orders. During the
three weeks since the storm, his health had deteriorated dramati-
cally, stripping another six pounds from his frame and causing
alarm in almost everyone who knew him. Even Phillip could see
that the loss of weight was beyond reason; his arms looked fragile
and thin, his pelvis stood out, and his shoulders had developed hol-
lows at the sockets. It was Colonel Westin who finally insisted he
go on sick call. Phillip lied to the doctor about his stomach and
about his emotional condition. He mentioned nothing of the dizzi-
ness which came from merely standing, or the frantic, fluttering
pulse that the mildest effort produced. He came away with a diag-

325

nosis of moderate hypertension, a prescription of muscle relaxant that temporarily grounded him, and a warning that his blood pressure was approaching a dangerous level.

Phillip looked around the dark room. He wanted to remain in bed, but had come very close to falling asleep, close to dreaming again. He needed to be up and watching. He eased his feet toward the floor, then pushed himself to a sitting position. He was very weak, but it was so easy to be that way, to lie back while life flowed past. He smiled feebly at the thought of the young doctor prescribing a depressant. He was taking the capsules anyway.

He stood with effort and lit a candle, then moved carefully to his corner chair where he could sit in deep shadow and watch through the one remaining window. The other two screened panels at the corner were covered now with plywood drops. Following that horrible night of lashing rain and thunder, he had tried to leave all three panels down, but despite it being December it was much too warm for that until very late at night. Even worse, he discovered, was the claustrophobic fright of sudden blindness; every sound, every bump, every muffled voice beyond the boards, became the creeping edge of terror. He *had* to be able to see outside. Before he became too weak, he removed the third panel and installed it inside his room so he could open or close it from there. With a drill borrowed from motor pool he made several small peepholes which he plugged with corks of chewed paper. He never lowered the panel until Pach was inside and the door of the hooch latched, and he never slept until the panel was down.

Though Billy Roark and the threat he posed had turned Phillip's waking hours into a nightmare, at least there was some defense against the man. But no wood panel or steel bolt could hold back the dreams. In one which had come several times, he awoke in his bed to find Roark on top of him, a knee embedded in his stomach, and the cold edge of a knife pressed lightly against his throat. Roark looked down and laughed a metallic, merciless laugh, then began a slow cutting stroke which always ended with Phillip's bubbling, soundless scream. Because it began in bed and ended there, it was especially terrifying, so difficult to know the boundary between dream and reality, to be certain when he was awake. Each time, his hands went to his throat to feel for the hinge of his half-severed head. Twice he had wet himself.

Another dream, more subtle, but equally powerful: It was a clear day, and when he heard a sound and looked out, there stood Pach and Brown and Klepper, and especially Colonel Westin, gathered with all the other officers Phillip knew, and they stared at him with accusing, unforgiving eyes, handing down a wordless verdict.

When the dream ended and he was awake, the eyes came into the room and hung projected on the ceiling, then on the red whorled patterns of his eyelids. The eyes bored into him, their explicit message worse than death.

Death was a real prospect now. Its consideration was no longer a game or a pastime, but had become a daily part of Phillip's life. For a time he had divided the issue, telling himself he was not contemplating suicide, but was instead wishing for death. There was a difference. Then he realized that the difference was passivity, that wishing for death was merely the cowardly form, hoping someone or something would take responsibility for the act. But what made it incomplete, what kept him alive, was the question why—if he really wanted to be dead—*why* did he fear Billy Roark so much? Perhaps the life that was in him was not yet ready to give up. But no matter; Roark would eventually come.

Once he had admitted that he was considering killing himself, Phillip discovered he was suddenly able to explore forbidden places. Disregarding recent events, which seemed only a natural progression, he wondered how it had happened, how the idea could have ever grown. It was tempting to say, *There! That morning at Leonard Wood on the edge of the bed, that was the instant it happened, that was when it began!* But he realized it was merely the moment of acknowledgment. Once it was done, he discovered, he could not go back and pinpoint the exact source. There was none. It was instead a slow rot, a corrosion of the soul, an internal decay undetectable until the collapse, undetectable because to even search for signs was in itself an admission. He was convinced that Billy Roark was not the explanation. In every part of his memory, clear back to his childhood, there seemed to be traces of discontent. But those memories, he knew, were now unfairly shaded, just as the neighbor who says, after a mass murderer has been discovered living three doors down, that he suspected something all along. It seemed funny now that in the smug security of more confident years he had invariably explained away people who killed themselves as being quite clearly insane.

He understood there could be no going back. Perhaps things could be suspended at the present stage, but there would be no reversal. It was the truth of shards: Nothing broken can be repaired beyond a shabby semblance of what once was, a wrinkled gathering of ragged pieces not quite meeting at the edges. Once accepted, he found, the knowledge of death's worthiness was not so easily renounced.

He looked at his hands and was surprised to see two letters. The thicker, softer envelope was the original one from Rita, marked all over with forwarding addresses from pursuing him to his destination. The other, also from Rita, had arrived only today. It was addressed correctly, and he suddenly realized that it meant his ex-wife had gone to some trouble to find out exactly where he was. But she had waited too long. He stood and held the envelopes together above the flame, then sat and studied the progress of blue and yellow and curling black. It was a positive move that made him feel good, briefly illuminating his dark corner. The ash crackled quietly as it grew, then fell in pieces like charred leaves, decomposing around his feet. Weakness made him want to open the letters, and he had sworn he would never go to Rita that way again, the certainty of fire more attractive than the eventual cost of salvation.

A movement outside caught his eye, and he leaned forward, squinting at a passing figure made hazy by the angle of the screen. It was not Roark; this man was too plump, and the fool was whistling. Roark moved like some skulking animal, slowly, silently, his back curved, head low, hands partially in his pockets, the cap pulled down so his watchful eyes would seem to be toward the ground. Three times Phillip had seen him creeping along the path, and always about this time of night. There could be no doubt of his intentions. The predator's eyes fairly glowed beneath the cap, silently promising that soon he would come, delivering the death that Phillip had earned. A shudder went through him then and squeezed forth a whimper of fear. At such moments Phillip wanted to run out, to find Roark, to grasp him by both arms and try to penetrate the glassy green insanity of those eyes, to explain his fear as far back as he could remember, as far back as Roark had known it, to beg his mercy by forgiveness or by instantly ending the agony of life. His entire body trembled as memory seized him, and his stomach folded like lead. "I never intended to kill that poor girl," he whispered. "I never intended that."

The blast was still loud in his head, more awful than anything, death and all its terminal ugliness compressed into a single ghastly sound. It was in his hair. Then he was a clawing, thrashing, falling silhouette, scrambling through an electric flood, framed and suspended against phosphor clouds by bolts of greenish white, photographed by heavenly light for all to know and see. It was not until morning mess, after a completely sleepless night, that he learned the horrible news. He would never know why it happened—how it happened—never understand how such an appalling moment could become a part of his life, never completely believe that it was not some bizarre segment of a full-length dream. There was a real sense of it having been planned and accomplished by someone other than himself. Some division of his mind had relegated the plan, even the execution, to a place where details were handled. Then the thunder awoke him, the rain began, and he was out in the storm. An act of living flesh determined to prolong its miserable existence.

He spent a harrowing day at his desk, too ill to eat, too distracted to work. But it was not until afternoon that total terror struck with the awareness that Billy Roark would know. He would know, and now he would come.

Someone else was on the path, and Phillip hunched forward, digging his nails into the arms of the chair. This time it was Billy Roark. He stopped as if to pick something from the ground, then the wind pulled his cap from his head and blew it in Phillip's direction. Roark followed it very deliberately, and when he picked it up, he dusted it against his leg and looked directly into Phillip's eyes. Then he turned and walked away, but not before speaking. "Crable," the voice said in the wind. "Crable."

Phillip sat frozen until the man had crossed the opening between the hooches, then quickly snuffed the candle before crawling beneath his bunk. A moment later he emerged clutching a grenade and a bayonet. Still on his knees, he peered out the window, first toward the lighted pathway, then back toward the inky darkness beside the hooch. There was no sign of Billy Roark. Frantic now, he looked around. The door was locked. This has to be the night, he thought. He could feel his heart pounding in his chest, and for a quivering moment thought he might actually burst into tears. Then a calm came over him. He felt for the splayed ends of the pin in the grenade and pinched them together. A gust of wind hit the hooch, rattling the door on the opposite end. But was it the wind? Phillip leaned toward the screen and listened, straining to hear. The ringing in his ears, and the distant music, suddenly seemed so loud.

There was a small sound on the opposite side of the building, and when he turned his head, he remembered that Pach's boards were up, his screens completely unprotected. Roark could get in that way simply by using a knife. Quickly he stood, and with two slashing movements of the bayonet opened his own screen with a zippered rush. Then he heard a faint laugh, and in one quick movement he was out the window, crouching in the tight space between the sandbags and the side of the hooch. Clamping the spoon firmly beneath his thumb, he slipped a finger through the ring and pulled the pin with a twisting motion. Then he gripped the grenade and waited for Billy Roark.

XIII

The Huey sound was wrong—the beat of blades too fast, the groaning engine scream not right. Then it was almost on me, coming low across the trees. I knew the fear and sadness, the helplessness when nothing's all that's left, the drunken, clinging desperation of the crew. Black smoke boiled beneath the cowlings, feathered flames behind.

It came much too fast, turning, dropping toward the strip. One skid reached down, but drifted over, finally gone unconscious. A lump stood up, and the aircraft stumbled, still going a hundred and twenty, belly showing, over left and forward. The blades dug in and the Huey cartwheeled through a belch of red-black fire, going all to pieces in a wrenching OOF! Scrap metal and men tumbled along the ground.

I must have been racing down the runway because I was suddenly there. I jumped from the jeep and ran among the pieces. One of the pilots was facedown and free, torn from his seat somehow, but with his helmet still on his head. I grasped his hip and shoulder, and when I eased him over to find out who he was, the pale dead face I met was mine.

330

CHAPTER THIRTY-EIGHT

FARRELL DUNNING frowned as the pilots filed from Operations. Normally by this time of day he was crossing the ramp toward his room at the Greenhouse where he would put on dry boots and dry socks before going to evening mess. But more was bothering Dunning today than just a change in schedule. Once again, Billy Roark was on the loose.

For a time it seemed that Task Force S-3, in charge of all operations, would veto Roark's request. But only two nights later Schueller was penetrated by sappers. One GI was killed, eight wounded, and two of the 155s were destroyed. The attack surprised everyone, stirring concern even in Nha Trang. S-3 was suddenly ready to try anything.

What Roark wanted sounded simple: to change the VR mission, normally scheduled for about 1030 each morning, to the late afternoon for a few days. He also asked for blanket free-fire clearance for most of the southern AO. He wanted to conduct high-speed reconnaissance, with the freedom to move unexpectedly from one area to another, reasoning that the enemy, accustomed to the regular mission time, was probably more active during the hours before sunset. Just like any hunted animal, he said. He said he

331

wanted to concentrate on the extremities of the AO where missions were so seldom allowed. The NVA lived every day in the jungle, and it would be the most natural thing for them to discover the areas where their enemies never came. Just like any hunted animal.

S-3 didn't care what time the VR was performed so long as it did not interfere with convoy cover. They did, however, object to the size of the area Roark wanted cleared, primarily because it challenged the impression of precision in their work. Other than insuring that there were no friendly troops in the vicinity—certainly easy enough—and alerting the artillery crews not to lob any playful rounds in that direction, there was really nothing to clear. It was a matter of perception, being able to later say, in case anything went wrong, that they had not done their work haphazardly. When sufficient time had passed, the clearance was handed down. Dunning did, however, manage to have it restricted initially to a single mission, a single day.

Though he only voiced one strong objection to the mission, Captain Dunning had several. He pointed out to McLeod and Roark, as well as the others during briefing, the obvious truth that if trouble came in the late afternoon they could very quickly find themselves faced with a nighttime situation. To Dunning's dismay, that possibility only heightened interest among the young pilots. He also believed that tactics should come from the top. It was no accident that scouts were young and daring; like the helicopters they flew, they were expendable instruments, designed to accomplish a particular task. No one expected them to think or, worse, to express an opinion. It seemed a most dangerous arrangement when one man of insignificant rank could affect the direction of the entire troop. Finally, there was the nightmare possibility that Roark might actually locate the regiment. Delta Troop was no more than a gnat against a giant, and all they could possibly hope to achieve was to get smashed flat. Underlying all of Dunning's reservations was a deep distrust of Billy Roark. The CW2 was obviously dedicated and proficient, but he was also fanatical and emotionally unstable. Dunning kept seeing the moment of barren madness beyond the blood of Brian Dailey, and through the blood the haunting something other that almost looked like triumph. He frankly didn't know if it was better to give Roark clearance, allow him to do his deadly work and simply hope that he ran out of time, or to try to hold him back once more and risk the inevitable explosion.

The ships were revving to operational RPM. Dunning stepped into a canted panel of sunlight and watched as the team of drumming birds hovered toward the runway, kicking up a cloud of colored dust. One by one they took the active and flew away on the dangerous hunt. Not until the last bird was gone and An Khe was silent again did the captain return to his desk.

The search began on the eastern edge of Delta's AO in the folded heights and lush canyons south of the Deo Mang—the area that it seemed should have been saved for last since it was the last to receive the sun's light. But from the beginning Roark made it clear that few of the rules of scouting were to be observed. The Little Boys moved up streambeds without checking the ground above, and darted straight into promising areas without the least precaution but speed. There was almost nothing on the radio beyond terse instructions to Huckabee. Blue and Lockhart swept their heads around, half standing at the edge of their seats, leaning back for protection from the wind. The heavy jungle would have been hard to scout even at lower speeds, but by now they understood they were looking for campfires, sniffing for traces of smoke or the scent of an evening meal. High overhead in the gunships, Mc-Cawley, Shadrach, and their front-seaters kept watch. Occasionally McCawley would say, "One-two, you're crossing the line. You need to move back this way." Each time, Roark would acknowledge with two quick clicks, always stalling a few seconds before slipping back over the line.

He worked the flight in a zigzag along the great lumpy back of mountains, occasionally dropping into a deep ravine above the Dak Pokor before turning back eastward, reversing directions behind a peak, then sweeping southward beyond the screening ridge. Locked in the intimate world of the treetop perspective, turning this way and that ten feet from the surging jungle sea, it was understandable to become completely lost. But Roark was beyond that now. He crossed the line again and again, but he always knew exactly where he was, exactly what he was doing. He worked reflexively, without thinking. He could fly a helicopter, lead a mission, scout a piece of jungle, find and kill the enemy now without conscious thought. A machine functioning on impulse. Decisions were instinctive.

They topped the two-toned ridge at the limits of the AO, and Blue turned to give Roark a silent look. Eastward, beyond the golden touch of sun, the jungle fell in a rippled V, coursing by shaded degree into a green and blue-gray basin, all in ARVN territory. Both men looked toward the place where the jutting tip of a hill hid a paddy, recalling another day. They had made the discovery the first morning they flew together after Saccharin was killed. Roark had cranked that day without a preflight, and they made their way toward An Khe ahead of all the other birds. Halfway there, he turned away from the river without a word and flew at altitude deep into the mountains to the south. Eight miles from any road they found the flooded paddy sprigged with rice, fed by a diverted trickle from a mountain brook. There was no question what they had found; Montagnards didn't grow wetland rice. They left it undisturbed and unreported, and didn't even discuss it. Three days later they went back. Roark made excuses that evening to the rest of the Lane-bound flight, and Blue, hearing him, raised a cowling and pretended to work beneath the engine. Then when the birds were out of sight, he buttoned the door and moved forward to get ready. Nothing had been said between them. While Roark punched the starter, Blue squirted white lubricant into his weapon and sat calmly working the action back and forth.

They departed along the highway in the usual fashion in case they were watched, and didn't turn south at low level until they were out of sight beyond the Deo Mang. Working the terrain to maximum advantage, they skimmed the treetops and held close to the tightest parts of the canyons, twisting and turning as they stalked the hidden paddy. When at last they burst into the clearing between the boughs of two great trees, they surprised only a single man dressed in khakis, his pants rolled into knots above his knees, a tan pith helmet tilted far back on his head. Without even looking around, he ran with stretching sinew, corded muscles flexed and clear, in one decisive dash toward the trees. A trail of churning tracks grew and lingered on the water, and his helmet fell among them with a soundless splash. Then the stinging, slapping bullets pierced his flesh, and the soldier-farmer fell. No one but his buddies ever knew.

Roark saw the scene again, but without excitement, just an image with a sense of rightness. The glance from Blue was what was important. It was more than merely a reminder; it was an effort at communication. It meant that Blue had begun to believe that the threat was past, that doubt or indecision had taken form, that fear would cause the plan to be forsaken; it meant that Blue believed they might be allies now in at least this single thing, if only because they shared a secret; it meant that Blue had made a mistake, and it would not be that much longer until Roark could collect the fatal debt.

Soon the scouts were in the southeast corner of the AO, passing the cindered scar where once the regiment had camped, then crossing a narrow canyon and climbing the steep face of another mountain. Ahead lay a circular green valley where several streams came together. Beyond stood another shouldered mountain mass—prime territory, but all within the sphere of ARVN neglect. Roark gave the valley an emotionless look, then turned the flight northward for a long, curving run above the Song Ba. Three times they detected smoke, and once even saw a tiny flame through the open face of trees near the river, but in every case Roark moved the flight onward, saying simply that it was not what they were looking for. The sun was nearing the western rim of the valley, casting dark streaks beside individual trees and throwing panels of amber light far back into places usually shadowed. Sluggish fish cut sudden, crazy trails through the shallow river.

Approaching the highway near No-Name, McCawley radioed with the reminder that only thirty minutes of station time remained. Roark acknowledged in a flat tone, then told Huckabee to switch his gunner's mike to intercom, flipping Blue's selector off UHF as he spoke. Blue gave him a look, but said nothing. "Roger, One-two," Huckabee said. Instead of talking to the entire flight, each gunner's comments were now restricted to his own pilot.

They turned past Alpha Two, then cut south along the base of the western mountains, crossing the undulating land in a roller-coaster ride. "Two-three," Roark called, "could you move your flight about six hundred meters to the east of our path so you won't be overflying the same territory?"

"Will do," McCawley said. "It's getting pretty hard to see you, buddy. How about turning on your beacons?"

"Negative, Two-three."

The terrain was different from that on the opposite side of the valley. The mountain rim was actually one narrow running ridge, marked in places near the peaks with gray outcroppings of tremendous rounded boulders. The crest marked the edge of the area of operation. The far side let down into VC Valley, while on the east the land fell away more steeply, sweeping quickly down through forest rather than true jungle, fanning past foothills where the trees gave way to savanna. In the lee of the mountain the shadow was changing, the luminescence of the sky lending a deceptive sheen to the waxy leaves of the forest, making the earth seem that much darker. As depth perception diminished, the scouts flew farther from the trees.

"One-two, we've lost sight of you completely. We're going to have to have a beacon."

"Negative, Two-three. We're still holding a straight line, just across the base of the slopes about two hundred meters inside where the trees thicken. We'll hold this course to the blue line, then call it quits and head to Alpha Kilo. You'll just have to pretend you can see us."

"Okay, fella, it's your butt."

"Roger, Two-three. I'll call when we hit the gap," Roark said, then he called his wingman. "One-five, tell your gunner if he sees anything here, not to shoot unless it's shooting at us. Don't point or yell or wave or do anything. Just be real cool."

"Roger, cool."

Blue turned around and looked again at Roark, but still was silent. When he turned back, the air was filled with the scent of wood smoke, and there were dim winking eyes of charcoal through the trees. *"Keep cool, keep cool,"* Roark said rapidly. Huckabee answered with a double click.

"What's happening down there, One-two?" McCawley said.

"Nothing, Two-three," Roark replied. They crossed a protruding ridge, and the campfires were lost. "We'll be turning toward the Song Ba in another three-zero, then we'll give you some beacons." Soon they reached the pass where the stream from VC Valley cut eastward through the ridge. The air was brighter there, filled with a fiery glow that flowed around the form of a dark and spreading mountain to the west. The land beyond the Central Highlands was all afire.

"You know a man named Phillip Crable?" George McLeod knew the answer, but wanted to see Roark say the words. He was quickly realizing that the kid he thought he had grown to know was still a total stranger. Roark stood surprised and dumbfounded, holding the screened door half open, the guilt on his face enough to send him to the stockade.

"What's this about?" he asked.

"It's about Captain Crable," McLeod replied, satisfied at penetrating the barriers; this was the first emotion he had seen from Roark since the killing of the girl. "Come on in, Billy. I was fixing to send for you." Roark stepped dumbly into the room, avoiding his eyes. He was just up from the flight line, still wearing his chest armor, his flight helmet dangling from one hand. McLeod waved toward the refrigerator. "Get yourself a beer and sit down. We got some talking to do."

Everything seemed to go out of Roark then, all the steel and stiffness; he suddenly looked tired enough to drop. He gave a sigh impaired by the armor, then lowered his helmet and pulled the Velcro from his waist. Numbly, he fetched a beer, then sat without looking at the major. "Tell me about Captain Crable," McLeod said, his voice deep and rumbling, but still with a certain gentleness.

Roark took a long drink, then met the major's eyes. He began with the night of the mortar attack at Evans and told of the night-time resupply to Hamburger Hill, then about the way Jim Tyler died. He told about the dreams and the phone calls, and finally about driving up to Leonard Wood. He told his story simply and honestly, doing nothing to justify himself or make what he had done look any better.

"I guess I wanted to kill him," he said, his face drained. "If he'd been stronger, I think maybe I would have. I was in the woods across the street that night in Missouri when he opened the door, and I saw his face. That was enough. Driving back I kept seeing it over and over, and hearing him scream until I finally began to feel ashamed and sorry. It eventually came that he was just another dumb dude who wasn't prepared for what he found in the jungle. The only thing he really did wrong was to be afraid."

"That's not something to kill a man for," McLeod said.

"That's what I decided. Crable just didn't know how to deal with it."

"Apparently not." McLeod's voice was no longer so gentle. "The man was killed last night by a grenade."

Roark stared at him blankly, not understanding. Finally it came. "Here?"

"Yes, here. Didn't you hear it?"

Roark hesitated, and his face changed. "I heard it," he said. "I was walking around, but it was a long way off." The way he said it made it sound like it no longer mattered if somebody got fragged every night.

"That was Crable."

"But he was in Missouri."

"You must have scared him pretty badly."

Roark rubbed his face. "I didn't know. I didn't have any idea he was here."

"Well, he knew you were. They found a note among his things, saying you were trying to kill him."

McLeod went on to tell him the rest. It was almost 0100 when Davy Pach got back to his hooch and found that the door was locked. He was accustomed to that, but Phillip was always awake, sitting up in his chair like a parent waiting for him to come home. But this time there was no answer when he knocked. He banged harder at the door, thinking Phillip must have fallen asleep. Then he yelled, and an instant later the side of the hooch blew in. Pach was carried to the hospital with an eardrum ruptured and splinters of plywood embedded beneath his scalp.

"I didn't have anything to do with it," Roark said. There was no

sorrow or sympathy in his voice, nothing frantic or crying or concerned.

"Well, you did, but you didn't," McLeod said. "But you lucked
out. The MPs were sending a bird to An Khe to pick you up this
morning when somebody found one of his hands stuffed between
some sandbags. The grenade ring was still around one finger. You
came that close, Billy."

Realization suddenly filled Roark's face. "Then it wasn't Blue."

"No," McLeod said. "It was Phillip Crable. Trying to defend
himself against you."

"So what did you want to see me about?" McLeod asked.

"Huh?"

"You came here on your own, said you didn't know about Captain Crable."

"No, I didn't know," Roark replied absently. He was still a moment, and a change came over him, a return to something separate.
"We found them," he said.

McLeod was right with him. "You didn't report it to Dunning."

"I didn't want it fucked up."

"So where are they?"

"Will you help me this time?"

"Goddamn it, boy!" McLeod was on his feet, holding a thick
finger before Roark's face. "Don't jack with me," he growled. "I
can ground your butt and still find out what I want to know."

"Nobody saw it but me," Roark said, uncowed. "Even Blue
missed it." McLeod flexed his big hands. Finally he turned around
and sat in the rocker and glared at Roark. The butchered mess of
his face, all scars and wrinkles and ruptured vessels, was impressive with color. His mustache looked whiter. "I did what you
wanted," Roark said. "All right? I did it all the way. So help me get
it finished."

McLeod's face slowly relaxed, and he lowered his eyes toward
the floor. When he looked up he said, "I'll do what I can to convince the colonel."

"I'll need to go with you, sir," Roark said. "Colonel Calvert is
going to have lots of questions, and you're going to be in trouble
the minute you walk in the door."

Clayton Blue was standing against the bar at the NCO club in a
knot of black and hostile faces. His hair was frizzed and pierced
with an ivory pick, and around his neck hung a doubled string of

puka shells. He wore an olive drab T that had been hacked into a vest with a knife. "This is where we come to get away from officers," he said.

Roark motioned to the bartender and ordered a bottle of whiskey. The spec 4 glanced at a sergeant seated on a stool near the door, then took Roark's money and placed the bottle on the bar.

"You're on enlisted turf," Blue said. The men around him slowly turned toward Roark, forming a threatening wall. At a nearby table, Grouper and Lockhart were whispering. Grouper shook his head, then stood and walked casually toward the bar. He leaned at Roark's side, saying nothing, not looking at anyone. Quietly he ordered a beer.

Roark opened the bottle and took a long, burning drink that made his eyes water, then turned and held the bottle toward Clayton Blue. "And I didn't kill your brother," he said.

It took a moment for everything to connect with Blue, then the cataracts of anger and hatred seemed to fade. Finally, he reached for the bottle, held it to his mouth, and slowly rubbed his lips all around the neck. The others made sardonic smiles. When he drank, whiskey trickled down Blue's chin and sparkled on his woolly chest. He shoved the poison back toward Billy Roark. "Motherfucker," he spat, but then began to smile.

Roark started to drink, then ground the neck beneath an armpit. The burn was very bad this time, and when he brought the bottle down his vision was blurred. He recalled the day they had fired machine guns at each other, and he remembered one of the first things he had ever said to Clayton Blue. Why would I want to kill my own doorgunner? he thought, but he decided not to say it now. He just handed the bottle back, then waited again for it to be his turn.

CHAPTER THIRTY-NINE

I T WAS almost like the old days. All around were helicopters, most tied and waiting, but a few loose and seesawing gently where work was being done. Scattered about were restless, waiting men. Along the taxiway at POL a Snake and a Little Boy were topping off, and beyond them above the palm-shaded hamlet, a Huey turning base seemed to skim the green, irregular surface of the farther mountains. The shrill sound of turbines and whirring, slapping blades produced the proper atmosphere, and the air was fragrant with jet exhaust, sun-dried grass, pisstubes, and dust.

The men had spent the morning working around the aircraft, later eating C-rations in the shade. But the only mission so far had been convoy cover, flatbeds stacked with crates of 105 shells for the ARVNs up at Pleiku. The standbys pulled the job while everyone else waited, futilely hoping things might kick off ahead of schedule. Mission time was tentatively set for 1400, less than thirty minutes away, but so far, despite Colonel Calvert's stated intentions, no one had yet said it was a definite go. At the morning briefing Major McLeod had spoken with a wait-and-see vagueness that surprised no one, all of them understanding that military plans have little bearing on what ultimately takes place. More than two hours had passed since McLeod disappeared into Task Force headquarters.

The men moved around the ships, doing things already done. Near the south end of the ramp four Cobras stood like bladed iron; skids spread and gouging ruts in the penaprime, wide blades flexed, shark's teeth gleaming, stacks of dozing rockets. The crew chiefs fiddled with the turrets, then moved to the pods, their hands eventually caressing the snout of each individual warhead. On the Little Boys the gunners lubricated their weapons, checked ammo cans for twigs and pebbles, and wiped at windshields. The pilots jiggled push-pull tubes, peered through access doors, and gathered with the gunnies to smoke and watch the front of headquarters. The slick crews, most not expecting to fly, lounged in the cool cargo bays. In the grass beyond the Hueys the rifle platoon lay scattered—weapons, men, and gear—like worn toys, some glancing at limp magazines, most simply sprawled with their shirts open, boonie hats pulled down as if they were sleeping. They had been told they would not be going out, but they were there waiting, faded and dark and ready.

Squatting with Gil McCawley gook style—elbows over the knees, butt almost touching the ground—Roark studied the scene from the center of the ramp. It seemed a long time since he had seen the birds with anything near wonder, but it was all there again like looking through new eyes. McCawley smoked the same unfiltered Camels that Roark did, and when he finished his cigarette he automatically shook two loose. They sat silent for five minutes before a scuff of footsteps roused them. Kirby Hockett had Shadrach and Corbish in tow. "Hey, Roark, how's it going?" he said.

"It's going."

Hockett went down on one knee, his face full of concern. "Say, Gil, Tom and I have been talking, and we think it'd make more sense for me to lead the first team with him on my wing, and you hang back here with the second guns."

"Screw both of you," McCawley said.

"Seriously, Gil," said Shadrach. "You're down to two weeks. There's no sense in you going out."

McCawley shook his head. "You kids can play when I'm gone."

Hockett laughed and looked at Shadrach. "Told you," he said.

Corbish showed his stained teeth. "Hang in there, Gil," he said. "You children just stand aside. This is a job for *real* men, CW2s."

When the shouts and insults had subsided, Hockett turned to Roark. "You think it's a go?" he said, fumbling at his shirt for a smoke.

"Sure," Roark said. "It's a go. The colonel said we'd do it. Simple as that."

"Never thought I'd hear you talk like that."

"Lord Calvert's not as big an asshole as I thought."

"Something about the rank does seem to attract the breed," McCawley said.

"Something occurred to me in his office the other day," Roark continued. "How'd you like to spend thirty years trying to get somewhere and end up as chief road guard in a butthole like this? Task force, my ass."

"Gotta be a bummer."

"So tell me, what's the grand plan?" Hockett said.

"The plan is that pissant Delta Troop is fixing to take out half a regiment," Roark said. "That's the plan." He and McCawley grinned at each other like it was an old joke they had heard many times, just not recently. Hockett had been glancing at McCawley, looking for messages and finding nothing. "Relax, Hock," Roark said. "Everything's cool."

"You through being weird?"

"Yeah, I'm through."

Smoke rolled out of Hockett's mouth, and he pulled part of it up through his nose. "You had us real worried," he said, looking anywhere but at Roark's eyes. "I never said so before, but I'm real sorry about what happened."

"You ready to go?" Roark said.

"I'm ready," Hockett said firmly. Rodgers, the wing AC of the second gun team, joined the group and stood with his back to the sun, which had just appeared from behind a cloud. "So I'll ask again, butthole, what's the plan?"

McLeod's briefing had been unspecific, giving little more than the target location, the hoped-for mission time, and the radio frequencies. Roark pulled a map from his pants leg and lay the folded section on the ground, then looked toward the revetments. Glenn Castle was watching them, slumped in the rear of his bird. Roark made a beckoning motion. "Is he your wing?" Hockett asked.

"Yeah," Roark said. "He wanted to go, and he's got time on Huckabee. He's really come around."

Castle went down on one knee beside them. He seemed to sense he was being talked about. He had a determined frown, but the set of his mouth was buried in the drooping mustache. Shadrach and Rodgers knelt with the others. Roark pushed his cap back so he could see the map and still glance up at the faces, then began speaking in a calm, steady voice.

"Everybody's going in low at first, even you," he said, nodding at the gun pilots. "We'll hold just south of the Ears until the fast-movers show, then Glenn and I will go straight for the target. The base camp is right here in this elbow, about two hundred meters inside the tree line. It's big. The terrain is a half bowl with a shelf in it, and the shelf is where the camp is. We're going to pop a white phosphorous trail across the flats, make a big arrow for the fast-movers. The gooks might hear us, but I don't think they'll figure out what's happening until it's too late to make a move. Glenn, Grouper will drop all the Willy Petes but two, and I'll be saying when. Meanwhile, Gil, give us about a mile head start from the river—they might not hear us, but I know they'd hear you across that open country. Then start climbing out toward this area." He indicated a place on the map northeast of the base camp. "That'll keep you clear and put you in reasonable position to make a run if you need to. The napalm should hit about the time you start your orbit. Glenn, you drop pretty far back before we hit the trees—be ready for a right turn and don't overfly my path. I don't like doing it that way, but it's our only choice. We'll drop one Willy Pete to the left, then another to the right. Shorten your turn so you don't overfly the grenades. Tell Grouper to start laying down fire as soon as Blue pops his first one." Roark looked at McCawley. "We'll link up below you then. The first load will be pure napalm, and he's going to punch it all off on the first pass. His wingman is supposed to be carrying a load of two-fifties. If that's all we're getting, he'll dump half, then I'll adjust. If there's more coming, I'll have him drop the whole load at once. I doubt anybody will be in a bunker before that point. The colonel said he would try to get more sorties, and if he does they'll be carrying heavier stuff to get whatever's underground, and more napalm."

Roark turned to McCawley and lowered his voice. "You know there'll probably be some fifty-ones up top," he said. It suddenly occurred to him that since he had been at An Khe no one had ever been fired upon by a .51. "I'm just guessing."

"They'll be there," McCawley said. "It might take a few minutes to get 'em manned, but they'll be there unless they get so confused they don't know what they're doing."

The circle of men became quiet. Castle and Roark exchanged looks, and it was all there without words. Roark looked around at the others. "Anyway, that's all I've got," he said.

Shadrach and Rodgers wandered away. Castle looked up at a rectangular cloud drifting across the sun, then found a toothpick in his shirt pocket and began absently tracing each tooth. Roark and McCawley exchanged quiet looks, and this time it was Roark who provided the cigarettes. He could feel himself tightening, getting ready. He filled his lungs with smoke and gazed around the ramp, smiling, knowing there was no place he would rather be, nothing he would rather do than what he was about to do.

Clayton Blue was still working, still finding things that needed doing. He slipped the belted ammunition through his hands, running a forefinger along the cartridge butts, checking alignment by feel. He smiled as Roark approached. "What's the word?" he said.

"Thunderbird."

"You mean Turkey bird, don't you?"

"Don't remind me," Roark said. "My head's just now getting right."

"Don't I know. Mine hurt 'til yesterday evening."

It had been a devastating drunk, leaving little more than fuzzy pieces halfway through the second bottle. Still later were misty recollections of singing, sitting arm-in-arm in the dirt outside, Lieutenant Colonel Westin walking past, and giving the important man a left-handed salute. *Evening, sir. Cav once, Cav twice, holy jumping Jesus Christ . . .*

Roark watched as Blue continued his preparations, thinking how easily it could have gone another way.

Blue finished checking the ammo, his third time today, then folded it neatly and left the end draping over the back of his seat. Hanging on the piano wire at the door were two white phosphorous grenades. Pale greenish white, shaped like the old pineapple grenades, they were a spectacular weapon, sending out great arching streamers in a gigantic blossom, beautiful fireworks suspending clouds of pure white smoke. Igniting spontaneously when exposed to air, the burning particles would eat into flesh, and the fire could not be extinguished.

As Roark began putting on his armor, Blue reached behind his seat. "Got a little something extra, just in case," he said. He held up a freshly built Super-C the size of a small shoe box.

Roark eyed the homemade bomb warily. "Don't think there'll be time for that nonsense," he said. He had never felt comfortable with the devices aboard. A man could sometimes avoid bullets, or luck might play a part, but there was no way anybody could dodge a Super-C.

In the next revetment, Grouper already had his armor strapped around him. As he moved to the tail boom and untied the blade, he yelled at Roark, "Today's going to make up for many a load of shit."

"You got enough Willy Petes?" Roark had already gone over every detail with both gunners.

"Got five," Grouper said.

"Lookie here," said Blue.

Roark followed his eyes and saw Major McLeod coming out of headquarters. "Get the blade," he said, and immediately began jogging across the ramp. A ring of pilots converged on their commanding officer.

McLeod stopped near the center of the ramp and waited for the stragglers. "Okay, we're going," he said, then he looked at Roark. "We've got two pairs of Fox-fours. The first will be on station in"—he looked at his watch—"twenty-two minutes. The second pair, five minutes later. Rigged out right. There'll be a third pair on standby that we can have if the target warrants it. And there's a possibility we can get a fourth or even a fifth—"

"All *right*!"

"Well, this is what the president calls a defensive posture," McLeod said dryly. "Putting troops in the field is *offense*, and we can't do that anymore, but bombing the shit out of the bastards is *defense*. Damned fine distinction, I'd say, but I'm no politician. Anyhow, I'll be orbiting just to the east. Roark, you'll direct at least the first four sorties. They'll be up Troop UHF. Your contact will be Gunfighter Zero-one—"

"La-tee-da!"

"The war must be over."

"Getting minimums."

"No, just another oak leaf cluster."

McLeod waited, then said, "Okay, cut the crap. The man's a colonel, so maybe he's got enough know-how to put the first load where it's needed." He looked around. "Who's leading the second gun team?"

"I am, sir," Shadrach said.

"Tom, you and your wingman wait for word from Operations. Same goes for the second scouts. I want to remind everybody that we're not going out there today to get involved in a war. We're grossly outnumbered. All we want to do is inflict maximum damage, then get out. I said it this morning, but I'll say it again—anybody goes down, try to move downslope and get to the clearing. I'm sure everybody has heard the rumor that we could be out of here by Christmas. So far, that's just rumor—you know as much as I do—but that's all the more reason not to screw up. We might all be as short as McCawley. And we might not. You know the Army; they won't tell us a thing until the last minute, then we'll have to jump through our butts. Don't do anything stupid, and don't forget we're on this plateau by ourselves. Guns, if you encounter heavy weapons, try to get a good fix, but don't go up against them. We'll leave that to the boys upstairs.

"There's one more thing," McLeod said. He looked around at the young faces. "In all the time I've been in the Army there's been one inflexible rule: You don't leave anybody in the field, ever. But we're in a situation where things are different. If it turns to shit out there, we're on our own. Somebody goes down, we're going to do everything we can to get them out, short of putting in troops. There's not going to be any help. All we've got is the rifle platoon. They're willing to go—they've been sitting down there all day waiting to do just that—but all that'd happen if we put them in is every last one of them would be killed, and more besides. So they're not going in, and neither is anybody else. Not under any circumstances. So if anybody wants to change their mind about going, now's the time. Nobody will say a thing about it."

Hockett looked at McCawley, but Gil just turned his head, casually stabbing a middle finger up his nose.

"Anybody got any questions?" McLeod said. Nobody did. "Then let's get cranked." The pilots scattered toward their ships.

Roark pulled the shoulder straps into place, threaded the heavy lap belt, and latched the buckle, then gave the free end of the webbing a sharp, snugging tug. With precise movements he pulled on his helmet and the leather-and-Nomex gloves. He didn't realize he was smiling until he looked across at Blue standing outside, then both their grins spread wide. Today it was coming together; the enemy would be there, the bombs would land just right, and something significant would finally be accomplished. This moment was what it was all about.

When the birds came to a hover and began moving down the ramp, Colonel Calvert, for the first time ever, came out to watch them go. He stood in front of headquarters holding his cap tightly on his head, squinting against the blowing sand.

Meeting the colonel had made all the difference. McLeod had not come around until noon, and then it was with a scalding beaker of heavy coffee he called axhead. The potent brew got Roark on his feet, but it was the flight to An Khe with the major at the controls that sobered him up. Before they landed, McLeod handed him three sticks of gum which he mauled, then left stuck to the side of the revetment. Even then, he was careful not to get too close to the colonel.

The man known throughout the task force as Lord Calvert seemed disarmingly ordinary, small and unpretentious behind his desk, though not unaware of his position. He was a pale but handsome man of about sixty who wore starched fatigues and Old Spice lotion. His skin, thin at the temples and showing a delicate slackness at the throat, had been spared the indignity of trapped fluid. His eyes were washed blue, the set of his mouth judicious but fair, and he projected the satisfaction of a man who was either honest or realized he appeared so. His eyebrows had been trimmed with scissors.

Roark decided that the colonel looked in every way like a good and reasonable man. It left him feeling suspicious. He noted that the fingernails were filed and sanitary, and that the gray hair was oiled and wavy and combed straight back like an evangelist. That made him feel better. He hid his thoughts behind a blank soldier's face, held his body taut, and gave the colonel a crisp regulation salute.

Colonel Calvert returned their salutes and said, "Stand at ease, gentlemen." His voice had an aged timbre, carefully modulated, his words unhurried and precise. An orderly stepped into the room, then backed out silently with the door. The colonel flicked his eyes over Roark, catching the nametag and the 101st patch, then turned to McLeod. "Yes, Major?"

"Sir, this is Billy Roark," McLeod began. "One of my lead scouts . . ."

Colonel Calvert looked calmly at Roark and nodded. "Mr. Roark," he said as if the name were familiar. "You're the young man who got Lieutenant Dailey killed." It was not an accusation, just a statement.

"Yes, sir, I am," Roark said. He held the colonel's gaze.

Colonel Calvert seemed on the verge of saying more, but McLeod cleared his throat. "Go ahead, Major," he said.

"Well, sir, Billy . . . Mr. Roark thinks he has located that NVA regiment again."

The colonel's eyes widened slightly and he leaned back. "When was this?" he asked, the gears turning.

"Uh, yesterday, sir," McLeod said.

"On the evening reconnaissance?"

"Yes, sir."

Colonel Calvert looked at Roark, then back at McLeod. "Why am I just now hearing about this?"

"Well, sir, there was a problem before . . ."

"What sort of problem? Specifically, Major."

"I can explain, sir," Roark said.

The colonel turned his head and leveled the full force of his command presence like an eight-inch gun. He glanced back at McLeod, then said, "By all means."

"Sir, I found this unit before . . ."

"That I'm aware of."

Roark stared at the colonel. Everything was about to be decided. "Sir, I worked hard to find this outfit. Everybody but Major McLeod kept saying it was just pieces of a platoon or a company we were running into. Then one day we stumbled onto them, purely by accident, at the tail of another mission. There were gooks everywhere. The biggest camp I've ever seen, the biggest I've ever heard about, and Captain Dunning says we've used up all our flight time for the day, we'll see about it tomorrow. So we go dragging out there the next day, and naturally the gooks were gone. I've been looking for them ever since. Last night we found them, but I don't think they know we did. We were real careful about that."

"So you didn't report this to your Operations?"

"No, sir," Roark said. He could see the color rising in the colonel's face. "I wanted to talk to my CO first, sir, because the last time this happened he was at An Son and didn't have an opportunity to take part in the decision. Also, the first time, I had no way of knowing if you knew anything about any of it until it was too late to make an effective strike, and I couldn't very well march over here and ask you. So last night I waited and talked to Major McLeod, and I asked to come with him today to explain all this."

Colonel Calvert hooked an arm over the back of his chair and slumped sideways as if whatever held him together were coming unhinged. He kept his eyes on Roark. After almost a minute he looked down at his desk, then up at McLeod.

Major McLeod was trying his best to look positive about the matter, but with one side of his face bound up in scar tissue and the other side an empty leather pouch, the results were awkward. It seemed his turn to talk, so he raised his eyebrows and said some things supporting Roark and the Cavalry and the hopeless effort. Knowing his struggle, Roark lost track of the words. The robust major was practically helpless before the seated gentleman; it seemed that a great deal had gone out of him in recent months. The colonel was listening patiently. Suddenly Roark could see the three of them: Colonel Calvert, the authority and measured control, the discipline and, hopefully, the wisdom; Major McLeod, the aging warrior, still angry and violent but beginning to feel useless; and Roark himself, the young fool caught up in the bloody work.

When McLeod was finished his face was red with effort. He flexed his big hands and rubbed his palms against his hips. A flicker of compassion crossed Calvert's face, then he sighed and stared across the room, appearing suddenly fatigued.

"Okay," he said. "Let's start over, Mr. Roark. What makes you think you've located your regiment?"

"Well, sir, it's really not my regiment. It's Major McLeod's. He told me about it the day I got here. He said nobody believed it was here but him. But I did. I kept thinking they were planning to hit An Khe. Then I realized it was just like the major said—they were training troops and laying in ammunition and waiting for us to go home. That put me on the right track. I heard VC Valley was bad when the First Cav was here, which means it probably still is if anybody ever went there. Since I've been here we've never been allowed to do a VR of the mountains at the edge because the ARVNs are supposed to be next door. But they're *not* next door, they're huddled in their bunkers at Blackhawk, and the NVA know that. Then I remembered the paths that cross the Song Ba. That's where we got the eight NVA that day. They fizzle out to the west and seem to go nowhere, but in the other direction they come together and are worn to bare dirt near the river. That's because a rock formation comes to the surface right there, and there's a ford. On the other side is where the Montagnards are with their pigs and chickens and corn. It suddenly hit me after the probe on Schueller that the paths are a lot heavier than they used to be. When we found the first camp, there was a sapper school there. The thing out at Schueller seemed more like a training exercise than a real attack; I'm sure they could annihilate the place, but they know we're pulling out soon. So to me that makes it look like training, maybe a graduation or just something to boost morale. Anyway, that's what got me to thinking in that direction. That's where the Frenchman—where the French were always getting murdered. Anyway, putting everything together, it finally hit me where the camp had to be. Then I spent some time with the map. After that, all we had to do was fly over it. I wanted the evening VR because I thought they'd be eating supper, and that was the only way we could spot them without them knowing for sure that we had. We went right over the camp at high speed, sir, and nobody yelled or pointed or turned or did anything."

Colonel Calvert spent a moment in consideration, then said, "There's one thing I believe you're mistaken about, Mr. Roark. I don't think Schueller was training. It was too well done. I am more inclined to believe it was a rehearsal, a test. It is true, as you say, that they know we won't be around much longer, but they also know we are not going to commit any men to direct combat at this stage. Which means they could cut short the waiting routine. Perhaps for morale, but also because if they could demonstrate that Schueller is untenable it would then be abandoned or manned by ARVNs."

"Which would be essentially the same thing," Roark blurted, then said, "Sorry, sir."

"In any case, Schueller is vulnerable," Calvert said. "Besides the loss of life, which would be tragic at this point, losing control of the firebase would impair movement to and from Pleiku as well as seriously affecting our ability to hold An Khe. So I believe we have no choice. We need to strike while we can."

"Most definitely, sir," Roark said, smiling.

"Very well, Mr. Roark. There's just one more thing . . ."

"Yes, sir?"

"You need to tell me where it is," Calvert said. Then the commander of Task Force 19 smiled, but Roark was digging for his map and missed it. Calvert noted the coordinates and briefly examined the surrounding terrain. "I'll see if I can set this up for tomorrow morning," he said.

"Sir? No, sir," Roark said without thinking. The colonel and the major both looked at him in surprise. "Not tomorrow, sir." Colonel Calvert gave him a curious look, but said nothing. "Sir, they saw us fly over. We were practically on top of them, so they're wondering if we saw them. My guess is that if they didn't leave last night, they left before dawn this morning. They know we won't insert troops, but they might expect an airstrike. They'll bivouac across the ridge, then tomorrow they'll send back a few men to check things out. Just to be safe they may not come back until the day after tomorrow. That's when I'd like to hit them if we can."

The colonel cut his eyes toward McLeod, who was looking at the ceiling, then back to Roark. "And what time of day would you like to do this, Mr. Roark?" he asked.

"Fourteen-hundred, sir. They know we're not normally out in the afternoon, and by then they'll probably figure that last night was a fluke. Which means they should be back to doing whatever it is they do out there on a regular basis."

Colonel Calvert leaned back again in his chair, steepled his fingers beneath his chin, and raised one groomed eyebrow. "I get the impression, Mr. Roark, that you also have an opinion on precisely how the mission should be conducted."

Roark stiffened and stared at the wall. "Yes, sir, I do," he said.

"Okay," Calvert said. "Let's hear it."

CHAPTER FORTY

S O THAT the sound of gunfire might not carry to the enemy, the scouts detoured across Camp Radcliff, tested their weapons, then circled Hong Kong Hill and headed south. The gunships trailed low level a quarter mile behind, looking ungainly and vulnerable so close to earth.

They paralleled the river. Roark let the Kiowa climb enough to get a look at the mountains down and across the valley, then drifted back toward the brush. The clouds ahead, thickened with the compression of miles, stood three thousand feet or more above the tallest peak. He turned his head hard right and saw Grouper dangling his leg in the wind and grinning. The gunner threw him a power salute with his clenched left hand and turned and said something to Castle. "One-two, my alpha said for you to keep your eyes on the road," Castle said.

"Ask him if he remembered to change his tampon," Roark replied. When he looked again, Grouper flipped him the bone. Blue was laughing. He had unclipped his sixty from the D-ring and was holding it in his lap, stroking it, talking to it with his hands. On impulse, Roark reached out, and they did an impromptu dap with fists and elbows.

The fastmovers were punctual. George McLeod, Shamrock Six, was just passing the Mouse Ears at the tail of the flight when Gunfighter lead announced their arrival. The helicopter crews looked skyward and soon saw the speeding specks racing beyond the scattered clouds. McLeod immediately passed the Phantom pilot off to Roark. Gunfighter Zero-one already had the coordinates for the target. Roark verified that he had the general area in sight, then gave a brief description of the terrain and base camp and how they intended to mark it. "Make your runs from east to west," he said. "My wingman will be with me, and we'll break right and hold to the northeast. We'll call clear, then you hit it as fast as you can. Are you carrying napalm?"

"That's correct, One-two. And my wing has two-fifties."

"Roger, Zero-one, dump it all on the first pass, maybe just a hair short; the trees are about sixty feet tall."

"Gunfighter Zero-one, wilco."

"Okay, we're about four klicks south-southwest of the Mouse Ears now, just crossing the blue line. Turning to a heading of two-four-five, about eight klicks out. I'll call ten seconds before the first Willy Pete."

"Fighter Zero-one, roger."

As the scout ships started across the green parkland, skimming the scattered trees, dropping to just above the ground in the open, the doorgunners lowered their clear visors, checked their weapons and belts and white phosphorous grenades, and stepped out onto the skids in the wind. "You ready, One-niner?" Roark called.

"Ready, One-two."

Ahead stood the triangular shape of the mountain spine where the ridge descended past the camp. The flat of the camp itself was still not in view, but the bowl behind it was. "Get ready with the Willy Pete, One-niner," Roark said. Castle answered with a double click. "Gunfighter Zero-one, ten seconds to first smoke."

"Gunfighter Zero-one."

"Now," Roark called. Grouper dropped the first grenade, and a burst of white erupted behind them. "Number two . . . Number three . . . Number four . . ." From the perspective of altitude, a white dotted line splashed across the green, an arrow pointing straight toward the base camp. "Number six, on target." Blue tossed his first grenade as they slowed and veered right, then instantly reached and pulled and dropped another. Below were flashes of bare packed earth, thatched rooftops, and upraised faces of astonished soldiers. Grouper's gun began to roar, and the muffled double *whoosh* of the grenades rolled through the trees.

"One-niner's clear," Castle called.

"Hit it!" Roark said, but he was not prepared for what happened next. Almost as if the snide remarks made earlier on the ramp had been overheard, the colonel dropped his load less than two seconds off their tail, and in exactly the right place. Liquid fire blew through a long swath of forest, baking it clean, then gathering in a boiling red and black hell surging skyward. Roark heard his neck crack in violent reflex.

"Jesus Christ!" Castle said.

"Zero-one, that was beautiful," Roark said. "Absolutely perfect. Have your wingman drop his entire load fifty meters north." The scouts moved clear of the dense forest and began a left turn, climbing for better visibility. Before the turn was complete, the second Phantom appeared between two clouds, hurtling toward the smoking black hole. Then he punched off and bellied out and was already climbing away before the bombs slammed down with a convulsive stutter. The mountain trembled and the forest flashed red, and a patch of trees disappeared in a roiling, cement-colored cloud. Led high by the rising smoke, the bombs impacted slightly long, some climbing the steep slope up the bosom of the mountain.

"Shamrock One-two, Gunfighter Zero-one, I've got two more birds on station now. Think you can do a quick BDA and adjust?"

"Affirmative, Zero-one. Wait one. Break. One-niner, One-two."

"One-niner."

"Okay, One-niner, we'll have to do it the same way to cover the slopes. Play it loose. Go hot when we do."

"One-niner, roger."

"Two-three, you got us?"

"Gotcha covered, One-two."

"Coming around." *Click, click.* "Again." *Click, click.* They were in position now, paralleling the descending ridge that wrapped the camp on the south. Then they were over the trees and looking down at hard-packed earth and banana-leaf rooftops. Blue began firing before they reached the burn, and at first there was nothing coming back. A long sweep of the complex lay charred and open to the sky, and all across it were little orange fires and splintered timbers and bunkers that looked like empty eyes; stairs descended into the holes. At the upper end of the burn was a long tangle of bodies, black and red with curling, bluish smoke. The air was thick with wood smoke and cordite and the distinctive odor of burning meat. Suddenly, as the Little Boys crossed the space that the bombs had missed, the NVA cut loose. "Taking fire!" Roark called, and he dumped the nose of the aircraft. Bullets swarmed around both scouts, and the gunners swept their weapons below, eye to eye with the gooks. Roark veered past the gray craters and saw muzzle flashes in the splintered shadows. "Coming right," he yelled, hoping Castle was giving way. Then they were clear and everybody was still alive, and they could hear the scream and thud of rockets, the grinding roar of the minigun. "You okay, One-niner?"

"Yeah, we took some hits, but I think we're all right."

"Us, too," Roark said. "You okay?" he said to Blue.

"Yeah," Blue said, turning around, looking like he had never smiled in his life. He slipped back onto his seat, pulled up some more ammo and checked everything over, then kicked some loose empties out the door. "They can't shoot for shit," he said.

"One-two, we're clear of the target," McCawley said.

"Roger, Two-three. Break. Gunfighter Zero-one, One-two."

"Go ahead, One-two."

"Roger, Zero-one, you got any napalm left?"

"I don't, One-two, but I have a bird up here that does."

"Okay, Zero-one, I need one canister in the area between the first two strikes, a little shorter, then some heavy stuff in the same area. The target is clear."

"One-two, Gunfighter Zero-one, how'd we do down there?"

"Real good, Zero-one. Probably eighty, maybe more." The napalm had hit about half of the main barracks, which were empty, but upslope it had swept through two long sheds that must have been classrooms; all around were bodies, fried where they fell, running for weapons or bunkers.

"One-two, here comes your nape." It looked like a miss from the moment it left the white belly of the Phantom, and it fell fifty meters short with only the farthest splash reaching the area of packed earth. Roark cursed to himself and called the adjustment. The gooks knew what was happening now and were either cringing deep in their bunkers or beating it out of the area as fast as their bandied legs would go. The longer this went on, the less effective each successive pass would be.

The scouts were holding in the same area as before—clear of the dense forest, away from the mountain ridge—with McCawley and Hockett circling overhead. They slipped forward and back and checked each other for damage. Castle said there was a wet place on the belly of Roark's ship, but that was all. They climbed to five hundred feet to get a better view.

There had been little time to think until then, but now Roark studied the mountainside and tried to project himself into the trees. No way would he be in a hole, he decided; he'd be doing his best to get the hell out of Dodge, in this case over to VC Valley. The mountainous spine behind the camp, gradually descending southward toward the Dak Pihao, was much lower there than farther north, but equally rugged. A tiny stream curved around and through the camp, and the ravine that fed it led up to a bony saddle. It seemed a likely route.

The napalm was on target this time, probably too late to hit anybody, but it opened up another portion of the camp to the sky and exposed more bunkers. Roark called Gunfighter Zero-one, who had remained on station, and told him to simply have his pilots put their heavier bombs in the center of the complex, and to work the remainder of their loads along the ravine from the top down.

"Shamrock One-two, Shamrock Six."

"One-two."

"One-two, I've got another pair of Fox-fours on the way. I'm just to your east now. Tell me what you've got down there, and I'll guide 'em in when they get here."

Roark gave McLeod a quick rundown, then watched the jets finish off their loads. Gunfighter Zero-one called, and they thanked each other in the standard effusive style, Roark promising to relay a more accurate BDA when things settled down enough to take a good count. Then the camo-painted Phantoms rushed away, leaving four pale streaks of charcoal on the sky.

The mountain was a smoldering mess. Most of the fires had burned out, but trails of smoke like cigarettes angled away from the splinters. An irregular crescent had been clawed out of the jungle, and the trees and earth were pulverized and dusted with ash. Rising beside the triangular peak, trailing southward, was a cloud variously tinged in shades of black and white, reddish gray and blue. The mountain looked defeated, but the job was only half done. "You ready, One-niner?"

"Whenever you are, One-two."

"Two-three, One-two."

"Go ahead, One-two."

"Two-three, we're going up top now, past the saddle and around the crown on the far side, then circle back."

"Gotcha covered."

Roark turned the Kiowa toward the mountain and began calling signals to Castle, getting clicks for answers. "Be ready with smoke," he said to Blue. Certain he'd be using it, Blue clamped the spoon and pulled the pin of a red smoke grenade, then eased his left leg out to the skid and got ready.

Remembering the likely .51s, Roark gained speed in a shallow dive, then slowed through a cyclic climb tight against the trees, skirting the edge of the bombed ravine. "We got a bunch of 'em there," Blue said. The leaning tangle along the edge of the blast zone was hung with shreds of clothing, and here and there the dust was soaked through, muddy red. "Fresh footprints, lots of 'em," the gunner added. "Headed uphill." Roark glanced quickly, but had to watch the rising treetops as they climbed the steep slope. The approach had left them facing the sun for a few seconds, but the only other viable option was coming in from VC Valley where no bombs had yet fallen. The windshield flared golden, then they were on top and turning left.

The top of the mountain ridge was a narrow, exposed spine of pale gray boulders, cracked and broken, weathered round. Winding through the jumble was a maze of footpaths. "Got a blood trail," Blue said. He looked down and beneath the ship then and completely missed the three khaki-clad men standing around a tripod in a natural pit.

"Nine o'clock!" Roark yelled, and Blue dropped his smoke and came up firing, but they were already hit hard. Two .51 rounds slammed through the nose beyond the panel, tearing half the right side out and kicking the aircraft sharply around. "Taking fire!" Roark yelled. Then he saw that Blue was gone. The gunner had been knocked loose from the skid and was hanging out of the aircraft against his belt with his left leg beneath the ship, his right stabbing upward across the radios. He thrashed about, cursing, still clutching his weapon, but Roark couldn't help him. Wind surged through the doorless cockpit; he kicked in pedal to bring the ship around.

Grouper had been firing from the first, but the boulders suddenly seemed to stand up and come alive. His ship was being peppered, but he stuck to the men in the pit and managed to take two down. Then there were others moving up, guns belching fire, then the big one swung around.

"Get out, Alphie! Get out!" Roark yelled. Blue was suddenly back in the aircraft, and it seemed the bird would still fly. Roark nosed it over hard and came left across the stony ridge, Blue gritting his teeth and firing his sixty again. Then they fell away down the side of the mountain.

"Alphie's down!" McCawley yelled. "Alphie's down!" The gunship aborted his dive and pulled back up to altitude.

Roark banked sharply left and pulled in power, then came up and over the ridge again. The .51 had disappeared. Only a few shots from AKs were fired at them as they crossed, but Blue held off. At first they couldn't see the broken ship, then they spotted the top of the mast protruding from a sloping green hole among the boulders fifty meters down the west side. The ship had landed hard, but almost level, then bounced and pitched forward into a gap. The blades were bitten off and the tail boom had done a complete twist before flopping downhill, still attached by the driveline. Castle was slumped forward with his mouth bloody, but there was no sign of Grouper. Then the gunner stood up from behind the wreck, lifting his machine gun, his helmet still on his head. He broke off a section of ammo, looked up and waved, then went around to see about Castle.

"Get the standby guns and scouts in the air," Roark said, eyeing the boulders. There were still no gooks in sight, but they had to be closing in. He moved the ship quickly forward and swept the area upslope. Immediately they were among about twenty NVA and taking hits. Debris rattled behind the seats. "Taking fire," Roark said, much calmer now. Blue had gotten a smoke out and put several men down. "Two-three . . ."

"Stand clear, One-two, we're coming in," McCawley said. Roark swung wide to the west as four pairs of rockets marched in explosive progression along the ridgetop. It took a man who knew what he was doing to work them that way. The covering minigun sent a tangle of red tracers careening off the boulders in every direction.

"Hold off," Roark said. "Too many ricochets." Hockett was already beginning his run, and he pulled out straight ahead and began to regain altitude. That left the ridge momentarily uncovered, with McCawley coming around on the east, broadside to the target. Near the saddle in a low clump of brush between two house-sized boulders, the missing .51 again began to boom. He had McCawley dead to rights; it was too late to do anything but watch. The gunship pitched forward, slowly at first, then sharply, turning almost inverted and coming down. The blades slowed and flexed, and the last eight feet of the tail boom was lopped away. Then one of the big blades bent and broke. The ship wobbled twice before the transmission came free. All the pieces came down together on the slopes of VC Valley, then some went back up with the explosion. The radios were silent.

Blue had a positive fix on the .51. They charged in, skimming the ridge line, turned between the boulders as if around a pylon, then Blue handed the antiaircraft crew his Super-C. When the concussion overtook them and the sky was raining pebbles, Roark heard him mutter, "Fucking pink."

Back at the downed ship, Castle was conscious but groggy. Grouper was trying to get him out, but the pilot's feet were wedged in the caved-in nose. Roark swept the high ground again, and Blue killed two men who were wounded. Then they moved back down and around, checking the cracks and pockets. The rest of the enemy had vanished. "Three-eight, be ready," Roark said.

"We'll be there as soon as you say the word," Corbish replied. The chase slick had moved in and was circling just east of the ridge, dangerously close. To the west, McLeod was unloading the Phantoms in ARVN territory. Suddenly three men with AKs jumped out from between two boulders downslope of the wrecked ship, reinforcements coming up from the valley. Grouper was bent over, working with Castle's feet, and he went down and rolled backward, hit high in the legs. Blue swung and killed two men, but in that moment about forty more rose up from the rocks downhill and fired their weapons together. The swarm of lead went through the ship like a continuous load of bird shot. Both chin bubbles and windshields and the floor and ceiling and radios all went to pieces at once, and the air was filled with debris and blood and bits of bone and flesh. Roark reacted by reflex, and the riddled aircraft moved away, still rattling with hits. He didn't try to call taking fire; he didn't yell or say anything; he just flew the aircraft, knowing it was over. Then the wind was moving past and it was quiet with just a heavy metal banging. He turned and looked at Clayton Blue. Blue was folded loosely forward, almost to the floor, held by the belt and caught inside the jamb by his shoulder. He had been hit in the legs and groin and throat and face, and the back of his helmet was gone. His right arm was broken and bent in a pool of brass; his machine gun swung on the bungee. Gravity caught the flapping ammunition; Roark watched dumbly as a length motored over the seat and out the door before finally snagging on the armor.

Feeling small and far away, he noticed the hydraulics were gone. Caution lights were flashing, the aircraft shuddering, and he dimly wondered if he had been wounded. He made a wide right-hand one-eighty and went back.

NVA soldiers were standing all around. When the helicopter slowed to almost a hover, they held their weapons at their sides and stared up at the battered ship. Grouper had been shot through the head. Glenn Castle was out of the wreck, NVA on either side, looking weak and frightened. He made a movement with his face as if to smile, but couldn't manage. Finally he jerked his head in a little backward nod.

CHAPTER FORTY-ONE

THE DOOR that George McLeod ordinarily kept open was closed. He sat slumped at his desk, his arms spread heavily before him, studying his hands as if they belonged to someone else. The look of them surprised him, heavy and rough with thick fingers wrapped in a hide resembling gloves. Mature hands, strong hands the way he remembered his father's when he was small. The knuckles and flats around the nails were densely scarred; thick blue veins covered the tendons. Hands that had worked, hands that wanted to work again before the rot of age and creeping death set in.

There was a discreet knock, then Kirby Hockett entered the room and saluted. His face was tired but impassive. "We just got another call from the tower," he said. "A shuttle bird on the way to Pleiku spotted a fifty-eight burning in the Mang Yang. They flew around it a few times, and finally hovered, but said they couldn't see anything that looked like a body. I've already checked the flight line. The bird that the tower said went out before dawn was one of ours—five-two-eight. I've checked all the hooches and talked to everybody. Nobody's seen him since last night."

McLeod was silent for a time, then said, almost to himself, "He burned it."

"What, sir?"

"Nothing. Exactly where was the crash?"

"The Frenchmen's cemetery, sir." Suddenly the emotion welled up in Hockett, seemed almost to overwhelm him.

"Thank you, Mr. Hockett," McLeod said. "I'll handle it from here."

When Hockett was gone, McLeod sat motionless, the skin of his face loose, feeling old and dry and wasted. Slowly his eyes wandered around the room, finally coming to rest on the watercolored stream. It was truly hideous, nothing but a few pencil scratches and a pastel smear on a scrap of paper; flat, impenetrable, meaningless. He crossed the room, removed the painting from the wall, and, without another look, dropped it into the trash. Then he took his flight helmet from its hook and left the room.

Delta Troop was standing down, a fact that was evident everywhere. Three enlisted men under the direction of the XO were working diligently in the orderly room, sorting and boxing files, stirring the odor of dust. The walls were already bare. Everything that could be burned was being carried to a smoking fifty-five-gallon container just outside the door. The XO, Captain Weatherly, looked up from a desk mounded with manila folders, then bent back to work.

McLeod paused on the front stoop, watching the last minutes of his command, searching for something to keep. It was a shabby place, these shanties of the 1st of the 10th, but it had never seemed that way before. A dry, complacent breeze moved aimlessly across the hill, stirring the dust on the grassless ground, tilting the smoky columns.

On the flat ground in front of Supply, Sergeant Lapp was following the incomprehensible instructions. Behind him was a growing mountain of equipment—flak jackets, web gear, rucksacks, canteens, gas masks, ponchos, cots, mattresses, even the treasured poncho liners that all the men had begged to take home—everything required to run an army that wasn't made of steel and would not explode. The sergeant stood with a clipboard at the head of a loose line of men, checking things off as they tossed them onto the pile. Occasionally he shook his head at a soldier.

McLeod stepped down from the stoop and walked slowly, looking all around. When he reached the pile, he bent and withdrew a wrinkled rucksack. The line of men had finally fizzled out. The major spoke to the sergeant a moment, then followed him into Supply. When he came out, the rucksack sagged with a small load. From there, he went to the mess hall, then to his hooch where he rummaged among his things. He came down the steps carrying his rifle.

He paused again to watch Sergeant Lapp. The thin man was walking around the pile of equipment, jerking a jerry can of amber fuel. When he had made a full turn and the can was empty, he looked in McLeod's direction, hesitated, then bent and used his lighter. The diesel burned sluggishly at first, then slowly fanned and spread until the mound was squirming with orange flames. Soon another dark trail of smoke moved across the sky, diminishing with distance. McLeod watched the smoke and flames and blackening ash until he was certain it would last, then he hitched the weight of the pack on one shoulder and limped down the slope toward the aircraft.

XIV

McLeod hovered around the ashes, then followed my trail to the trees. He dropped a ruck and his CAR-15 wrapped up in a poncho liner and nearly crashed trying to one-hand the controls. He kept acting like he could see me, but I know he couldn't. I heard him yell my name. He switched hands on the cyclic again, and this time did it right. He started to salute, then just held up his hand. He hovered all around. I felt the wind from the blades and heard his voice again. He made a couple of orbits, then flew away. A few minutes later he came screaming over the hill low level, taking one last look. Then he was gone.

I know the truth about the Frenchman now. The man was never crazy; he just ran out of options, made all the decisions that were his to make, did the only thing he could.

Jim Tyler is still hanging upside down, Colonel Blackburn is facedown in the Z, Saccharin is waiting, and down at the end of the A Shau somebody's hands are wrapped around some bamboo bars. The man in the Gahan Wilson cartoon is looking at everything he won.

But, like they say, everybody dies. That's no joke, they sure as hell do. When it gets a little darker I'll cross the highway.

362

AUTHOR'S NOTE

Twelve years after I left Vietnam, while I was groping for some way to turn my experience into a novel, I suddenly realized how deeply immersed I still was in the war—not to the debilitating extent which has become the popular image of the Vietnam vet, but rather to a degree which never allowed the memories to be anything less than immediate and real. To say that after twelve years those memories were as fresh as if they happened yesterday would be a misstatement; they were actually stronger. A part of me was still there. I realized then that there must exist an invisible, speechless army of men with feelings similar to my own. Those men, and the part of each of them that never came home, are what Billy Roark is all about. He is the collective commitment, abandoned in the jungle by those who sent him there, and he will always be in Vietnam, still trying to win the war.

GLOSSARY

8-inch—a self-propelled howitzer capable of firing a 200-pound projectile 16,800 meters.

12.7—a 12.7mm antiaircraft weapon used by the NVA. Also called a fifty-one, for .51 inch.

13—OH-13 helicopter.

23—OH-23 helicopter.

37mm—an NVA antiaircraft weapon.

.51—see *12.7.*

58—OH-58 helicopter.

105—a 105mm howitzer, fired a 33-pound projectile 11,500 meters.

122—a 122mm rocket used extensively by North Vietnamese and Viet Cong elements to attack large bases.

140—a 140mm rocket, used by the NVA, but less frequently than the 122.

155—a 155mm howitzer, usually towed, range 14,600 meters, 109-pound projectile.

175—175mm howitzer, self-propelled, range 32,700 meters, 147-pound projectile.

4F—Selective Service classification for persons considered unfit for military duty.

AC—aircraft commander; left-seat pilot in a Huey or Chinook, back-seat pilot in a Cobra.

ADF—automatic direction finder, navigational aid that includes AM radio.

AFVN—Armed Forces, Vietnam; in-country radio station.

Air America—pseudo-civilian company operated by the CIA.

AIT—Advanced Individual Training, the training that took place following completion of Basic. For most men, this was infantry training.

AK—AK-47, 7.62mm automatic rifle used by NVA and VC.

Alphie—nickname for the scout wingman.

AO—area of operation.

ARA—aerial rocket artillery, a Cobra armed with 76 rockets.

Arty—artillery.

ARVN—(ar-vn) Army of the Republic of Vietnam; the South Vietnamese soldiers.

Autorotation—emergency procedure for landing a helicopter without power, as in the event of an engine failure.

B-40—rocket-propelled grenade used by NVA.

B-52—Stratofortress, heavy U.S. jet bomber.

Bangalore—linear explosives, used by both sides.

Battalion—military unit, two or more companies.

BDA—bomb damage assessment.

BDO—battalion duty officer.

Beaucoup—much or many.

BG—Berchtesgaden.

Blivet—black rubber bladder, container for fuel or water.

Blue line—a stream.

Boom-boom—sexual intercourse.

Boonies—the bush or jungle.

Brigade—military unit of which divisions are composed; sometimes organized as independent combat units.

C-4—plastic explosive widely used in Vietnam. Resembled dense marshmallow mixed with synthetic fibers.

CA—combat assault.

Camo—camouflage.

C&C—command and control.

CAR-15—(car-fifteen) a carbine version of the M-16.

Cav—cavalry.

Cayuse—OH-6 helicopter.

CCN—Command and Control North; one of three branches of MACV's Special Operations Group.

CDO—company duty officer.

Chaine Annamitique—mountain range that runs much of the length of Vietnam.

Charlie—phonetic C; also, Viet Cong.

Chieu Hoi—Vietnamese for "open arms," a program whereby NVA and VC could turn themselves in for reprogramming.

Chinook—CH-47, a twin-rotored Boeing helicopter. Also called a Hook, short for shithook.

Claymore—remote detonated antipersonnel mine, used in ambushes and on defensive perimeters.

CO—commanding officer.

Cobra—the AH-1G attack helicopter; also called a Snake.

Collective—the control stick held in the helicopter pilot's left hand, for adjustment of throttle as well as the angle of attack of the main rotor blades.

Company—military unit consisting of two or more platoons. Called a troop in the cavalry, a battery among artillerymen. Size varied greatly according to application, but generally involved 120 to 200 men.

CONEX—(con-ex) containerized express; steel containers for storage and transfer of equipment and supplies.

Control touch—a refined feel for the controls of an aircraft, gained only by experience.

Crew chief—left-side gunner on a Huey; in charge of the mechanical and operational well-being of the aircraft.

Cush—easy; from cushioned, as in the cush life.

Cushion—a supporting layer of air between a hovering helicopter and the ground.

CW2—warrant officer, grade two.

Cyclic—the stick held in the helicopter pilot's right hand, rising from the floor between his legs; controls the tilt of the main rotor plane.

Dap—ritualized handshake.

DEROS—(dee-ros) date eligible to return from overseas.

Dang-dang—explosives or ammunition.

Delay—a variable, timed fuse on an artillery round or bomb that allows the projectile to penetrate trees or earth before detonation.

Diên cai dâu—Vietnamese slang for crazy.

Dinks—the enemy; this term became dominant, as opposed to gooks, later in the war.

Division—basic military combat unit consisting of brigades or regiments, approximately 20,000 men.

DMZ—Demilitarized Zone.

Dustoff—medical evacuation helicopters, name derived from the call sign of Major James L. Kelley, killed in action.

E&E—escape and evade; to make it through the jungle on your own.

EM—enlisted man.

ETS—estimated termination of service; the date of scheduled release from active duty.

Evac—medical evacuation.

F-4—Phantom; fighter-bomber manufactured by McDonnell.

FAC—(fack) forward air controller.

Fastmovers—jet aircraft.

Firebase—temporary artillery bases established in operational areas in support of ground forces.

First sergeant—the senior NCO at company level; grade E-8.

Flak vest—a heavy vest designed to stop shrapnel.

Flareship—aircraft rigged with million-candlepower parachute flares for illumination missions.

Flechette—beehive-type round used in artillery and rockets, composed of thousands of steel darts surrounding an explosive charge.

FM—frequency modulation; the low-frequency radios used for ground-to-ground and ground-to-air communications.

FNG—fucking new guy.

FO—forward observer; someone who directs an air or artillery strike from either ground or air.

Fox-Mike—FM radio.

Freak—radio frequency.

Gook—the enemy, Viet Cong or NVA; also used generally for all Vietnamese.

Group—military unit composed of battalions, subordinate to a brigade.

Guard—emergency radio frequency.

HE—high explosive.

Higher—higher command, usually meaning Group, Task Force, or Division.

H-model—a later, stronger version of the UH-1 Huey.

Hook—Chinook.

Huey—UH-1 helicopter.

I Corps—(Eye Corps) the northernmost of four geographical divisions of South Vietnam, designated for military convenience.

IFFV—I (Eye) Field Force Vietnam.

IG—Inspector General; an inspection conducted by that office.

IP—instructor pilot.

JP-4—refined kerosene used by turbine-powered helicopters.

Jungle penetrator—a metal device with a fold-down seat, for the vertical extraction of personnel.

KIA—killed in action; a dead soldier of either side.

Klick—kilometer; .621 mile.

Loach—see *LOH*.

Log—logistics. The term also refers to logging—accumulating and recording—flight time.

Log bird—aircraft on logistics assignment.

Logistics—nontactical assignment involving movement of personnel, munitions, food, mail, etc.

LOH—light observation helicopter; although several aircraft fit this description, the term came to mean the OH-6 Cayuse, called a Loach.

LRRP—(lurp) long-range reconnaissance patrol; members of such a unit; freeze-dried meals designed for such teams.

LZ—landing zone.

M-16—standard infantry rifle in 1967; 5.56mm.

M-60—standard U.S. light machine gun, 7.62mm.

M-79—40mm, single-shot, break-open grenade launcher; it looked like a sawed-off shotgun with a fat barrel.

MACV—(mack-vee) U.S. Military Assistance Command, Vietnam.

Matel Messerschmitt—nickname for the Hughes TH-55 trainer.

Medevac—unarmed medical evacuation helicopters; Dustoff.

Mike-mike—millimeter.

Minigun—a six-barreled Gatling gun, electrically driven. On Cobras, could be set to fire either 2,000 or 4,000 rounds per minute.

Montagnards—aborigine tribes of the Chaine Annamitique.

Mule—a half-ton four-wheel-drive cargo platform.

Murmite cans—insulated food canisters for serving hot chow to troops in the field.

Napalm—*n*aphthenic acid and *palm*etate; jellied gasoline. Developed in 1941–42 for use in flamethrowers.

Nape—napalm.

NCO— noncommissioned officer; a sergeant.

NDP—night defensive position.

Nomex—flame-retardant material, a polymide fiber developed by DuPont, used in flight suits and flight gloves.

O-2—twin-engine, push-pull Cessna, used by some Air Force forward air controllers. Also called an Oscar-Deuce.

OD—olive drab; nickname for the Army.

OH-6—Cayuse, light observation helicopter produced by Hughes, used as aerial scout and to carry VIPs. Called a Loach.

OH-13—Sioux, Bell Helicopter, the familiar "bubble" aircraft of early television. One of three types then employed as trainers by the Army. Employed in the Korean War, and in the early years of Vietnam.

OH-23—Raven, produced by Hiller, one of three training helicopters used at Fort Wolters, employed in the Korean War as well as in the early years of Vietnam.

OH-58—Kiowa, light observation helicopter produced by Bell, used late in the war as a scout and VIP bird.

Operations—the segment of an organization in charge of planning and accomplishing the tactical mission.

Ops—Operations.

Oscar-Deuce—O-2 airplane.

P-38—folding, bladelike can opener used on C-rations.

PA&E—Pacific Architects & Engineers; U.S. civilian contractor in Vietnam.

Pathfinders—trained infantrymen who were inserted in the field to assist in air operations; identified by black baseball caps.

Penaprime—a dust palliative; black, sticky oil when applied, it eventually dried to a semihard tar.

Peter pilot—name used to designate the right-seat pilot in a Huey as opposed to the aircraft commander who flew left seat.

Phantom—F-4 fighter-bomber.

Phougas—(foo-gas) jellied gasoline, napalm, generally used in 55-gallon drums in perimeter defenses, rigged with a claymore mine for dispersion.

Pink team—a scout covered by a Cobra.

Pisstube—urination point for male personnel, usually a 55-gallon drum or an artillery canister embedded at ground level and covered with screen wire. Normally included a narrow modesty screen at genital level.

Pitot tube—hollow tube projecting from the front of aircraft to determine airspeed.

Platoon—formed by two or more squads; two or more platoons form a company.

POL—petroleum, oil, lubricants; generally used to refer to the refueling point for aircraft.

Poncho liner—a lightweight, camouflaged quilt intended for use inside a poncho, but commonly used for bedding.

Poz—position.

PRC-25—"Prick" 25, most common FM field radio in Vietnam.

Prep—preparation of a landing zone by artillery or gunship bombardment prior to the insertion of troops.

PSP—perforated steel plate; sectional, interlocking steel panels used to produce a hard surface for runways or flight lines.

PSYOPS—(sigh-ops) Psychological Operations.

Push—radio frequency.

PX—Post Exchange, a retail facility.

PZ—pickup zone.

Quad-fifty—a four-barreled .50 or .51 caliber weapon.

Ramp—flight line or aircraft parking area.

Ranch Hand—defoliation operation in Vietnam, flown by Air Force C-123s.

R&R—rest and recreation.

Recon—reconnaissance, air or ground.

Regiment—in cavalry, two or more squadrons.

Revetment—minimal protection for aircraft, consisting of two low, parallel walls.

ROK—Republic of Korea; Korean troops.

ROTC—Reserve Officers Training Corps.

Rotorwash—the wind given off by a helicopter.

RPG—rocket-propelled grenade; enemy antitank weapon, later versions of which could penetrate more than twelve inches of armor; also known as B-40 rocket.

RTO—radio-telephone operator.

S-1—Personnel.

S-2—Intelligence .

S-3—Operations.

S-4—Supply.

SAM—surface-to-air missile.

Sappers—enemy commandos.

Satchel charge—explosive devices carried by sappers during an attack, usually in a canvas pack with a carrying strap which facilitated throwing the device.

Seabee—Construction Brigade, Navy.

Sergeant of the Guard—the NCO in charge of a guard detail.

Servos—electrically activated hydraulic assist mechanisms which reduce the force required to manipulate the controls of a helicopter.

Seventeen-pounders—a 2.75-inch rocket fired from U.S. aircraft.

Shitcan—half a 55-gallon drum, used in latrines; these were burned periodically with diesel fuel.

Sit-rep—situation report.

Slick—a Huey armed only with doorguns.

Snake—Cobra helicopter.

SOI—radio code booklet carried by pilots.

Sortie—one round trip, one load of troops or supplies.

Spec 4, 5—(spec-four, etc.) specialists, grade E-4 and E-5.

Squadron—cavalry equivalent of a battalion.

Standdown—a unit withdrawn from action for refitting and repair; withdrawal of a unit from Vietnam.

Stars and Stripes—newspaper produced and distributed by the armed forces.

Strings—ropes.

Sucking chest wound—a wound which penetrates a lung, through which air is forced as the victim breathes.

Surg—surgical hospital.

TH-55—one of three models of training aircraft at Wolters; manufactured by Hughes. Nicknamed the Matel Messerschmidt for its toylike appearance.

Ti-ti—(tee-tee) a little bit, soon.

Translational lift—an aerodynamic lifting force applied to helicopters when a relative airspeed of about fifteen knots has been attained.

Troop—cavalry equivalent of a company.

TWs—lightweight, tan summer uniform that could be worn in lieu of khakis.

UH-1—Iroquois, called the Huey, produced by Bell.

UHF—ultrahigh frequency.

Uncle Ho—Ho Chi Minh.

URC-10—a compact emergency UHF radio, included an emergency beeper tone and a voice capability.

USO—United Service Organizations.

VC—Viet Cong.

VHF—very high frequency.

VR—visual reconnaissance.

W-1—warrant officer, grade 1.

White phosphorus—an element that ignites upon exposure to oxygen, producing volumes of dense white smoke. Employed in grenades and artillery shells.

Wilco—will comply.

Willy Pete—white phosphorus.

WO—warrant officer.

WOC—(wock) warrant officer candidate.

WP—white phosphorus.

XO—executive officer; second in command at company, battalion, or brigade levels.

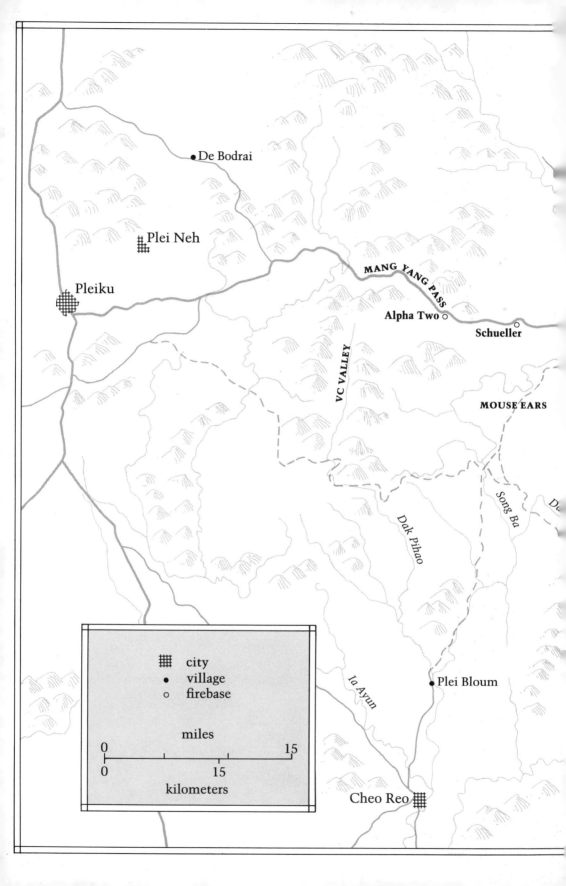

De Bodrai

Plei Neh

Pleiku

MANG YANG PASS

Alpha Two ○

Schueller

VC VALLEY

MOUSE EARS

Dak Pihao

Song Ba

Du

Ia Ayun

Plei Bloum

⊞ city
● village
○ firebase

miles

0 _____ 15

0 _____ 15
kilometers

Cheo Reo ⊞